the
ALIGNMENT

the
ALIGNMENT

KAY CAMDEN

THE ALIGNMENT

Editing by Debra Argosy
Photography by Keith Lee Studios
Cover art by Damonza
Book interior design & typesetting by Bookery

ISBN-10: 099100440X (paperback)
ISBN-13: 978-0-9910044-0-9 (paperback)
ISBN-10: 0991004418 (eBook)
ISBN-13: 978-0-9910044-1-6 (eBook)

For more information about Kay Camden go to kaycamden.com

the
ALIGNMENT SERIES

The Alignment
The Two
The Oak and the Moon
The Catalyst
The Warrior

CHAPTER 1

LIV

I STAND ON THE shoulder of Montana's U.S. Route 2, staring at my flat tire. Having a blowout in the last fifty miles of a fourteen-hundred-mile drive hints of a bad omen, but I'm thankful for the distraction. Another tractor-trailer roars by, shifting into the empty oncoming lane so it doesn't pick me up like one of the scrubby plants embedded in my grille. The big trucks thunder past me, but every car and pick-up has stopped since I pulled over.

"The tow truck's on its way," I've hollered into twenty lowered windows, mentally recording each driver's physical description and license plate in case there's a serial killer among them—although those details would only be useful if I escaped. Unlikely out here. Any sicko could drag me off the road and dump my body in the woods. No one would report me missing. My friends in Chicago don't expect to hear from me again. They all know what happened. Why I'm here.

I open the trunk to free my spare, trapped under the tightly-packed jumble of my belongings. Like luggage unloaded by airport security, it will never go back the same way again, and there's not an inch in the crammed interior for overflow. I could postpone the task longer, but that deflated tire wasn't doing much for my entertainment.

I don't notice until it's already on me—a black motorcycle headed in the opposite direction, its engine winding down like an angry wasp. Eye contact would suggest I need his help, but I'm staring before I can stop myself. The rider remains curled against the bike as the shiny black helmet tilts toward me. No way to know what he looks like behind the tinted visor. The police sketch artist would have to draw him with a glossy black bulbous head and only one enormous insect eye. A lot of help that would be. He shifts down a gear, then another. In that fraction of a second, his scrutiny becomes too prolonged for comfort. A glint from the sun blinks at me—a visible nudge to force my attention away from him, back to the boxes and bags. I need to get to town. Somewhere with witnesses.

He revs the engine and blasts by me. My stomach invades my throat. I stumble away from the trunk, clinging to the bumper with one hand and bracing myself on the ground with the other. Losing my lunch on the side of a Montana highway would make this delay extra special. And that bad omen harder to ignore. Somebody needs to tell that bad omen my life can't get any worse.

"The tow truck's on its way," I say to the departing motorcyclist. I cough. I wipe my mouth with the back of my hand. Guess I wasn't his type.

The wave of nausea passes as quickly as it came on, and I resume my unloading, pleased I get to keep my lunch. *Dwell on your positive moments*, my counselor had said. Not throwing up definitely falls into this category. *Positive moments reap new positive moments.* Not getting murdered by a tow truck driver on a road curling around mounded earth and evergreen forest is also a positive moment. Let's hope it comes true.

The tow truck arrives in the motorcycle's wake and makes a U-turn to park behind me. I squint at the windshield, trying to make out human features behind a pane of glass that reflects blue sky and the green bristly side of the mountain. The driver climbs out of the truck. I could easily outrun him. I could also curl up and take a nap on his belly.

"Joe's Towing," he calls.

A shaggy-haired kid jumps from the passenger side. No way could I outrun him. He looks to be over eighteen, so at least he'll be tried as an adult. They approach. The driver writes on his clipboard. "I'm Joe. You need a tow or got a spare?"

"I have a spare. Just need to dig it out."

He takes my information while the kid jacks up my car. My old name rolls right off my tongue. "I'm sorry. It's Liv Gilchrist," I correct.

His pen pauses on the paper longer than it needs to. I return to my trunk. The more I unload, the more there is to unload. Everything smells like the old wood of my abandoned house.

He whistles under his breath. "You coming or going?"

"Coming."

"To Casper?"

"No, to Black River."

He takes the box out of my arms and sets it on the stack beside us. "Well then I'll give you an early welcome. Got family there?"

I duck into the trunk, shaking my head.

"You plan to stay?"

I hand him another box. "We'll see."

I pay Joe cash as the kid lowers my car back to the pavement. "Go easy on that spare," he says. I watch them drive away to stall my repacking of the trunk, now even more impossible with the addition of a full-size wheel. I could just drive away from the whole stack, watch it disappear in the rear view mirror like I watched the Chicago skyline a few days ago.

Then I see the box I couldn't label, the layers of packing tape hugging it, so thick at the seam it tilts the box at an unnatural angle. I can't leave that behind.

I shove the box all the way to the back of the trunk and bury it under the four trash bags packed with clothes jerked off hangers and scooped out of drawers. I should have paid attention. If I rip these bags open to find cocktail dresses and nightgowns instead of jeans and T-shirts, I'll be living in my scrubs. The trash bag of scrubs goes in next, white, so I know which one it is—a convenient result from unloading the contents of the clothes dryer straight into a bag yanked from the pantry. I'd already been living in scrubs.

Work, dance, bed. Three repeating tasks. A simple routine to cling to so I wouldn't fall apart. Now, a new goal. A new life.

When I squash the final bag in and slam the lid, I almost expect applause. I take my seat at the wheel. I'm really doing this. I pull onto the road. My old name repeats in my head. The driver's pen, pausing on paper. An eternity before it moves again. My heart awakens in the way I don't want it to, thudding and hot, reminding me of questions I don't want to face. I'm supposed to be running away. My past wasn't allowed to tag along. Has he started looking for me?

Tires throw gravel, and I straighten up to jerk the wheel just in time. I need to stop thinking about him. It brings everything else with it.

My finger finds the button for the window and the glass lowers, breaking the calm with a blast of wind that tosses my hair around my shoulders. Out of nowhere, a motorcycle blows past me in a blur of noise that claws up my backbone. As the high-pitched whine of the engine subsides with the growing distance between us, a chill rushes along my skin from scalp to toes. I sure didn't see him coming. Not that I had much time. He must be doubling the speed limit. Black sport bike carrying a man with a black helmet and jacket. It's the same guy. I watch him round the next curve and realize I need to take a break. I should be coming up on that town soon, whatever its name is.

The gas station is a little shabby. No, minimalist. I'm trying to work on my optimism. I take the pump closest to the entrance and turn off my car. When I look up, there it is again, stationary this time and missing its rider. The dust on the bike's tires is the only part of its anatomy not shiny black. I lean across the passenger seat to read the letters scrawled on the side. *Ninja.* But why remember details? It looks like I'm the one following him. And he doesn't even have a trunk for my corpse.

As soon as I open my door and step out, my knees plunge into gravel, followed closely by my palms. A metallic flavor washes from my throat into my mouth. Now I *am* going to be sick. The explosion of the bike's engine growling to life snaps my head up just in time to see gravel fly as it rockets away. Knees attached to boots appear in the dust cloud, and I am pulled upward.

"You okay, ma'am?"

My head swims for a few seconds until my eyes focus, and I find myself clutching a man's flannel-covered arm. I clear my throat. "I think so. It just passed. I've been driving too long I guess." And apparently have a new allergy to motorcycles.

"Come inside and sit down. I don't need no one passin' out in my lot."

The old man offers me an orange plastic chair and a bottle of water and goes back to his crossword puzzle. There is something to be said for the people in these small towns. They have a graceful way of showing their humanity that leaves you feeling like you owe them nothing, because they know they can expect the same of you. Out here, there are fewer distractions to clutter the mind, there is more focus. It's stripped down and basic. Simple. And exactly what I don't need. Peace and quiet seemed like a cure but

I've overlooked one crucial detail. I can't be left alone with my thoughts.

I finish the water in a long gulp, try my legs again, and settle on stable ground. I push the chair back into its spot against the wall. The old man looks up, chewing on a plastic straw.

"Fully recovered?" He smiles, and his eyes crinkle.

"Fully recovered." I smile back. It's such a foreign sensation to me now, but for once, it feels natural.

"Jimmy pumped your gas for you, ma'am. Hope you wanted it full. It's on me if you didn't."

I pay, but he won't take money for the bottle of water. The intensity of the sky hits me when I step outside, and I notice it's not so much the brightness of the sun, but the amount, the spread of it. Its warmth touches my skin through my clothes. The cool breeze blows into the ripped knees of my jeans. Someone once told me these jeans make me look like a teenager. I should've gotten rid of them. All they do is remind me of someone I'm trying to forget.

Back on the road, I feel like a night has passed and the day is new. My destination is close enough for unexpected hope to replace the nausea I felt earlier. It was either anxiety, or some abrupt sickness that starts a blender in my stomach just to turn it right off again like the power cut out.

Downtown Black River pops up on both sides of me like a Hollywood set. The classic wall of joined buildings common in old Westerns updated with twenty-first century touches—new windows, modern signs, an ATM. I pass the address so I go around the block. This town can't be more than a few stoplights wide. Its flatness seems a human invention, but the town's founders probably chose this land for that natural feature. I wonder why I chose it. It seemed obvious at the time, like a gut feeling I no longer have. I spot the real estate sign on my second drive-through. Two women holding takeout coffees chat on the sidewalk as I slip my Civic into a row of pick-ups and SUVs angle-parked along the curb.

Nancy, my real estate agent, is on the phone when I enter her office, so I busy myself with an Avon catalog. She's a real estate agent by day, Avon lady by night. Or maybe vice versa. It probably depends on the day. Or night. Her energy and positivity are not human. The pages waft perfume samples at me, and I close my eyes and picture a hot bath. There's something about long drives that makes me feel so grimy and worn out.

Nancy slams the phone down and spins her chair around, making a dramatic gasp. "Liv, you made it!" Her turquoise earrings swing with the momentum of the spin.

"Yes. I'm committed. Were you worried?"

"Not in this lifetime." She reaches into her desk, pulls out a key, and shakes it in the air next to her spirited smile. "How about you follow me?" I know her good mood is going to be contagious, even with my powerful immunity.

Nancy leads me through a small town more active than I would expect for the middle of Montana. I navigate the Civic around logging trucks, women with strollers, and UPS making a delivery. My Chicago real estate agent hooked me up with Nancy because she said this town was peaceful and remote, and "has everything you'll ever need and nothing you don't." A little past the railroad tracks that seem to mark the edge of the downtown, we go over a narrow bridge above the Black River, the town's namesake.

The river is narrow enough for an untrained swimmer like me to swim safely across, but wide enough for the fear of some flesh-eating creature to keep me on shore. Its water dances with reflection, but below the refracted light is a darkness that confirms its bottom consists of slate or some dark rock. After five double thumps from my tires on the bridge, we're on the other side.

From the main road, Nancy turns onto a narrow road cutting through a thick forest, and I feel the walls close in, like each tree is reaching its branches toward us to have a taste. It's a striking change from the openness of the interstate. Our elevation is increasing. The clouds seem closer, and the rearview mirror shows the landmarks of our path in miniature form, far below us. Pavement turns to gravel, and I follow Nancy's SUV up the incline toward the house.

I park beside her and reach for the door handle, but the tops of two pointy ears and a furry tail have appeared between our cars. She gets out, and motions me out of my car.

"I'm told the dog comes with the house," she says.

"Dog?" The animal looks too wild to be a dog. I'd have guessed it was a coyote.

"He's friendly. The sellers told me their father befriended him." She offers her hand to him. "He still sticks around, but he's maintenance-free. No one comes by here but me, and he won't eat the kibble I bring. You probably won't need to feed him."

He doesn't look too friendly to me, but I'm sure the same could be said about me. He glares at me before slinking off to sniff my car.

Nancy chuckles. "Well, give him a little time to warm up to you. But I have been told he doesn't get along with other dogs."

I turn to look at the house. It's more enchanting than the pictures from the listing which showed a rustic log cabin surrounded by pine trees. The large front porch, complete with two rocking chairs, is lined with hanging baskets full of late-summer flowers. White drapes billow outward from the windows with the breeze as if they are waving to me.

"I opened all the windows this morning to freshen it up. I know the contract says everything in the house is yours, but the seller said he'll haul away anything you don't need."

"That's very nice of him." My hand slips into my pocket to finger the folded paper that should still be on my kitchen counter in Chicago. I was wrong to take it. Leaving it would have been the mature thing to do. But who would blame me?

The front door is already unlocked, and we go inside. You don't see a lot of knotty pine in homes in Chicago, and I love it. The cathedral ceiling in the main room makes the house feel much bigger inside than it looks. He would hate this house.

We walk through the main room to the kitchen where a vase of wildflowers and a yellow envelope greet me from the table.

"Nancy…" I should've known she was going to do this.

"Liv, I don't have a lot of clients like you. This is special. I'm honored to help you during this…time…in your life." Her eyes mist over, but she contradicts them with a grin. "Just humor me, okay?"

Inside the card are two gift certificates—one for the town spa, one for Avon products. I manage a smile. "I guess you're trying to clean me up?" I know I must be grateful for her kindness, but the feeling slips through me and I can't get ahold of it again. People like her are going to help me get through this. Hopefully this town is full of them.

"Never. But everyone loves to be pampered." She squeezes my arm. "Now let's take a look at that view."

We step out onto the back porch, and I am struck by the panorama. Evergreens stiff and straight, crowding every possible space like the bristles of a brush. I focus on the sky above them and they turn into a rolling green sea, its waves gently falling away in the distance to reveal the snow-topped Rockies on the horizon. To my right is mountain-side, pointing straight up. To my left, open air extending out to the face of a small white bluff interrupting the thick pine forest. A shoulder of the Black River peeks through the trees below it. The pictures did not do this justice.

"Pinch me," I say. I can't tell her it's all too new, too foreign, to feel real. Someday I'll cherish this view like it deserves to be cherished.

Nancy gives me a sly look, her eyes smiling. "I can't believe this place sat as long as it did. Surrounded by all this conservation land? This is the very definition of peace. You can pretend all of this is yours and there won't be anyone around to complain."

"It's perfect." I've made an awful mistake.

"You do have one adjacent neighbor but..." She turns toward the river and squints into the distance. She waves the thought away. "He's too far away to borrow sugar."

I thought the quiet would kill me in Chicago. Out here, it's going to slowly skin me alive.

"And this is where I'm going to leave you. Cell phone service is great up here. Please call me if you need anything. I mean that."

I give her a hug, and she lets herself out. I hear her tires on the gravel, rolling down the hill. And then, nothing but the wind.

This must be what it feels like to be the last person on earth.

I envision my old house. My front door. Shoes in the front hall. The switch for the light with the spent bulb too high for me to replace, but I always try to turn it on anyway. Yet somehow, the unforgiving solitude under this sky, surrounded by these snowy mountains, is less lonely than being back home on my busy street where I knew every neighbor. I will go back someday, but not before I'm prepared. He could be there right now.

I should not be so pleased the paper in my pocket is not there with him.

When my arms fall asleep on the railing, I remember how much I have to unpack. I go back through the house and out the front door. The coyote dog is sitting next to my car as if he finally has his greeting prepared. I feel like I need to shake his paw. He watches me intently while I unpack the trunk.

"I could use some help," I say, on the twentieth trip back to the car.

The coyote dog stands, looks into the woods as if hearing someone calling his name, and saunters off. I stare after him and wonder if he just pretended to hear something in order to get out of helping. See, I am already going crazy out here.

As if longing for him to find me isn't crazy enough.

TREY

River greets me at the driveway with her tail wagging hard enough to bend her body to the side. It's one of her more obvious signals for no visitors. I pull the Ninja into the garage, take off my helmet, and tug the door closed. Halfway to the house, I halt. Something feels different. Something is off. I turn on my heel to glance at River—surely she would feel it too.

She cocks her head in a "What?" I notice the bloody trail carved into the gravel from the back of the house to the garage. This sloppiness will drive me out of town, force me to do what I'd rather not do. It's my own damn fault. I just don't remember it being so messy.

I look at River. "Is someone here?"

She lowers her tail and gives me a defensive look, and I know what will happen if I don't trust her—the silent treatment, for hours, maybe days. Since I'd rather not be without her help, I nonchalantly grab a piece of firewood off the porch like I was planning to bring it into the house, open the front door, and listen.

All clear.

And I am so whipped. By a dog.

I go inside but the surge of blood through my veins persists in its effort to warn me. Something feels vastly different. I'm never wrong. It doesn't really matter, though. If he wants to wait and surprise me, that's fine. I'm always game for that, in fact, I welcome it.

My phone buzzes in my pocket. I dig it out. "Hey Mike," I answer.

"Trey. Last time I checked, you owe me a favor."

"Is that right?" It probably is. I can never remember these things.

"I've got to pick up a big load tomorrow. I could use your truck and your manpower."

"What time?" I ask.

"Late. They're going to finish up during the day and whatever's left at the end of the day is mine."

I turn toward a sound picked up by my unoccupied ear. "All right. Call me tomorrow afternoon."

"Will do. Thanks, man."

"I'm just glad we'll finally be even."

He hangs up, cutting off his laughter. I end the call and listen. That sound must have been nothing. I'm getting paranoid. I need a drink.

I toss the firewood on the hearth and untie and kick off my boots. When I look up, I notice the mess in the kitchen I was too tired to clean up last night, too tired to clean up this morning. And too tired right now. Being tired has become a disease. Its symptoms range from apathy to complete mental drain. I'm its victim and its expert and I've known it's winning for a long time now, but I can't be bothered to think my way free of it.

The most unfortunate part is I have an eternity to be tired.

I move to the doorway of the kitchen to stare at the mess. The kitchen faucet drips, and my shoulders sag. That's the reason I left this morning. I can't stand another night of that dripping. How could I have forgotten? My lack of focus gets worse every day. It should surprise me, but it doesn't. Nothing surprises me anymore.

I turn away from the pile of broken dishes, kitchen table on its side, blood splattered on the wall, knife drawer upside down on the floor with knives scattered. I pull my boots back on, drag myself into my truck, and head back to town. I'm barely going to make it before the hardware store closes.

While waiting at a red light at Fifth Street, I feel the familiar rush of adrenaline. It's that gray Acura again, parked across the intersection on the other side of the street. The car starts to pull away and I know they realize they've been spotted. They make a right on Fifth so I turn left and floor my truck in pursuit even though they already have a big lead. The light shines green at the next intersection and I blow through, hoping the next light will change to green before I get there. The red light gets closer but I know I won't stop. Nothing will make me stop this time.

I enter the intersection just as I see another car coming at me from the right. Against my will, my foot slams on the brake, but it's too late. Metal smashes. My truck sends the red car spinning into the curb where it stops and sways. We're about twenty feet apart but I can smell the red car's antifreeze. I smell my burning rubber. I pop the steering wheel with my fist. That gray Acura got away.

I step out of the truck and notice the other driver doubled over as if she's about to throw up. As I approach, she appears to collect herself and takes a big breath. Here we go.

"Are you insane?!"

"You aren't the first person to ask me that." People often mistake the bitterness in my voice for sarcasm and think I'm making a joke, but as soon as the words are out I can see she's not one of those people.

She throws her hands in the air while shaking her head, her eyes wide. "Did you not realize you had the red?"

"I did realize that. I was hoping you'd see me." I wonder if she'll believe I'm telling the truth. People rarely tell the truth when the collision is their fault. What else am I going to say anyway? I'm a bad liar.

Her eyes narrow. "Is this a joke?"

"I wish it was." Maybe then I'd have something to laugh about for once. I glance at her car. "You're driving on a donut. No wonder you couldn't stop in time."

"Me? Not stop in time?"

I crouch to look at her other tire, hissing as it loses air. "And this one's worn to hell. You have no tread. Are the backs as bad?"

She opens her mouth to say something but breaks off as if the words catch in her throat. Turning away from me, she takes a few long, deep breaths while staring back down the road past her car. I watch her and wait until she finally turns back.

Her voice strains. "I'm calling the police."

"No need. I admit fault. I'll pay to fix your car."

"And then you just walk away with no consequences? I don't think so. You can't just blast through a red light with no regard for other people's lives, cause an accident, and get away with it!"

She is determined, I'll give her that. Punishing me for this may seem appropriate to her. I can't blame her for thinking a ticket, a fine, or even jail time would bother me in some way, teach me a lesson of some sort. I doubt she's capable of grasping what little effect it would have. She turns toward her car. My first reflex is to grab her hand.

"Do *not* touch me." She yanks her hand away like I have a disease. How ironic.

"Be reasonable. I'm being reasonable." It's becoming an effort to keep my voice calm.

"*I* need to be reasonable? You're a psychopath!"

"And you're starting to get on my nerves." Barely realizing I spoke aloud, I begin to fantasize about telling her how she made me lose the gray Acura. How her being here at the same moment I was stopped me from catching it. Maybe she would calm down if I told her exactly what had been at stake here.

She opens her mouth again but no words come out. She must not be from around here. Not many people who live in this part of the country overreact when faced with such a simple problem, a problem that has already been solved. I close my eyes to gather my thoughts and imagine the relief I could feel by telling someone about the gray Acura. And I wouldn't have to stop there. What would it feel like to tell someone, a complete stranger, about everything? Doesn't matter if it's her. Just any other human being capable of listening. The sound of another car pulling up breaks me out of my trance.

"Is everyone okay...*Liv*?"

It's Nancy Carter, the town's one and only real estate agent. Using her presence as an out, I make my way around the crash. My truck looks untouched, but her car looks like it needs a shitload of work. The axle is definitely bent, and the flat tire holds onto the rim for dear life. I'll have it towed to my mechanic. Body and mechanical damage. That's going to be one hefty bill. Before I turn away, the Illinois license plate catches my eye. So I was right.

I return to the women and take a deep relieved breath when I see that Nancy appears to be having better luck than I am. Shit, I could use a drink.

Nancy turns to me. "I'm taking Liv home, to the Joseph place right across the river from you."

"Liv...what?" If she's moved into that house I need to get her full name.

"Liv Gilchrist. She's going to need a car at some point, preferably sooner than later, and this mess needs to be taken care of. I'm assuming you can handle all of it?"

People around here seem to trust me. Hell if I know why. I nod my answer—that was my plan from the beginning anyway. The other driver just wouldn't listen.

Nancy closes the woman into her own car. Then she's in my face again. She lowers her voice. "She's alone in that house. She doesn't know anyone here and she has no one to help her. It's all you, Trey."

"Got it." The first time. I'd say it, but she'd probably smack me.

She gets in her car and drives away. My truck starts confidently, so I pull over to the side of the road. After grabbing an empty box out of the bed, I head back to the other car and wrench open the passenger door. It groans a complaint and buckles in the middle. Great, more to fix. Her car is a stick, so I know she can drive my truck when I leave it for her. I grab her stuff from inside the car and throw everything in the box. I try not to notice the economy-size bottle of Pepto-Bismol and assume she doesn't need it right away. She can get more if she does. Not my problem.

I get back in my truck to wait for the tow. A hot trickle runs down my cheek, and I brush it away. My hand comes back with a smear of red. I turn the rearview mirror toward me. Crap. The gash above my eyebrow has opened again, oozing blood down my face. I look down. And my shirt. I knew it needed stitches and shouldn't have put it off. I have to honor the promise I made to myself that I can sew up any part of my body except my face. I'm neither skilled nor patient enough to do a decent job, and I don't want to end up looking like Frankenstein's monster.

I wipe the blood on my jeans. Just what I wanted to do tomorrow—drop by the clinic for stitches. At least this time I have a good excuse for the gash. Too bad I don't care.

The tow arrives, and I give him instructions. I manage to get the bleeding to stop, so I drive to the hardware store in Casper that's open an hour later. Figuring I won't have a useful vehicle for a while, I run some errands while I still can. My appearance inspires a variety of strange looks, but nothing I'm not used to. These people should know to expect it from me by now, but apparently this little amount of blood is enough to throw them into a panic. If they had any idea the amount of blood I see regularly, my appearance today wouldn't be worth a second glance. Maybe the next time I have a really good run-in I should just come straight out into public without cleaning up first. Now *that* reaction might give me something to laugh about.

With my errands complete, I drive my truck home to unload my ladder and replace it with my ramp and tie-downs. I'll need to haul the Ninja when she's done with the truck—I'll be stuck with two vehicles in the same spot and only one driver to get them home. Then I'm off to the Joseph cabin. It's late, and I don't want to encourage any obligatory greeting, so I pull up and kill the engine imme-diately. The mutt on the front porch stands but makes no attempt to approach. I leave the key in the ignition and head down to the river on foot. Once I reach the shore, I look up to the night sky for Orion to guide me home.

My weary eyes open to the morning sunlight that hits hard at the back of my head. Another killer headache and I only have myself to blame. After a bowl of cereal and a mug of coffee at the counter, I shower, throw on a clean white T-shirt, jeans, and work boots. I slip on my riding jacket and grab my helmet. It's a quick drive to the clinic on the Ninja, and I know getting this done first thing is the only way I'll follow through. I dread this. The clinic itself doesn't bother me. It's the concentration of cheerful people that really gets me down. I've been alone so long it's hard to remember how to get along with people the way everyone else does. I'm incapable of putting on a smile and making small talk. I feel like I'm dragging people down into my abyss.

While I'm signing in to see the nurse, the frosted window slides open. Ann takes the clipboard and initials by my name. "What have you done now?"

I tilt my head so she can see.

"That's a nasty one. You just missed your eye. Still self-pay?"

I nod.

"Same credit card?"

I nod again.

"Have a seat."

I drop my helmet on a chair and sit next to it. I stare at the magazines on the wall rack, too lazy to get up and retrieve one.

"Trey Bevan?"

I rise.

Rachel beams at me. "Again so soon? Fell off another ladder already?"

The ever popular running joke with the nurses. Every time I show up it's because I've fallen off a ladder. I gave up trying to provide good excuses a long time ago. She walks me to an exam room where the nurse is waiting for me in the perfect personification of my crappy luck.

"This is Liv. She's new, so go easy on her. Okay, Trey?" Rachel hurries out, closing the door behind her. It's like I've just been locked in a cage.

Liv Gilchrist looks as sickened as I feel. "Too bad she didn't ask that of you yesterday," she mutters, turning away. "I assume you got this cut in the crash? The one you caused? By driving like a reckless idiot?" Her words aren't any less offensive spoken to my chart in her lap.

"I'm surprised you don't remember." It's pointless to try to hide the disgust in my voice. Every one of my fingernails could have just been ripped off and it would only begin to explain the degree of pounding irritation now alive in my brain.

"I was a little distracted." She hasn't opened my chart but it's still holding all her interest. She puts a hand to her mouth. Swallows hard.

I toss my helmet on the chair and catch her annoyed glance when the back of the chair hits the wall with a thud. I lean against the exam table. She stands and reaches for the blood pressure cuff on the wall.

"Just the stitches."

She drops her hand. Opens my chart, skims a few pages, closes it. "Okay."

There must be a note in there that says to leave me the hell alone.

"How did you get the laceration? Was it the car accident?"

I didn't realize I'd have to break in a new nurse today. I should have asked for one of the regulars.

"I'm only asking in case you need a tetanus shot."

"Just the stitches." How many times am I going to have to say it?

She presses her lips into a tight line.

How did I not notice my own truck in the parking lot? My apathy will be the death of me if I don't recover my focus. Maybe I need a change. I've been here what—ten years? Twelve? I can't stay much longer. It seems a good time for a change of scenery. Putting that plan in action may prove to be a problem with my current state of lethargy and indifference though. It would be a hell of a lot easier just to lie in bed at night and wait for them to come for me. Get it over with. My thoughts make it seem so simple, but I know I could never allow them to win again.

The silence hits me and I return to the present to find Liv Gilchrist's blue eyes boring holes into mine.

"What?" I ask, feeling as if there is an unanswered question hanging in the air between us.

"Do you want to wait for the doctor or would you like me to give it a try?"

"Usually one of the nurses does it," I answer without thinking. Give it a try? Fuck. I'm probably better off doing it myself.

The look on her face tells me she expected a different answer. Or she's just been sentenced to the electric chair. "That would be me. But we don't suture a head wound. We usually—"

"Just do something."

Her pause feels twenty minutes long. "Lie down on the table and keep your eyes on the corner of the ceiling."

I slip out of my jacket and drop it on top of my helmet. As the paper on the table crinkles under my weight, it occurs to me this might be a bad position for me considering what I did to her car yesterday. She rummages through the drawers then abruptly exits the room. When she returns, she's empty-handed. She leaves the door wide open. My discomfort in this closet is either obvious or contagious. She selects supplies from the drawers, and I realize she's not going to fill the time by talking my ear off. With me captive on this table, she could really chew me out—or worse. Endless trivial details about children, friends, or boyfriends—she keeps it all to herself. Reluctantly, I give her bonus points for that. And it sure beats the hell out of waiting around all day for the only doctor. She finishes in half the time I expected and starts to clean up, so I stand.

With her back to me, she says, "All done. You can check out with Rachel up front." She stiffens and covers her mouth like she's about to sneeze.

I grab my jacket and helmet and head out.

Outside, the glaring concrete blinds me, and I pause in sudden awareness of the bright and vast blue sky. The clear air fills my lungs as my eyes adjust, and I try to remember if the weather was this nice on my way to the clinic. The skin on my forehead feels itchy and tight, but the relief I feel walking away from the clinic is a potent amphetamine injected straight into my heart. I swing my leg over the Ninja and start it up. The ride toward the highway passes in slow motion. As soon as I hit the entrance ramp I open it up and fly.

CHAPTER 3

LIV

T HANK GOD TREY Bevan is no conversationalist. I wasn't sure how to break it to him that his truck and I don't get along. I may not be able to forgive his driving, but it doesn't matter. It's going to take a lot more than a nonfatal car accident to shake me. It was nice of him to let me borrow his truck, even nicer that he thought to grab my stuff out of my car. Especially the Pepto-Bismol. My volatile stomach turned on me again at the clinic. No warning, just like the last time. I can't believe I chugged the rest of the bottle.

I sit in the truck preparing myself to drive it again, wishing I had demanded a rental car. I should've asked him when I had the syringe poised over his face. But right now, I need to run by the pharmacy and pick up another bottle of Pepto.

Maybe this nausea is a new spin on the torment, the latest method to keep me reminded of my solitude. I can't deny it seems at its worst when I'm around other people. It's like some torturer has taken over my life, assigned to the duty of keeping me on my toes. Preventing comfort. Hindering rest. And now I've conjured up some bogey-man to explain what must be simple nerves resulting from a cross-country move and a run-in with the jerk of the century. The only prescription is time. Everything is better with time. Not perfect, but better.

I start the engine, jam it into first gear, and the truck lurches forward. Luckily, I can pull forward through the empty parking space in front of me. As I shove it into second, the grind of the gears shakes the whole vehicle. I miss third, and the engine revs so loud it sounds like it's going to explode. I stomp on the clutch and try to find second again. I'm not sure if I hit second or fourth but finally I'm cruising, if you can call it that. I try to avoid red lights as I hit the pharmacy and drive home.

Coyote Dog rises from his lookout on the porch to greet me but ducks and lowers his tail when I miss another gear and the truck shudders and dies fifty feet from the house. Close enough. Maybe I should call a cab tomorrow—but I doubt they have cabs here. I drop down from the truck and trudge up to the house, immediately nudging the thermo-stat up a few degrees and changing into jeans and an old thermal shirt as soon as I get inside. I pull off both socks.

Wood floor and bare feet. A pleasant combination to make me feel at home when home has never been so far away.

I go to work cleaning, starting with the dirty windows obscuring my mountain view so still and perfect it seems to be painted on the windows instead of dwelling outside in real life. Throwing myself into the task relieves me like a deep meditation. The Zen of a rag and some window cleaner. Doctors should prescribe it.

Night approaches, but my appetite lags too far behind to be noticed for dinner. I make some oatmeal—my fallback when the idea of eating a meal seems more like punishment than pleasure—and go outside to the back porch with a piece of cheese in my palm in case Coyote Dog comes around. With my bowl empty, I stand and notice Coyote Dog peeking at me from around the side of the house. I'm an awful throw but I try anyway, and the cheese lands close enough for him to snatch it up after a calculating look at me.

I wander to the other end of the porch, and suddenly I'm knee deep in floor boards, crying out and cursing as if there's someone around to hear me. The knee that didn't plunge through the rotted boards slams into hard wood. I sit and tug my injured leg out. Deep, wide abrasions full of splinters run the length of my calf where the hole's jagged sides pushed up the leg of my jeans. Then the blood comes, welling up through the wounds and joining forces to run a river down my leg. I've seen worse, but I can't keep the tears from stinging my eyes from yet another setback. Especially since the rotted boards were noted in my home inspection. My mind was simply too occupied to retain these critical bits of information. As I lie down on my back, Coyote Dog inches to my side.

I stare at the darkening sky and feel sorry for myself for a few minutes. That's all I'll allow. Every minute brings me closer to the edge of that pit I know too well. I won't make it out a second time.

Coyote Dog inches closer. I pretend not to notice, hoping he'll stay. He lies down like a Sphinx a foot away. I owe him a whole block of cheese.

Time's up.

Tomorrow, I'll have to call someone to fix this. Right now, getting myself into the house is top priority. I hobble inside and carefully slide out of my jeans. Sitting on the edge of the bathtub, I remove every splinter with my tweezers. It's a good thing I've got a strong stomach for this, even when it's on the fritz. After washing my leg in the tub, I apply ointment, wrap my calf in a bandage, pull on some cut-off sweatpants, and limp into the living room.

A pain reliever would be a good idea but I'm already on my back on the couch, staring into the wooden beams in the ceiling. The skylight is a dark square that reflects a portion of the room back at me. I could kill the lights and watch the stars, but the light switch is too far away and my leg has become a chaos of sensation—the bone-deep throb of a future nasty bruise, the tight, crawly rawness of exposed dermis.

I cross my elbows over my eyes. Falling asleep on the couch is a bad habit I broke long ago when its only purpose was to get me closer to that sound of his key in the lock. One night on the couch becomes two, then a week, and before I realize I'll be fused to the thing again and unable to breathe without falling apart. I start to drift, knowing that when I wake up sore and disoriented, I'll remember this moment when I should have stopped myself. I'll remember every day and night spent on the couch, and how I'm not going to repeat that. And I'll get my ass up and take a shower and get dressed. Eat. Go to work. Function.

A heavy air settles on me. A pressure change, but I haven't moved. My arms fall off my face to allow more breath to flow but all it does is make me feel more smothered. I sit up. Saliva floods my mouth like it does when your last meal wants back out the way it went in. I should have my blood work done at the clinic, maybe run my symptoms by Dr. Wu. Just as I lie back down I hear a knock at the door.

I push myself up and shuffle toward the front door, gripping the wall as another wave of nausea overtakes me. This sure is getting old. I hop into the kitchen and down a swig of Pepto-Bismol. Another knock. I know I look a mess with unkempt hair, cut-off sweatpants, and bloody, bandaged leg, but there's really no one I need to impress. I reach the door and look out the window to see Trey Bevan on my porch. Swallowing bile, I pull the door open and try to hold it together.

He's visibly taken aback by my appearance. "Did that happen yesterday?"

He sounds a little guilt-ridden. Good.

"No, just now. I fell through a rotten spot in the back porch." Damn. I should have told him I fell off a ladder. My attempt at humor is always one sentence too late.

"Oh." He looks past me into the house. "Are you in for the night?"

"Why?"

"I need my truck for a few hours. I'll have it back by the morning."

He's changed his clothes. The jeans are probably the same, but his T-shirt has been replaced by a thick flannel shirt and a puffy nylon vest.

"I'll get the key." I open the door wider. "Come in."

I never realized how tall he is, or how he seems to have a permanent scowl on his face. To be fair, most men are taller than me. Just not as tall as him. And I'm sure my own scowl could easily outdo his. He stands awkwardly in the foyer while I retrieve his key and hand it over.

"Have a good one," he mumbles, and he's out the door, scowl and all.

On my path back to the couch I hear the truck start, grind, then start and grind again. Crap. What did I do? The slam of the hood sounds through the front door, followed by loud footsteps back to the house, and rapid, angry knocking. Holding back my churning stomach, I open the door.

"A bit vengeful, aren't you?" he says.

"What?" Should I be surprised by his vicious expression?

"An eye for an eye? I trash your car so you trash mine?"

"Are you serious? You think I did that on purpose?" I tighten my grip on the door. He's too close, and I'm not letting him get any closer without a fight.

"Yes. I think it was sabotage. I should've seen it coming." He turns his back to me like he's looking for someone out in the yard to strangle.

"It's not my fault your truck is a piece of shit. Maybe next time you total someone's car you should give them a vehicle that's drivable." My stomach rolls. It's certainly not helping the situation, or my attitude.

He places both hands on top of his head as if he's trying to figure out who to kill first. Me, or…well me. He turns back around slowly. I try to look intimidating, but his eyes cut through me.

His arms drop to his sides, fists clenched. "Well played."

I'm at a loss for words. This guy is something else. There's nothing for me to gain by ruining his truck. He glares at me for so long I can barely stand it then turns and storms back to the truck. After grabbing a motorcycle helmet out of the bed, he stomps behind the truck to a black motorcycle I didn't notice was parked there. *Kawasaki ZX-14.* I've seen that somewhere before. Gravel flies as he spins the tires and shoots down the road. Don't know how I missed the sound of that thing coming toward the house.

Call me a coward, but I've given up on this day. It's a lost cause. Although it's still early, I take a sleeping pill and tuck myself into bed. Yeah, I said I'd quit the pills. Three nights without them is a great achievement but it's also three crappy nights of sleep. Somehow I'll have to talk my doctor into another refill. I stare at the ceiling, counting backward from one thousand until the pill takes hold of me.

I awaken to the alarm clock and groan as my sore leg reminds me of yesterday's events. I can't call in sick on my second day, and I can't stay home and feel sorry for myself. But I can get myself out of bed and go to the medicine cabinet for pain reliever. I manage to wash up and dress, pull my hair into a ponytail, and pack myself a lunch. A bowl of cereal and a banana serve as a breakfast I hardly taste. I grab my bag and step outside into the cool, clean morning air. Coyote Dog rolls happily in the dew-covered grass while birds sing to one another across the forest.

Oh yeah. The truck is broken. And he probably took the key.

Coyote Dog wanders up and looks at me, his head cocked to the side. I sit on the stoop. A vehicle passes on the road through the trees but instead of growing quiet its sound gets closer. Coyote Dog sneaks into the woods. Seconds later, a bright red pick-up drives toward me. As it comes to a halt, the window rolls down to reveal a large, bearded man in red flannel and a baseball cap. I'm going to need to buy more flannel to fit in here.

"You Liv?"

"Yes?"

"I'm your ride." His window rolls back up without my answer.

I shouldn't look a gift horse in the mouth. Is the gift horse going to take me somewhere and torture me and bury my dead body in the woods? Entirely possible. Hell, I have nothing to lose. I limp over to the open passenger door and climb inside.

"Trey wanted me to tell you he doesn't go back on his word, no matter how difficult the other party is. Normally I wouldn't want to get involved, but he pays good." He snickers and pulls out onto the road.

He glances over at me and grins. "Well, Trey didn't exactly use the word 'difficult,' but I edited for your benefit."

His laughter seems to shake the truck. I imagine the sound repeating later, when he and Trey can have a nice laugh together at my expense. But that would require Mr. Crabby to lighten up. Somehow I don't think that's going to happen since he's too busy throwing tantrums in my front yard.

Work is uneventful, nothing like the ER in Chicago, but it's a pace I hope to fall into with time. I'm showered with sympathy about my leg, and I quickly tire of reliving the event for every single person I encounter. If my injury is the most exciting thing that happens around here, I'm going to have to find a hobby. Another nurse named Jennifer removes my old bandage and puts on a fresh one while she describes the clinic's most eccentric patients to my honest attempt at interest. I desperately want to fit in here despite my rough start in this town.

I run into Dr. Wu as I'm getting ready to leave, and he insists I take tomorrow off. I try to explain that I'd rather come in than sit at home but he tells me my shift has already been covered. The red pick-up is waiting outside for me, and Jennifer walks me out and helps me into the truck. She closes the door and waves as we pull away.

"I won't need a ride tomorrow," I say to my driver.

"Yep."

Figuring there's no way he could know I have tomorrow off, I assume he's just acknowledging my statement. We drive in silence, and I stare out the window at the zigzag of the tree line against the sky, rising and falling as if oblivious of the road lying flat below it. As we near the driveway, I spot Coyote Dog pacing near the entrance. He follows the truck to the house and stops to turn and look at me in exasperation, like he's really being put out.

Trey's truck perches on jack stands with a pair of legs sticking out from underneath. I want to laugh—the half-tamed wildlife and I seem to be getting along better than I am with my own species. I give Coyote Dog an *I know* nod. He makes three tight circles and curls up by the porch, not taking his wary eyes off our intruder. He must be more frustrated than me. This was his house before it was mine.

I reach for the door handle. My stomach heaves. I slide out of the truck and hobble inside without even a look in Trey's direction.

"Trey, man! Pay up!"

I slam the front door before I have to hear his voice. The bathroom seems a mile away but when I reach it and flip open the toilet lid, the trek has settled my stomach back into place. I change out of my scrubs into an oversized T-shirt and the same cut-off sweatpants I wore yesterday. Staring at myself in the mirror, I try to relax the guarded expression I wore all day.

In the kitchen, I glance out the window to see the red truck gone and Trey standing over the engine of his own truck, twisting a rag in his hands like its motion is turning rusty gears in his head. No one told him he could use my driveway as a repair shop. Maybe I should give him the phone number for Joe's Towing.

My stomach starts to churn in a mild threat of what's to come. Food might help. I shake out a bowl of cereal, grab an apple and a piece of cheese, and head toward the back porch.

I step outside, testing the boards as I go. I forgot to make that phone call to find a handyman. Pale sections of the flooring catch my attention, and my eyes move from one board to the next until it dawns on me. He fixed them. He replaced all the rotten boards. There's a tightening in my head when I realize something else. This guy thinks he's god's gift to women. That's what this has been about all along.

He causes an accident. Instead of calling the police and the insurance companies, he wants to handle it himself. He wants to pay, he wants to take my car to his mechanic, he wants full control. He gives me a vehicle to drive. He goes to all this trouble because I am just a helpless female, incapable of handling anything too complex. And this is why he's made himself at home in my driveway. He probably thinks he's entitled. Like I'm indebted to him in some way. Like he's welcome here. Well he was right about one thing. I am a sucker, because I fell for the whole thing. Until now.

I plop down in a chair and set my apple on the armrest. Coyote Dog wanders around the corner of the house, so I toss him the cheese, and he hangs out closer to me than he ever has. I finish my cereal, take a bite of my apple, and gag as my stomach violently resists. The sound of the outside faucet squeaking sends a wave of relief. He's probably cleaning up and will leave soon. The faucet squeaks again. A heavy tread vibrates through the porch. To my surprise, Coyote Dog moves in front of me.

He comes around the corner in a grimy T-shirt and jeans, soaking wet from head to waist. The nurse in me cringes as soon as I notice he got grease and dirt in the gash I treated at the clinic. One of the butterfly bandages is already missing. His eyes meet mine, and I stare him down.

He breaks the silence. "I guess I should probably—"

"I didn't ask you to fix this." I gesture toward the new boards.

"No…" he agrees, standing up straighter like he's been caught off guard.

"Did it occur to you to ask first? That I may not be as incompetent as you think?"

"No, but it *did* occur to me that in your current state it would be impossible for you to fix it yourself."

His wet hair falls onto his brow so he runs the back of his hand across his forehead to brush it to the side. I'm about to be sick. I'm not going to last this time. I take a deep breath as the pressure on my chest intensifies. Maybe it's altitude sickness.

We glare at each other. I have nothing to say to him. I wish he'd just leave, but I know if I tell him to get off my property he's just going to get more confrontational. He probably expects me to back down, look away, apologize. So I hold his eye until he mutters under his breath, "Not even worth it," and turns away.

"What?" I demand.

He faces me. If it's possible for him to look even nastier, he does. "I came back here to tell you the truck was already fucked. You didn't do it. So I owe you an apology, but really…now? It's not even worth it." He waits for my reaction.

I boost myself up and limp into the house, sliding the glass door closed behind me. This is just too much. I don't have to take this abuse over something that's his fault to begin with. He opens the door, and I spin to face him. I should have locked it.

"Apology not accepted." I really hate to be childish.

"Fine by me." He tosses the truck key on the table and yanks the door closed. Any harder and he'd be cleaning up shattered glass. I should tell him these displays of aggression are lost on me. I hear his heavy boots stomp off the porch, his motorcycle's engine start up and buzz away.

Good thing I'm off work tomorrow. I'd rather die than drive his goddamn truck.

CHAPTER 4

TREY

I KNOW I SHOULDN'T let my temper loose like this. I gun the Ninja hard into the turn. Nobody closes a door in my face. And to think I was going to apologize. Her car is supposed to be ready tomorrow, and it can't come soon enough. Once her car is returned I'll never have to see her face again.

River greets me in the driveway with an "all clear" so I park the Ninja in the garage and unwind the garden hose. The herbs are doing great this year. Potatoes always do great. The cabbage and kale seem to be having a hard time but I'm having a hard time caring. After watering, I go around the house to make sure nothing has been tampered with and all my traps are still in place. River knows exactly which spots to avoid. The wildlife does too. I've made sure of that. No need for her meals to get caught in a trap. That takes the sport out of it for River.

The first thing I do inside is pour a drink. I make a few calls to my current jobs to explain my truck has been out of service and work will resume shortly. People aren't uptight around here. They don't mind a few delays now and then. Leaving this laid-back lifestyle will be a shock to the system when I do find a new place to live. I'll at least wait until after harvest so none of my vegetables will go to waste.

I finish my drink and stare at the blood-splattered wall. It takes several minutes to will my legs to move me from the counter. The kitchen is still a mess. How long has it been like this? Two days? Three? I sweep up the broken dishes and spilled food. What an unruly dinner guest he was. It was stupid to wait for him to come into the house for me, but I'd do it again just for the amusement. Two in a row seems out of the regular pattern. They're probably trying to throw me off. A challenge would be a welcome reprieve from the monotony of my life, but I know it's not going to happen. I'll always be too good for them. They obviously haven't figured that out yet.

After returning all the knives to the drawer and picking up the fallen chairs, I boil some water for the herbs and let them steep. Every time I do this it reminds me of my mother. Dabbing the brew onto the gash on my brow cools the nerve endings, the annoying tickle of split skin. My mind drifts back to when I would sit on the kitchen counter and watch my mother work. It was the only safe place in that house.

I dump some of the brew into a shallow tray to soak my hands, scratched and cut from working on the truck. The skin on a few of my knuckles is busted open and full of grease, but it won't be like that for long. Once my hands feel better, I pour the remaining brew into ice trays and stash them in the freezer for later.

These spikes in my temper are gaining ground on feelings I've worked hard to repress. My mind wanders to that day—the day I came home to an empty house, belongings strewn everywhere, unmistakable signs of struggle. My rage, demanding answers no one would give me.

I shove my feet back in my boots and go outside calling for River. We walk to the riverbank and follow it to the old footbridge. I consider crossing it but remember who's on the other side. We continue on my side of the river and reach the clearing with just a sliver of sun left above the horizon. We sit until the moon and stars are bright enough to lead me home, and my wrath has been stuffed back down where it belongs.

I take a different route home, one that takes us higher into the bluffs. A clear night like this offers the best view, an opposite palette from the colors of the day, a negative image counteracting the day's positive one. Shadows in varied shades of black ground the highlights of the moon and stars and their reflections on the water. My boots settle on flat rock. I walk to the edge, losing the cover of the trees. Illuminated rectangles of yellow light glow below me, unfamiliar, my brain not making the connection until I see her rise from her seat and move toward the railing, her bandaged leg bright white in the moonlight. I never realized this bluff overlooks the side of the Joseph place. It hasn't been lit up at night for a long time.

I'm too far away to read her expression, but I know she can see me. My sound night, my privacy, invaded. But I feel like the voyeur, caught at his own game. Although this meeting was completely unintentional, it probably validates her belief that I'm a creep. Or whatever she thinks of me. She'll have to work much harder to validate what I really am.

I could jump. A late night swim. That would give me a reason to be up here. I can't remember how deep the river is at this point. River growls and I turn, sensing it too, as a coyote charges from the trees and River meets him head on. He just wants to provoke her. If a coyote had been tracking us we'd have a perfect reason to be up here. His pack must be nearby, and they must be bored tonight. I retreat into the aspen on the other side of the bluff and descend until I reach the river. I follow it toward home, stalling a little so River can catch up to me. Soon she does, panting hard, in high spirits.

We arrive home and I let River do the rounds. I'm wiped out, physically and mentally. She returns to signal everything is okay before running off into the woods. I devour some leftovers from the fridge. Untie my boots. Fall onto the couch.

My first waking thought the next morning is who am I going to call to help me pick up her car? It's a two-hour drive one way. I can't ask Wayne again, and everyone else I know is working. I am not putting this off until the weekend.

My only option is to take the Ninja out there and drive her car back myself, then drive the truck out there again this weekend to pick up the Ninja. But, if I'm going all the way out there today, I really should bring the truck and make a supply run. That means I'll have to drive her to work. And pick her up in her car after work. Suck it up. It's better than letting this go on until the weekend. I need this behind me.

I take a quick shower and dress. It's a short drive on the Ninja to her place, and as I ride up the driveway I see the truck still parked in the same spot so I know I made it before she left. I park the Ninja and toss my helmet in the bed of the truck. I'll give her fifteen minutes. If she hasn't come out by then I'll knock.

She probably heard me pull up. Damn, this is becoming far more complicated than it needs to be. I go up to the door and knock. Patience is not my strongest trait, and it takes her forever to come to the door. She moves the curtain aside and stares at me long and hard before opening the door.

Her voice is all business. "Can I help you?"

"I need to use my truck today. I'll have to take you to work."

"I'm off today."

"Okay. Then I'll take the truck. Unless you need it?" I try very hard to be polite. I can't allow my temper to escape from its confinement again.

"No. All yours. Let me get the key." She goes inside.

If she's off work, she could come with me, drive her own car back, and put an end to this nightmare. She returns and hands me the key. I start to ask her then think better of it, but she catches on. Apparently nothing gets by her.

"Are you picking up my car?"

"Yes. I'll be back in a few hours."

"A few hours? You towed my car that far away?"

I'm not telling her he's the best mechanic in the state. And he'll rush a job for me if I need him to, without taking any shortcuts.

"Who's going to drive the truck back?"

"Me."

"How?"

"I'll go back for it this weekend." Ramp and tie-downs are already in the bed. It's all ready to go. I turn to head toward the truck but her voice stops me.

"I'm coming with you. You're not doing me any more favors. Let's just get this over with, okay?"

Finally something we can agree on.

She accepts my silence as a bargain. "Give me ten minutes to get dressed."

I can't control a snort of disgust. No woman could get dressed in ten minutes. She closes the door in my face, again. If it happens one more time, I'm ripping it off its hinges and beating her with it.

Back in the truck, I wait and watch the clock for my own entertainment. Fourteen minutes later, she hobbles out with her wet hair in a ponytail. I check the clock again. I must have timed it wrong. She even took a shower. As she gets closer I notice a giant bottle of Pepto-Bismol sticking out of the top of her bag. If she gets sick in my truck, I swear I'll kill her.

Shit. My supply run. I can't go while she's with me, and I won't have time on the way back.

"What?" She pauses with her seatbelt halfway to the buckle.

"Nothing."

We coast down the road in silence. As I accelerate onto the highway, the sun blasts from behind a cloud and we both flip down our visors. I put on my sunglasses, and she puts on hers. She opens her window all the way and pulls a book out of her bag. Thank god. No talking necessary.

Fifteen minutes into the ride, her shifting around in the seat makes me want to strap her down. It's distracting and annoying and she doesn't seem to care. When she finally settles down, it only lasts a few seconds. She squirms again, reaches down for her big pink bottle and takes a king-size gulp. That can't be good for you. But she's a nurse, she should know. I hear a sharp intake of breath and whip my head around to look at her, worried she's about to blow.

She looks back at me, her eyes huge through the tinted lenses of her sunglasses. "You make me sick!"

I can't contain an outburst of hollow laughter. It took her this long to figure that one out? "I hate to say it, but the feeling's mutual."

"No, you literally make me sick!" In her excitement, her voice rises to a frequency that makes my teeth grind together. "I just figured it out. Every time I'm around you, I get sick to my stomach. I think you were even there the first time it happened." She turns to stare out the window, animated by her theory. "The gas station…" she whispers.

"That's great news. Once this is over you'll have a good reason to avoid me." What an encouraging thought. And I'll have to modify my hiking routes.

But she can't really be serious.

"Can we pull over? I want to test this."

I guess she is serious. "No. This is ridiculous." I can't keep the disgust out of my voice.

"Okay then. I have to pee."

I exhale hard to voice my disapproval.

She glances at me. "I know if you try really hard, you might not be such an asshole."

"Don't you get sick of hearing your smart mouth?"

"Don't you get sick of your inflated ego?"

My hands clench the steering wheel hard enough to keep me from killing her, and I turn off the highway at the next exit. I pull up to a quick shop and she gets out. She disappears into the store and emerges with some snacks about ten minutes later. When she climbs back into her seat, I go for the ignition.

"Wait," she demands.

I lean my head on the back of the seat and stare upwards. Several minutes pass. She opens her door and gets out again. I watch her gimp back toward the highway until I can barely see her. A few minutes later she heads back, triumphant.

She opens the door and gets in. "It is totally you. You make me sick."

"You are so full of shit." I turn the key, jam the truck into gear, and floor it toward the highway. DOOR AJAR illuminates in the instrument panel.

"I wish I was. That would be easier to explain. This is going to be a very long ride." She laughs under her breath.

"I could have told you that before." I stare at the DOOR AJAR warning when I should be watching the road. The warning becomes a biting offense directed straight at me. I don't know how anyone could get in a vehicle and not realize they hadn't closed the door all the way.

"What cologne do you wear?" she asks.

"I don't wear cologne."

"What deodorant?"

"Whatever's on sale at the store."

"Which would be?"

"I have no idea!" I feel an urge to rip the steering wheel out of the truck. I should've never agreed to let her come. Not only have I become lazy and careless, but I'm growing stupider by the day. And if that DOOR AJAR doesn't disappear, I'm going to explode. I lean over her and yank her door closed. She freezes and remains that way until both my hands return to the wheel.

"You could have asked me," she hisses.

"You failed to do it the first time."

If she continues this attitude, she's going to be a lot more than just sick to her stomach. She offers me some peanuts, and I ignore her. She seems jubilant in her discovery, satisfied at hatching this idiotic explanation of the pattern she's built in her mind. Her body language suggests a better mood due to this. I think I prefer it when she's in a bad mood, so I start thinking about things I could say to make her mad. When she pulls out her book, I put it to rest and try to concentrate on the road stretching out in front of us.

The drive drones on. The flipping of pages in her book mark the time. We make a few short stops to give her a break from her "sickness" and I humor her, unconvinced it's me causing it. Every noise she makes, every movement, combines to create my own customized torture. The more time that passes, the worse it gets. Her breaks become mine as well, allowing respite from the treatment so perfected I pray it remains secret. If my enemies could reproduce this, I wouldn't last a day at their hands.

By the time we stop to eat lunch at a fast food place, I want to strangle her. I lost count of how many exits we passed before agreeing on where to eat. I finally give up and give in—I'm so hungry I could eat my own arm. Even a simple routine like eating lunch has to be a difficult, complicated ordeal with this woman.

In the restaurant, we pretend not to know each other and choose tables at opposite ends of the room. It's a seamless arrangement, like we had the same idea. She finishes before me and goes back to the truck without a glance in my direction. She must be ready to get this trip over with too. Thank god it's only one way.

When we return to the road, every familiar creak and rattle of my overworked ten-year-old truck adds to the mounting tower of pressure ready to blow. Although the noises never bothered me before, I doubt I'll be able to drive this truck again without them reminding me of the soaring aggravation I feel now with her a foot away from me. The sound of the tires on the pavement could be the sound of sandpaper on my skin and I wouldn't be any more bothered by it. The atoms making up every object around me merge into a microscopic army specializing in my personal persecution.

"What?" I blurt, caught off guard by a question fired my way.

"It would be nice to have some background music."

Too consumed with my discomfort, I don't bother answering. Her loud, disgusted sigh in return almost runs me off the road, murder-suicide style.

"Fine." I pound the stereo knob with my fist. It comes on to pure static. I punch each preset until something comes in.

"That wasn't too hard, now was it?" I can sense her snotty expression. I don't need to see it to know it's there.

The music does nothing but apply another layer of agony onto my hell. I wonder how it would feel to kill an innocent person. A helpless woman. There are so many ways I could do it, right now. I wouldn't have to stop the truck for some. My buried conscience whispers a warning that I would regret it once I was removed from this situation. Being here now, regret is hard to imagine. When we enter the Missoula city limits, I can already taste the relief I will have when she's out of my truck and my life.

My mechanic is his usual talkative self, and I nod and agree to everything he says while eyeing Liv as she looks her car up and down. If she makes one complaint, I will surely snap. I can't expect her to notice the four new tires she got out of the deal—tires she should have bought a long time ago. She returns to us, visibly pleased, so I go inside the office to pay. The bill is brutal. I'm paying for my sins with both my sanity *and* my wallet. Some of them at least.

The whole trip home I'm not far behind her. I'm not trying to follow her, but it seems as soon as I think she's lost me, I turn a curve or go over a hill and there she is again, her red car throwing the sun's reflection like a beacon. Alone in my truck the time passes quickly and soon we're back within Black River city limits. If I don't pick up the Ninja now, I might have to face her again tomorrow and ruin another perfectly good day. It will take me five minutes to load it into my truck and I'll be out of there.

I trail her up her driveway and to the house, and park behind her as she gets out of her car. I'm sure she's already figured out why I'm here. She heads straight for the house, so I sit in my truck to let her get inside. Out of nowhere, her dog darts in front of her legs. She stumbles a few steps before steadying herself. Her irritated curse carries across the yard to me. Poor dog doesn't know she's been in a bad mood all day. The dog continues crisscrossing in front of her in an obvious attempt to impede her path, and I can't help but chuckle. She stops.

I follow her gaze to her wide-open front door.

I'm out of the truck before I can think, defenses up. She turns around, and I'm already across the yard grabbing her shoulders.

"Did you leave your door open this morning?" I try to keep my voice low.

"No…" she says, in slow motion.

"Get in the truck." I push her between the shoulder blades toward the truck and slip up to the house, my senses in overdrive. There's an audience out there, and whatever happens inside must be quiet and clean. I move around the house, checking every room, noting the destruction they've left behind. Every box is emptied, every drawer upturned. The guilt is a plastic bag over my face. My truck has been here too much, overnight even. They don't know the situation. They thought I was staying here, with her. Do they think I'm that fucking stupid?

It doesn't matter what they think. I've carelessly drawn an innocent person into my purgatory due to my own negligence. I thought my apathy would be the death of me, but I was wrong. It will be the death of her.

CHAPTER 5

LIV

H E MATERIALIZES AT the front door and crosses the yard toward me. As he gets close, I notice his green eyes, intense, fierce, and a strange rigid poise to his body. He yanks open the driver's side door and slides inside.

"I'm taking you to my house."

"No! Why?"

"It's not safe for you here. They think I'm here. They're after *me*. If I leave you here they will come back." He grips the steering wheel but stares straight ahead, not meeting my eyes. His jaw muscle tenses and rolls like he's grinding his teeth. The steering wheel looks like a toy in his fists.

"Who?" I laugh. "I can't just leave. I live here. I'll be fine." I pull the door release to get out. He's crazy.

He grabs my wrist. "Please. Listen." His eyes struggle to convince me. This violent change in him compared to the expression he wore all day is like a plunge in an icy lake.

I twist out of his grasp and he returns his hands to the steering wheel. If he crushed it in his fists I wouldn't be surprised. A primal fear builds inside me. His alarm is contagious. I have to see what he saw inside.

"Can I at least get some stuff from the house?" I'm startled by the sound of my own words. I can't really be going along with this.

He shoves open his door, jumps out, and walks around the truck to open my door. He leads me to the house but at the last minute, he turns. His face is close to mine. My adrenaline must be working to calm the sickness—it's hardly noticeable now.

"Are you sure you want to see this?"

"Yes."

He pulls me inside behind him and I gasp, covering my mouth with both hands. My belongings litter the floor as if a cyclone had raged through the house. Every drawer, closet and unpacked box ransacked and their contents scattered. Shock numbs me and empties my mind, every thought flushing down a massive storm drain.

He looks at me. "Get what you need quickly. We need to go."

I nod. I step into the middle of the room and glass crunches under my shoes. Trey and I both look up to see an empty hole where the skylight used to be.

"They came in through the skylight." He points out the obvious.

"Why not the door?" I hear myself ask.

"They were trying to ambush us."

With this knowledge, I get to work sorting through my things, throwing what I need into a plastic trash bag. On my way out I grab a pillow and blanket. With tears clouding my vision I look at Trey, catching his arm to stop him.

"What if it rains?"

He puts me in the truck and slams the door closed. I hear him rummaging around in the back of the truck as I stare at the house, unable to process the scene stamped in my memory. I see him dart toward the house with a piece of heavy plastic and a hammer. He disappears around the side of the house and re-emerges on the roof, where he nails the plastic over the hole and disappears again. Then he's at my door. "Will you be okay driving if I lead you on the Ninja?"

I swallow my tears. "Yes." I scoot over to the driver's seat and start the engine. The motorcycle fires up behind me and advances ahead, skidding in the gravel. I put the truck in gear and follow.

My mind is devoid of thought and emotion during the drive toward town, over the bridge, down a winding road to a gravel driveway. I go through the motions without thinking. I park the truck behind him and turn off the engine. When I look up, he's already at my window.

His voice reaches me through the glass. "Stay in the truck until I come back."

I sit and stare until he returns, a dog on his heels. He pushes the motorcycle into the garage and walks back toward me. Halfway, he stops and looks straight up into the sky for a drawn-out moment. He seems to mold into the scene. I find myself holding my breath until he moves again. He opens my door. "Everything is okay here, but you have to stay right behind me. There's only one path into the house, and you have to stay on it. Got it?"

I don't know what he's talking about, but I follow him anyway. He zigzags his way to the front door and closes it behind us. I stand in the entry clutching my pillow to my chest as he carries my things into the house. He returns with some wadded up sheets and takes them to the other side of the house where I hear the washing machine start up.

When I see him coming back I blurt out, "My car is back there. Is it okay to leave my car there?"

His shoulders slump. "Yes. Your car needs to be there."

He grips the back of the couch with both hands and leans over it, head bowed. "Do you know, if I hadn't let you come with me today..." He sounds like he's talking more to himself than me. His eyes meet mine. "You only have to stay here until I have a plan. I'll come up with a plan. The long-term plan is I leave, but I can't leave until we have steered them away from you. Do you want a drink?"

I follow him into the kitchen and take a seat at the table. He removes two glasses from the cabinet and pours a few inches of amber liquor into one.

"Just water for me." It comes out in a whisper.

He fills the other glass with water and drops it on the table in front of me. I take a sip and look up. His glass is already empty.

"I'm going to be sick every day I'm here." My voice has no emotion.

"It can't be helped."

I stare into my glass. My life has somehow spiraled into a new form of turmoil ever since he ran into me a few days ago.

"Are you in the witness protection program or something?" I sound accusatory without meaning to.

He searches my face and replies, dragging out the word, "Yes."

"What's your real name?" I try to make it come out softer.

"I didn't change my name."

"You can't be in the witness protection program and not change your name." My shrill voice doesn't sound like it's coming from me.

His face morphs back into the face I sat next to during our drive together this morning. His eyes narrow and his mouth sets into a harsh line beside a tense jaw, settling the permanent scowl back into its natural position. He pours more liquor into his glass and drinks it in one swig.

My stomach turns, and I stand suddenly, shoving the chair backward with my legs. "Can I go outside?"

"No."

"So I'm a hostage?"

He exhales loudly. "Yes."

I stare at him.

"But please, make yourself at home."

I need to get out of this room. I turn to fix the chair and notice he has a back porch similar to mine. "What about the porch? Is the porch okay?"

He looks at me as if he's surprised I'm still talking. "The porch is okay."

My thoughts clear. "So, everything outside is boo-by-trapped except for the porch."

He addresses the ceiling instead of me. "Yes. Just don't get too close to the railing."

I escape outside into the early evening air. The land here is lower in elevation, close enough to the river for me to hear the gurgle of water over rock, even though it's mostly drowned out by the cacophony of chatty birds in the trees looming over the house. Unlike my cabin which is high on its own slope, this cabin lies deep in the elements—hunkered under pine trees, sidling next to the river. The only view is coniferous forest rising up on all sides.

A vegetable garden spans most of the gentle slope behind the house until it drops away and changes from trimmed lawn to overgrown grass to forest bursting skyward. Flat wooden boxes with slanted glass covers are built into the earth past the farthest row of plants, some of their lids propped open with wooden blocks at the corners. They look like miniature greenhouses. This guy is dedicated to whatever he's growing.

A wide trail is worn in the grass along the length of the garden, and at the far end rests a huge tractor tire on its side. I've seen rural yards with abandoned farm equipment, but usually nature is trying to reclaim the metal and rubber. This tire is clear of all weeds and plants, like it dropped straight out of the sky then skidded down the grass on its side, exposing a path of dirt. I peer over the railing to see that the trail ends at a pile of sandbags at the house. I can't imagine the river would flood all the way here. But if it does, a dozen sandbags aren't going to save much. Maybe he uses them for his booby traps. Trip a wire, get a sandbag on the head.

I sink into a chair, roll my pant leg up over my knee and unwind the bandage from around my calf. Scabs are beginning to form, but the skin still feels tender. More noticeable are the dark purple bruises mottling my leg from ankle to knee. I wonder when I'm going to think about why I'm here, what just happened, and who did that to my house, but it just feels like a bad dream. There's no reason to dwell on a bad dream.

The twisting in my stomach has eased in a way I know is only temporary, so I sit and enjoy the breeze until I start feeling restless. I suppose I could unpack my things so I can get ready for work easily tomorrow. And I need to do something about dinner. He can't expect me to eat dinner with him. I stand and turn back to the door. Dried flowers and herbs hang in the eaves along the entire length of the house. I'm surprised I didn't notice that before.

I slide the glass door closed behind me, sealing the sounds of nature outside. He's standing in the silence, in the same position I left him, his back against the sink with his hands gripping the counter and his head bowed. I can tell he's grinding his teeth again.

His eyes rise and center on my unbandaged leg.

"I'm airing it out," I mutter, making my way in front of him into the other room before my stomach has a chance to protest. I wander into the only bedroom and find a bed stripped of its sheets crowding the whole room. A small dresser is crammed next to it, my bags perched on top. The floor is bare, but the window has a heavy curtain. The room hardly looks lived in.

I press my nose to the mattress and notice no discernible smell, so I lift it to view the underside. Nothing hiding under there either. Although it doesn't remove my disgust—I have to sleep in his bed. Fortunately, the mattress itself doesn't nauseate me. So far at least. I hope he doesn't mind the couch, but do I care if he does? He should be sleeping on a bed of nails for the grief he's given me.

I unpack my things, filling the two bottom empty dresser drawers and unloading my bath items on top of the dresser. I stare at my handiwork, wondering when I'll be able to go home, wondering why I'm complying with any of this madness in the first place. Suddenly I'm aware of every sore muscle in my body. I'd kill for a hot bath.

The bathroom is the next door down the hall. It's barely big enough to turn around in. There is a tub, but not one I'm getting into. I find some bathroom cleaner under the sink and spray the entire tub including the tile walls. I also spray the sink and the outside of the toilet. I grab a rag from under the sink and go to work. Having a task to occupy my hands offers an excuse to not think about what I'm trying not to think about.

Once finished, I spray the entire floor and scrub it on my hands and knees. Everything sparkles like a TV commercial for bathroom cleaner. I wish I had worn gloves. Too bad they'd never protect me from contracting his toxic disposition. That's what I seem to be trying to scrub out.

Back in the bedroom, I pick out some clean clothes and gather my bath stuff. I hesitate in the doorway, unsure of proper etiquette between captor and hostage. But he did say to make myself at home. I can hear him moving around in the kitchen, so I shuffle within hearing range. It doesn't take much in this tiny house, so sparsely furnished there's little to absorb the sound.

"Is it okay if I take a bath?" My voice cracks.

No answer. The floor creaks, and he appears in the doorway throwing a bath towel at me. It lands on my shoulder but I grab it before it hits the floor. It's still warm from the dryer.

I return to the bathroom and close the door. I stare at the doorknob. No lock. This can't get any better. I stuff the wet rag I used to clean under the door, hoping it will act as some kind of obstacle. The tub faucet squeaks loudly as I turn it on. I undress, throwing my clothes against the door as well. I let my hair down and study the person in the mirror, a face too pale and eyes too bright. It's the look pasted on faces of family members of the trauma victims I treat at work. I try to relax my face. What is wrong with me? I'm in a strange man's house, preparing to take a bath in his tub after scrubbing his entire bathroom without asking. I must be in shock.

An electric jolt rips through my body as a knock sounds on the door. I press my palm against the crack of the door, holding it closed. "What?!"

"Something out here to soak your leg."

I hold the door until my breathing returns to normal. I turn off the tub faucet and listen. There's no way to know if he's still out there. I wrap a towel around me, shove the pile of clothes aside with my foot, and crack the door. Seeing no immediate threat, I open it some more and find a shallow tray filled with a dark liquid on the floor. I grab the tray and push the door closed with my elbow. The hot tray threatens to burn my hands, so I set it on the floor. The rising steam smells sweet, like apples. And something else. Mint?

There are two possibilities. One, he's trying to poison me. Or two, he's actually trying to be nice. If option one is true, I am a sitting duck. I'm stuck in his house, and he's going to get me one way or another. But it's hard to believe he would poison me with an herbal bath when he could have easily let those people kill me today. Unless that was all a setup to lure me here, and he wants the satisfaction of killing me himself. But he's had so many other opportunities. There's no need to go to this trouble.

As for option two, maybe he feels guilty about ruining my life and he's trying to redeem himself. If I don't use the herbal bath, his feelings might be hurt. Do I care about his feelings? Hardly. Maybe it's a test. If I pass, he doesn't kill me. If I fail, he kills me. I'm not offended at his disregard for my medical knowledge to heal my own leg. He let me treat his brow, so he must think my experience is good for something. I could dump it in the toilet and pretend I used it. But why bother lying?

Holy shit I'm neurotic.

I get in the tub. The herbal liquid sits there demanding my attention.

Surely something that smells like a mixture of sweet herbs must be harmless. The drying flowers and herbs hanging on the eaves on the back porch pop into my mind. Modern medicine began with folk remedies such as these.

I lie in the tub and soak but it doesn't last. The brew's heady smell has permeated the room and won me over. His intentions make no difference. If he poisons me, so be it. No one will miss me.

I drain the tub and set the tray inside. I dip my shin into the tray until the water covers my entire leg. The warmth of the water itself offers instant relief since I'm soaking wet and cold. Although it might be a placebo effect, the soreness in my leg seems to ease. I let it soak for as long as I can stay in position before I dump and rinse the tray.

It's hard to deny my leg feels better, but it's impossible to know if it was the herbal bath and not just the warm water. Regardless, I tried. He can't expect any more than that, and I don't really care if he does.

I dry off and get dressed in a thermal shirt and cotton pants. Putting weight on my leg seems easier, but it still could be my imagination. I take my things back to the bedroom. The bed has been made up with clean sheets and an old quilt. Everything smells fresh from the laundry.

Hearing no sign of him in the house, I follow the smell of food into the kitchen. I let out my breath, relieved to find him absent from the room. A pot of rice sits steaming on the stove next to a pan full of mixed vegetables. I open the lid of a third pan. Scrambled eggs, bright yellow and fluffy. A clean plate and silverware wait beside the stove. My attention zones in on my hollow stomach. It seems like weeks since I've eaten a real dinner. I said I didn't want him doing me any more favors, but I already ruined that pledge with the herbal bath. This meal is impossible to turn down, and much easier to accept if I don't have to eat it with him.

I help myself and sit down at the table shoved against the wall with no better place to go in this small room. The vegetables taste so fresh they must have just been picked from the garden outside. I'm too caught up savoring the food to hear him come in but suddenly he's here, shrinking the room even smaller. Either he needs to go, or the refrigerator. These are quarters too close for strangers to be comfortable. Riding in the truck with him was bad enough.

"If I make you some tea for your stomach, will you drink it?" His face seems sheepish. Or is he hiding something?

My stomach twists in reply. "Yes," I hear myself say around a mouthful of rice. My hunger won't let me escape this cramped room, or say no to the provider of these perfect veggies.

He sets a bucket on the counter and pulls a cutting board from a drawer. When I've cleaned my plate, he removes it and sets a mug of steaming tea, a bag of sugar, and a spoon in front of me.

"Sugar will make it taste better."

"Does it taste bad?" I peer into the dark liquid in the mug.

"Hell yes." He turns away. Was that a smile? Sadistic bastard.

I put in two spoonfuls of sugar, stir, and take a sip. Bad, but not too bad, considering I've consumed how many bottles of Pepto-Bismol in the last few days?

CHAPTER 6

TREY

I FEEL A LITTLE guilty about spiking her tea, but the relief to see her drinking it is enough to make up for the guilt. It *will* soothe her stomach, so there's really no harm done. Once she has it in her bloodstream, she'll be more agreeable to what I have to tell her.

"Is your leg better?"

"Yes. What was that you gave me?"

"An old recipe of my mother's."

I don't want to go there, so I turn and start on the dishes. Knowing I have some time to kill before I can drop the news, I take my time cleaning up. I stow the ingredients from the tea and take my bucket back outside. She stays at the table, sipping away. This is too easy. I thought she'd put up more of a fight.

On my way back into the kitchen, I pause. Nothing about this situation should remind me of the second woman whose memory I avoid, but somehow, it does. Thinking about my mother is one thing. Thinking of the other woman is strictly off limits. The pain tempts me. Her face starts to come into focus.

The sound of Liv setting her mug on the table pulls me back. She stands. Her chair grates against the floor. Ah, she still irritates me to no end.

"You shouldn't grind your teeth," she says.

"I don't grind my teeth." What the fuck does she know? A resonating hum fills my ears. I need to hit something. "Did you finish it?" I open the cabinet for my scotch and take a long drink from the bottle.

"Yeah, it wasn't so bad." She starts to leave the room.

"Wait, do you want more?"

"No thanks." She sways and clutches the table. "I knew it. I knew you were poisoning me." She starts to smile then catches herself.

It's time.

"Can you sit? We need to talk."

"I'd rather not." She sits anyway.

"I changed my mind. I'm going to walk over to your place and bring your car back. You need your car to drive it to work."

"Sounds good to me." She looks at the splattered blood on the wall. Guess I should have been more attentive with my cleanup.

"You can't tell anyone you're staying here. You can't tell anyone about what happened at your house. No matter what happens. You can't say anything about any of this."

"Oh I can't? I think I can."

"No, you can't." I sit in the chair across from her.

She looks away. "God. What did you put in that stuff?" She blinks several times as if to clear her vision.

"Nothing. Listen. If you say anything to anybody, you're putting yourself in more danger. We'll sort all this out. Just give me some time. You can blab all you want after this is all over." I look at her hard, trying to convey the magnitude of what I'm telling her.

"Blab?" She giggles. "That's funny."

"Promise me."

"Okay I promise. Jeez. Can I go now?"

"Promise me you won't tell anyone about what happened with me, or your house. Say it."

"I promise not to tell anyone about what happened with you or my house." She can hardly keep a straight face.

"Will you be okay until I get back? I'll give you my number. Call me if anything out of the ordinary happens."

"Mmm…okay." She looks at the wall again, takes a clump of her hair, and twists it in her fingers.

"Listen. Are you listening? If you hear a doorbell, you need to hide. There's a trap door in the closet of the bedroom. Close the closet door behind you and hide inside the compartment until I come back."

"They're polite enough to ring the doorbell?"

"It's rigged. It's a proximity alarm. If they get within—"

She reaches toward me and plucks a piece of grass off my shirt near my shoulder. "How did that get there?" She furrows her brow.

"Do you understand everything I just told you?"

"Yes!" she says in a huff. She stands, steadies herself on the table, and wanders into the living room. I follow her. She drops onto the couch, leans her head back and closes her eyes, a contented smile on her face.

After jotting my number on a piece of paper on the table, I grab my phone and dig her keys out of her bag. I jog outside to the riverbank and all the way to the footbridge where River catches up to me.

"Go home. Guard the house."

She makes a U-turn and bolts toward the house.

I jog the entire way there, and by the time I reach the cabin my endorphins are rushing. It would make my day if one of them was here. A high like this can only be satisfied by a good messy fight.

Too bad it looks like I'm out of luck. I survey the back yard and head up the side. The front yard is clear too, and I can't see any sign anyone's been here since my last visit.

Suddenly feeling I'm being watched, I whip around to survey the forest. The wind picks up, tossing branches. I close my eyes and listen. I hear my heartbeat in my ears.

"Come on…" Bring it on. I open my eyes, combing the land, hungry for some action. The wind settles. Everything remains still. Damn.

Inside the house I grab a duffle bag from the debris and pack it with an assortment of books and magazines and more clothes. I go into the bathroom and grab whatever is in my reach. In the kitchen, I find some wadded grocery bags and fill them with all her food. I'm thankful it isn't much. I set everything near the front door and go to work at my next task.

It would be a lot easier if they hadn't trashed the place. I wonder why they did. There's no point. Once they knew we weren't here, they could've simply left with no trace to make another ambush possible. Maybe they had already made a mess of the skylight and knew their presence couldn't be concealed. They could have been looking for something, just like I am right now. But they have no reason to care about her besides her connection to me.

My purpose is different. I'm trying to help myself make a decision. I need to see what effect it would have if she weren't around anymore. I sort through the clutter trying to find anything that could give me a clue: a photo album, a bank statement, a checkbook. Evidence of elderly parents or grandparents who rely on her for money. Children, maybe living with their father. Any family at all.

Frustrated, I come up with nothing. It's a little unusual not to have any family pictures around the house. But look who's talking. I dump a pitcher of water in each of her flower pots on the front porch and the half-dead one out back. I've been gone too long, so I take one last look around and lock the front door behind me.

When I get back home, I pull Liv's car into the garage. Her car needs to stay hidden while it's here. Inside the house, I drop the duffle bag in the entry hall and put the groceries in the kitchen. In the living room I find her curled up on the couch, her knees tucked practically up to her chin. I could leave her on the couch and sleep in the bedroom, but I need to be out here to be on guard.

Praying she doesn't wake up, I slide my arms under her shoulders and knees and lift her up. Her head flops and her arm dangles toward the floor. Halfway to the bedroom, she stirs. I hasten my steps to get her on the bed before she wakes up, but when her head rolls I see the waste of my effort.

Her eyelids flutter. "Umm…You? You stink."

As I lay her in the bed she turns over, hugging the pillow. I jerk the sheet over her, then the quilt, and pull the door closed. I take a quick shower because, apparently, I stink, then I fall onto the couch. Still high from my jog, I stare at the ceiling. My brain won't quit. It's working too hard trying to plan. I just don't know how I could have been so careless, how I couldn't have seen what it looked like to them. They think I'm seeing her. So now they aren't just going to be after me. They will be after her too.

I should tell them the truth, but they won't likely believe me. They'll think I'm trying to lead them off her. They won't listen to the details if I try to explain. They believe too much in their foresight. They'll think it's finally happening.

It would be so much easier to let them kill her. I'll give it a week. If I don't have a plan in a week, they can have her.

CHAPTER 7

LIV

A CONCERT OF CHIRPING birds outside makes it impossible to go back to sleep. Not that I even want to. I'd rather lie here in this bliss as long as possible. An infinity has passed since I've felt this healthy, this vibrant. My whole body hums with such contentment that it's hard to imagine being mad at him for drugging me. Especially since his drugs are so much better than mine.

If I get up now, I can get ready and leave before I have to encounter him. It's worth sacrificing this relaxation. I throw the covers aside.

My legs are bare. I didn't take off my pants last night. I spot them on the floor, but my reaching hand freezes in midair. I didn't get in bed last night either. I fell asleep on the couch. I vaguely remember him moving me to the bedroom, but the hazy memory feels like a dream.

He took off my pants. He's out of his mind. I have good reason to storm in there right now and chew him out. Who does he think he is?

I dress in clean scrubs and finger-comb my hair. I pull it back in a low loose ponytail, put on my shoes, and grab my bag. Tiptoeing into the hall, I'm bewildered by my ability to put full weight on my leg.

The sound of heavy, even breathing grows louder as I move toward the front door. I can't avoid seeing him lying on the couch on his back, his feet hanging off the end, arms splayed. He looks as if he just fell backward on the couch and stayed that way all night. My temper flares. I bite my lip and head for the door, almost tripping over a lump in the path. I recognize my purple duffle bag so I unzip it slowly to keep the zipper from making too much noise. It's packed full of my belongings from the house.

I'll deal with that later. I ease open the door and step outside, but as I take a deep breath, my mood quickly crashes and burns. I can't leave! I have no idea how to get to my car without falling in a pit of snakes or stepping on a land mine. And I don't even see my car. He was supposed to get my car! I drag myself back inside my prison and sit on the bed, numbed to the bone.

All of this, from the moment our cars collided, is his fault. The people after me—his problem. Yet I'm the one suffering. He's peacefully sleeping on his own couch. Nothing in his life has been disrupted, while mine has been shaken until the already broken pieces have shattered into rubble. It seemed impossible to repair before. Now, it's hopeless.

I force myself up and over to the window to pull the curtain open and let in some light. As soon as I see the bars on the windows I almost laugh out loud. This can't get any worse. My threat of laughter chokes in my throat when I hear a raised voice, coming from outside. It's him. I wonder who he's talking to. He must be on the back porch. I strain to see him but it's impossible from this angle. I crack the window, hoping it doesn't make a noise. It slides easily.

"…can't explain the situation? It's not what it looks like… so what if they don't care, I'm just trying to save them some trouble…I *know* they can see everything. Can they see my middle finger?"

I strain to detect a response but hear no other voice. He must be on the phone. He makes an exasperated sigh, obviously listening to the person on the other end.

"Just do me this one favor, I'm sure you owe me for something…I don't fucking know, but there's got to be a way to explain…"

He's silent for a while until a burst of laughter surprises me. It's such a strange sound from him, maybe there is someone else out there whose laugh I can hear but whose voice I can't.

"For real? Tell them their guys are getting worse. It's hardly a challenge anymore…Yeah, maybe I shouldn't complain. The practice is good. My dad must be eating this up. Maybe it's some sick way for him to keep me in training."

He pauses again. Another laugh. I press my cheek against the screen, hoping he'll walk into view, hungry for proof that the sound is coming from him. "Okay yeah. Call me either way… You're sick…yeah, you wish. Okay. Later."

I slide the window closed and sit down to digest what I just heard. I'm involved in something, and I'm not sure I want to know what. A sharp knock on the door propels me to my feet.

"You up?" he asks through the door.

Trying to clear my expression, I open the door.

"I pulled your car out of the garage. If you're ready, I can walk you—what?" An innocuous sentence transformed into an accusation complete with narrowed eyes and a bitter scowl.

I guess I wasn't successful with my attempt at a blank look. "I'm ready." I grab my bag and squeeze past him and go out the front door.

He catches up and leads me across the yard in the same zigzag pattern as before. I try to memorize the route, but it's hard to concentrate while trying to bridle my impatient tongue. When we reach my car, I spin to face him, unable to hold back any longer.

"Did you enjoy undressing me?"

"What?" He straightens up in surprise.

"You didn't think I'd notice that you took off my pants?"

He leans into my face. "I did *not* take off your pants."

"Well they were off. And it only could have been you." I glare back at him, holding my ground, even though he's uncomfortably close. He expects me to recoil from his aggressive stance, but I won't. We can stand here like this forever.

He makes a lightning-fast movement to grab my shoulders but catches himself.

"Try it." I will scream bloody murder and aim for the groin.

He stares at me through narrowed eyes, his chest heaving. There's a scar running into his upper lip and another across his cheekbone. Old scars. Like something very large and sharp skipped across his face. His attitude must be a source of trouble with people much bigger and less civilized than me. It's bad news to be face to face with someone like him, but I refuse to break eye contact. I watch him struggle to recover. His mass looms over me. He obviously has the physical advantage, but I know the human nervous system. And where to strike to cause the most pain.

"You don't have to believe me. But I would not do that." He holds my eye to drive his point. He turns and stomps away, his boots making huge prints in the wet grass.

He's a grown man, trying to intimidate someone smaller than him like a bully in grade school. When he's not doing that, he's drinking like an alcoholic. He has the scars to prove he hangs with losers just like him.

So much for this morning's brief bout of contentment.

The front door of the house slams. I get in my car, doubling over in pain as my stomach catches up with the hours I seemed free of the sickness. I don't even care. I'm just not going to talk to him, ever. I'll give him until Monday to figure a way out of this. If I'm still stuck here Tuesday, I'm going to the police.

I start the engine and floor it, putting distance between my stomach and him as fast as possible.

Walking into the clinic is like walking into another world where everything is bright and cheerful, where people talk pleasantly, laugh often, and smile for no real reason. I feel like an imposter trying to conform to some other dimension. People ask me questions and I answer, I fall into routine. I go out to lunch with Jennifer and Rachel, or at least my body does. The rest of me is still immersed in the disorder of Trey Bevan's world. I ask around offering to work someone's weekend shift, but no one accepts.

Driving home, I wonder what could be stopping me from going to the police. I could drive to the station right now, ask for a chaperone, and go home to my own bed. Instead I pick up some groceries and drive straight back to my prison in some hypnotic coma.

There's no sign of him or his truck when I arrive. I park and turn off the car. I don't know how I didn't notice the note stuck under my wiper blade. I open the door and pluck out the note.

Liv,

Front yard is clear. It's
safe to go straight inside.

Trey

I feel like I just won the lottery.

The hearty aroma of food hits me as soon as I step inside. As savory as it smells, I refuse to eat anything he cooks, and I'm sticking to it this time. I check the kitchen anyway and find a crock pot full of thick stew. Steam rises when I open the lid, carrying the tang of tomato, carrot, onion, black pepper. A clean bowl, spoon, and ladle are set out beside it.

Damn him and his stew. His teeming vegetable garden. His soothing herbal bath soak. If this domestic shit gets any more profound I might have a problem. Funny that I'm okay with the blood-sprayed kitchen wall but if he starts making scented candles and potpourri I'm out of here. The ingredients for a cold sandwich in my grocery bag are no match for this home-cooked meal, but I willfully throw one together, resisting the seduction of the stew by trying not to breathe in.

I return to my bedroom, yanking my duffle bag along with me. I shove bites of my sandwich into my mouth, barely chewing. Yes I'm stubborn, and proud of it. I put my hands to work unpacking the contents of my bag, a collection of random things from the house. As I start organizing the room, something sticking out from under the bed catches my eye. On my knees, I pull out a piece of white gauze.

Realization hits, forcing me to swallow a lump in my throat. Sometime during the night I woke up, determined to re-bandage my leg. I must have given up and gone back to sleep. But not before I removed my pants. This crucial memory was missing this morning, but now it's there in full shaming color. A sickness burns in my stomach in a completely new way. Being wrong is one thing, but after accusing him of something like that, I can't face him again. Any normal person would apologize, but it's useless. Perhaps it's better just to leave things the way they are. We aren't ever going to get along.

Boredom catches up to me when I find nothing else to busy myself with in this little room, even with his attempt to entertain me by bringing some of my things. It's not fair I'm cooped up in here while he's free to go where he pleases. And now I know he's home because I can hear him out there, stomping and banging around like some rogue giraffe. Screw him. If he wants to keep me here I'm going to make it as difficult for him as it is for me.

I change out of my scrubs, grab my nail kit and go into the kitchen. He's at the table, eating. My unused bowl and spoon sit untouched on the counter. I help myself to a glass of water. He doesn't look up, but I know he notices me from the severity of the tension in the air. After a deliberately slow consumption of my water, I wander back into the living room and start filing my nails, trying very hard to relax and put myself in the mental state I would be in at home. After a while I hear him cleaning up in the kitchen. A few minutes later, his footsteps close in on me.

"Do you want some food?"

"I'm fine." I refuse to look at him. The apology wedges in my throat. I think of different ways I could phrase it as he hovers.

"You're not hungry?"

"I already ate." Although twisted in a million knots, my stomach still longs for that stew. Maybe I should just give in and eat. I have nothing to prove to him. He's an asshole and he knows it. He's made it a career.

"Would you like some more tea for your stomach?"

His audacity doesn't surprise me in the least. I'm learning to expect it. "You mean your special roofie tea?"

"Yes."

I can't help but laugh. He isn't even ashamed. I look up at him to read his face.

"It did help your stomach. You have to admit that."

"Yes but it also made me drunk! High! Whatever."

"That can be a side effect."

"Thanks for telling me that beforehand." My tone is sharper than it needs to be.

He's scowling again. "Maybe you should be more careful the next time a stranger offers you a drink."

I stare up at him. What a creep. I've never met anyone so unapologetically crude. "Maybe I should call the police to check up on what kind of illegal substances you're growing out there." I go back to filing my nails.

"Look. We don't get along. Fine. You don't have to talk to me. But there's no reason for you to suffer. I'll make some tea, for both of us. I drink a mug and you drink a mug. It will be ready in five minutes." He goes back into the kitchen.

I sit frozen, staring straight ahead. But the thought of putting the mug to my lips wins, and like a drug addict, I drop my nail file and follow him into the kitchen. He's busy at the counter, so I take a seat at the table. All I can think about is that mug in my hands and the warm liquid flowing down my throat.

He gets the mugs out of the cabinet and sets them on the counter. I can't tear my eyes away from them. He puts the tea leaves in to steep and leans back against the counter. Folding his arms across his chest, he shoots me a condescending look.

I can't hold back. "You're a goddamn psycho."

"As I'm aware."

My fingers drum on the table. Has it been five minutes yet? He ladles some stew into the bowl still waiting for me on the counter.

CHAPTER 8

TREY

I CARRY THE TWO mugs over to the table, set one down in front of Liv and the other at my spot across from her. She immediately reaches for hers.

"Wait for me," I tease.

She tries to pull back nonchalantly, but I know the effect this tea has. I was addicted to it for seven years. I bring the bowl of stew to the table and set that down in front of her as well. She doesn't take her eyes off me. As I sit across from her, she takes a few bites of stew and a sip of tea. I take a sip of mine. We set our mugs down at the same time and our eyes lock.

"I am such a lightweight," she says. "And I take no responsibility for anything I do tonight."

"Likewise." I hold my mug up to hers, and we toast.

She must have been starving the way she's devouring the stew. I grab the newspaper from the counter and open it. Hopefully the tea will allow us to get along. I'm counting on it to tame my nerves so her irritating quirks don't bother me as much. When she empties her bowl I put down the paper and refill it. She thanks me.

"I bought a piece of replacement glass for your skylight. I was going to install it tomorrow. Would you like to come with me? I could help you clean up your house, and we could secure it better until you can go back."

She looks at me like an animal that's just been freed from a trap—an emotion she would have been able to hide a moment ago. "That would be nice."

Several minutes of silence pass. She gets up and sets her bowl on the counter and returns to her chair. "Isn't it ridiculous we both have to get drunk to get along?"

"Who says we're getting along?" I don't mean to flirt, but I do anyway. I catch myself about to grin at her so I look away. I must have made the tea too strong.

She sighs. It doesn't annoy me.

"I'm going to dilute this a little." I stand.

"No! Mine's perfect." She grabs her mug with both hands and smiles impishly up at me. I stare into her brilliant blue eyes and start to lose myself. I sit back down.

"How old are you?" she blurts out. Her forehead wrinkles in confusion, and she adds, "I don't know why I asked that. I wasn't even really wondering it."

I chuckle before my answer comes out on its own. "Thirty." It really doesn't mean anything anymore.

"I'm older than you. I'm thirty-two."

I would have guessed late twenties. Or maybe not. I can't remember.

She puts her forearms on the table and leans forward, her eyes round and serious. "I have to tell you something."

"Oh, god. Is this the tea talking?"

"No. But it's easier now. I was wrong this morning. About what I accused you of. And I'm sorry." She looks genuinely sorry.

"Don't worry about it." I stop myself from saying more. I actually don't want to piss her off. That's a first.

She stares at her nails. "I missed one."

"What?"

"A nail. I missed one."

"You missed one?" For some reason that's funny to me. But I can't laugh. It's stupid.

She absentmindedly pulls the rubber band out of her hair and massages the back of her head. Her hair falls in waves down her shoulders. She puts the rubber band on the table. Then she looks surprised it's there. She takes another drink and frowns. "Empty."

I realize I'm staring at her. I go back to the paper. I look at the pictures because it's too much work to read the words. She flicks the back of the paper, and I almost laugh but stop myself before it comes out.

"I'm empty," she announces.

"You can't have any more."

"Why not?"

"It would put you over the legal limit."

"This is legal?" She pantomimes shock. "Now it's no fun anymore."

"Is your stomach better?"

She acts like it's the first time she's thought about it. "Yes." She peeks into her empty mug. "What is this stuff, anyway?"

"It is a natural remedy for stomach ailments and anxiety. Sometimes it's called Honesty Tea, because of its side effects." I pause for her to reply, but she doesn't. "It's also called Lover's Tea. And some other names I can't remember." Is that me talking so much? I need to shut up.

"But what exactly *is* it?"

"If I told you, I'd have to kill you." Ironic. I'm sure I'll have to kill her anyway.

She scoffs.

"Hey, do you want to go for a walk?" I sound like an eager child.

She twists around in her seat to look outside but quickly turns back to me with disappointment creasing her brow. "But it's dark out."

"All the better. The moon is full tonight. There will be plenty of light."

"Okay!" Now she sounds like an eager child.

I put on my boots and pull my flannel jacket out of the closet. She disappears down the hall, so I clear our mugs, throw the remainder of the used tea leaves in the trash, and hide the rest of the tea at the back of the cabinet. She'll be looking for more when she comes down. So will I, and I don't want to make it easy for either one of us to find it. I glance out the window. The moon is not very high but it will be soon.

I sit on the couch to wait for her. The sounds of her stumbling around in the bedroom carry down the hallway, and I watch the fluctuation of light on the wall, wondering if she needs any help. Several minutes later she appears in front of me in jeans, a flannel shirt, and hiking boots. Thank god she knows how to dress for the occasion.

I pull another one of my jackets out of the closet and throw it to her. She makes no attempt to catch it, but it lands on her shoulder. She looks up, as if wondering where it came from. I shake my head and stifle a laugh. We head out the front and I lead her in a wide arc around the property, to the back.

"I can't see!" It's too giddy an exclamation but it must have come out of her. She stumbles, reaching out for me in reflex, but recovers without my help.

"Your eyes will adjust. Give them a few minutes."

We walk without speaking until we reach the river. She moves closer to the water, watching it break and roll over rocks. It's not reasonable to be impatient because my sense of time is warped. Like the unending flow of water over rock, my thoughts consume me. Spending time with someone I'm setting up to be murdered can't be a good idea. Maybe it's the most humane thing, to be nice to her in her last days. But I'm not capable of being humane. I should know better than to even begin to befriend a woman, but at this point it doesn't matter. They already know about her. Or think they know. They just don't know how mistaken they are.

A better way out of this isn't in my grasp. Incompetent. Disgusting. Losing my game, with no motivation to do anything about it. This mental drain worsens every day, nurturing an apathy I know from past experience will go undefeated. A change in scenery will only stall it. After I get settled somewhere else, it will come back. It always does.

She turns around, her face bright. A slight breeze stirs her hair around her face. She pulls my jacket from around her waist and puts it on. It swallows her. She tucks her hair inside the collar and raises the hood over her head.

"That cold?" Again, my flirting is involuntary. Damn tea.

She climbs up to where I'm standing and looks up at me in anticipation. I hold her gaze longer than I should, pushing it. Being with her reminds me of someone, of better times. It fills the barbed hole in me with a steel abrasive. I find myself savoring the pain. Wanting more. Wishing I could go back to that time when it almost broke me.

"Where to next?" she asks.

Her words yank me from the irresistible lust for that pain. I should know better than to give in to it while in the presence of others. I can't trust what I will do.

We walk along the river to the footbridge and cross over. The terrain becomes more rugged, and I let her in front of me so I can watch over her. We head higher and higher. She should be tired by now, want to turn back.

"There better be a payoff," she says, twisting around, almost reading my thoughts. I give her a look that tells her to be patient. She takes another step and loses footing, sliding down under me on her stomach until I catch her by the jacket and pull her upright. She looks at me apologetically and wipes her hands on her jeans. Her pupils are huge. Mine probably are too. This is dangerous and stupid. But it feels like heaven.

"Your boot is untied." I point.

"Oh." She crouches to tie it.

"Double it," I say when she stands.

She rolls her eyes and leans down to double the knots on both boots.

"So demanding," she mumbles when she stands again, but I refuse to meet her eyes.

When we reach the bluffs, the moon is high and so bright it illuminates the whole valley. I walk out to the edge like I usually do, and she gasps.

"Too close! That makes me nervous."

I turn around to face her. I could snap her neck and toss her over right now. Tomorrow would be a pain in the ass, but in a week I would forget any of this happened. Everything would be back to normal. Shit. I've got to be more creative than this.

I return to her side. She takes my hand and sits, pulling me down with her. We sit cross-legged and enjoy the view. The nagging feelings return, poking holes in my weakened resistance. Making the tea strong seemed like a good idea for earlier reasons, but now I see the error. I forgot the power it holds over me, the images it releases. Images of her I can handle. But I pity whoever is unlucky to be near me should my thoughts ever dwell on him.

"Are you a ballet dancer?" I ask.

She looks surprised I spoke. "Yes."

"For how long?" I'm not sure why I care, but it seems important for some reason.

"My whole life. How'd you know?"

I saw those ballet shoes when I was snooping through her house. Time to shut up before I incriminate myself. "Just a hunch."

The air is thick with sounds of the end of summer. I pick out individual noises—a rabbit's scamper across pine needles, the creak of tree branches, the undulating breeze—before combining them one at a time until they become a chorus once again.

"Do you get in a lot of fights?"

Fights. I can't control my laugh. "Why would you think that?"

"Your lip is split. The bruise on your neck. The cuts on your knuckles. Telltale signs. I'm a nurse, remember?"

I look away. "Yes, I remember." And I'm not going to answer the original question.

"It can't be healthy."

I shrug and look at her. It's hard not to laugh.

"I hope you know your way back." She scans the landscape around us.

"Sure don't. I was hoping you did," I joke. She doesn't buy it. "It's easy. Tonight, you can find Orion, and then use the rest of the stars as a guide."

She raises her eyebrows. "You're kidding, right?"

"Nope."

She shakes her head, the tip of her tongue clamped between her teeth like she's physically suppressing it.

"There was a time when people used the stars…" I'm talking too much again.

She looks up at the night sky and releases a deep breath. "Will I ever know?"

Her words stab me without motive. "What?" I ask, already knowing the answer.

"Who trashed my house."

I hesitate. The temptation of confiding my secrets overwhelms me in sudden lucid possibility, especially knowing she's not going to be around much longer. I look over at her. The hood has fallen down, and her hair has freed itself with the breeze. I feel my mask return. I look away. "No."

She opens her mouth again, and I silently cringe. Please just let it be.

"So which one is Orion?" She searches the sky.

It takes me a second to recover. "You have to look for his belt. See those three bright stars right there? If you follow the line they make with your eyes, you can find Sirius."

"Where?" She looks in the wrong direction.

I grasp her head and point it correctly.

"Oh those three there? I see them now. And which one is Sirius?"

"There." I point.

She tries to follow my finger but misses. God, I could go swimming in those pupils. She had as much as me and she's half my size. Overdose. Wouldn't that be funny.

"You are impossible." I grasp her head and move it again.

"Ah. The bright one." Her long bangs catch on her eyelashes, and she brushes them aside.

"Yep, the really bright one."

"Do you know them all?" she asks, still looking up.

"Yes."

"How did you learn?"

"Self-taught," I lie. "Should we head back?" I stand.

She stands and sways, grabbing my arm for support. "Head rush," she explains with a grin I try to ignore.

I let her get her bearings before we begin our descent. The ground is steep for a while, and I lead the way until it levels out and we can easily walk side by side. Now the air feels peaceful; the energy we had on the way up has been replaced with a strange tranquility that puts me at ease. It's a nice feeling I wouldn't mind more of. I'm better off without it.

River blasts through the underbrush, and Liv jumps backward.

"A warning next time? My god!" She tries to catch her breath. "I thought we were being attacked by wolves."

"Where have you been, girl?" I ask River. She looks like she's been up to no good. She follows us all the way back to the house and takes her usual spot by the garage. We go inside and I flip on the living room light.

"What?" she asks in response to my gaze.

"You have a million leaves stuck in your hair."

"I do?" She reaches up, and her fingers find one. She pulls it out and examines it.

"You've got your work cut out for you." My words sound dead. It feels like we have already lost our alliance.

She goes back out on the porch, and I watch her shaking out her hair, combing it with her fingers. When she finally turns to come inside, I collapse on the couch, roll onto my back, and stare at the ceiling. She goes straight into the bedroom. My eyes close before my hands make it to the laces on my boots. I untie them by feel and kick them off. I don't hear them hit the floor.

CHAPTER 9

LIV

I WAKE UP IN utter bliss once again. Knowing it won't last, I get up and get dressed to make the most of it until my stomach becomes aware of its subdual and strikes back. Along with the sickness, the clouds of doom have also lifted, and I feel like a criminal, cheating a well-deserved fate. I know this happiness is only temporary, and chemically-induced, but it's impossible not to enjoy this reprieve just a little. Waking up from sound, natural sleep is a luxury I never thought I would feel again.

The silence in the house tells me he must still be sleeping, so I make my bed and head to the bathroom. It's a surprise to see my face in the mirror while brushing my teeth. This unguarded expression hasn't surfaced in almost a year.

When I pass through the living room, I try not to make the floor creak so I can enjoy the morning alone. He's on the couch in the same position as before, lying on his back with his arms open and feet dangling off the end. I try to control my stomach from growling as I tiptoe into the kitchen.

Everything in the refrigerator looks sparkling and delicious. I pour some orange juice and stare out the window, trying to make sense of last night's events.

The couch creaks in the other room, then the floor. He appears at the doorway, rubbing his face with the palm of his hand. Hair sticking up in all directions, shirtless, barefoot, with sleepy eyes and a goofy look of surprise as he sees me. I bite my lip, trying not to smile. It's hard to detest him when I feel so well again. Without a word, he turns around. The sound of his footsteps recedes down the hall. A moment later I hear the shower running.

Mr. Control Freak would probably kill me if I made breakfast. For some reason, knowing this makes me want to do it more. The cabinets are as spartan as the rest of the house, but I find a skillet and some eggs. I set the table, start the coffee, and go back to tend the eggs as pieces of last night come back to me. Whatever we drank made everything so easy. I might go so far as to say I had fun. Okay maybe not fun. A pleasant time. But that's not saying a lot considering the state of my life.

"You don't need to do that."

Nothing clears the head like an early morning panic attack. "God! Don't sneak up on me like that."

He snorts. "Sneak up on you? You must be deaf."

Still on my high, I satisfy a simple need to laugh at him instead of adding another scar to his face. He holds open his hand for the spatula. Just as I thought, a total control freak. I pretend I don't see the open hand and turn to finish the eggs and turn off the burner. He's behind me the whole time.

I step around him and serve the eggs to the plates on the table. I pull two pieces of toast from the toaster and put two more in, pour the coffee, and bring milk and orange juice to the table.

He still hasn't yielded his position.

"Do I have to wait for you?" I mock, echoing what he said last night. I might be crazy, but I swear I see the corner of his lip turn up.

His toast pops up, so he retrieves it and sits. We eat in silence, awkward in our own thoughts. When only the coffee remains, he slides open the back door. Birdsong fills the room. He should have done that sooner. We sip our coffee, working hard to avoid each other's line of sight. He lets me help him clean up. Once everything is put away, he clears his throat. "I have a few things to load in my truck. If you want, you can ride over to your place with me."

Weighing my options, I don't see why not. "Okay."

I sit in the truck while he loads the bed with various items from his garage. On the ride there, he seems different. Like his usual blatant hostility has been replaced by human thought, yet withdrawn. Depressed. Almost like the fire went out. But I don't find the voice to ask.

When we park at my house, he turns in his seat and searches my face.

I know what he's wondering, so I answer his look. "I'm fine." And I am. I've been through much worse. Comparatively speaking, this is nothing. I don't mind seeing the house trashed again. In fact, I'm anxious to get it all cleaned up so I can forget this ever happened.

I go inside and get to work. Before long, his footsteps are thumping on the roof, and leftover glass rains onto the floor beneath the missing skylight. Once I move all the furniture back to its proper place, I replace all the contents of the boxes I hadn't yet unpacked and refold and rehang all my clothes, trying to ignore how violently they had been ripped from the dresser and closet. I know this isn't personal. It only feels that way because it's such an invasion of privacy.

Hearing voices outside, I freeze to listen but can't determine who it is so I peek out the front window. Nancy!

Outside, she's hugging me before I have a chance to say hi.

"Liv you look great! I just wanted to drop by and see how you're doing. Sorry for my bad timing…" She gives me an exaggerated wink.

"Yeah, I guess he kind of owes me a favor." Try to make light of it. That's all this would be, if we weren't here to repair a home invasion.

"Hon, all the single women in this town are going to be jealous when they hear you snared Trey Bevan."

"Oh no, it's not like that." Other women must not know what a pain in the ass he is. I hold back a smile. She would only think I was giving something away that couldn't be farther from the truth.

"Right. We'll see. Wouldn't it just be fate though? Considering how you met?" As usual, her laugh is almost contagious. But I would be laughing for a completely different reason. I'd have to commit a heinous crime for fate to pair me with him.

"I would invite you in but I have the whole place torn apart. Kind of…reorganizing everything."

"Oh no I don't want to intrude. I was just nearby and thought I should check on you. So everything is okay? You're enjoying the place? Making friends?"

"Everything is great." I can't help but smile now. Making friends all right, with home invaders who might want to kill me.

"Well, I'm thrilled. I knew you'd love it here. Okay, I've got to run. Take care and call me." The last two words she drops to a loud whisper, jerking her thumb toward Trey on the roof.

I wave as she drives away. Trey is standing, looking down at me from the roof. I meet his gaze and hold it. He's probably wondering if I snitched. Well, he'll just have to wonder. I'm intent on making him miserable.

I just about have the kitchen in order when a searing pain in my stomach seizes me. My knees buckle, and I grasp the countertop and lower myself to the floor, pressing my forehead against the cabinets, tears streaming down my face. This is the worst it's been. I'm immobilized. I feel like I'm dying.

Something turns me around and through my tears I see two green eyes. I hear his voice but it sounds far away. I feel myself being lifted up, and I cry out, twisting in agony. A sudden softness cradles my body. A warm hand brushes my hair off my face. And then darkness.

It is so bright. My eyelids feel unnaturally heavy but I struggle to open them. As I turn my head, my vision comes into focus. He's here. Sitting on the chair, staring out the window. I look at the ceiling. The skylight. He fixed the skylight. I try to clear my throat. "Trey?"

"How do you feel?"

"So tired."

"Can you sit up?" He moves toward me to help me sit up. He returns to the chair.

"How long was I asleep?" I blink the dried tears from my eyes.

"Three hours."

It seemed so much longer than that. I feel like I should be asking what day it is.

"Were you here the whole time?" I ask instead.

"No. I had to go home and get something to help you."

His voice is a cold wind blowing through the dead grass of a barren winter landscape, lifeless and bleak. The vivid imagery in my mind surprises me.

"I think it helped." I wonder what it was he gave me before I realize I don't care.

"Yes, but it's only temporary."

I stretch my legs out in front of me, looking around the room.

"You finished cleaning?" I ask, already knowing he is the only one who could have.

He doesn't answer.

My eyes focus on an object resting in his lap, the sight of which lowers me into that pit. The one I won't escape a second time. My mind goes over the object's soft cover and the silky pink ribbon surrounding it as if it is again in my own hands.

Suddenly, he's next to me, his face inches from mine. "You have a child?" He sounds like he's choking.

I shake my head. My heart has frozen, spreading a painful chill to the rest of my body.

He lifts the album, still in his hands. "Is this your child?" His voice is the cold winter wind.

"Yes." I gasp for air. My lungs are failing.

He lays the photo album on the couch next to him and stares into the room. I cannot breathe. When he turns back to me, his eyes are a harsh green expanding all around me like duplicate tunnels in a fun house—it doesn't matter which one I pick, they both drop me into the darkness of his pupil. I close my eyes. The dizzying motion settles into a tight ball in the back of my head, turning prickly hot. "Stop it." I don't know why I say it. He can't subdue a chaos that's inside me.

"You lost a child?"

"Yes." I want the tears to flood my burning eyes, but I cannot cry. I have cried too much already.

"I did, too." His voice is a desolate whisper I feel more than hear.

We stare at each other, motionless. Time passes but I can't break away. Our suffering cements us in place. His pain is my pain. I can see his soul. We are in a lifeboat, together, in the middle of the ocean. I can feel the waves, the gentle rocking of the boat, the sun warming my hair. We are exposed, alone, lost. No one will ever find us here. We will die here.

The boat begins to rock harder. I'm unable to sit still anymore. I have to grasp the sides of the boat to keep myself upright. And like dominoes falling, one by one, I start losing my hard-earned control.

"Where did you find that?" I say. It's his fault I'll be imprisoned in the pit again, buried under the weighted darkness. I packed that album away. I wasn't ready to see it.

He blinks. He can't speak.

"I want to know where you found that!" Who is that screaming? It hurts my ears. I point to the album.

He looks at the album. He looks back at me, his lips parted, his face expressionless. "In the clutter. On the bedroom floor."

My ears pound. Someone screams again. "You had no right!"

I lash out, and my wrists are caught. He yanks me to standing. The vertebrae in my neck pop from the force.

His pupils are dilated, his breath comes in short bursts. I see an unstoppable fury unleashed before me. With it comes a clarity, a lightning strike. I was wrong about him before. He wasn't hostile or menacing. That was a guard, a protective layer. It's missing now and something's been released—his temper is now armed with bare emotion. What I see now has put it all in perspective.

I try to twist out of his grasp but his hands are iron shackles. His face is the vicious mask of a killer. Blood to my hands is cut off. My legs are tingling hot with the urge to run, but when facing a predator of his power it's the worst thing to do.

"Trey." His name spoken in a way I didn't plan. Not just an appeal, but a recognition. An understanding.

He drops my wrists like they've just burned him. He stumbles one step back. The broken look on his face is my reflection in a mirror.

My breath leaves me and I choke. I cover my mouth, attempt to control a sob but it's too late. Once it starts it will never stop until I'm a dried husk, blowing away, all my moisture cried out.

"Do you have any more of that tea?"

He swallows hard. "It's habit-forming."

"I don't care."

I follow him out to the truck. He drives like we're in a high-speed chase.

Inside his kitchen, he combines three jars of different tea leaves into one and dumps half of it into my palm and half into his. We stare at each other in a silent count of one, two, three. He crams the whole thing into his mouth, and I follow.

CHAPTER 10

TREY

I WAKE UP ON cold wood, a wet nose under my hand. I roll onto my back. The sky is a kaleidoscope, each point of color shrinking down until I see they're merely stars. I'm not sure how I wound up on the porch. The temperature must be low but I don't feel it. River claws my arm, a numb limb now alive with four distinct lines of pain. I'd stay out here and die if she wasn't so insistent.

I feel my way inside and trip over a body in the kitchen. When I see her I'm glad it's no one I killed, no body I need to drag from the house. Then I remember what we did. I kneel to find her pulse. Hell, she should be dead.

She's not. I carry her limp body to the bedroom and lay her on the bed. Only I could survive a handful that size but

I gave it to her anyway. Maybe this is how it ends, this is my out. If she dies here instead of at their hand, she won't feel the pain of death.

It will be easy to make it look like an accident. I'll take her body up to the bluffs. I'll be sure to be part of the search party. If I'm there when she's found, I can make sure they won't question. It's a simple effect—quick to prepare, effortless to dole out. My power might be rusty but I've succeeded at this more times than I can remember.

I pack all her clothes, gather her things from the bathroom and comb the house, removing every trace of her. Once her body is gone, I will wait for the harvest, and I will leave.

I collapse on the couch, too exhausted to remove my shoes.

I awaken to River's howl in the night. Two more howls, followed by a pause. I wait for it. One more howl. Her warning call. Someone is here. My adrenaline is slow to kick in because the tea's still in my system. It's worse than being drunk but I'll have to shake it off. I roll from the couch to the floor in a squat, listening. I can't let them get to her. If they find her before I can deal with her, it will be more difficult to cover up. I don't have a plan prepared for that, and I don't have the desire or motivation to come up with one.

Using the shadows to conceal my motion, I slip over to the large bureau. Common sense pleads a good case, but I stopped listening to common sense a long time ago. I stand and shove the bureau down the hall and up against the bedroom door with flaccid arms and a swimming head. It makes a lot of noise, but it can't be helped.

I prefer to face him outside. There's more room to move around and it's easier to clean up. My head start was taken by moving the bureau. I open the door and walk outside, offering myself.

A yelp sounds from the woods. River. I jump aside as a knife flies by me, cutting my arm and sticking into the ground nearby. I retrieve it, making sure my movements appear strong to hide my insobriety.

"Thanks," I say aloud.

Instinct shifts my attention to a black outline crouching in the shadow of the garage. I take off running. Better to get this over with. He moves behind the garage and climbs up the back of it, so I follow him up to the top where he grabs my shoulders, flips me hard onto the roof. I roll and get up, but he's already around me, grabbing me from behind. A wire cuts into my neck. I flip him over my back, using the split second his body is airborne to aim the knife for his throat as he lands. He dodges. I twist my arm, stabbing downward, and the knife makes contact with his thigh.

The exertion leaves me momentarily blind. He rolls to the edge of the roof and drops to the ground. I take a running start, leap off the roof and flip midair, landing on my feet. He's already running to the house. Fatigue takes hold, but I push it away.

"Oh no you don't." I know what he wants. I'm on his heels. This has become personal. They are so insistent on making my life difficult. I am not cleaning up their mess again. This is *my* mess.

Reaching him at the house, I kick his legs out from under him. When we land, I poise the knife to meet his fall. It plunges deep into his lower back. He grunts but obviously still has some fight in him. His elbow makes contact with my cheekbone, and I fall back, catching myself with my elbows on the ground. I leap up to see him scaling the side of the house, so I follow him up. When he reaches the peak in the roof, I leap for his waist. We fall together, our bodies crashing against the shingles.

He manages to get the knife to my throat, and I feel my strength waning. The fatigue has grown more difficult to deny. This is just a bad night for this. I press the knife away from my skin, but it isn't quite enough. The tip of the knife slices my chest from collarbone to hip. I use the momentum of his downward thrust and turn the knife back on him, catching him somewhere in the leg. He rolls off me, and I pounce. His open palm slams into my freshly cut chest, but I manage to get around him and roll him over to the edge of the roof, slicing his throat open from ear to ear. He doesn't let go of me in time, and we both plummet to the ground. I wait for the impact, but it never comes.

CHAPTER 11

LIV

My eyes open to darkness. I take a slow breath. Shadows, dim images come into focus, monopolizing my concentration until suddenly my ears adjust. Something's above me. On the roof. I sit up and look around, straining to make sense of the sounds and my surroundings.

Everything around me shudders under the impact of something crashing hard against the roof, and I jump off the bed and duck next to it. Whatever it was, it can't be good. Violent commotion continues on the roof while I grope blindly in the dark. My fingers settle on the closet door. Somehow I know there should be a trap door in there where I can hide. My stomach roils, driving all the air from my lungs, and I double over with my hands on my knees.

Something massive scrapes down the length of the roof and slams onto the ground. I freeze, overtaken by a shifting, a twisting, like the core of my body is turning with a force of which I have no control. A prickly heat cups my head. I flatten both palms against my temples yet it won't ease. I know this feeling, but I can't place it. Something foreign is in my head and it's spreading lower, into my chest, down my arms and abdomen, sweeping my stomach clean. Once it reaches my feet it's gone, my body freed from under a weight I didn't know was there. With the release of this pressure I'm thrust forward, like a tree branch snapping upward when a clump of melting snow finally falls.

I open the bedroom door and catch myself before walking face-first into a large piece of furniture blocking the doorway. I put my hands against it and push. It has to move out of my way now. Leaning into it, I push as hard as I can but the damn thing only slides an inch. I push again, putting all my weight into it, and gain another six inches.

I try to squeeze between the object and the doorway in the tiny space I created but it's not enough. With my back against the wall, I keep at it, a painful fraction at a time until I finally flop into the hallway. Gasping, I burst through the front door into the yard. The night sky captures me in a way it never has before, every star shimmering for me alone. Orion, so new to me just a few days ago, shines upon me like I've known him my whole life, drawing me into his world as if I'm just as much a part of the celestial realm as he is.

River runs up, weaving anxiously back and forth in front of me. I follow her around the corner of the house and see him. His body stained dark with blood. Filled with a pure, potent sweetness, I rush toward him and land on my knees in the grass next to him.

Flat on his back, he's so covered in blood I can't tell where he's injured. Blood pools around his head, and his shirt hangs off in pieces. I check his airway, his breathing, his pulse. His heart beats faintly. His legs are bent under him at the knees, so I feel for broken bones and finding none, I straighten his legs.

A search of his skull reveals no clue for the source of the blood. It's impossible to know if he has a neck injury, but looking at how he landed, I'm going to have to take a risk and assume he does not. Fresh blood trickles out of his nose and right ear. Not a good sign. I check his pupils, but it's too dark to see. A shiny slash glistens across his chest, offering a reason for some of the blood soaking him and the ground around him. I'd rather it be from that than from his head.

I stand to assess the situation, knowing somehow I have to get him into the house. It's an instinct strong enough to overcome my training that should be telling me not to move him—bleeding from the nose and ear could mean a bad head injury. River is standing over a dark crumpled heap in the grass. I rush toward her to find a man, dressed completely in black, lying in a dark puddle of blood so thick it looks more like a mirror of the night sky.

My arm halts on its way to find a pulse when I see his throat has been cut. I check for a pulse in his wrist and find nothing. He has bled out.

There could be more of them out here. Head injury or not, I have to get us both inside.

I run to the garage and yank up the door handle. It roars upward and out of my way. There's just enough light to spot a big square of folded tarp. Perfect. I tuck it under my arm. I unfold the tarp on the ground next to Trey and roll his body onto it. It's an easier feat than I would've thought. I seem to have a superstrength, yet even though my muscles are working overtime I know it won't last. I manage to slide him to the edge of the driveway where I lose my footing in the gravel. The tarp budges on my second attempt but I begin to realize the futility of this. After a progress of only a few feet, I collapse on the ground, take a few seconds to catch my breath, and run back to the garage. I find a board with wheels on it, the kind mechanics use to work under cars, and I grab a rope as well.

On my way back to Trey, my run slows to a stop. One familiar dog has been replaced by a pack, all standing next to Trey but staring at me. I try to pick River out but can't tell which one she is. One of them barks at me, tail wagging. I drop the board and the rope, run back to the garage, grab the broom, and walk straight toward them. They part as I approach.

With the broom raised, I look around at them and recognize they're not dogs, but coyotes, all calmly watching me as if they are waiting for my orders. He must feed these animals for them to be this tame. I don't have time for this. I'm going to have to ignore them, and they are just going to have to get out of my way. I toss the broom aside, and one of them runs forward, grabbing the tarp in its mouth like a game of tug of war.

"Shoo!" I shout, frantic. This is no time to play!

All at once, the others grab hold of the tarp and I topple backward, catching myself on the ground with my palms. As a perfect team, they drag the tarp, with Trey aboard, all the way to the door. This must be a very bad dream. I will wake up soon, and I can eat breakfast and go to work and forget about this night.

The coyotes dash away. I run to Trey. I lift his head up onto the step and slide my legs under his armpits. I wiggle myself underneath him, brace my feet on the porch, and heave. Once we're both inside the door, I kick it closed. I don't want to think about how many times I'll have to do this until I get him to the couch.

Halfway there, I slide out from under him and run into the bedroom. I pull a couple blankets out of the closet and pile them in the living room. I return to the bedroom and strip the bed of its sheets and pillows and drop them in the living room on the rest of the pile. In the kitchen, I rummage for a pot in the cabinet and fill it with hot water. I lug the pot, soap, and towels into the living room, flipping on the main light with my elbow on my way.

But the effort is for nothing. The darkness was masking a dead man. Now in the light, he has the look of a trauma patient who didn't make it—pale skin covered in blood, that limpness to his frame which only means one thing. My eyes fill with tears but my hands are too full to wipe them. I have no reason to cry, except my chest has caved into itself and the world has broken away from me.

In the silence there's a thin breath, and I know it's not mine because mine is stuck in my lungs. Another breath. I hurry to find his pulse. It's so faint it must be my own pulse in my fingertips. But it's too slow to belong to my pounding heart. I put my ear against his chest and count the beats. He's not gone yet. And he's not going to die on my watch. I need to clean him up. I need to locate and treat his worst injuries.

I need to call an ambulance.

The blood in his ear has dried enough to tell me it's through bleeding. I check behind the ear for a bruise that would indicate a head injury. It appears normal. And so far, no evidence of raccoon eyes. I cut what remains of his shirt off, carefully picking it from the open wound on his chest. I take off his shoes and unbutton and unzip his jeans. With my feet braced against the floor, I pull the ankles of his jeans until they slip all the way off.

He's clean from the waist down, so I cover his lower half with a sheet and two heavy blankets. I soak a towel in the warm water and begin to clean him up. The water turns quickly red, so I take the pot back in the kitchen and dump it. While it's refilling, I dash into the bathroom and find bandages and ointment then hurry back into the kitchen to retrieve the water.

I get the rest of the blood cleaned off his chest and arms. Several gruesome cuts and scrapes run along both fore-arms and a nasty gash divides his bicep. After refreshing the water again, I move on to his face and delicately wipe his forehead. His eyelids. His lips.

His swollen right cheekbone is already developing a large bruise. I clean out his bloody ear and do as much of his back as I can reach. Washing under his chin exposes a shallow cut across his throat, as if a knife skimmed him there. It makes me think of the man outside.

Standing to look at my work, I realize I need to do something about the blood caked in his hair so it's easier to see when the bleeding stops. With so little color to his skin I must assume he's lost several units of blood and may need a transfusion—something I can't do here. I hurry back into the kitchen for fresh water. While the pot fills, I take a bag of frozen peas out of the freezer and find the shallow tray he used for the herbal bath for my leg. I grab a flashlight from the top of the refrigerator.

I take everything back into the living room and rinse his hair until it's possible to examine his head in the light. There's a two-inch gash, no longer bleeding, and several lumps but nothing too concerning. The lumps remind me of the frozen peas, so I balance them on his swollen cheek, trying not to apply too much pressure. His pupils respond normally to the flashlight. His irises glow back at me, purely and perfectly green.

With the back of my hand I check his temperature—not good. I quickly wash each of his hands and dry them. They look like they've been through a wood chipper, the knuckles scraped almost to the bone. My fingers move faster than my mind, applying ointment and bandages to all the wounds I can see. I pull the blankets up to his chin.

Standing up leaves me dizzy and drained, but I drag myself to the laundry room for the laundry basket and return to the living room to place all the dirty towels in it. I wipe as much blood off the floor as I can manage. I roll him onto his side and unfold one of the heavier comforters on the floor next to him. I roll him to his other side and do the same with another, creating a makeshift bed when he's settled back in place. I tuck a pillow under his head, curl up next to him under the blankets, and fall fast asleep with no willpower left for a second thought.

My face is buried against his arm when I wake up. The scent of his skin is an illegal substance, and I'm a criminal, stealing one last fix before the cops haul me away. It's wrong, and I know it, but I can't stop. My sickness has fled with my good sense, but now I'm sick with something new: a need to be curled up next to him for eternity. The world has turned upside down.

I sit up. His face—I know it, but not like this. It was different before. This upside-down world must have different lighting or special effects to give his face a rough charm. Features both foreign and familiar, they give me a warmth I've never felt. I'm glad he's asleep so I can stare. I place my palm on the uninjured side of his chest to feel the rise and fall of his steady breath. His heartbeat is stronger than it was last night. Some life has returned to his skin, and the swelling in his cheek has been replaced by a dark purple bruise.

I slide the blanket to his waist and examine the cut on his chest which seems to be already healing, among older scars I didn't notice last night. Lacerations long-healed by bad suture jobs and what look like gunshot wounds—too many for one person to have so they must be something else. I take his right hand and admire its mass, its strength, its masculinity in proportion to mine. I lean over him and examine his head for the swollen contusions and find them significantly shrunken, and no open wounds. I gently run my fingers down both sides of his face, admiring the cut of his cheekbones, the curve of his lips, the way his hair falls onto his forehead. I pause to stare at his closed eyelids, his lips inches from mine, and wonder how long I have until he wakes up and I have to pretend I still hate him.

CHAPTER 12

LIV

I FORCE MYSELF TO get up. Two hours spent lying beside him, and I'd do it longer if I could. I've become a Trey Bevan fangirl overnight, and it's not due to his stimulating conversation. He's half-dead on the floor and the least I could do is give the man some space, but it feels much better to be burrowing against him. He'll never know unless he has this house under hidden surveillance. If that's the case, I'm busted. Although I would like to see the footage—maybe a replay of this scene will give me a clue. I can't figure out this pull he has on me. It's too ingrained, too primal, to even feel new.

I place my hand on his forehead. He's a little warm, but his breathing and heartbeat both feel normal. There's no way to know how long he'll be unconscious. Or how long I can possibly let this go on before taking him to the clinic.

Down the hall the bureau blocking my path into the bedroom remains a nuisance. Pushing so hard my feet slide away proves to be a waste of energy when I notice one of its feet stuck on a slightly raised floorboard. I squeeze through to the bedroom the same way I got out.

At first glance, the bedroom looks empty except for a few black trash bags on the floor, so I paw through them and find my clothes and bath stuff. I open a dresser drawer, and it's empty. I don't remember packing my things, and I don't know why I would have. All I remember is fighting with Trey.

Oh yeah. Fighting with Trey. Over what he found. That explains the bruises on both my wrists. If I saw these on a patient, I'd notice each bruise looks like the mark of a finger and immediately think domestic violence. Until now, I blamed my struggle to get Trey into the house last night. A cold flush runs through my body in forewarning of what will happen when he wakes up. But one thing is sure, I remember nothing after fighting with Trey. I must have been so mad that when we got back here I packed my things. To go where? Back to my house I suppose.

On my way through the living room, Trey's jeans buzz on the floor. I reach into the pocket and retrieve the phone to see 'Christian' displayed on the screen. My thumb hovers in position to answer the call. There's no way to know if Christian is a good guy or a bad guy. I wonder if he could help me. I glance at Trey's comatose body, as if he has a say.

And I know it doesn't matter. Whether this guy Christian would help me or kill me, I'm not going to answer Trey's phone. I place it on the hearth and take his jeans to the laundry room.

In the kitchen, I down a cup of coffee, wishing he was awake so he could sit with me, bad attitude and all. Maybe he could show me how to cook a fancy risotto, or make a Christmas wreath. His get-over-yourself-dude domestic talents that made me want to gag before…well what can I say? Now I'm game. I wet a washcloth and sit cross-legged next to him in the living room. I gently wipe his forehead, his cheeks, and his neck. The cloth comes back bloody. I roll his head to the side to find his ear bleeding again.

Swelling of the brain means he might need burr holes. He needs a neurosurgeon in a hospital for that. To determine any of this, he needs an MRI or a CT scan, that I know for sure. How long do I wait? Until he's brain damaged, or dead? There's no doubt if he were awake he'd refuse the hospital. And with him unconscious and unable to explain his side, I have no excuse for his injuries. Police would get involved in something my gut tells me is above them. The little I know about him is enough to guess police and hospitals would make this situation more dangerous. My gut might change its mind if his condition worsens. Hopefully I'll get enough of a warning.

I check his ear for a cut that would explain the blood and also end my worries, but I find nothing. I put a clean towel under his ear to catch the blood. His hair is darker than mine by a shade. Brown so dark it could be mistaken for black. Like the color of the strongest dark chocolate. Or the tea he gave me. Maybe I missed these physical traits the first time we met. Spinning into the curb from the force of a Ford truck could have jarred my brain a bit. But it's a little strange to be living in a man's house, eating meals with him for days, and not notice the color of his hair until he's limp on the floor.

I pause in front of the sliding glass door in the kitchen to notice the day for the first time. Leaving the safety of the house gives me a bad feeling even though it's ridiculous to feel safe inside. If they wanted me, they could come straight through the front door and there would be nothing I could do about it.

A squirrel bounds along the porch railing, flaunting its freedom in the beauty of the day. I can imagine how the air smells outside. Thick and heady, with a crisp edge indicating fall is just around the corner. Cracking the window over the sink offers a compromise when the sounds from outside permeate the room.

After a thorough exploration of the cabinets and the refrigerator, I decide this guy must be on some psycho diet. There's not an ounce of processed food except for my own groceries which he must have brought from my house. Stew from the other night is still in the refrigerator, so I spoon some into a small pot and put it on the stove. All of a sudden it occurs to me that I have to leave him when I go to work tomorrow. There's just no other way around it. I'll have to somehow smuggle an IV, a bag of fluids, and a catheter from work.

The stew is just as delicious as it was the first time and I eat slowly, savoring it. Just yesterday, I was suffering with unending stomach sickness. I don't know how it could be gone, just like that. If it was related to emotional distress, it seems like it chose the most stressful time to disappear.

I can't keep my mind from wandering back into the living room. It's a betrayal, sleeping next to him when he can't refuse. I imagine him awake and aware while trapped in a comatose body, mentally kicking and screaming as I snuggle up next to him. I wonder what he'd do if the situation were reversed. If he'd care for me like I'm caring for him, or if he'd have left me out there to die.

When I return to Trey, he looks the same. He could remain like this for weeks, possibly months. I'd have to get someone to help me move him. He'd need medical supplies I couldn't easily take from the clinic more than a few times. And this would all require explanations. Overwhelmed, I push that thought to the back of my mind.

I never examined his back, the one area I wasn't able to clean yesterday. I roll him onto his side.

His back is much worse than I thought. He must have bled for a while last night without my knowing. A wide abrasion runs from his right shoulder blade down his spine to the bottom left side of his back. Untreated, it glistens in the light. I wash it with soap and water and pat it dry. Clean skin reveals more old scars similar to the ones he has on his chest. I dab the wound with ointment and apply bandage after bandage until the whole abrasion is covered. It's really not good he's going to be lying on this for who knows how long. I spread a clean bath towel over the stained bedding and gently roll him back.

I start searching the house for more blankets. The bedroom closet contains nothing but his clothes. A check of every closet and every piece of furniture leaves me empty-handed. The door in the kitchen opens to basement stairs, so I feel for a light, flip it on, and descend into the basement.

Shelves and cabinets line the wall nearest me, and a large workbench occupies the central area. I search around for another light in the semi-darkness. A string hits me in the forehead, so I give it a pull and the area is bathed in light. It's immediately obvious this is not a place to store blankets. I reach for the pull chain but pause, my eyes catching the wall closest to the stairs.

I've never seen a gun this close in person, and there are so many here I'm almost afraid to move. Knives and other weapons mix with the guns and hang on the wall above. Some shiny new, some rusty, some I can only imagine a use for.

A half-empty bottle of liquor sits among it all like a lighthouse in a choppy metal sea. I spin it by the cap so the label faces me. Scotch. Scotch and guns. What a combination.

Morbid curiosity pushes me along the wall to the next set of shelves which holds dozens of jars. Like his herbs upstairs, some are labeled, some are not, but of those that are labeled, many are in a language I don't recognize. I see liquids, powders, herbs, gelatinous substances, with labels identifying some names I recognize as medicines, some as poisons. Thankfully, the amount of dust on most of them gives me hope they haven't been used recently.

The wooden workbench in front of the shelves is littered with tools and containers one would find in a chemistry lab—beakers, tongs, stirring rods. A loose end of a rubber hose continues somewhere to the storage area underneath. Can anyone say meth lab? In the center a heavy stone mortar and pestle holds the remnants of something brown and flaky, like crushed peanut shells.

Moving toward the far end of the wall reveals a library of books, some in English, some in Latin, some in an undistinguishable language. They don't appear to be organized and the subject matter varies. Cooking, gardening, martial arts, weaponry, herbs, chemistry, medicine, botany, astronomy. I pull out an ancient-looking one with a Latin title and flip it open. The entire book is handwritten. I study the drawings, trying to understand the subject matter, unable to decide if they depict an ancient form of medicine or an ancient form of torture. If it's the latter, he certainly has the tools for it. Hopefully he isn't planning on using me for practice.

If some of these books are really as old as they look, they're probably worth a fortune. Did he rob a museum or something? Sending assassins seems an awkward way for museum curators to get their stuff back. I remember the body of the man outside. I have no idea what to do about that.

I circle around to the other side of the basement, conventional in its assortment of power tools, camping gear, workout equipment and free weights. A door in the wall appears to lead to the outside, but several two-by-fours have been nailed over it. I return to the shelves and pull out a modern astronomy textbook. I tug the light chain and climb the stairs to the kitchen where a mountain of laundry awaits me.

Another check of Trey reveals the towel under his ear is soaked with blood, so I replace it with a clean one and settle myself on the couch with the book I brought up from the basement. Maybe by the time he wakes up, I can teach *him* a thing or two about astronomy.

The room dims with the sinking sun. It's already time to check my patient's back. I roll him over and remove the bandages. With each one my astonishment grows. The open flesh has been sealed by a healthy scab. I have never seen a wound so inflamed heal so quickly in my life. After poking and prodding the sealed wound in awe, I lower him back down.

A sharp rattle fills the room and my head jerks toward the noise. Silence. With a second sharp rattle, Trey's phone hops off the edge of the hearth. I cross the room and pick it up. Another call from Christian. Surely someone with a name like Christian must be good. He knows Trey isn't answering his phone and must be worried. Maybe Trey didn't show up somewhere. Maybe Christian is checking one last time, making sure Trey is unable to answer his phone before he comes to kill me. I notice three new text messages before I power off the phone to eliminate any future temptation of answering it. Several days from now, I may be too desperate for help to care about what kind of person I'm inviting here. My only option should be the police.

In the kitchen I close the window against the chilly gust blowing through. It's going to get cold tonight. I find a box of chamomile tea and brew a mug. The sight of the mug compels me to open the herb cabinet and stare inside. When I realize what I'm doing, I slam the door and return to Trey's side.

The chill from the kitchen has crept into the living room. It can't be too difficult to build a fire. I've seen it done enough to know how to start it. A layer of ash covers the base of the fireplace—good, that must mean it's okay to use. I open the flue and put the solitary piece of firewood on the grate. There must be more outside, and there is—a pile stacked to the porch ceiling. I take an armful inside.

There's a box of pine cones next to the wall. I add more wood and pine cones and light them with a match I find on the mantel. The fire blazes high, hot on my face, and I imagine it exploding out of control and the house catching fire. And here I am, with a half-dead man and no coyotes to help me this time. The flames settle down like they've just read my mind, lapping at the wood as if it's a tease before fizzling out. I try another match, but it burns down to my fingers before anything catches. My gas fireplace in Chicago was a lot easier than this. We had a remote control.

I find his newspaper in the kitchen, the one he pretends to read to avoid talking to me. The paper catches fast, curling and writhing and igniting everything else. I close the screen and return to my book on the couch, hoping he won't be too mad I burned his precious newspaper. How could he be? He's still limp on the floor, as unthreatening as a tranquilized animal. Maybe I should tag him and release him back into the wild.

The flicker and crackle of the fire is like another sentient being in the room, a comfort in the stillness I didn't realize was missing. But there's something else missing from this house. This man has no TV. I can't decide what's more strange—the vast collection of firepower and medieval torture books in the basement, or the lack of TV. He's a single guy living alone. I've known men who have one in every room.

I read about Ptolemy and Galileo then flip pages until I see a chart of the night sky. It's easy with the constellations labeled and drawn with lines, but I don't know how anyone could make sense of this outside in the night, with or without the chart in hand. I check on Trey. Surprised again at his vitality, I can't find anything I can do for him. A tiny spot of blood marks the towel beneath his ear. It's a good sign, but I can't let it fool me. It could always start up again. I put my hand down on the floor on the other side of him and lean over him, memorizing the unpolished perfection of his face. It's as if I never looked at him until this day. I wouldn't have been able to pick him out of a line-up or recognize him in a crowd. Now his face has characteristics I both see and feel, like he's someone I once knew, changed by time, the core elements of him still familiar. A part of my memory. My life.

Lines between his eyebrows speak of hardship. If I saw these before, I'd guess he was the cause but now I know better. They remind me too much of me. Maybe that's what draws people together—one person's recognition of self in another. A common pain, different in detail but identical in feeling. Once you've been there you share a spot in the world with others who have lived through the same. It's a bit selfish—to sympathize only because you can relate— but that's human nature.

I need to stop obsessing. It's moving into stalker territory.

And there's a pile of bloody blankets and towels beside him that needs my attention more than him. If anyone sees it, they'll think someone was murdered. Everything needs to be scrubbed. Tomorrow. I'm done for the night.

The switch on the thermostat in the hall points to off, so I flip it to the on position. The furnace kicks on in the basement. I put a few more logs on the fire and wait for the furnace to heat the house. Impatience causes me to wander back into the kitchen, where to my utter surprise I find myself looking in the herb cabinet again. Infuriating! And I must admit a little comical—Trey Bevan is a drug pusher, and now I'm addicted to some weird plant that's probably illegal. I wonder about his intentions. Was he innocently trying to relieve my stomach, or is it more like a "first one's free" deal? When he wakes up, I'll have to fake my nausea to get some more of that stuff, whatever it was. Dr. Bevan's going to have to write me a prescription for a year's supply. And after bathing him and doing all his laundry, I'm not paying him a dime.

Bored, I look in the refrigerator then the freezer and find a giant carton of cookie dough ice cream that seems out of place among all the healthy food. I guess everyone has their vice. I hope he doesn't mind sharing. I'll be sure to tell him ice cream is going to undo all his effort. It's going to lead to worse things, like chili cheese corn chips and—oh god—white bread. What then? He'll lose his special parking spot at the monastery. He'll be shunned by his Paleo Diet crowd. Utter ruin.

Back in the living room, the warmth of the fire reminds me how cold the rest of the house still is. The furnace should be running. I strain to hear the hum through the floor, but it's as quiet as it has been all day. I flip the thermostat off then back on. The furnace kicks on again, so I find a floor vent and stand on it. It blows cool air. After a minute or so, it shuts off. Great.

I head back downstairs. Staring at the furnace does nothing but remind me how not mechanically inclined I am. Isn't there some kind of pilot light that has to be on? I look the thing up and down and peek in all the vents but see nothing obvious. I've no idea what a pilot light even looks like. I see a power switch, so I switch it off then back on. It starts up. I'm halfway up the stairs when it shuts off again.

"Crap," I say aloud.

Trey needs the one clean quilt in the house more than I do, so I squeeze past the bureau back into the bedroom and start layering on his clothes—a sweatshirt over a thermal shirt, sweatpants, and a pair of his thick socks. It's so much material I can barely walk. Tomorrow, I'll need to go by my house and pick up my winter clothes. Montana temperature changes are more drastic than I expected. I put as many logs on the fire as seems safe, and, respecting what I know would be Trey's wishes, I make myself comfortable on the couch.

CHAPTER 13

LIV

THE CHATTERING OF my teeth wakes me up in the middle of the night. My half-asleep reflex reloads the dwindling fire with logs and stokes it until wood hisses and flames flap high. I climb under the quilt on the floor, snuggle up to Trey's blissfully warm body, and fall into instant sleep.

Not much later I wake up covered in sweat and strip off all the extra clothes. The air outside the quilt chills my damp skin before I slide back underneath, pull it up to my chin, and press against him. The pulse of the fire's glow gives every shadow two legs, shoulders, and a head. I fall back asleep knowing if anyone is coming for us, I'll die knowing there was nothing more I could do.

Extracting myself from my pocket of warmth under the covers when the alarm goes off seems like some horrible injustice. The cold silence and smell of ash in the room confirm the fire's been out for hours, even though I woke up several times to feed it. Turning over, I try to ignore the sweep of his skin against my back and notice the pile of my discarded clothes. How cliché this is. Two people who hate each other, forced to conserve body heat in the cold. Only I don't exactly hate him anymore. And there was no force necessary because he's not exactly conscious.

The strangest part, though, is my quality of sleep. Unmedicated sleep. On the floor, in the cold, next to Mr. Scowl. This must be the longest I've gone without a sleeping pill. By now I should be wanting to choke down the whole bottle.

I flip the quilt off, sit up, and look at his face. His slightly parted lips, his eyelashes brushing his cheeks. If he finds out about the change that's evolved inside me, I don't know how he'll react. Or how I'll hide it from him. My stomach flips at the thought of telling him. The biggest asshole I've ever met, and I have a thing for him. I hardly believe it myself.

I get up, make coffee, get dressed, and eat a quick breakfast. I tend to Trey, making sure he'll be comfortable while I'm gone. He looks impossibly vibrant, almost more alive than when he's conscious. If anyone saw him now, they'd never believe the extent of his injuries only two days ago. My own memory of it seems more like some illusion.

Stepping onto the front porch, I scan the yard. If they wanted me they had all day yesterday to march in and kill me. I'm not any more exposed outside even though it feels that way. Once safe in my car, I shut the door and lock it. Fear for my own personal safety dissolves under an onslaught of worry for Trey. This is going to be a long day.

My first task proves it in an unexpected way. I'm sent straight into my own emotional war—attending a birth. There's a quiver in my legs when I near the patient's room. I want to get lost somewhere. Hide in the air ducts. I want to go home to Trey. I should've told them no Labor and Delivery, but then they'd ask why. This isn't the kind of place you can make requests like that. We all have to cover for each other. If I can't suck it up and put my patients' needs first, I'm a failure. I square my shoulders and open the door.

Dr. Wu looks at me over his spectacles, surprised. A gray-haired woman stops mid-sentence to squint at me from the exam table. I'm in the wrong room. I stammer an apology and let myself out. The room's number tells me I'm on the wrong damn floor. I start walking to dispel the sickening heat on my skin, my broken cool threatening to send me home like a coward. I find the correct room in a daze and knock before pushing my way in without a second thought.

The nurse inside tells me the mother wants no meds. We're checking mother's vitals and baby's heart rate every fifteen minutes and otherwise staying out of the mother's way unless she or her doula asks for something. I'd love to keep much farther out of her way, but something makes me think of Trey and for some reason I'm able to give her the thumbs-up. Every check of the baby's heart rate is like a kick in the stomach. I try not to imagine that heartbeat slowing down. Becoming still.

After two hours another nurse comes to relieve me. A panicked run from the room would only prove how unstable I am, so I take each step with defiant care. On my way down the hall, I pause in front of the supply closet. The hallway is empty in both directions. Now is my chance. I go to the break room and grab my bag. After slipping inside the supply closet, I shove a catheter and IV supplies into my bag then return it to my locker. Somehow, I'll figure out a way to replace it.

Now alone with my thoughts, I can't put a damper on my paralyzing worry for Trey. They could have been waiting for me to leave so they could finish him off. A silly idea—I'm no obstacle for them. But maybe they thought I would call the police, so they patiently waited for me to leave so they could carry out their sick plan with one less complication.

"Liv, I have a patient waiting to have a cast removed. He's been waiting a while now. Can you take him?" Rachel's voice invades my fantasy world. "Liv?"

"Sure." I remove the cast for a little boy who's elated to be able to see his skin again. As I'm cleaning up and trying not to check the clock every minute, Dr. Wu sticks his head in the room.

"Liv, our laboring mother is asking for you. Could you stay with her?"

"Absolutely." It's the last place I want to be but at least it will take my mind off Trey. I gobble down my lunch then return to the room. The clock has been removed from the wall. I have no opportunity to leave her, no chance to slip out and go check on Trey like I'd planned. When Dr. Wu and another nurse come in, I ask for the time. It's been three hours. That means Trey's been alone for seven.

No one's more relieved than me to see the baby born wiggling and crying. In my dreams they all die. At birth, as crawlers, as toddlers. Just when I think one has survived past the red X on the calendar, I open the door and find another baby dead in a crib. On a rug. In the grass. In a car. My dreams like to be creative.

Everyone is crying—mother, father, baby. Except me. I can't begin or I'll never stop. Eight fingernails digging into my palms keep it on lockdown. Until I can escape.

It's an hour past my shift. I get my bag and head to the entrance of the clinic, trying hard not to break into a run. Rachel catches me before I make it through the door.

"Liv, I know you're leaving, but no one else is available to give a tetanus shot. Could you do it really quick?"

"Sure, Rachel." I reach for the chart, feeling suddenly short of breath. My desperation to get back to Trey intensifies with every passing second.

Fifteen minutes later I'm running to my car. Forget going by my place for more clothes. I am sick with worry for Trey.

Everything looks normal when I pull up to the house. River greets the parked car, and I hop out and pat her on the head in an attempt to slow my frenzied pace. I go inside, step out of my shoes, and drop my bag to the floor. With the borrowed medical equipment in hand, I hurry into the living room.

All I see is a rumpled blanket on the floor.

He's gone. Oh my god he's gone. I look around frantically. Every object in the room has turned unfamiliar and menacing. Shadows alive with murderers. My breath sounds hollow in my chest. I recognize panic and push it far away. I have to find him. He could still be here, need my help. My footsteps pound into the kitchen. Back to the living room. Into the bedroom. The bathroom. I run back outside to the front yard.

"Trey!" They got him. And if they got him, they'll get me too.

"Trey!" I scream again, knowing no one will hear. The wind answers, shoving the trees around like it's just a warning. Like it could do so much more.

"Hope you weren't planning to use that stuff on me."

I whirl around. He must have come around the house. He's wearing the sweatpants I discarded in the middle of the night and nothing else. I follow his gaze and realize I'm still holding the catheter and IV.

He smiles. I didn't know he could smile. It turns my stomach into one of those trees, tossed around like a plaything.

"What are you *doing* out here?" I demand.

"Had something I needed to take care of."

"With no jacket on? No shoes?"

"Okay, mom." He walks toward me. A gentler gust of wind ruffles his hair.

The earth under my feet has gone spongy. Someone, please, slap me out of this. "It's like forty degrees out here."

"Feels good to me. I'm burning up."

"You probably have a fever." I quickly close the gap between us to feel his forehead.

He lowers my hand. "You really don't need to worry about me."

I fall off a cliff into his eyes. I don't find my voice until he looks away. It takes much too long. "Well I wish you had told me that this morning. I could have saved myself the worry all day. Oh, but you couldn't have told me. You were in a coma."

"I was?" His eyes dart back to mine. He's playing with me.

"It's not funny." I force myself to glare up at him. He stares down. Eyes inhabited by the dusty green of coniferous forest. And that soft dark hair. My stomach does a pirouette without me. He's going to draw this moment out again, and I won't be left standing.

I turn and go back into the house. I drop the supplies in my bag to return to the clinic tomorrow and notice my damp, grass-stained socks. I hold the wall to remove them one at a time. Montana's biggest asshole is awake, and I went running outside in my socks like a fool to find him. I can't imagine what has made him so undeniably appealing to me now.

He comes in behind me. "I see you took the opportunity to raid my closet while I couldn't protest."

I stop to look at him. This has to be the most he's ever talked to me when we're both sober. He's actually pursuing the conversation, if you could call it that.

"Well considering your furnace is broken, and you were lying on all the blankets, I really didn't have any other options."

"The furnace is broken at the clinic too?" He gestures toward what I'm wearing.

Now I can't tell if he's playing with me or actually irritated. I pause, wondering if I should control my tone. "Did you really want people to see this?" I push up both sleeves to reveal the bruises on my wrists, which I know must be somehow connected to him.

His smirk fades into a look of alarm. He drops his eyes and looks away so I can't read his expression. When he speaks, his voice is thick. "I'm sorry. I didn't know." The set of his jaw becomes harsh. He walks past me into the living room.

I follow him and start cleaning up what's left of the makeshift hospital room. My emotions catch up to me, and I search for strength to cover the loss that washes over me, forcing me to acknowledge a painful truth. I'm back to where I was with him. Only now, everything has changed for me, but nothing has changed for him. It was easier when I hated him. Yet I can't begin to understand this illogical affection I have for him now. It's become so integrated it's a struggle to question at all.

I continue cleaning but can't help feel like I've been fired from a job I love and I'm cleaning out my office, waiting to be escorted out.

CHAPTER 14

TREY

I KNOW I SHOULD stop talking to her. She probably wants me to leave her alone, but I can't help myself. I have to know how much she remembers about the other night, and what she can tell me I missed the last couple days. As soon as I know I can leave her alone.

Being out cold for two days must have made me delirious. Once I get my bearings back, things will be back to normal. I hover, feeling like I need to say something to her.

"Thanks for—"

"You don't need to thank me."

"…not leaving me out there to die."

She tilts her head, sizing me up in a strange way. Then I notice her wrists again. My guilt is a cancer growing inside me. I don't know how I could be capable of hurting her like that. My hands on her is one vivid memory I have of that night. An action so normal to me I rarely second guess it. My hand now cups her wrist. I'm not sure how it got there.

I am losing it.

"Sore?"

"Not…too bad," she answers slowly.

She's obviously trying to figure out why I care. *I'm* trying to figure out why I care.

"Have you been drinking that tea?"

"What? No." I let go of her.

She eyes me for a moment before resuming her cleaning. My first reflex is to help her, but I feel like I'm overdoing it. She doesn't need my help anyway. It makes no sense. I should make dinner, so I break away and head to the kitchen. I'll get the information out of her, one way or another.

There are no fresh ingredients so I snatch some red potatoes and zucchini from the garden. River is gnawing on something behind the garage. I chuck a potato at her just to give her shit. It hits hard, inches from her paws. She doesn't flinch but raises her eyes like I've got mine coming.

While I chop, I try to organize my thoughts, but there are too many things I need to ask her. Should I start with more recent things, like what did I miss this morning? Or should I ask her how much she saw of the fight after she woke up the other night? And how the hell did she move that bureau to get out of the bedroom? She materializes next to me, hands on hips. I look over at her to acknowledge her.

"What happened to all the dirty laundry?" she asks.

"I burned it."

"You burned it? I was going to wash it!"

"Not worth the effort." I look away. "It was a gorefest. There was more blood than fabric." She doesn't answer, so I add, "I'll pick up some new stuff tomorrow." I have no idea why I'm trying to appease her.

"Then what are we going to do about bedding for tonight?"

I glance over at her and just can't help myself. "We could do the same thing you did the past two nights. You didn't seem to have a problem."

After the words are out, I wish I had phrased them as a question because, as much as I hate to admit it, I'm dying to know. There's an unfamiliar thrill in my blood. I try to keep cool.

She changes the subject. "Can I put some ointment on your back? I don't want it to get infected."

Since she's already unscrewing the lid to the ointment, I understand it was a rhetorical question. This is the nurse in her, doing her job, and nothing else. She cared for me for two days, so I can understand she wouldn't want her hard work to go to waste.

Her cool fingers soothe my burning skin. "You must have a fever. You need to take a fever reducer. Okay, turn around." It's an order that should annoy me.

Tempted by that strange thrill, testing it, I oblige. I watch her face as she works on the cut across my chest and the one across my neck. Her bangs are swept to the side, out of her eyes, blending into osprey-brown hair streaked by the summer sun. I had myself trained not to notice these things about women. One blow to the head, and all that training went to shit? It can't be possible. It isn't me.

When she goes for my cheekbone, I feel like I'm being a pushover, so I swat her away. "That one's fine."

"No, it's not. It's going to split."

"I'm cool with that." I turn back to the stove.

She leaves the room. When she returns, she offers her balled fist to me. "Here."

I take the pills and set them on the counter. This is getting to be too much. I need to put a stop to it. She fills a glass with water, sets it down next to the pills, and looks at me impatiently.

"Just leave it there." I'm surprised at the lack of irritation that usually accompanies this kind of exchange.

She raises her eyebrows and nods toward the pills.

"I'll take them later if I still feel warm." God. Pushover.

I grab an onion and go back to cooking, doing my best to ignore her. She's left the kitchen which is good since she's a pain and I prefer my space—but her absence feels like a problem I need to fix. When the food is ready, I mound my plate, pour a scotch, and sit. I don't need to call her. She'll come when she's hungry.

Several minutes pass and I'm halfway through my meal. I slow my pace. But it would be ideal to finish quickly so I don't have to eat with her. Somehow that just doesn't seem right. I toss back the rest of the scotch and refill my glass.

She finally joins me, wearing the jacket I let her borrow the night we took our walk together. She helps herself in silence. I offer her some scotch but she shakes her head. I can tell she wants to say something, but I try to ignore it and concentrate on my dinner.

"Are you going to fix the furnace?" Her words are gentle. An obvious effort not to nag.

"I doubt it's broken. It's probably just the pilot." I open the door to go downstairs.

"When can I go back to my house?" There's an unmistakable sadness in her voice. How I recognize it is beyond me.

"You can go back to your house whenever you want. I just don't think it's safe. For reasons you're well aware of now."

"Don't you think if they wanted me they would have come yesterday?"

She's right. They should have killed her and it would have been easy. It's not something they'd overlook though, unless they thought I'd already done it. There's no easy way to explain that to her. It's something I'd rather keep to myself. It's something I'd rather erase.

"They must have thought you were…gone."

"Why?"

I search for an explanation that would satisfy her and exonerate me, but why am I bothering? I shrug and go down the stairs before she can respond. I don't need to explain anything to her.

The pilot light is indeed off. I light it, go back upstairs, and set the thermostat. As soon as the house warms up, I'm going to burn my ass off. I return to the kitchen and take both pills on the counter as she watches.

She still seems upset. What do I care?

"So it works?" she asks.

"What?"

"The furnace."

"Yeah, I just had to light the pilot."

"But that still means we have no sheets or blankets. And I'd really like to pick up some of my warmer clothes so I don't have to keep wearing yours."

There it is again, that thrill. A long lost excitement rises inside me and I concentrate to suppress it. I need to get back to my normal self. This can't go on.

If I wanted to be logical, she does have a valid point. "Okay. Let's make a run to your place."

I pull on a jacket and my running shoes and grab my keys. She's already waiting at the front door. The unseasonable chill outside suggests a cold night ahead. I don't know how she managed without heat last night. Well, I have a hunch, but I try to put it out of my mind while we both climb into the truck.

As I back out, she strains to look out her window toward where that body was. "Did you—"

"I took care of it."

The sun has already set, leaving a sleepy blend of color in the sky still powerful enough to light the landscape with a soft glow. I look over at her. She appears to be lost in thought, staring out the window at the blur of scenery. It's hard to control the need to strike up a conversation and ask her one of the many questions looming in my mind.

"I'm sorry," I say without meaning to. I wasn't even thinking it.

She abruptly looks at me but it takes her a moment to respond. "For what?"

"Everything."

My eyes return to the road, but she continues to watch me. I crack my window, and the wind stirs her long hair around her shoulders.

"I just…moved out here to escape. To simplify my life. To get away from…everything." She takes a deep breath and turns away from me to look out her window again. "I think it was the worst thing I could have possibly done. And now I'm trapped."

She makes the last sentence sound so final, so hopeless. Like she has been defeated. My guilt eats her words up, relishing them, licking its fingers. I pull up to her house, and we both get out of the truck. Her dog stands from his watch on the porch as if he had been waiting for her for days. He probably has been waiting for days. As we get near, he comes toward us, and she stiffens and stops walking.

"What?" I search her face.

The dog licks her hand. "He's never done that. He's never been this friendly."

"There's a first time for everything. He misses you." I find myself squinting in confusion at my own strange optimism.

"Is it awful that I'm afraid of him?"

"Why would you be afraid of your own dog?" A laugh stirs in my chest, and I breathe it out.

"He's not my dog. He just lives here. He lived here before me." Her eyes catch mine and hold them in a gentle captivity. An alarming comfort surges through me, like the ebb of a strong tide. Instead of swimming against it, I take a deep breath.

Instinct jolts me to reality. Something doesn't feel right. I take her arm and pull her toward the front door while analyzing every object, shadow, and movement around us. As she rummages through her bag for her house key, I notice. "The lock has been picked."

She looks up at me, then at the door. "How can you tell?"

I push the door open with my palm. It wasn't even closed all the way.

"God, no," she whispers.

Side by side, we peer inside the house beyond the creaking open door. Nothing in our line of vision looks to be out of place. The dog probably wouldn't be here if someone was still around, but I pull her behind me as I check each room. At least they didn't trash it this time. They must have found what they wanted the first time. They weren't so lucky when they came back for something else.

I lead her back to the living room and let go of her hand which falls lifelessly to her side. She stands silent, motionless, so I spin her to face me. Tears streak her face, but she makes no effort to wipe them. "I'll never be safe here," she whispers.

When her eyes meet mine, it's too late. Her grief has somehow infiltrated me. My control is lost. I crush her against me, my face in her hair. It's that moment when whatever chemical you've consumed has finally saturated your brain, planting you in place with no desire to argue. Setting you free.

Too comfortable to fight it, I simply let myself be. The soft warmth of her body feels delicate against me. I feel her give, molding to fit me. Her hair smells like a forbidden pleasure, and I take a deep breath, savoring the lusty scent of female skin mixed with body heat. I never want to let go. Because it's not just any chemical but *that* chemical. The one you've been craving. It's settled in, lulling your nerves back into harmony, and you realize it's more than a recreation. You've become too attached. You can't live without it.

Reality hits me like a floodlight flipped on in the darkness. I unwrap my arms, grasp her shoulders and hold her out to arm's length. She looks as shocked as I feel. I release her. She wipes her face with her sleeve. I need some time alone, time to think. This is madness.

"What are we here for again? We should get it and go." My voice is not mine.

She blinks a few times before heading down the hall. I follow her. She loads my arms with sheets, blankets, a big comforter. I wait outside her bedroom as she shoves clothes into a bag. Then she's in the bathroom grabbing things out of the cabinet and tub. We carry her stuff outside to the truck and drive back to my house in amplified silence.

Dusk has descended on my house, bringing my attention to the air that has dropped several degrees during our absence. River raises her head from her station by the garage but doesn't bother getting up. The house is warm when we enter. After I heave the bureau back down the hall, we both go into the bedroom. I help her make the bed up with clean sheets and a comforter. Then I put one of the remaining blankets at the foot of the bed. She gives me this grin—it goes through me like a guided missile.

And I'm left standing alone in the room, staring at the wall like some dope who's never had a woman smile at him.

I take the other two blankets out to the living room with me. Water rumbles through the pipes beneath my feet to the shower as I collapse on the couch. I take off my shoes, unzip my jacket and shrug out of it. The corner of something catches my elbow, so I pull it out from between the cushions. It's one of my astronomy books from the basement. She must have gotten bored watching my stupid ass sleeping off a concussion for two days. This also means she went downstairs. I try to think of anything down there she shouldn't see, but it doesn't matter. She's already seen too much.

Pulsing with energy yet unable to think, I know I could probably use a good run, but I don't want to leave her alone. The only coherent thoughts I can manage are the nagging questions I'm dying to ask her. How did she get me in the house by herself that night? Did she see the other guy or what I did to him? What did she do to me while I was unconscious?

I try to clear my head and relax when I hear her emerge from the bathroom and go into the bedroom. I'm holding my breath as I entertain the image of walking in there, pulling her against me, and kissing her hard. Something tells me she would kiss me back, and it wouldn't have to end there. I'll allow these thoughts for now. But when I wake up in the morning, I will forbid them.

The fantasy plays itself out in my mind, and I don't stop it. Common sense makes a good argument, distracting me with the image of my likely swift rejection, but I shove it aside to watch the vision continue. My repressed sexuality is like a wild animal, clawing viciously at a newly weakened spot in its cage. Suddenly, she's in the room with me, wearing my flannel robe, carrying a pillow which she drops on the couch next to me. I sit on my hands.

"How did you move that bureau by yourself the other night?" I ask, in desperate need of something else to occupy my mind.

She studies my face a moment before she answers. "It wasn't easy."

"You just pushed it?" It doesn't seem possible. Her body is so small. I find myself laughing. "What are you, five foot three? About a hundred twenty?"

She gives me a look. "Something like that." She cinches the robe tighter around her waist. "Sorry, but I forgot my robe at home. All that stuff I just brought and—"

"That's okay." It should not be such a challenge to avert my eyes. I never had this problem before. She turns toward the kitchen, but I can't let it go. "Tell me what you heard when you woke up that night."

She doesn't answer right away. I can see her going over it in her head, deciding how much she should tell me. I'll just have to keep after her until I get all I want.

"I heard noises on the roof. I started to hide in the closet, but then, I don't know. I was compelled to get out. I don't really know why." She sits down at the opposite end of the couch, folding one leg underneath her.

"And then you went outside?" I try not to notice how the robe rode up her leg when she sat down.

"Yes. I went outside and walked straight to you. I felt a strong…" She lowers her eyes for a moment. "River was there."

"You weren't afraid?" I look away, but her image remains etched on my retinas, feeding a continuous transmission to my brain.

"No. You needed help. You were lying in a pool of blood. I couldn't tell where you were hurt, and I took a big risk moving you. You could have broken your neck." She exhales hard, like this risk weighed on her more than it should have. I'd think she'd be glad to see my sorry ass half-dead on the ground.

"Did you see anyone else?"

"Yes, I checked on him too. He was already dead."

Good thing she wasn't out there when I cut his throat. But I don't know why it matters. She obviously knows what I did. What surprises me most is her willingness to hang out with a murderer. Her tea-induced promise of secrecy only covered what had happened before it. An oversight, since she was free to leak future events like me killing someone in my backyard. Most people would have run screaming to the police. "Why didn't you turn me in?"

"Turn you in for what?" She furrows her brow, genuinely wondering what I mean.

"Murder."

"Hmm," she answers without breaking eye contact. "I just didn't think of it that way. I guess I probably should have. I guess I still can. Where's the phone?"

There's that spunk. I knew she still had it in her. Her eyes light up playfully, and my body aches to touch hers. My restrained hands slide out from under me on their own. With only a few feet of space separating us, all I'd have to do is slide toward her—

"Is there any way I could convince you to come to the clinic tomorrow to get a CT scan?"

"It's not necessary."

"You bled a lot out of your right ear."

"I'm not worried about it." My dismissal is automatic. Maybe I should just explain it to her.

She rolls her eyes, an action that would have been like a splinter under a fingernail to me three days ago. I watch her for a moment, fascinated by this new tolerance for a woman so repulsive to me before. Tolerance? Fuck it. Who am I kidding? It's more like infatuation. Pushing every sexual button I have.

When she raises her eyebrows in response to my stare, I return us to the subject. "How did you get me into the house?"

"I was hoping you wouldn't ask me that. You're never going to believe it."

"Try me."

She looks at her hands in her lap. "I rolled you onto a tarp that I found in the garage. I tried to pull you inside, but you were too heavy. I went back to the garage to look for something to help me, and when I got back to you River was there, along with some coyotes, and they dragged you all the way to the door." She looks up at me and shrugs.

I can't hold back my laughter.

She turns away. "See, I knew you'd think it was ridiculous. It was probably all a hallucination anyway. So, I really don't know how I got you in the house." Noticing her exposed leg, she pulls the robe down to cover her bare skin.

"It's not that I don't believe you. I just think it's funny they did that."

She continues on her own, probably wanting to move away from the subject of the coyotes. "And then, somehow, I got you in here. It took me forever to clean you up. You were a mess. By the time I was finished, I was exhausted, and I fell asleep."

She cuts off there, looking away as she runs her hand through her hair.

I knew it. "You fell asleep on the floor?"

"Yes." She looks back at me with a challenge in her eyes.

Like a coward, I refuse to accept her challenge. I know I'm teetering on the edge of losing self-control, and I can't trust myself anymore. Not tonight.

"Guess I owe you" is all I can muster.

"I didn't find out about your back until later. It was pretty bad at first. But the next day…" She squints at something only she can see.

I remain quiet, still unable to collect my thoughts. A long moment of silence passes.

"Why are they trying to kill you?" she asks.

"They aren't trying to kill me," I answer without thinking.

She raises her eyebrows in disbelief.

"It's a long story." That would feel so good to unload. But not tonight. Not ever. I need to ground myself and restore my self-discipline before I make any more foolish mistakes.

CHAPTER 15

TREY

W HEN THE ALARM goes off, I'm already wide awake. The buzzer's throbbing rhythm pounds my brain, still fuzzy from a night of fitful dozing through thoughts I couldn't turn off. Hopefully she'll be safe going to work and coming home by herself. She'll think I'm crazy if I suggest escorting her, and that will make two of us. After a full night of asking myself why I care whether she lives or dies, I still don't have an answer.

Too much to do today, on not enough sleep. It isn't the first time. I get up and take a shower. I pull her car out of the garage and load up my truck with the stuff I'll need for the day. I leave before she wakes up. A day without her will give me the chance to recoup and find my sanity again. Or, my insanity, depending on how you look at it.

I stop by the gas station. Fuel up, grab a newspaper, a couple bananas, and coffee. My old routine is a welcome friend. Strange looks and wary eyes meet me everywhere I go due to my busted cheek and cut up throat, but it's not anything I haven't experienced before. At least it gives people a good reason not to talk to me.

When I arrive at my first job, the foreman slaps me on the back in a greeting. I had forgotten about my wounded back until then. The bitterness of the reminder makes me feel like myself again. Two billed hours of wiring go by and before I know it, I'm taking one last look at my finished work. On my way back to my truck, I run into Wayne carrying some lumber so I drop my stuff to help him.

"Trey, man! How's your lady friend?"

"Real funny, Wayne."

"Always the ladies' man, never wants to brag."

"I don't know who these ladies are you're always going on about." Wayne seems to think I get a lot more action than I do.

I head back to my truck. As I turn the key in the ignition, I check the clock on the dash. She'll be at work now. Not that it matters.

Next job is the Lietz place. On the way there it starts to rain. Mrs. Lietz answers the door as I'm shaking the water out of my hair.

"Oh dear, you're all wet. Let me get you a towel."

"No need. I've got the parts for your toilet."

She takes me to the guest bathroom and hovers in the doorway while I get to work.

"What in heaven's name happened to your eye?" Attempted concern, covering good old-fashioned nosiness.

"Just a little car accident. No big deal."

This is the part I hate about the small jobs. Dealing with customers who think they're paying me to have a conversation with them instead of do what I'm there to do. In the beginning, I took these jobs to keep me busy. The same rule applies—busy is exactly what I need to be right now. Suck it up.

"Oh, well I hope you went to the hospital. You know you're always hearing about folks who get head injuries and don't go to the hospital and twenty-four hours later they're dead."

"Yep." Real uplifting conversation. And she figured it out, without realizing there was anything to figure out. She also managed to return my thoughts to the woman who took care of me while I slept off that head injury.

I ignore her. After a while she wanders away. The job is a pain in the ass, of course. I find three problems to fix instead of just the one. Sometimes I wonder if these people break stuff on purpose just to get me out here to entertain them. And she's got her heat cranked up to at least eighty degrees so by the time I'm done I'm sweating like I'm back in Phoenix digging ditches in July. But I shouldn't complain—the aggravation is good for me. It makes me feel right again.

Walking to the door, I holler to Mrs. Lietz to tell her I'll send her a bill. I hear her start to get up and walk me out but I'm already out the door before she can corner me.

It's pouring now. One of those heavy, constant, cleansing rains that turns the earth to mush, fills the creeks and seems to go on all day. And will. I sit in my truck and eat lunch, watching the water roll down the windshield, trying my hardest not to wonder where she is, what she's doing—because why should I fucking care?

No doubt the roofing job is off for today, but I swing by the site just to let them know I haven't ditched them. A couple of other guys show up too, and we stand under the porch for a few minutes discussing whether it's going to let up. My prediction wouldn't be any more accurate to them than their own.

"So Bevan, what's the other guy look like?"

I laugh. If they only knew.

"Man, I'd never take you for a brawler, you're always so chill."

"You always catch me in a good mood." I could laugh so they think I'm joking, but I don't.

"Hey, we're going out for drinks later on, you should join us."

I tell them I have some stuff to take care of.

"Oh yeah? Blonde or brunette?" They all laugh but I have a hard time joining in.

My next job is a one-hour drive out of town. I try to use the time to figure out how I'm going to get her out of my house without getting her killed, but the more I think about it, the more impossible it seems. She's already in too deep. If I'd just finished her off that night instead of falling asleep, this would all be behind me, and I wouldn't know the difference. It would be done. I'd have my house and my life back.

Conjecture is pointless though, especially in hindsight. The smallest, most trivial change of events could cause a drastic change in the result. If I'd been five minutes later and hadn't spotted the gray Acura that day I would have never turned to follow it, and never run into Liv Gilchrist. And it's not always a change for the better. If Liv hadn't been able to push that bureau they could have gotten to me before she did.

When I arrive at the site, I find them short a few guys, so I offer to take up some of the slack because that's what I would've done two weeks ago before I had someone living in my house. It's good hard labor, the kind that promises to wear me out so I can sleep. There will be no need to run off excess energy tonight. And with no familiar faces, there's no one to bug me or stir up my mind any more than it already is.

Before I know it, it's late, and I still have the commute home. I drive through the hard rain, feeling good, like my old self has settled back into my bones. I pull up to the house. Her car is missing. I squash my disappointment. I should be glad to have the house to myself.

The rain soaks me on my walk to the door. A light shines inside, and I curse aloud. She's at the kitchen table, already changed out of her scrubs. Cold sandwiches prepared on the counter, a plate set out for me like I do for her.

She looks up at me in the doorway. "I waited for you, but I got hungry and wasn't sure when you'd be here."

I avoid her eye. "You don't need to wait for me." She's filled the fridge door with yogurt, the kind I buy. I take two and put them on the table. "Where's your car?"

Her face shows no emotion. "I put it in the garage."

I should have stayed gone longer. I pour some scotch, grab the newspaper, and sit down. Between bites, I flip pages, reading nothing.

"I can't stay here much longer." Her voice sounds drained.

I have nothing to say to that. I stare at the paper. Wind knocks against the house, creaking the door in its frame and throwing a sheet of rain against the window. "What do you expect me to do." It's really not a question.

"You said you would figure it out."

"Yeah, well I'm trying."

"It's not good enough. The only thing I can do is go to the police. Because if I just go home and try to forget all of this happened, some strange people are going to kill me. I could go back to Chicago, but then I have to give up the house I bought here, and my job. Not very practical, is it."

I know I shouldn't, but I look at her. I feel myself slipping. I need to focus. "Be patient."

She raises her voice. "Patient for how long?"

My voice rises in response. "It's not that easy to sort this out. It's going to take time."

"You don't have a plan!"

"I have a plan, it's just not a plan you're going to like. I'm working on a better one. It takes time." I unclench my jaw. I really need to relax. I take a long drink, lean back in my seat, and fold my arms across my chest. Her lips...

"What's your plan?"

I close my eyes. Stretch my neck to the left, to the right. *Shake yourself out of it, dumbass.* "I'm going to leave. I'd been planning to leave anyway. Just have some things I need to wrap up first. Once I'm gone, you can go back to your normal life."

"If you're leaving, I'll be alone here. So what's the difference if I just go back to my house now?"

"By the time I leave, they aren't going to be interested in you anymore."

"Why not?" She's standing now.

I imagine running my thumb over her bottom lip. There's nothing stopping me from getting up and doing it right now. I stand. My hands are not my hands. She holds my gaze, lips parted. If arguing with her is going to feel like foreplay from now on, I'm a dead man. Without a word, she pushes past me and disappears into the living room, leaving a palpable disturbance of air. I hold up my hands and stare at them. Maybe I should get that CT scan. But brain damage isn't my concern—I've lost my mind altogether.

I clean up the kitchen and find her on the couch in the living room with a book in her lap. Her loose hair is pulled to one side, hanging against her chest, exposing the back of her neck and a hint of shoulder that damn wide collar is doing nothing to hide. I take a step forward but press my palm against the wall to stop myself. I'm in a virtual wind tunnel with the full force of the wind hitting me from behind. I swivel my feet in slow motion, as if they were mired in wet concrete. To turn from her, to get the hell away.

I force my legs down the basement stairs. If I find something else to soothe her stomach, she'll be more comfortable and more patient. Standing at my workbench, flipping through my books, I struggle to keep focused on the pages in front of me and not the woman upstairs. I find some options and bookmark them, now very annoyed by my lucid intensity. Any other day, I'd drink myself stupid and pass out on the couch. I set the books on the stairs and pull off my shirt. A quick hard workout should do the trick.

I hang on the pull-up bar from my knees and do sit-ups until I feel the strain. Pull-ups follow, draining my arms and shoulders but the full-on fatigue I need never comes. Gloves go on. I box and kick the hell out of my heavy bag. Most of the time it's a poor substitute for human flesh and bone. Tonight is no exception.

Still pulsing with energy that seems indifferent to this exertion, I load up my barbell with weights. Squats, dead lifts, and finally I'm about to break. Although physically tired, I still feel wound-up, but it will wear off. I grab my shirt and the books and climb the stairs. My wadded shirt sails from my hand into the laundry room, and when I turn around she's standing right in front of me.

I clear my throat. "I found some other options. For a stomach remedy. Something that isn't as strong as the last one."

She shakes her head.

I throw my hands in the air. "You are impossible. Suffer all you want."

"It went away."

I turn back to her. "It went away? When?" Intrigue is not a strong enough word for what I feel now, possibly because it seems like decades have passed since I've felt intrigued by anything at all.

"The night you got hurt. All of sudden, it just stopped."

Sweat runs into my eyes, so I wipe my face with the kitchen towel and throw it in the laundry room. "Do you remember *exactly* when it stopped?" I wonder if that's what brought her out of unconsciousness.

"Yes. I heard noises on the roof, and I was trying to find the trapdoor in the closet so I could hide. Then it just stopped."

"And?"

"And I pushed the bureau so I could get out of the room."

"Did you still hear noises on the roof?"

She watches me like someone does when they're having a phone conversation with one person while trying to carry on a simultaneous conversation with another. "No, the noises had stopped. I heard something fall off the house. That was probably you." She closes her eyes. Opens them again to look straight back into mine.

I'm not used to all this eye contact from her. "And your stomach pain just stopped after I fell off the roof?"

"Yeah. I think so. Why?"

Her words take a moment to reach me, like something important has happened and my brain's just catching up. So, she wakes up, hears our combat on the roof, goes for the trapdoor, I fall, her nausea disappears, and she decides to get out of the room.

"Just curious." Her collarbone is a work of art. She shouldn't wear that wide-necked shirt.

"Well it's pretty amazing, because I feel so much better, it's almost like I was never sick in the first place." She smiles, her eyes lighting up.

God, I can't concentrate around her anymore. I have to get out of here. Leaving her in the kitchen, I head to the shower. I stand and let the water roll down me, trying to clear my mind yet again. I'm putting a lot of effort into keeping a clear head and it's dominating my mental resources. I can't repeat the past and must do everything in my power to make sure of that. I have to think of a way to get her out of my house. The only problem now is it's impossible for me to kill her. I know I couldn't do it, whether I wanted to or not.

I put on a clean T-shirt and some flannel pants and stop to stare at my face in the mirror. It seems lately my old wounds don't have time to heal before I rack up new ones. They must be really worried about her. They have definitely stepped it up. And now I'm worried too. She's withdrawn inside the bedroom so I go straight to the couch and fall sleep.

At two a.m. I sit straight up and throw the blanket off, the need to know now uncontrollable. I hurry down the basement stairs and yank on the light. I run my index finger along the spines of the books until I find the one. Careful with the old pages, I scan until the passage is in front of me. My translation is rusty, but undeniable. I close my eyes. A series of potent feelings pass through me at once. Anger. Dread. Injustice. Exhilaration. Excitement. But the most pervasive, the most resilient, is acceptance. And it's going to take every ounce of my willpower to deny it.

CHAPTER 16

LIV

H E'S BROODING AGAIN this morning. This man is the CEO of Mood Swings, Inc. and his product outperforms all competitors. I wonder if I should ask him what he was doing in the basement at two in the morning, but from the look on his face I know it's not a good time. The return of the scowl brings its earlier absence to my attention. I wonder how long it had been missing.

My efforts to lighten him up are only making it worse, but I just can't help myself.

I start packing myself a lunch. "Do you want me to pack you a lunch?"

"No."

I do anyway. I try not to smile at the venom crammed in that one simple word. What should be offensive is kind of adorable. I should go by the grocery store on my way home tonight. I feel like I need to contribute more food to the house since I've been eating here so long, though I doubt that's expected of a hostage. I hand his lunch to him as he starts to leave the room. He pauses, not looking at me. I stare up into his face. It's hard for me to be demanding since he's so much taller than me.

"My feelings will be hurt if you don't take it."

He looks at me, his jaw tense. My smile is involuntary. He jerks the bag out of my hand and storms out the front door.

I gather my things and go out to my car. Two deer standing in the driveway make little effort to move out of my way. The rain has stopped, but everything still looks soggy and wet, and my car cuts through patches of fog all the way into town.

"Did he ask you out?" is the first thing out of Rachel's mouth when she sees me come in the door.

"No, but I had a really hard time getting away from him." I don't know what it's going to take to get the medical supplies delivery man to leave me alone. He's good-looking and hilarious and could very easily be my type—and I'm of course not interested. Yesterday when I turned him down he didn't seem discouraged in the least. He'll probably try to ask me again today. The truth would conveniently send him running, but I left it at the state line. And that's where it's staying.

I take a few easy patients before my first real emergency here turns the whole clinic into organized chaos. Paramedics bring in a man who got his leg caught in an auger. His friend stands by, clutching a camouflage cap in his hands, looking like he's about to faint.

"Can you take him to a room to lie down?" I ask Rachel and point to the friend. We don't need a second emergency on our hands.

She drags him away, and I remove the patient's clothing. Dr. Wu comes in dressed for surgery. We lift the patient onto the operating table and the paramedics take their stretcher away. It looks like someone dumped an entire bucket of red paint on it. I start to leave, but Dr. Wu calls me back in, telling me to scrub up for surgery. I'm flattered yet horrified. I don't know my way around the OR, and from the sideways glances I'm getting from the other two nurses, I doubt they'll be very forgiving.

The surgery takes about an hour. Afterward, I take the patient to his room and get him comfortable. I can't help but be reminded of caring for Trey when he was unconscious. Rachel brings me a fresh pair of scrubs.

I eat a late lunch in the break room by myself, wondering if Trey ate the lunch I packed or tossed it and got something else. Although he's unapologetically rude and unreasonably stubborn, I can't envision him wasting food. The rest of the uneventful day settles into a routine. As I'm gathering my things to leave, Dr. Wu finds me.

"Liv, I wanted to tell you that you're an asset here. I know this isn't much, just a small thank you for your great work."

He hands me an envelope and steps away before I can thank him. No reprimand for walking into the wrong exam room the other day and now this? They must be more desperate for help than I thought. Inside the envelope is a gift certificate for a dinner for two at one of the restaurants in town. I wonder if I could use it on a dinner for one, twice.

Walking to my car, I can already spot the delivery man by his bright red hair. He's leaning against my car, waiting for me.

"Hi, Shawn."

"Liv." He gives me a slow, playful wink.

I stop in front of him. His hair is cropped short, and his blue eyes sparkle. "You got a haircut," I point out.

"Yep." He smiles and throws his arm around me. "Surprised you noticed."

"Shawn…I have some errands to run. I need to get going."

"Skip the errands. Let's have dinner. Come on. Nothing formal. I just don't feel like cooking tonight."

I realize I don't either, and I'm sure I'll beat my roommate home again. The gift certificate Dr. Wu gave me must be alive for all the whispering it's doing in my ear. Eating at a restaurant by myself is always so lonely. At least I could have someone with me.

"It might be your lucky day. I have this gift certificate…" I dig it out of my pocket and show it to him.

"Perfect. That place is real casual. We can go as we are." He's thrilled, with no attempt to hide it.

"But we're going as friends. Just because neither one of us wants to cook."

"Got it. I'll drive."

"No, we'll both drive. I'll follow you." I get in my car before he can complain.

The neighborhood pub is more crowded than I'd expect for a weeknight. A jovial mob lines the bar, and several families with children fill the booths nearest the door. My mood lifts as soon as we take our seats. This is going to be so good for me.

Shawn's sense of humor has me laughing before I have a chance to realize I'm having fun. Our light conversation makes no threat of getting anywhere near my new secrets or the old ones. Two friends of his join us from the bar, and I find myself laughing harder than I have in a long time.

When the bill comes, Shawn insists on paying. The waiter takes Shawn's cash and won't accept my gift certificate. He tells me to "save it for next time" and high-fives Shawn as he walks away. It's hard for me to be mad though, after so much unexpected fun.

The cold, wet air outside turns my high mood giddy and far too accepting of Shawn's warm arm around me. My teeth chatter but I can't stop smiling. Fog hangs heavy, dulling the street lights.

At my car, Shawn gives me a bear hug. My feet briefly leave the ground. I unlock my door, he opens it, and I slide behind the wheel. Before he shuts the door, he leans in and says, "Next time I'm kissing you. Drive carefully."

It's late when I get to Trey's. His truck is already parked in its spot. I drop my bag at the door and head to the kitchen toward the only light. He's sitting at the table in wet, dirty clothes, eating out of the cookie dough ice cream carton.

When he sees me he slams his spoon onto the table. "What the *fuck*."

"Hello to you too."

"I thought I was going to have to start looking for pieces of your body."

"Sorry. I went out."

He exhales loudly. I can't help but smile at him. I'm in too good a mood.

"Have a good time?" It's too sarcastic to deserve an answer, but the look on his face doesn't match. His expression is too mixed, like he can't quite decide something.

"Awesome time. Too bad you didn't come, it would have been good for you. Actually, I was going to use this gift certificate but Shawn insisted on paying. So if you want to join in next time we could both go free." I drop the gift certificate on the table next to him.

That mixed expression hardens. His eyes blaze. "Shawn?"

"Yes. Shawn…hmm. I don't know his last name." I slip out of my jacket and hang it over the back of the chair next to him. I catch his eyes running the length of me when I return my attention to his face.

"You went out with some guy and you don't even know his last name?"

"Oh, please. I see him at work every day."

He grunts, staring into the ice cream carton. I get a mental image of a bear holding a big jar of honey and stifle a laugh. The pub's atmosphere still clings to me. He looks up at me as if I spoke.

"Care to share?" I ask.

I'm not trying to flirt with him, but it's impossible to curb it before it happens. I seem to have very little control over my increasing desire for him. I take a spoon out of the drawer and pull the chair closer to him. He looks at the chair like it's going to attack. I sit, holding my spoon straight up in the air. He pushes the carton toward me.

"I'd never take you for someone with a sweet tooth." I dig in. It's partially melted, just how I like it. I stick a spoonful into my mouth and notice he's staring at me. "What?" I ask around the spoon.

He scoots his chair back, stretches his legs out under the table, and folds his arms across his chest. There's a smudge of dirt across his cheekbone like he rubbed it with a grimy hand. And that scar running into his upper lip. How can something like that be so sexy on a man when it would be so unbecoming on a woman? I touch the scar on his bicep out of reflex. He eyes me warily.

"How are the other wounds? Can I check them?" I might be pushing it.

"No. They're fine." He focuses on something below my face. It's so straightforward, I can't believe it's an open admiration of my chest—but what else could it be?

I duck into his line of sight. "What did you do today, roll around in the dirt?"

The corner of his mouth turns up in the slightest way. I'm wearing him down.

"Roofing."

"Sounds exciting."

"It was." He holds my eye.

"So are you going to take me out to dinner?" I don't know why I'm flirting. It just keeps happening, ignorant of good sense.

"With your gift certificate?" He looks away, but he can't hide his sudden amusement.

"Hell yeah. I swear I won't tell anyone." I put my elbow on the table, put my chin in my hand, and smile at him alluringly. There is something so gratifying about playing with him sometimes. A danger smolders deep inside me, walled behind the brightness of my mood and my undeniable attraction to him.

His eyes lock with mine. He swallows.

A loud howl sounds outside. He sits up straight in his chair. Another howl and he's charging down the basement stairs, and before I have a chance to question him he's back and putting a gun in my hand.

"Shoot anyone who tries to come in here."

My spoon rattles onto the table. I need to tell him I hate guns, that I don't know how to shoot a gun, that I won't, but all I do is sit and stare at the heavy, ominous object in my hands. He's long gone anyway.

The doorbell rings. I stand. I'm afraid to put the gun down, but afraid to hold it. And what is it he told me once about the doorbell? I'm usually so calm in emergency situations, but this gun is clouding my thought process. If this is an emergency. I don't know what is going on.

And then I remember. *If you hear a doorbell, you need to hide.*

Should I hide? Does holding a gun nullify the need to hide? I put the gun on the table and sit back down on the edge of the chair.

The front door opens. A flood of adrenaline propels me from the chair.

"Liv, it's just me. Don't shoot."

I exhale.

Trey enters the room carrying a long knife. Blood drips from his lip, staining his chin glossy red.

"Are you kidding me?" is all I can say.

"Everything's fine. And check out this blade I scored!"

I clamp my mouth shut. He's like a child on Christmas morning. Now I understand the source of all the weapons in the basement. They're his war bounty. He rips a paper towel off the roll and wipes blood off the blade, apparently oblivious to his own blood dripping down his chin and onto his shirt.

"Do you even know you're bleeding?"

"I am?" He reaches up to touch his mouth. "Crap."

"Just sit down." I pull his hand and he willingly sits, dropping the weapon on the table with a metallic clang. He is still breathing hard.

"*Oderint dum metuant*," he says to the knife.

It sounds like Latin. I wait, expecting a translation.

He notices my silence. "This one thought he'd mouth off before I took him down."

Chills scatter up my back. "Who was it?"

He watches me but doesn't answer. He doesn't mind I know he kills people, but he can't tell me who they are?

I change my approach. "What did he say?"

He turns away, laughing under his breath. Dismissing my question. "They're getting out of control. It's never been this frequent. I'll need to be more alert."

"More alert?" I laugh. I can't help it. I manically grasp for anything to distract me from the weapon on the table. From whoever's blood has soaked the paper towel he dropped in the sink. The injured, possibly dead person outside. The person I'm not helping. The phone call I'm not making for an ambulance. "I don't like guns, by the way. I have no idea what to do with that thing and I have no desire—"

"I'll have to teach you." He picks up the gun without looking at it and makes something on it click. He sets it back down. Unconscious movements. He seems a little distracted. Blood strings from his chin to the dark stain on his shirt.

"I'd rather you not." I catch his filthy hand just before it wipes his mouth. "Don't. Wait just a second."

I dampen a clean towel and pull up a chair to face him. Careful not to look in his eyes, I wipe his chin and dab the blood off his lip, already fat and swollen. It's an atrocity they always have to get him in the face. But I guess any part of his body would be an atrocity—I need to stop thinking about his body. "What languages do you know besides Latin?"

"English." He keeps a straight face even though he must know he's being a smartass.

"There's more than Latin and English in those books downstairs."

His eyes cling to mine. His lips part. He appears to be on the verge of words, but I'm unable to be patient long enough for him to gather them.

"Welsh?"

His lips seal shut, but his eyes do not leave my face. Just when I think he isn't going to answer, he does. "Good guess."

I don't know if that's a yes or a no, and I don't understand why it's a big secret. Being multilingual must break his tough-guy image. I can see he wants to say more, but he's holding back. Something tells me if I push him, he'll shut me out forever. I focus on his wound. "Are you hurt anywhere else?"

"I don't think so."

His breathing has slowed, and I become aware of him studying my face as I work on his lip. I stand to put some ice in a towel, and his eyes follow me the whole time. I sit back down facing him and lift the ice-filled towel to his lip. His expression becomes strange, unfamiliar.

Soft.

I look into his eyes.

He lifts his hand and lightly runs his thumb across my bottom lip. In that moment everything shuts down. There is nothing in the world except his thumb, and my lips.

As if realizing what he's doing for the first time, his expression hardens, and he pulls his hand away. He takes the ice from me and stands. "Sorry. I don't know what I was doing."

"Trey?"

"What." His voice is gruff.

"I need to know something."

He doesn't answer. He's turned away from me, his eyes focused through the glass of the back door although it only reflects the room back at us.

"I need to know what happened to cause the bruises on my arms."

He looks at me as if I've slapped him. Then he lowers his eyes, shaking his head slowly. When his eyes meet mine, they are cold. Tormented. He doesn't speak.

"Please. I won't be mad," I urge.

"Maybe you should be mad. Maybe you should have me arrested."

"So it was you?"

"Of course it was me!" He slams his fist down on the countertop, causing the dishes in the sink to jump. "We fought. And I almost lost control. Before we came back here and you blacked out. Don't you remember? I could have killed you."

Even though I already knew, it startles me to hear the rest, to imagine what could have happened.

"Things were different then," he continues. "I'm a monster. I know that. I'm usually very undiscriminating. You were no different from anyone else then."

It takes a few moments for his words to sink in deeply enough to stun me. "And now it's different?" The innuendo behind my own question throws fuel on the smoldering danger inside me.

Could it be different for him like it's different for me? My mind replays the last few days to help me understand, but it's impossible. If anything, in the last few days he's been more distant, more rude. Except for that night at my house, but I've already labeled that as pity. And the move he pulled just now which I haven't been able to process yet.

"It's just different. I told you what you wanted, so please drop it."

Something slams into the back door and I jump a mile.

"It's only River. She wants her treat." He pulls a turkey leg out of the freezer and takes it to the back door. Two sets of eyes glow.

"Looks like River has a friend. That's your dog, isn't it?"

I can't be sure. "I told you he's not my dog. But Nancy said he doesn't get along with other dogs."

"River gets along with anyone."

The simplicity of this exchange seems out of place after everything that just happened, but I yield to it as if caught in the undertow of events moving forward without my input. He goes back to the freezer for another turkey leg and hands them both out the door. The disgust has left his voice, and his movements seem more at ease. I need to keep him talking. It seems to be the only way I'll be able to process all of this.

"So I guess now I know where you got all those guns downstairs."

He snorts. "Yeah, a lot of them."

"And the rest?"

He leans back against the counter, preparing his response. "Some are family heirlooms." He should be avoiding my line of sight, ignoring my question. But the pointed stare and unmoving stance make him appear open, even anxious for me to respond.

"The books too?"

"So while I was in a coma, you ransacked my house? Do you do that to all your coma patients?"

I think he's teasing me, but I'm not sure. Although it feels out of character for him, nothing would surprise me tonight.

"Yes. And I went through your mail and hacked into your phone." My desire to play with him returns in full force.

"You are ruthless. I didn't sign up for this." His lips move to the verge of a smile.

Now I'm sure he's teasing me. Maybe if he had the opportunity to kill someone every day he'd always be in a good mood. The prize of his smile becomes my goal.

"You have no idea what's in store for you. What I'm capable of." The possibility of witnessing his smile again eggs me on.

"Oh, there's more to come?"

"Yes, much more to come. I am your biggest nightmare." With the last two words, I cross the room toward him and poke him in the chest with my index finger for emphasis.

There's the smile. And I am its captive. The world shifts. I watch in slow motion as his face morphs into a version yet unseen by me, eyes intense, smile gone, and then his arms reach around me pulling me toward him. His head bows, and his lips settle on mine. As our bodies make contact, my arms circle his neck and draw me upward, our kiss becoming untamed, ravenous. His hands drop lower to pick me up, and I wrap my legs around his waist. He spins, setting me on the countertop. I cannot get close enough. I need him on me. I'm a wilted, fallen husk baked into the earth. And he is the rain.

Something in my mind has become frantic. Screaming, out of breath, demanding that I think about what I'm doing. Stop! And this voice sends its power to my arms and pushes me away.

"Are we going to regret this?" I can't seem to catch my breath.

"Yes," he says, tugging me back to him.

My arms latch around his neck, my hands find his hair, and I feel myself being lifted and carried, but it's impossible to pay attention to anything but my hunger for him. He rests me on the bed and I impatiently reach my arms up for him. He pulls his shirt over his head, and pulls mine up over my head, then he's back with me, his lips on mine, the warmth of his body quenching my skin.

CHAPTER 17

TREY

I'M NOT SURE what makes me more livid: the fact that I let it happen, or the fact that now, the morning after, I have no remorse. That I would do it all over again. I turn and wrap myself around her, savoring her scent, her softness. I have gone too far, and I don't care.

The most significant knowledge I have gained is that I'm powerless to be away from her now. We're going to have to make this work together, which means I'll have to get her comfortable around a gun. I don't know how much I can risk telling her.

She turns toward me in my arms and opens her eyes. They are endlessly blue, like a beam of light in space going on and on. I lift her arm and kiss the inside of her elbow. Just as I expected, the bruises are completely gone.

"You're good," she says.

"Likewise," I return.

I unwrap my arms from around her and get up, watching her as she snuggles into the bed with her eyes closed and a contented smile on her lips. From the hall, I notice her bag on the floor near the front door. I go for the inner pocket and touch the amulet I put there the other night. It gives me a little peace of mind knowing it's still there.

I take a shower and get dressed next to the now empty bed, still covered in a tangle of twisted sheets that looks so out of place in my bedroom. This bed has only known one occupant at a time as long as I've had it. Last night must have been a shock. Strangely, it's not a shock to me. It felt more natural than my hunger for breakfast. I rub the remaining water out of my hair on my way to the kitchen. She's standing in my flannel robe at the stove scrambling eggs. After throwing the towel in the laundry room, I sit to tie my boots.

She comes to the table with two plates of food. I get up and pour us each a coffee. She pauses, a forkful of eggs aimed at her mouth, and gives me a radiant smile. I can't control my smile back.

I also can't help myself. "Want to go again?"

"Anytime." Her eyes hold a dare.

"What time are you going to be home tonight?"

She laughs, a deep, heartfelt sound I've never heard before. I want to hear it again—but there's more important things—

"We're starting gun training. Tonight. What time will you be home?"

"A little after five. But I'm not getting anywhere near a gun."

"I'll try to be home at five."

I get up and open the window above the sink so we can hear the sounds outside. The sun is back, illuminating the tiny particles in the air just outside the window. My garden will be in desperate need of work. I unfold yesterday's paper and skim it, and she finishes her breakfast and cleans up. As she walks by me, she runs her finger up my arm and across the back of my neck. It takes all my willpower to remain seated. A few minutes after the shower stops, she returns to the kitchen while I'm packing a lunch.

"My bruises are totally gone." She holds her wrists out straight for me to see. From her expression, I can tell she thinks I'll be surprised.

"Yep."

"What do you mean 'yep'?"

"To be expected. A little added bonus from being with me. You're welcome." I look away from her. My self-preservation voices a violent complaint in my mind, but I don't have it in me to keep this from her. Not after last night.

"What are you talking about?"

I turn around and face her. "I know you can't believe it, but it's true. Trust me."

She doesn't speak. She continues staring at me, her lips slightly parted, eyes narrowed, head cocked to the side.

"I'm not messing with you. Did you look at your leg? It should be healed, too."

She lifts up her pant leg and examines her leg. Sure enough—cuts fully healed, bruises gone. I knew it wouldn't take much. They were old bruises.

"Can I bring you to work with me?" She drops her pant leg and straightens up.

I'm caught off guard by the change in subject. "Why?"

"You'd make my job a whole lot easier. I could sit around and do crosswords all day."

She doesn't exactly look convinced, but at least she has a sense of humor about it.

"You want me to sleep with all your patients? That's a lot of work."

"Have you considered charging people? You could make a killing at this."

"I don't think that's legal in this state."

"Well you wouldn't be charging for sex. Just for the healing."

I laugh. "Are you trying to pimp me out?"

Her eyes dart to the side, and she places an index finger against her lips. "Yes, I think I am. I want twenty-five percent. No, fifty."

"Fifty percent. You're out of your mind."

She studies me for a long moment. The original idea is starting to settle in her mind, I can tell. If she doesn't accept this, she'll never accept any of the other things I'll eventually have to tell her. Although I should know better than to get my hopes up, I feel there's a chance she'll understand some of it, and this burden of secrets may be lighter the next time we're together. It's impossible to imagine.

"I've got to get to work!" I hear the front door close. The amulet should keep her safe until she's back here with me.

The house feels dead without her, so I load up my truck and head to the jobsite. The weather has completely cleared up, mocking me with a cloudless blue sky that reminds me of her eyes. The cool air clings to me, fighting the sun that heats my skin through my clothes. Perfect weather to be stuck on a roof all day.

I'm early, so I get started, hoping to get a lot done before the other guys show up. Maybe we can all leave a little early today. I feel renewed, like I've just awakened from hibernation. Fifteen years of celibacy. She has no idea what kind of commitment I broke, and what is at stake now. It won't be easy news to give her—that I should be fifteen years older even though I'm physically the same age I was fifteen years ago. And that's the least of it.

The anger I felt at myself this morning is only a memory now. It disappeared as soon as I looked into her eyes. It almost seems worth it in a way, breaking my commitment for her. All my dedication at remaining single, at keeping my distance, has now been for nothing. But it was easy until I knew her. I never had any reason to give in, and I never had something so strong working against me.

The situation borne from last night is all my fault, a product of my carelessness, a lapse in my own judgment and self-control. I knew the power of what we were up against, and I let it defeat me. Although the consequences may have bothered me in theory, in action they take on a whole new meaning. I know I'm gloating, but I have no shame. Impulsive sex does wonders for the mood. But it's not just that. My strategy has shifted from lazy defense to hard-nosed, ambitious offense. It feels amazing to finally stare real danger in the face.

Everything has changed, pushing me beyond the point of no return. I never would have believed that I'd welcome it. I've raised two middle fingers and walked into their crosshairs for her, and if given a chance to go back, I'd do it again. I just need to make sure she understands everything. So she knows what she's getting into. It would be unfair to her otherwise.

"Hey man, snap out of it." One of the guys slaps me on the back.

My eyes focus on the mortar lines in the brick chimney jutting from the roof. I didn't realize I'd stopped working. The nail gun pops to life in my hand, and I move along the row of shingles while blocking all thoughts but the task in front of me.

The day seems painfully longer than it should be to a person who has learned to ignore the passing of time. We make good progress and I stay until half the crew has left. I then say goodbye to the remaining guys and head for my truck. After loading my gear in the bed, I pour a bottle of water over my head and let it run down my face. There's no need to think about it anymore. I've already made up my mind. I wipe my face on the bottom of my shirt and drive home.

I spot the unusual car parked next to Liv's before I'm up to the house. The seat belt and truck door impede me in my haste. I can't get out of the truck fast enough. A few long strides take me to the front door, and as I throw it open I hear voices. Her voice, and a man's voice. Laughing. I storm into the kitchen. Instant relief floods me, followed by a contaminant that burns hot. If he's told her *anything*—

"Trey! Slow down bro, no need for an assault, I come in peace!"

"Christian."

Our handshake turns into a hug.

"You look good," I say. It seems like forever since I've seen him. Has it been a whole year? Two years?

"And as always, you look great. Very young for your age, how do you do it?" His smile is reserved for me alone.

I give him a warning with my eyes. I doubt he wants to die today.

He laughs. "What's got you all riled up?"

"Didn't recognize the car. Don't fuck with me. You could've called first." I punch him hard in the arm. Hopefully that will leave a bruise.

I look at Liv, searching her face for clues of how much damage he's done already. She smiles back at me, the same radiant smile from this morning. My mind flashes the image of her last night, leaning in for more, her lips already swollen from being kissed so hard. Me pulling her toward me. The feel of her hands on my back, drawing me in. Her legs wrapping around and holding me tight. Deep. Inside. If Christian wasn't here…

"So no need to introduce us, your lovely housemate and I have already met. We've been talking about you."

I love Christian like a brother, but sometimes he really needs to be punched in the mouth. I stifle the need. "I'll be right back. Talk about the weather or something, for god's sake."

I change my clothes faster than I've ever changed my clothes in my life. I return to the kitchen as Liv is pouring three glasses of iced tea. I'm going to need something stronger. I help myself to the pizza on the counter. Christian's contribution, no doubt. I down the entire glass of iced tea, pour a scotch, and join them at the table.

Liv breaks the silence. "You didn't tell me you have a brother."

"That's because I don't. Don't listen to anything this guy tells you. He's full of shit, pretty much all of the time."

"You ass, we're brothers and you know it." Christian shakes his head at Liv, like they have some shared understanding.

"We're cousins, Liv. We grew up together," I clarify for her. And it's good to paint him as a liar, just to save myself if he's told her other things.

"That makes more sense. You two look nothing alike."

And she's right. Christian is a blond-haired, blue-eyed pretty boy. Overdressed for every occasion and soaking up the attention.

"Sorry I haven't made it out here in so long. It's been… weird." He unbuttons his cuffs and starts to roll up his sleeves.

I shrug. I don't need him for anything. "Did you drive?" It's quite a long drive considering I'm going to have to kick him out tonight.

"No, I flew into Missoula. Only decent flight I could get. Your mother sends her love."

My mother. A different kind of guilt twists inside me. I change the subject. "You know there's nowhere for me to put you tonight."

Before Christian can answer, Liv speaks up. "We can figure something out. I'll take the couch."

Christian's laugh fills the room. "I'm not sharing a bed with this dirty bastard. I'll take the couch. You two share the bed." He cannot hide his devious expression.

Here's where it gets tricky. I'm not sure I can trust Christian to know Liv and I would willingly share a bed, even though I trust him with everything else. I wasn't purposely vague with him on the phone; I just thought I didn't need to explain much back when everything was simple. I was putting up with her temporarily so she wouldn't have to die. She meant nothing to me. I was just trying to save an innocent life, and save them some trouble. That's all I thought I needed to tell him.

Liv doesn't answer. She must know to leave this up to me.

Christian speaks without waiting for my answer. "Hey, I'm just trying to get you laid, man. I know it's been a while."

Liv lowers her eyes, a hand covering her smile.

"You're already starting to piss me off. You're lucky I don't kick you out right now." I shoot him another warning look.

He knows me well enough to know when I've been pushed enough. He throws his hands up in surrender. Good. Now he'll behave.

We eat the pizza, and he fills me in on family drama without giving away too much. Liv takes our plates to the sink. "I'm sure you both have a lot of catching up to do, so I'll leave you to it."

I hear her move through the living room and into the bedroom. The door shuts audibly, like she wants us to know she's not listening. I look long and hard at Christian.

"What?" he says. It's more of a laugh than a word. "God, chill out. I'm not going to say anything."

"You came close enough."

"I always forget you have no sense of humor anymore."

"Why didn't you tell me you were coming? You know how dangerous that is."

"Maybe you should answer your phone. And if it had been a test of your little fort, it failed. Not only did I make it to the house alive, she let me in eagerly. And you didn't tell me she's hot! How the fuck could you leave that out?"

I make no attempt to cover the rage on my face. "What did you tell her?"

"Nothing! Come on, it's me. You know you can trust me." He goes for his sleeve again like he forgot he already rolled it. Picks up his glass instead. "Anyway, you said she was nothing to you. That they're misunderstanding. But I sense something different going on." He takes a drink, studying me hard over the rim of his glass. "You didn't tell me she's living here."

"She's not."

"Unless you've started using vanilla-rose scented conditioner and a pink razor, her stuff is all over your bathroom."

"No it's not." Is it? I should have noticed.

"You are either stupid or in serious denial."

I hesitate. It's Christian. He's the only one I can trust. Besides my mother.

"Dude. She's a nurse. Do you know how hot that is? If you don't there's no hope for you." He looks toward the living room. "Can I have her?"

"Things have changed, I guess."

"Oh yeah?" He raises his eyebrows.

"Yeah."

"Nice. It's about time. Like riding a bike…"

"It just happened," I add, ignoring him. "I wasn't lying when I called you before."

His smile falls. "I'm not saying you were. I'm just…I wish I had known. Makes what I came here to tell you a little more complicated." He rubs his forehead. "A lot more complicated."

I watch him and wait. He's got about two seconds.

He stands and goes to the back door. "Shit," he releases in an exhale, bowing his head. He turns back toward me. "Kate…"

"What about Kate?"

"Kate is alive."

I'm in his face before I realize it. "Do *not* say that unless you are very, very serious."

He backs up a step, both hands in the air. "I wouldn't play with this, Trey."

I sit back down and put my face in my hands. A million thoughts ricochet inside my head. I take a few long breaths to slow my heart rate.

"How do you know?" I ask without looking at him.

"I saw her."

My head snaps up and I stare at him, not believing. It's impossible. She's been dead for fifteen years.

"She came back," he says.

"She was dead!" I yell.

"Apparently not." He takes his seat again at the table. "She wants to see you."

"And my son?" I choke, trying to contain the landslide of my grief.

Christian looks away, sighs. Looks back at me. "Aaron is with her."

This can't be happening. I stand, looking for someone to punish. Christian grabs my arms, holding me back. He's not as strong as me but I don't fight him.

"Trey, come on. We can make sense of this."

"How long have you known?"

"She came back Tuesday. I wanted to tell you in person."

"Where has she been?" Control is here somewhere, I just have to find it.

"You'll have to ask her."

"She didn't explain anything to you?"

"She just said she wanted to protect you."

"She leaves, and keeps my son away from me for fifteen years, his whole *life*, because she wanted to protect me?!" I grab the table. Christian holds it down.

"It's not her fault. I think there's more to this than I—" Confusion crosses his face just before I cut him off.

"She couldn't have found me? Called me?"

"They wouldn't let her."

"They?" I am blinded by my fury. They. They are behind this. I already knew, but hearing it spoken aloud fuels the rage that's lurked within me for so long.

Christian puts a second glass of scotch in front of me. I swallow the whole thing in a gulp.

"She still could have called. Fuck them. She owes me that." My voice is dead.

The room remains silent for a long time. With a shock, I remember Liv, in the other room. I'm at a complete loss. I have no idea what to do. I leave Christian and go downstairs. I pity the heavy bag, but I give it no mercy. I only stop when the bag has split in two, covered in blood from my bare knuckles.

When I climb the stairs, Christian and Liv are on the couch, talking quietly. I take off my shirt, wipe my face with it, and throw it in the laundry room. Something crashes to the floor in the darkness.

One thing keeps running through my head. She should have contacted me. If it were reversed, I would have done that for her.

They both turn to look at me standing in the doorway. Liv's face is a mask of worry. This badly timed, impossible situation is going to hurt her too. One more day of following my own ground rules would have prevented an added complication to this mess. Chalk it up to another failure on my part. Something finally feels right for once and it couldn't have been more wrong. I've given myself a vulnerability. I've put Liv right in their sights. My control slipped but I'll get it back. It's all I have. And I can't give them anything else they can take from me.

"It's a good thing you stopped. The house was about to fall down." Christian. Always trying to lighten it up. An army of their men could be rushing toward us and he'd still be spewing jokes.

Sweat's dripping into my eyes and down my back. I go past them into the bathroom to take a shower.

Does this mean I've cheated on my wife?

Does it even matter after fifteen years?

Is Aaron going to remember me?

All that grief—that love—I've harbored for Kate these fifteen years vanishes to leave a staggering void in my mind that quickly fills with dross. She has done this, she's a part of it just as much as they are. If she loved me like I loved her, she would've found a way. She wouldn't have let me go this long thinking she and Aaron were dead. I know what she's capable of, but even she couldn't have been so cruel.

I should have known, but I've been the fool all along. I've been played. And she only wants to see me to prove it worked. To extract the power.

When I step out of the shower onto the cold tile, it dawns on me. If Aaron is alive, and has been alive the whole time, then the prophecy is wrong. I am not under the effect and never was.

CHAPTER 18
LIV

I'M NOT GOING to get any useful information out of Christian who's chatting me up like nothing happened in the kitchen. Like he didn't hear the violence in the basement. He couldn't be more different than Trey if they had been born into families on opposite sides of the world.

When Trey returns to the room and drops heavily into the chair without meeting my eyes, I realize I won't be getting any answers from him either. Whatever set him off isn't going to be brought up again tonight. I rise from the couch and get the bandages and ointment from the bathroom. He doesn't object to my examination of his hands. The skin on every knuckle has been peeled away.

"Ever hear of gloves, man?" Christian says.

I get to work. I don't know how he's survived this long without a live-in nurse. They start talking about sports and I tune out. By the time I'm done, he's got a bandage on each knuckle, two per finger, except for his thumbs. It looks ridiculous. In a break in their conversation, I say, "Please at least keep them on overnight."

He agrees with the slightest nod. He still won't look at me.

I clean up the mess and retire to the bedroom. Curiosity is killing me, no matter what I try to do to occupy myself or how many times I tell myself it's none of my business. A strong need to do something constructive pecks me to pieces, but no ideas materialize to satisfy it. I try some stretching on the bed but can't relax into it so I collapse on my back. When I've memorized every square inch of the ceiling, I decide to call it a night. On my way to the bathroom, I can't help but overhear.

"I can always tell her you've moved on."

"No. Don't tell her anything. She can be in the dark just like I was."

Although I don't know who they're talking about, it's an easy assumption that things are about to change yet again. I've been on a roller coaster for two weeks. This ride just ended and I'm standing in line to board again. They're silent when I return to the bedroom. I flip off the light and lie in bed, staring at the ceiling in the dark, longing for him to join me, but he never does.

It's about fifty degrees in the house in the morning. I wake up too early, but can't fall back to sleep. After taking a shower and getting dressed, I creep past Christian on the couch and Trey on the floor, both sound asleep. I start coffee and breakfast for three. Christian joins me, yawning, his blond hair flat on one side. "Scrubs. Hot."

As if he didn't flirt with me enough yesterday. I set a cup of coffee in front of him.

He reaches for it through the blanket wrapped around his bare shoulders. "Is Trey trying to be green or something? I know he likes to torture himself but his guests might appreciate some heat."

"It was warm outside. He must have turned the furnace back off. I didn't think to check it before I went to bed."

Obviously reading my expression, he says, "He'll be okay. He just needs time."

I nod, not sure what to say. He probably thinks I know a lot more about his cousin than I actually do. The few things I do know about Trey would've made a normal person flee the state and hire a bodyguard a long time ago.

Christian continues, more to himself than me, "He has the worst temper." He looks at me. "Sometimes you don't even see it coming. He seems fine, and with no warning, bam. You're dead."

I'm all too familiar with that. Feeling strangely exposed and on the spot, I look away without answering him, but his attention remains on me as I make breakfast. I wonder if Trey told him about anything that happened between us. Specifically, the narrowly avoided assault. And the sex. It's silly of me to feel uncomfortable for Trey's own bad behavior. I know I can't be judged for that. I can be judged for not calling the police. And for sleeping with him, a violent murderer who almost attacked me not long ago.

I steal a glance at Christian and catch him in a wide yawn.

His eyes squint as his yawn turns into a sheepish smile. "I'd help, but I'm pretty useless in the kitchen."

Maybe I shouldn't be so paranoid. If he's disgusted by anything Trey or I did, he must be very good at hiding it.

"You could set the table," I suggest.

He drops his head in a loud, weary groan, and I can't help but laugh.

"Never mind. You're the guest, right?"

"You're not?" He raises his eyebrows with overdone innocence. It's an obvious taunt. He knows something, and he's playing with me.

I hold his eye for a moment before I answer. "I'm a useful guest," I say, deadpan.

He laughs and looks away. "Well if you're *useful* to him, I'm *definitely* useless, in the kitchen, and every other room in the house." Before I can think of a comeback, he adds, "Unless you have a sister. I could be very useful then." He takes a sip of his coffee, leaving me the floor and daring me to reply.

I'd feel the urge to roll my eyes if he wasn't so charming. I return to my cooking before he can see me smile. He's much better at this game than I am. My underlying worry for Trey won't let me put much effort into it anyway.

Just as I hand Christian a plate of eggs and toast, Trey joins us, but I can't read his expression. I make Trey a plate and set it in front of him.

Christian says, "I'm heading out after this. I think I've done enough damage."

Trey just nods and we eat in silence. I clean up our dishes, and they remain at the table with their coffee. As I'm leaving the room, I hear Trey say, "Don't you want a shower first? You look like hell. And you didn't even have to sleep on the fucking floor."

His sardonic tone floods me with relief. To kill some time before work, I make my bed and tidy up. I hear Christian get in and out of the shower. Their voices sound a little more congenial through the walls. Finally Christian calls my name from the front door.

"It was nice to meet you. Don't let this brute give you any trouble." He takes my hand and kisses it lightly.

Good looks must run in the family, but Christian got all the good manners. "It was good to meet you, too."

Christian slaps Trey hard on the back. "Call me when you're coming."

"Now why the fuck would I want to do that? You certainly couldn't manage a phone call before you came." Trey grabs the back of Christian's neck playfully and walks him out to his car.

I collect my bag and collide with Trey coming in as I'm going out, his face weighted with so many emotions I can't separate them all. He looks back at me but he's far away.

"Please take care of your hands today," is all I can think of to say to him.

He looks down at his hands as if he forgot all about them. "I will."

A killer cold front has moved in. I turn the heater on in the car and aim it at my hands. I never thought I would need gloves at this time of year. The clinic is quiet when I enter, and I can already tell it's going to be a slow day.

After my shift, I find Shawn leaning against my car. He gives me a big hug. "Want to go out?"

God, he's warm. It's hard to be mad he's causing a delay. "It's not a good night."

"It can be. If you go out with me." His smile reminds me of what he said last time. *Next time I'm kissing you.* He must remember too. Nothing could compare to Trey's lips, and the thought of accepting a substitute—even from someone as likeable as Shawn—leaves me cold.

"I've just got to get home."

"On a Friday night?"

I get in my car. He closes my door and waves. Life would be blissfully simple with Shawn, and impossible to settle for after what I had with Trey.

I'm not sure why I end up at my house, or why I go inside. Everything is too quiet and too still, my footsteps sounding like they're about to set off some screeching alarm. Being here is asking to be killed.

The jeans I wore on my first day in this town are at the bottom of the hamper, the note still in the pocket. I pull it out and read it one last time.

I can't stay in this house alone anymore. I'm moving to a town in Montana called Black River. I'll come back if you do. Please call me.

I'd written my new address at the bottom. He doesn't deserve to have my new address. He doesn't deserve the note at all. Had I left it, he could've shown up here anytime. With that expectation every day I'd be a slave to a fantasy and never be able to live.

I take the jeans and the note and a box of matches outside and set it all on fire in the driveway. It burns wild as if fanned by a strong wind, but the air is calm. A thin column of smoke rises high above the trees. I have a sudden urge to call him just to tell him something so stupid and pointless. *Remember those jeans? I just burned them. That's all. Good-bye.* Everything we'd gone through and that's all I have to say to him. I can't forget the hundreds of calls I made to him after he left and how every one went to voice-mail.

There's a rustling in the woods that's coming at me fast. I gauge the distance to the house and to the car but the car keys are in the house so I have to get there first. Then I see a brown and white shape leap from the woods. River.

I take a deep breath and shake out my arms and legs. Yeah, it's stupid to be here alone but there's no point in getting all panicky. She slows her pace to circle the yard with her nose to the ground. She sniffs my car. The garage. The porch. Then she comes back and eyes the fire and then me. I look up at the smoke still rising into the sky. He must have seen it at his house and sent his scout.

"You snitch," I say.

She opens her mouth to pant, that tongue flopping out like she knows how cute it is. I pat my leg. She comes close and I rub her ears. She's as trained to want to help him as I am.

"There's something wrong with us, you know that?"

She licks my hand and bolts back into the woods. I look at what's left of the fire and feel a sharp tug in my stomach. Regret. I can't fathom why. If the dirtbag ever returns to our home in Chicago he'll be confronted with an empty house and no explanation just like I was. It's what he earned. I stomp out the fire, feeling sick and wrong and missing him more than anyone should ever miss a person who abandoned them.

I lock up the house and drive straight to Trey's. He's waiting for me in the driveway.

"We need to talk," he says.

I nod. For some reason now I can't look at him.

"First, I need a promise from you. I've decided to tell you everything. Promise that at any point, if it becomes too much, or if you just want out, you'll leave. No explanation necessary."

It's such a harsh shift from my past to my present that I don't know what to say.

"Promise me."

"I promise."

"And also know that if you do decide to leave, you'll have very little time to get away from here. They will find you, and they will kill you. That's not a threat, it's just the truth. If you want away from me, I won't force you to stay. But I can't protect you unless you're with me."

I don't remember hearing him say so much at once. His intensity takes me captive all over again. I wonder if he'd let me kiss him.

He goes into the house and I follow. He starts building a fire, so I sit on the couch. When the fire roars, he sits next to me and looks into my eyes.

"What provoked this?" I have to ask, although I think I already know.

"Christian. And a day to realize I want you to know everything. Because I want you with me. And join me in what I have to do."

His words awake a thrill in me. "You just made that decision today?"

"Yes. Why?" He furrows his brow.

I watch his face. "Most people don't make decisions like that…" I trail off when I realize I don't know how to finish.

"My instincts are usually pretty good."

I wonder if he will let me kiss him now. I need my present to quell my past.

"I'll start by telling you what I knew before Christian came. His news makes things complicated."

I grab a pillow and hold it in my lap. He looks away from me for a moment, takes a deep breath like he's clearing his head, and returns to me.

"I stopped aging when I turned thirty. By now, I should be forty-five."

He watches my face as I digest this. He doesn't look a day past thirty. With his physical fitness, he could easily pass for twenty-five. I pick up one of his hands to look at his knuckles—the wounds he created yesterday look like they're a week old. The image of his back, after healing so quickly when he was in the coma, flashes in my mind. "This must be why you heal so fast."

He squints, watching me like he wants to say something but he's hoping I'll say it first.

"It's hard not to notice," I explain. "Especially after…"

He nods and shifts his weight, laying his arm across the back of the couch. "After I should have died. But there's a catch. Once I have a child, I begin to age again. And I did have a child. But he and his mother, my wife, died fifteen years ago. So I stopped aging."

He pauses again. I do remember him telling me he had a child. It was the night we fought.

"Why?" I ask. "Is there a purpose to this?"

"Yes. This is the part that's hard to explain. You'll think it's crazy."

"And what you just told me isn't?"

"True."

I wait for him to continue, my mind open. It's apparent he's not used to explaining himself. He's probably not used to talking this much to anyone, about anything.

"I'm part of an ancient family. We've been around a long time, and we've kept practices alive that no one knows about. Like the ability to manipulate our environment, use certain things in unconventional ways."

He allows time for me to respond, but what can I say to that?

"Magic."

My eyes widen uncontrollably.

"My people have certain beliefs. Prophecies. They're a bunch of religious zealots. Only, more times than I'd like to admit, their prophecies come true. One of them involves me." He pauses. "Should I open the door for you?"

"It can't be that bad."

"They believe that I, or actually, my heir, will lead to their downfall. The bargain was, they give me immortality, I never father a child." He studies my face for a moment before turning away. "I never asked for it, but you don't really question them. They considered it a fair trade. I met Kate when I was twenty-five. We got married a few years later. We were careful, followed all the rules, but she got pregnant. No one seemed to mind at first. They said they would find a way to make it work out, that the prophecy could be wrong. The baby was born. A son. We named him Aaron. Four weeks later, they took Aaron and Kate away from me, and they killed them."

My hands cover my mouth in reflex. I lower them, searching for his. He takes both my hands and leans toward me.

"Don't get upset just yet. Let me finish. There's no easy way to put this. When I found out it was them who did it, I lost it. I killed so many—I was better trained than all of them. And then I left. They've been hunting me for fifteen years, but as I told you before, they aren't trying to kill me. They won't because of the effect. That's what they call it. My gift of immortality."

"Could they kill you if they wanted to?"

"Sure. A couple well-placed bullets and I wouldn't have time to heal. But they'd never do that."

"Why not?"

"I'm too valuable to them. They expect me to get over it all and come back. And my father. He won't let them."

"What are they trying to do? Capture you?"

"No. They don't want me back unless I'm their servant. Unless they can trust me. They want to make sure I never have children. It's their agenda to destroy any woman I show the slightest interest in. They've made it clear this will continue, as a punishment for disobeying them."

The danger settles heavily into my heart. I'm not just rooming with the target anymore. I am the target.

"So now I'm cursed, too."

"You could call it that. But there's more to it." He stands.

"More to what?"

"Us."

Memories of that night pulse through me. That first unexpected, perfect kiss. The husky scent of his skin. His soft hair, brushing against my arm. His gentle lips moving down my back. The strong force of his body against mine. His hands, grasping my hips. Falling asleep against him. The greeting of his satisfied smile in the morning.

"I have proof," he says. "It should be my fault for bringing you into this. But I can't take all the blame, if you believe in their bullshit, which I normally don't. This particular one just explains too much. It's stuck with me."

He walks over to the armchair and brings a book back to the couch. The book, bound in a faded fabric cover and wound with a strap, must have come from the basement. The gold seal on the cover looks like an ancient Celtic symbol.

"This is one of our texts. A few nights ago I remembered a passage from it. To help make sense of things."

Interested, I scoot toward the book in his lap. It's also a good excuse to be closer to him.

"Make sense of things?" I prompt. He seems to have forgotten what he was going to say.

"Yeah. Of what happened to us. After hating each other like we did." He opens the book, finds the page, and turns it around so I can see it.

The words are not any language I recognize.

"I can't read that." I point out the obvious.

"I was going to translate." He spins the book back around and studies the page. Flips forward a page, then back a page. "A lot of this doesn't translate well into English. But I can give you an analogy."

"Okay." If he's dragging it out to build suspense, it's working.

"Imagine people as magnets. If you take two magnets and try to stick them together with the same poles facing, they will repel one another. But if you turn one around, so their poles are opposite, they attract." He pokes the page. "Similar concept, only it's biological. Human."

I cock my head at him. He's lost me.

"I'm a magnet. My energy is flowing positive side out. Your energy is flowing positive side out, too. We can't stand to be around each other. Then I fall off the roof and hit my head, and my energy flow is switched. Now I'm negative out. We attract."

"How…" I lose the question among too many others.

"It's more complicated than that. Not simply positive and negative, but many different types of human energy determined by each person's bloodline. But stripped down that's the concept."

"So it's out of our control."

"According to this, yes."

"And that explains why I was so sick around you all the time. We shouldn't have been so close."

"Yes. And you irritated the hell out of me. Then after I woke up, everything was different."

"Wow," I say again.

"Yeah, wow." The excitement in his face is unmistakable.

"So you're off the hook?"

"Not completely, but a little." He grins.

"Because you still ran the light."

"But I'm saying that was fate." He's suddenly serious. "I normally don't believe in this stuff, but it's the only thing I can go on right now."

"I didn't think there could even *be* an explanation." It shouldn't excuse what he tried to do to me, what he would've done if I hadn't stopped him. But something about me must have changed too, because the man I saw that day doesn't exist anymore. I've somehow slid under a gate. I'm on the inside now, standing beside the monster instead of confronting him. It's a different story when he's on your side. When his loyalty is so strong it's shifted your place in reality.

He stares off into the room and I worry he's about to withdraw like he did last night.

"So you felt the difference right from that day you woke up too?" I ask.

The moment draws out. His eyes remain focused on something far away only he can see. Just when I fear he's closed himself off to me, he returns. "Yes, but I was in denial. I wanted to fight it, because I was dead set on not repeating the past. I didn't want anyone I could lose to them all over again. But now? Screw them." A menacing smile hits his face. "Want something to drink?"

CHAPTER 19

TREY

S HE STANDS WITH me. My analogy proves to be more realistic than I thought—her body has some kind of intense magnetic pull on mine. She needs to know the entirety of our situation before I so much as touch her again. To explain that, I need a drink.

There's a focused hunger in her eyes that takes me back to that night. Is she trying to seduce me, or am I that deprived? I look at her hard. "Sit."

"Just a glass of water then," she says, sulking. Definitely trying to seduce me.

I bring my scotch and her water back and set them on the coffee table. I throw a few logs on the waning fire. She's examining her newly healed leg.

"Unbelievable," she whispers.

"You get used to it."

"What else can you do?"

I watch her a moment. She seems genuinely interested, not just hoping for a freak show. Or maybe she wants me to prove it in live action. I take a handful of ash from the fireplace. Her expression is neutral when I sit beside her and push her sleeve up to her shoulder. I slide my ash-coated palm down the length of her arm, leaving a trail of curling design etched on her skin like a henna tattoo. It's a technique of my ancestors. I don't remember its purpose.

She twists her arm, admiring my work. "Nice. But can you do anything…more useful?"

"If you stick around, you'll find out." I blow off the excess and wipe my hand on my jeans.

"I think I have already decided. I'm staying. At least until the lust goes away." She traces the design absentmindedly. If she notices it disappearing under her finger, she gives no indication.

"Don't decide until I tell you what I learned from Christian." I take a drink, followed by another. She pulls her knees up, resting her chin.

"Christian and my mother are the only members of my family I can trust." I try to gather my thoughts. There has to be a way to speak these words and keep my calm. "He came here, to tell me in person, that Kate and Aaron are both alive."

She makes no initial response. She looks down into her glass for a moment before looking back up at me. Her voice is thick when she speaks. "I am so sorry."

"How did you know?" Her unexpected reaction has managed to flatten something coiling inside me.

"I didn't. But I accidentally overheard you and Christian yesterday. I'm sorry this happened to you."

"You don't need to be sorry!" My voice rises without my consent. "You don't need to be sorry," I repeat, softer this time.

"I just… I can imagine how it would feel if I found out people I loved were alive this whole time." She has a far-off look in her eyes.

"How would you feel?" I hear myself asking.

"Robbed," she says without hesitation.

"That's a good way to put it. Especially when you know who to blame." My words grind together, grating against my calm. My train of thought lurches forward, causing my fist to slam against the coffee table. I take another deep breath. I didn't want this to turn into me raging. I'm taking it out on the wrong person.

We sit in silence as I try to repel the wild fury taking command of my mind. It's minutes before I can speak again. "So, I'm still married."

"Yes." The light in her eyes is dim. "And your wife and son are alive."

"My son won't even know who I am!" My voice rises again, and I reflexively reach out to take her hand in an effort to subdue the rage held behind a paper thin wall. "I'm sorry. *Fuck*."

"It's okay." She places her free hand over my knuckles.

A fresh layer of guilt settles on me. This news can only make her feel like a decision has been made. Like there's one natural outcome. I don't know how to make it better, but I have to try. "She left me. That's how I see it. I have no ties to her anymore."

Her expression turns thoughtful for a moment. "But you don't truly know the situation."

"No, I don't. But I know her. And until I know any different…" I'll have to hear it from her. She has to tell me she wasn't involved. I won't take it from anyone else. And her explanation better be damn good. Not that it even matters now.

"What are you going to do?"

I pull my hand away. "I don't know yet. But she's completely insane if she thinks I'm going to come running back to her." I stop, bowing my head. I don't know why I keep doing that. "Tell me what happened to your family." I want to know her past now that she knows mine.

She gives me an uneasy look and drops her feet to the floor. "It's very dull compared to your story. I was married, too. I had a daughter. Six months ago, she died. She was nine months old. And then my husband left me."

"He *left*? Nice guy." I can't imagine anyone leaving her after something like that. There are so many ways I could make him suffer. It's hard to visualize specifics without knowing what he looks like.

"Yes. With no explanation. He was just gone one day. He must have come home from work early, packed his things, and left. He wouldn't answer my calls. I never heard from him again."

"So we're both married and screwing around." I could crush his throat with my hand.

"I suppose so." Her voice sounds like it will tear in two.

I can't decide if this makes it better or worse. The similarity in our stories feels like some sick joke. "How did we find each other?" My laugh is cold.

"You ran a red light." She looks up at me with that teasing look in her eyes.

My control fails. I take her face in my hands and kiss her. A wildfire spreads through my body. She leans into me, weakening my restraint further. Her arms wind around me, and as my back makes contact with the seat of the couch, I know this can't happen. I have to stop it, but I am powerless. She runs her hands underneath my shirt, and I remember something I have to tell her.

"Wait," I gasp, holding her away from me. She opens her eyes. Her lips are parted, her breathing heavy. There's no word in any language I know to describe her beauty.

"Wait," I say again, more to myself this time. I sit up, moving her back into a sitting position. "I'm forty-five." I struggle against the memory, the feeling, of being wrapped within her legs. I can't live with myself until she knows it all.

"What?"

"I'm forty-five years old."

"No you're not."

"Aaron is alive. The effect didn't apply to me this whole time. I thought I wasn't aging, and I was."

She shakes her head. "There must be some mistake. You look too young—and what about the healing?"

She's right. The healing. And my effortless survival, when I should have been killed so many times. I'm so used to my superior state of health, it's hard to remember it's not normal.

"Can you really trust what they told you?"

She has a point. "So you believe all this?"

"Hmm. I guess I do. I just don't see why you'd make it all up. Is that foolish of me?"

"No." I smile at her. "We can't have sex anymore," I add, dropping my smile.

She doesn't look convinced. She unleashes her eyes on me. The pull is almost unbearable.

"Please. You can't do that."

"Do what?" she asks innocently.

She can't be unaware of what she does to me. Maybe it isn't her fault at all. Maybe it's all me, and my pathetic lack of self-discipline.

"We don't have to take it all the way." It's an offer. An irresistible seduction.

And I know myself well enough to know it doesn't work that way with me. "Yes, we would. I have no self-control. And you can't stop me."

"Sounds like fun." She's turned my comment against me in order to tempt me further.

"Stop talking about it." I rub my face with both hands—a vain attempt to vaporize the mental images of her bare skin against mine. "I have a bad habit of getting women pregnant when there's no way I could have. There could be other magic I don't know about. There could be—it's just not worth it to screw around. You probably shouldn't even be sitting so close to me."

She pouts.

Silence creeps between us, and I reflect on how drastically my life has changed since our first encounter. That day feels like a dream, like those memories belong to another person, a person who had no reason to exist. I have a purpose now. I feel vibrant and alive.

"Do you need some time to absorb all of this?" I search her face.

"Actually, no. I feel very much at ease. Settled. Is that weird?"

I wonder if I should give her time anyway. But that time could be used in other ways. If she agrees, we have a lot of work ahead of us.

"Nothing's really changed," she adds. "I knew there was something strange about you the whole time. Now I just know the details."

"So you're okay with me dropping another bomb on you?"

"If I've made it this far, I don't think there's anything left that could surprise me." She seems lifted, eager for me to continue.

"I need to see Aaron. Seeing him involves seeing Kate, and I do have some words for her. I have to go see them." I look into her cool, patient eyes. "And I want you to come with me."

Finally something that seems to surprise her. "You want me to go with you to visit your estranged wife?"

"She left me. Remember that. She hid from me for fifteen years."

"Yes, but—"

"And I can't leave you alone here. I can't go unless you come with me."

"Where would we be going?"

"Virginia."

Pressuring her may be unfair, but I know it's the only way we can move on together. I'll never allow myself to be with her with this looming over me. But I have to be honest. "And before you agree, I have to tell you it's going to be dangerous. They'll be expecting a fight."

She laughs and leans back against the pillow behind her. "You can't be serious. Do I look like I'm capable—"

"I can make you as capable as you need to be."

She smiles at me, shaking her head.

"They'll have zero chance against the two of us." I can't help but feel excited by the image of Liv and me, storming in there, side by side. I've always worked alone. This is going to be new for me, too.

"I don't know what you're talking about. But you're cute when you're keyed up like this."

"So what do you say?" I ask.

"I'm not exactly sure what you're asking me. But it sounds like I have two options. Stay here and wait for them to hunt me down, or go with you and walk into a war."

"I never lose."

"How do I know that's true? I barely know you."

"You'll have to trust me."

She places her elbow against the couch, rests her chin against her fist, and sighs. "I trust people too easily. I made a promise to myself to stop doing it. To be more careful. And I was doing pretty well until you came along."

"You *can* trust me." I lean forward, driving it in. I understand her hesitation. I don't exactly have a great track record with her. Or anyone.

"Anybody can say that. How do I know you're not a psycho homicidal maniac?"

"You already know I am a psycho homicidal maniac."

She laughs and shakes her head. "True."

"But at least I'm honest," I add to strengthen my argument.

She looks at me for a long time before she asks, "If you were me, would you say yes?"

"Without a doubt."

"Okay then I'm in. I have no idea what I'm in on, but I'm in. I have nothing to lose. And you might need me to save your life again."

I stand abruptly, pulling her off the couch. We have much to do in the coming days. "Bedroom is yours tonight. I'll take the couch."

She gives me a pained look before retiring to the bedroom.

"Close the door," I holler. I don't need the enticement of that open door, even though a locked door would only slow me down.

Back in the living room, I lie on the couch, envisioning my life at a crossroads, only I'm already proceeding down my chosen path. And I have never felt more confident about anything in my entire life.

We stand in front of the garden lit by slanted morning sun.

"You're really going to make me do heavy labor? What does this have to do with visiting your crazy relatives again?"

"Gardening is not heavy labor. It has to be done before we go. I've been neglecting it too long. Just think of it as combat training warm-up."

She gives me a what-have-I-gotten-myself-into look.

I aim my thumb at the tractor tire, the best exercise aside from actual combat. "Unless you'd rather flip that tire down the yard a few times."

She looks back and forth between me and the tire before stomping off toward the potatoes. After I've worked my way down one row of herbs, she hollers, "I have no idea what to do!"

I head toward her. "You're such a spoiled city girl, aren't you?"

She punches me in the stomach and I fake pain. "Now you're going to have to do it all yourself. I'm injured." She starts to kick me and I catch her leg. Her face breaks into laughter—a lure that traps me again. It's a fight back to freedom when all I want is to be stuck in that trap.

After removing the covers of the cold frames, I show her how to dig potatoes and carrots, and how to pick ripe squash, cucumbers, and cabbage. Once she has the hang of it, I go back to weeding and working on the herbs. I can't help but notice she's enjoying herself.

"There's something very gratifying about this kind of work," she says when I kneel beside her. "I would've never thought."

"Nah, you just enjoy it because of the great company."

"Yes that's definitely part of it." Her tone is too serious to be teasing me back.

"Tell me about ballet. You said you've been doing it your whole life?"

"Mm-hm."

"How old were you when you started?" This will give me something to tap into.

"Five years old. They put me in lessons just to give me something to do. They said I was a natural, but I think I just enjoyed it enough to work hard. Classical lessons at first. I do mostly contemporary nowadays. I took gymnastics too."

Ah, gymnastics. Bonus. "Your parents must have seen something in you." Just like I do.

"Not my parents. The people at the children's home. I didn't have a family."

"You were an orphan?" I'm surprised I haven't found this out already. "You never knew your parents?"

"No. I never knew any of my biological family. But someone left a trust fund in my name, and I used it for the best ballet lessons money could buy. And then medical school. Years and years of medical school." She claps the dirt off her gloves and sits back on her heels like she's ready to clock out.

"Medical school?" I flip open the tops of two more cold frames and hand her the shovel. Two more varieties of potatoes to dig and we're not going in until it's done.

"I was studying to be a doctor. But then…I lost interest. I already had my nursing degree so I just left it at that." She stabs her shovel into the ground. "You had no idea there was more to me, did you?"

"No, I just wasn't expecting it. I should've done better homework before taking you as my captive."

"Oh, so this was all deliberate? That car accident was no accident at all?" She pulls out a potato that's almost as big as her head and holds it up like it's a trophy. "This one needs to be measured for a world record. Look at it."

"It wasn't an accident. I ran the light on purpose."

"What?!"

I take the potato from her. "I was chasing someone. I didn't want them to get away again."

"Who was it?" she asks, more gently.

I stall by fetching a couple more empty buckets from under the porch. Evasion has become second nature to me. Like all my bad habits it's a hard one to break. I have to keep it up with everyone else. Not with her. "It was the car that was parked near the house the night Kate and Aaron were taken. I've seen it around a couple times, but it always gets away."

She shields her eyes from the sun and looks up at me. "There's a reason for everything. You can judge something with your own eyes, but to someone else, it's completely different."

"Yep. And you just happened to be at the wrong place at the wrong time."

River darts from the woods at the far end of the yard and I curse under my breath. I have too much to do today without having to deal with one of them. Or two, according to River.

"How far away, girl?"

And then I see that glint in her eye. She's messing with me. Getting me back. I point at her and she scurries past us and around the house.

"She's just playing around," I tell Liv, who's frozen in place, a potato in each hand like she's ready to clobber someone. Not a bad idea, but it would be a waste of good potatoes.

We carry the loaded buckets up to the kitchen. After washing, drying, and storing all the vegetables, she rinses the mud down the sink and I set the empty buckets outside on the porch. When I return to the kitchen she looks at me expectantly like she knows something's up.

"This is where it gets weird. You can stay up here in the normal world if you want, or you can join me in the basement while I prepare a few things."

"Are you going to mix up some potions?" She clasps her hands together, exaggerating her excitement with a wide smile.

"Exactly." I'm unable to contain my own grin.

CHAPTER 20

LIV

Ducking to avoid the low ceiling beams, he turns on all the lights in the basement and drags a stool to the workbench for me. I sit and watch as he scans his books, his fingers tapping a number of volumes before pulling three of them out.

Each book has its own unique fabric cover, but they're all equally faded and worn with age. One was formerly a deep maroon with a gold stripe, another a fuzzy gray that must have once been silver velvet—the material hinting of another century, or some lost world. Inlaid in each cover are nearly identical bronze medallions about the size of a quarter, suggesting these volumes are part of a series.

He stands next to me at the workbench and flips through the first book. The pages are thick and stiff, their edges uneven. Apparently finding nothing, he slides it in front of me. I study the faded indigo cover and age-worn medallion before gently tying it closed with its cord.

"Here it is," he says.

Handwritten words from another language fill the page in front of him. He runs his finger down what looks like a list before turning to the shelves holding the jars of unknown substances. I take each jar he hands to me, lining them up on the workbench.

He carefully measures ingredients from the jars, double-checking the book each time. The new mixture in the clean jar morphs into a brown, gluey substance. After tightening the lid, he sets it in front of me.

"What is it?"

"Binding agent."

I hold it up to the light. "For what?"

"To bind our minds." He squats to search underneath the workbench.

I set the jar down. "What are you looking for?"

"This." He sets a Bunsen burner on the counter.

"Oh my god."

He attaches a rubber hose connected to a tank of gas to the burner. He flips through his open book, stopping on a new page with a new list. The handwriting on this page is different, and small notes are written in the margins. After making selections from his inventory, he sets a beaker on the counter and adds the ingredients, glancing back at the list each time. He lights the burner and holds the beaker over the flame with the tongs. He whispers to himself, fixated on the task before him. I feel like a spy in the room.

He removes the beaker from the heat and holds it in the air to cool. A thin curl of smoke rises from it and the thick scent of gas becomes flavored by something spicy and pungent that gives the slightest sting to my eyes. It smells like peppermint.

"Were you chanting a spell?"

He grins and looks at me. "No, I was counting. Twenty-five seconds."

"Oh." I chuckle at myself. Stupid.

He searches my face as if to gauge my level of seriousness. "We'll do that later."

He turns the beaker upside down on a piece of brown paper, and out slides a little round glob. "That's not what it's supposed to look like." He goes back to the book, leaning over it on his elbows.

I spin away from the table. This shouldn't feel so normal. If someone relayed this exact scene to me in conversation, I'd never believe them. I'd want them to get their head checked. Our attraction has stripped my defense, making everything he does seem safe when I should be cautious. He's not someone I would have ever trusted, but I've never trusted anyone more. I'm not sure what I've signed up for, what I'll be party to. Somehow, it doesn't matter as long as I'm with him.

I notice the glob has shrunk to half its size. "It looks different now."

His concentration takes a moment to break. "Good. And now I'm supposed to..." He takes a knife and cuts the round sides off the glob to make a perfect cube. He wraps it up in the brown paper and ties a string around it like a tiny gift.

"For you, for later." He hands it to me.

"For what?" I ask a second time.

"Roughly translates as 'mind sleep.' To turn off your active mind. Usually tastes like shit. I added something that might make it better."

I stare at the tiny package in my palm. This is what I'm going to be party to.

He takes it back. "But I'll hold on to it in the meantime. I know about you and your lack of restraint."

"Me? I hope you're kidding. You've started it every time."

"I have?" He glances away as if to think about it. "Well, you provoke me."

I laugh. "I do not!"

He puts one palm on the table and turns his body to face me. The simple action sends a fluttery rush from my chest downward, like a wad of feathers floating through me. He's about to start something and prove me right. "See, you're provoking me right now."

Knowing I'm not, I decide to taunt him anyway. "What are you going to do about it?"

He leans down, his lips an inch from mine. "Absolutely nothing." He smiles. He is so handsome I almost fall off the stool. Sure, there's a textbook definition of our attraction he seems to accept as pure irrefutable science. Even without that, he has a rugged charm he wears well. Hair dampened by sweat from our work outside, strong blue-collar hands, an obvious finesse with this craft. And the confidence he emits while in his element.

I stretch up to him but he backs away just in time. I wonder what he'd do if I really did try to provoke him.

He returns to his work, leafing through another book. More meticulously measured ingredients go into the beaker and over the flame. He counts to himself again, removes the beaker, and dumps the contents out on brown paper just like before. Again he cuts it into a cube, wraps it in the paper, and ties the string.

"What's that one for?"

"For me. Translation is something like 'projection effect.' Also tastes like shit."

"Yours sounds more exciting than mine."

"That's because I have to do all the work. There's one more thing we need…" He opens a cupboard below the shelves of jars and pulls out a massive book. It drops onto the counter in a cloud of dust. "This is going to take a while."

I wander to the other side of the basement and find his boxing bag split in half and covered in dried blood. What is wrong with him? I know he has a temper, but this is unreal. It's like he doesn't know when to stop.

I turn around with a reprimand on the tip of my tongue. His broad shoulders are slumped over the book as he copies something to a piece of paper, and I decide not to break his focus. Nothing I say will change who he is. The way to protect a self-destructive person from hurt is to remove the triggers. Go to the source of the trouble. Make the person happy. It's going to be a long road.

Returning to the stool next to him, I notice his knuckles, which look almost healed now. Maybe that's why he doesn't stop. He knows whatever damage he does will fix itself before it has a chance to render him vulnerable. Maybe now that he knows he's mortal, he won't be so brutally self-destructive. But if he's mortal, his wounds shouldn't heal like time-lapse photography.

I trace the scar on his bicep, now just a discoloration. He's so deep in thought he doesn't notice. The scar on his neck is no longer visible. The wound on his forehead I Steri-stripped at the clinic is only evident if you know to look. His cheekbone scar is still a tender pink line, but it looks much better than it should considering how bad it was.

I shouldn't be doing this. I'm cheating on my husband. I've gone to bed with another man, and I don't feel bad about it. He could be at our home in Chicago right now waiting for me, worried about me, sitting by the phone just like I did for him. I'm as bad as he is.

"Done." He folds his slip of paper and puts the book back in the cupboard.

I start to hop off the stool but he stops me with a warm hand on my knee. "One more thing."

He opens my hand and places a gun in it. I stare at it.

"How does that feel in your hand?"

"Like an accident waiting to happen. Can you take it back?"

He puts it on the workbench and heads for the stairs. Apparently he sees no need to explain and I'm in no hurry to ask. I shrug it off and follow him upstairs.

He starts rummaging through the kitchen and I glance at the clock. Time moves at a different pace when I'm with him. And I've been in these dirty gardening clothes the whole time. I change into clean leggings and a loose cotton shirt. I push the couch a few feet back so I have room to do some stretching on the floor.

Not much later I hear him walk up behind me so I turn to face him.

"You need more space." His face is hard. Brooding.

"It's fine. I can work with it."

"Let me move the furniture for you next time." The flatness in his voice seems out of place after the light-hearted day we spent together.

I can't grasp what got him in this mood. "Okay," I answer to indulge him.

"Are you hungry?" He turns toward the kitchen.

I follow him. The exchange seems forced, and I can't pinpoint why.

As we begin to eat, the silence weighs on me. I know he's brooding, but I can't imagine what happened between coming up from downstairs and now. With nothing to say, I simply put down my fork and look at him. When his eyes meet mine, they are troubled.

He stops eating. "No good?"

"No, it's great, as usual. Where did you learn to cook?" Conversation couldn't hurt, and seems a much better strategy than outright asking him what's wrong—he'd take it as an accusation and become defensive.

He pauses before answering. "My mother."

I have a feeling he was debating whether he should answer honestly. I'm certain it's a touchy subject, but I can't stop myself. "Your mother taught you a lot. Will you tell me about her?"

A whole minute passes and he doesn't answer. Maybe I should change the subject. "You're still wearing those dirty—"

"My mother is nothing like them."

Relieved he used the present tense, I say nothing. I can almost hear the clock ticking when he finally takes a breath to speak again.

"*I* am nothing like them. My mother and I have always been the black sheep. Christian—he's the only one who's ever felt like family besides her." His eyes slide past me, to the scenery outside the sliding glass door.

He mentioned his father once, and maybe it's a touchy subject, but I need to know. "And your father?"

"He and I never got along like I did with my mother. She taught me everything I know except combat. That was all my father. He pushed me very hard. I should be grateful. Without him, these last fifteen years would have sucked." He laughs. His laughter is like a gift to me. "But, they're all his family. I've never met anyone on my mother's side. Not even sure there are any. She gave me her last name. I don't even carry my father's name."

"Really? That's unusual."

"Never seemed to matter. We aren't like everyone else."

"When was the last time you saw your mother?"

His gaze drops. "Fifteen years ago."

And just like that, he's withdrawn from the conversation. I want to keep him talking, but I'm not sure what to say. "Why are you so close to Christian?"

"My mother watched him when we were kids. His mother died when he was a baby."

"You said you two are cousins?"

"Yes. His father is my father's brother."

It feels like the conversation has turned into an inquisition, so I drop it. He cleans his plate and waits for me to finish, staring past me again out the back window.

When I stand to clear the table, he doesn't break out of his trance. I feel so helpless. He's stressed about something and keeping it in. The running water and clanging of dishes amplify the silence instead of filling it, and I consider changing the subject to something lighter but fear it will close a door that has been left standing open for me.

Has he really lived alone here for fifteen years? No one to share a meal with? No human touch?

I slip behind him, grasp his shoulders, and squeeze. His body tenses as the contact of my hands breaks his trance, so I squeeze again, working the knots in his muscles.

"You don't have to—"

He tries to protest by turning in his chair, but I turn with him and continue to squeeze, marveling at his muscle tone. "Take off your shirt."

His wary green eyes question my motive. Yes, I'd love to drag him to bed and show him how much I want him. But not now.

"It's filthy. Come on." I tug it halfway up his back.

He reaches behind his back and pulls his shirt over his head in one fluid motion. I try to ignore the rush I feel.

"Now come in here." I pull his hand.

"Oh no you don't."

"Do you want to make me stand the whole time?"

He doesn't look convinced.

"This is purely professional," I explain, to him and to myself.

He gives me a long, hard look, and stands. I lead him into the living room and spread a blanket on the floor.

"Lie down on your stomach."

"I'm trusting you," he says slowly, clearly aware of his own fragile state.

I drop a pillow on the blanket.

With him flat on the floor, I use my elbows and my palms, which are more suited to his frame than my fingers. I work his neck and shoulders then move down his back.

"Oh my god you have no idea…" He groans.

I lose myself in the rhythm. I'm vaguely aware the room has turned dark, the decreasing light so gradual I didn't notice the sun was setting. I turn on a lamp and lie down next to him. "Are you alive?"

"Barely." The softness of his voice is my reward.

After a few minutes he rolls to face me, pulling the pillow over so we can both share it. "Thank you," he says, his face inches from mine.

"My pleasure."

He rolls onto his back to stare at the ceiling. "I'm using you."

"No, you're not."

"Yes. I'm using you to carry out my own revenge."

"No you're not. I agreed. Remember?"

"But what other choice did you have?" Disgust fills his voice, and I know he's right.

"But I want to help you."

He rolls to face me. "Why?"

Good question. "I…think we make a great team. Why do *you* want me to come with you?"

He smirks, his eyes lighting up. "Because I think we make a great team." He drops his smile. "And I don't ever want to be away from you."

I look away from him. There's a flutter in my stomach, and my thoughts turn to mush.

"I shouldn't have said that."

"No," I begin, trying to think. "It's just, you can't say something like that and expect me to remain professional."

He laughs, a symphony in my ears. "Good point." He pushes himself up and holds out his hand. The muscles in his arms flex as he pulls me to standing. "I'm going to explain everything that'll happen tonight, so you can choose if you really want to do this."

There's a defeat to his voice, like he's already decided I won't commit. He has to believe I'm with him. Our trust has to be strong in both directions or this team won't last. If he's blaming himself for dragging me into this, well, I'm just as guilty. "I've already told you I'm in."

"You don't know what you're—"

"Trey, listen. I could've walked away from this a long time ago. I could've driven to the police station and explained the entire situation at any time. But I didn't. And in the beginning, even I don't know why I didn't. So my involvement is just as much my fault as it is yours. I have nothing else in the world right now, and staying with you just feels right. Can you accept that?"

"God, where did you come from?"

"Snack time?" I ask, because the intensity in his eyes needs to be squashed before I think too hard about that question.

In the kitchen, he cuts open a watermelon with an enormous knife better suited to clearing a jungle path, and I take a seat at the table. I try not to wonder if that blade has killed. He brings a plate of sliced watermelon to the table, the ripe fruit so perfect that the first bite leaves juice running down my arms.

"Okay." He pulls out his chair across from me. "The process I planned for tonight is a mind sharing process. Your mind will go to sleep, opening for input. My mind will project to your mind." He takes a few bites of watermelon while watching for my reaction.

I wonder what my expression looks like.

"It's not as crazy as it sounds. It's just a quick way for me to teach you certain things I know. Once those things are in your mind, we'll work with them so your mind and body can adapt to them.

"So, those tablets I made? We'll take them together. You'll go to sleep, and I'll stay awake but on a different level of consciousness. I'll enter your mind and apply my knowledge. Don't look so freaked out. It's easy."

"And then I wake up and know how to install a roof?"

He allows himself a moment's smile but remains serious. "Do you want to know how to install a roof? I can include that."

"Is this for real?"

"Yes. But the tricky part is we can't do it here. We have to go somewhere they can't easily find us."

"Why?"

"Because if one of them comes when we're busy—I can't protect us when I'm in that state. The process could take hours."

Hours, under his control, at the whim of his mind. "What exactly are you going to teach me?"

"Combat, weapons, and tactical knowledge like how to escape. And…I'll have to think if there's anything else. But once you have the knowledge, you'll need to learn to apply it, to sort of customize it, because physically you're so different from me. Your existing physical abilities with your dance and gymnastics background will help."

"So when we're done, I'll know everything you know but with my own personal stamp on it."

"When we're done, you'll be a highly-trained assassin." His sudden radiant smile carries a sinister edge.

"You're going to enjoy this, aren't you?"

"I'm not going to lie."

"How can you do this? Can anyone do it?"

"Anyone can receive. But to project, you have to be part of my bloodline."

"Your bloodline." I'm repeating it more to myself than to him. At some point, I'm going to wake up from this dream. These things he's told me, this talk of the supernatural and ancient prophecies and bloodlines that should not exist in reality are going to come crashing down.

He watches me with the attentiveness of a dog waiting for a treat. What does he expect me to say? Yes, I will take some mind-altering tablet you made in a beaker in your basement and let you program my mind while I'm unconscious? And that's just the beginning. He could probably do so much more, and I'd never know.

Will I end up a killer, like him?

He leans back in his chair, breaking his focused intensity with a smile. "The suspense is killing me."

Killing him. What an interesting choice of words. "I'm not doing it on purpose. I just don't know what to say."

"Are you afraid?"

"Not afraid of what will happen tonight." I wonder if my honesty will offend him. "I'm afraid of what I will become."

He nods slowly, closing his eyes for a moment as if he's already considered this idea himself. "Don't worry. It won't change you as a person. It won't make you like me."

"That's not what I was saying. I didn't mean—"

"It's a valid point. But it's no different from me teaching you kickboxing every night after work. If we did that, you'd just know how to kickbox. You wouldn't become a killer."

He answers my questions almost to the word. Is he already in my mind? "You missed your calling. You should be in sales. Either that, or I'm the biggest pushover alive."

"You're not a pushover. And I'm not selling it. It's just a damn good idea and you know it."

He's got something there. I'm not sure who could complain about learning a lifetime of skills in just a few hours. And all you have to do is take a nap. Forget magic. Consider it something ordinary people do every day. Who knows, someday they'll probably invent it. Pretend it's possible now, with technology instead of an ancient bloodline and strange words from an old book. Who wouldn't agree?

"Okay."

"Okay?" He leans forward.

"Okay I'm in." I reach out my sticky, juice-covered hand and he takes it in his.

Sometimes you just have to go with your gut feeling.

CHAPTER 21

TREY

"I'LL GET YOU back for that." I wipe my sticky hand on my jeans and stand.

"What?" Her attempt to look innocent falls short because she can't contain her smile.

I debate telling her the part of the prophecy I left out earlier. I swore I would, but I don't want to add any complications to this day. Putting it off now means I have to tell her soon. If it comes up for the first time when we're facing them, she'll think I deliberately kept it from her, that I betrayed her. I will not betray her.

She probably doubts what I said about not wanting to be away from her. I wanted to say more. It's such a struggle with her. I've possessed unfaltering willpower my whole life. Then Liv Gilchrist shows up and it all goes to hell.

"Should we get ready for our adventure?" I ask.

"Is that what you're calling it? I like that." Her blue eyes shine.

"Dress in layers. It's going to be cold tonight, and we'll be outside for most of it." I follow her into the bedroom to get some extra clothes from my closet. "If you need more clothes, help yourself." I leave the closet door open and go gear up.

I pack a bag with our tablets, the jar of the agent, bottled water, matches, and a blanket. I stick the sheet of copied notes into my pocket. Liv joins me in the kitchen wearing jeans and one of my flannel shirts over my thermal under-shirt. I curb my thoughts immediately. She doesn't mean to look so cute in my clothes.

"Settle down. Your clothes are just so comfy, and you offered." She rolls up the sleeves.

Nothing gets by her. I should know this by now.

I pull one of my sock hats over her head and slide her hair out of her eyes. She smiles up at me, and a tingle runs through me, charging my blood. I pull a sock hat over my own head, and we both sit to tie our boots.

I open the back door and click my tongue for River. Leaves rustle, paws pound the decking, and she stops in front of me, tail wagging. "Go scout."

She runs off eagerly. I grab my sheathed knife off the top of the fridge. It wouldn't hurt to bring a gun too, so I go downstairs for my nine millimeter. I'm slipping into the shoulder holster as I reach the top of the stairs, and Liv's eyes go straight to the gun and settle there.

"Are you sure you're not taking me out in the woods to kill me? I'm kind of making it easy for you."

That hits a nerve. I know she's kidding, but it feels like I've just taken a bullet to the chest when I imagine how easily she could've overdosed on that handful of herbs. How it would've been my fault. How my only concern that night was how to dispose of her body. There is no amount of gratitude I can pay to whatever caused me to sleep on it instead of toss her body off a cliff. I grab my heavy jacket and River appears at the back door with her friend from Liv's house. Both tails are wagging, signaling the all clear.

"Looks like River had some help tonight." I get two pieces of cheese from the fridge and hand them out the door. "Ready?" I turn around and hold her coat for her.

She slips her arms in the sleeves. "Do you have any gloves I can borrow?"

The smallest pair I have are the fleece-lined ones, still way too big but she'll need the warmth. She laughs as she puts them on, and I make a mental note to buy her some new gloves. I sling the bag onto my back, and we head out the front door and circle around toward the river. Both dogs catch up.

I point to her dog. "What's his name?"

"I don't know. I guess I call him Coyote Dog. When I first saw him I didn't know if he was a dog or a coyote."

"He definitely has some coyote in him."

"He probably had a name. I should ask Nancy if she knows."

"Want me to ask him?" I try to be nonchalant. I don't want to sound cocky.

She glances at me, her eyes big in the moonlight.

"Or, we could just give him a name, so I don't have to freak you out any more than you already are."

"Well if he's hanging around with River now, he needs to fit in. How about Brook, Creek, Stream, Tributary?"

"Tributary. Now that's a name."

We walk for a while, both lost in our own thoughts. Wet pine needles on the ground offer a damper to our step. The cloudless sky creates a dome of stars over our heads, and the moon casts enough light to guide our way. The temperature is crisp and invigorating, keeping us moving. We couldn't have asked for a better night.

I lead her to the footbridge and across, the dogs' gallop on the wooden planks breaking the serenity. We head into the woods, and when we reach the ravine it's filled with an inch of standing water just as I expected.

"I'm going to have to carry you for a while."

She stops and turns toward me. "Why?"

"The fewer footprints we leave the better. I can make my own hard to track."

I slide the bag around to my front and squat down, and she hops on my back without complaint. I can feel her breath on my neck, and I'm thankful for the layers of clothes separating us.

"Why don't we just go the rest of the way like this?" she asks in my ear, her arms secure around my neck.

Halfway up the ravine I break into the woods again, and about fifty feet in I let her down. I lead her toward the bluffs and up the gently sloping side, the side we'll retreat down if anyone meets us up here. This way she'll be somewhat familiar with the trail. At the top, I take a look around. If we stay under the shadow of the trees, no one can see us.

We can see two hundred and seventy degrees around us, leaving only one side where someone can sneak up. River can camp out on that side.

It wasn't very long ago I had a completely different idea for bringing Liv up here. The thought of what I could have done makes me sick all over again. A coyote calls, followed by two more. River sprints up the steep side of the bluff, panting hard.

"She's got the whole pack working for us tonight," I say to Liv, grateful for the distraction from my dark thoughts. I lower my hand and River licks it. She looks at me with her head cocked and one ear sticking up. "Get to work," I tell her, and she runs off to her friends to keep guard.

Noticing Liv's silence, I glance at her. She's hugging herself and watching me with guarded eyes. And something else, something new. Doubt? Mistrust? Fascination? In a few minutes I can find out. "I need to gather some rocks and place them in a circle. Want to help?"

"As long as I'm not the human sacrifice."

"Not tonight." I play along. She has no idea how true that would've been.

"So what are you? What do you call yourself?"

I start making a pile of rocks. "Trey." I know what she's getting at, but I'm going to make her work for it.

She throws a rock at me. I catch it and toss it in the pile.

"I'm referring to your…heritage. Your abilities. What can I call you? Witch? Warlock?"

"You can call me Master." I can't help myself.

She throws another rock at me, and I dodge, laughing.

"You'd get off on that, wouldn't you?"

"It depends on which abilities you're talking about."

She straightens up and stares at me, trying not to smile.

"Do you disagree?" If we didn't have work to do, I'd take her hard right now, and after it was over she'd have no reason to disagree.

"I'm not sure. I need another run-through before I make a decision." She goes back to her work, walking along the edge of the pine forest surrounding us.

Before I can think of a comeback, she calls my name in an urgent whisper. When I see her looking into the trees, I move to her side. I should have warned her.

"There's a coyote right there!"

"She's just curious." I take a rock from her hand and lead her by the arm to our pile. "She's with River." It may be simplifying the truth, but it is the truth. Liv watches me again with that same look from before while I arrange the rocks in a large circle on the ground and spread the blanket in the middle. "Ready?"

"As ready as I'll ever be."

We sit on the blanket cross-legged, facing each other. I take the tablets out of the bag, remove the jar and unscrew the lid. "You're going to have to take off your gloves."

I unwrap the tablets, placing hers on her knee, and mine on my knee.

"How can you tell them apart?"

"I just can. Hold out your hands, palms up."

She offers her hands and watches me as I place a drop of the binding agent on each of her palms. I pull the page of notes out of my pocket, unfold it, and smooth it out on the ground. I pick up her tablet, and she opens her mouth. I drop it on her tongue.

"Just let it dissolve slowly. Don't bite it."

She nods. I place a drop of the binding agent on each of my palms.

"Now, hold your hands up, palms facing me."

I press my palms against hers and close my fingers, binding our hands together. Her fingers close along with mine and I read the words from my page three times. She can't understand the words, but she doesn't ask me what they mean. I pick my tablet off my knee with my teeth. She calmly watches me while our tablets dissolve, and I observe the gradual change in her expression.

When her eyelids blink several times then fall, I gently lay her down, pushing her legs out from under her with my own so she can lie on her side and face me without breaking our joined hands. Her face is peaceful and her breathing slow, and I start to feel myself rising out of my own body, each of my senses strengthening and extending beyond what is normal for me. The rustle of leaves nearby is suddenly inside my ear. The brightness of the moon blinds me. The clothes on my body caress my skin with every microscopic fiber. The smell of the wet earth becomes a taste on my tongue. And then all my senses join together in one singular entity, not sight, sound, smell, touch, or taste, but something entirely new. A new dimension.

Chaos. Surrounded. I try to get my bearings, but I can't see. I remind myself not to panic. Stimuli from my ears mix with stimuli from hers. All the fragments of sound become a din, nothing making sense. I relax, try to settle into it, and slowly, my vision adjusts.

Movement, all around me. I hear voices, traffic, a dog barking. I look to the right where cars are passing along a street. I look down and see I am wearing a silver ring carved with a complex design on each of my middle fingers. I turn my hands over and there are dark stains on both palms. Below them, my brown work boots. I look up and I'm in the middle of a busy sidewalk in a city. I start walking with the crowd.

Why am I here? For her. I have to find her. There are some things she needs to know. In all these people, how am I going to find her? I'm lost in this mass and it feels wrong. I try to move on my own but bodies force me along in their direction. She wouldn't be here in this crowd. It's just not right.

I see a grove of trees up ahead, and I cross the street toward them. Wait. There's that dog again. That barking. It's getting closer. My senses zone in on it in the way a familiar sound would capture my attention. I walk toward the barking and enter a small city park. Children are making wishes at a fountain. I pass them and see a row of Austrian Pine. There's something red on the other side, and movement low to the ground, like a dog. I push through the pines, the sappy needles brushing against my face. A woman wearing a red coat is crouching down, petting a little black puppy. She throws a ball, and the dog bounds after it. She looks up. She smiles. It's her.

Seeing her face in this unfamiliar city park deepens the throb of my heart. I take her hand. "We have work to do."

"I know." Her cheeks and nose are rosy.

"Is it always so busy around here?" There's a chill in the wind I didn't notice before.

She gives a slight shrug. "Not always."

"Would you like to go somewhere quieter?"

"I'd love to."

We're standing on a deserted beach. I'm wearing cutoff jeans and a white T-shirt. She's wearing a white skirt and sleeveless top that ties behind her neck. Her hair is twisted up on top of her head, and her bangs are swept to the side by the breeze. She's looking down at our bare feet as the tide touches us, stealing the sand from under our toes. She lifts her arm to admire a bracelet of delicate pearly-white shells.

"So pretty." She looks up at me. "You have good taste."

I'm not sure how I knew she would like that. I raise my face to the sky. The sun's position tells me it's late afternoon. Time should pass at the same rate in here, and we'll probably be done by the time the sun sets. Four, maybe five hours. I take her hand, soft and cool in mine. "Are you cold? I can make it warmer."

I hear her answer like a reversed echo before she speaks. "No. It's just perfect." She looks out to sea.

We walk along the beach, the tide stroking our feet in its uneven rhythm, and I collect my thoughts. When I've been silent for a while, she looks at me.

"What am I supposed to do?"

I squeeze her hand. "Nothing. Just enjoy the scenery. I'll let you know when we're done."

With my thoughts organized, I begin my work. As we walk, I feed her information, with the most crucial pieces first in case I run out of time. The work isn't difficult, but it requires my complete concentration. It seems easier since I know this will be successful. Her mind is completely open to me, and so similar to my own that I make a mental note to think about it again later.

When the sun touches the horizon, I search my mental database to make sure I haven't missed anything important. I'm tempted to throw in something about roofing. It would be a good way to prove this worked.

I stop walking and turn her toward me.

"You look so tired!" She places both palms against my cheeks. Worry seeps from her voice.

Her worry washes through me as if it were my own, and I push it away, knowing it only belongs to her. "It's okay. We've been walking for a long time."

"I don't think it was the walking. Otherwise I'd be tired too." Her easy smile tells me she must have just been dosed with my calm.

"I have to leave now. You can stay here as long as you want. I'll be waiting for you, out there."

"Okay." She's disappointed this has to end. Her disappointment touches me, mingling with my own. She tilts her head and looks away, still smiling with her eyes full of contented wonder. She feels it too.

I let go of her hand and start walking back the way we came. I don't allow myself to look back.

My eyes open to the dome of stars above me. Cold air fills lungs that expect the warmth of the sea breeze. It was so straightforward. Effortless. I didn't expect it to be this easy.

I sit up, unclasp my hands from hers and wipe my palms on the ground. She's still asleep as I scatter the rocks to erase our presence. River bursts out of the woods to check on us.

"We're fine, girl. Go back to what you were doing."

I strike a match and burn the page of my notes. I wipe off Liv's palms to put the gloves back on her cold hands. It must be about three a.m. We need to start heading back so we can get a few hours of sleep.

I wonder how much she'll remember. Whether it's every last detail or nothing, it won't change what's in that text or how it just got handed to me in concrete proof. She's harboring a piece of me that's been gone so long I forgot it was missing. It's a component in what drives a person forward, powers the will to live. And it's at home inside her for the same reason I was. It's meant to be there.

No place I've ever lived has felt like home because she was never there. She's my home. She found me, drove across this wide country like a bullet to a bull's eye, and her timing couldn't have been better. The text is right.

A breeze builds, ruffling Liv's hair and bringing my attention back to her. There's no way to avoid explaining the rest of the prophecy to her now that I know it's the truth. I could spend eternity in her mind and never want to leave.

She stirs and I clear my throat, afraid my voice will give me away. "Liv? I'm here. You can wake up now."

"Hmm?" She mumbles something and sighs. She abruptly raises up, resting on her elbows. Looks around, squinting her eyes. She focuses on me.

"Do you feel okay?"

"Um. Yes. I think. What time is it?"

I check the sky. "About half past three."

She rubs her eyes. "That was…amazing. No word to describe it."

"Do you remember it?"

"Maybe not all of it, but enough to know it was amazing. God. Just amazing."

I laugh. I can't help it. "Do you think you can walk back to the house?"

"Um. Yes." She starts to get up so I stand and help her. "I guess we didn't get ambushed."

"Nope." I shake out the blanket and fold it up.

"Whoa. I think I need to sit back down for a second."

I start to spread the blanket out again but she stops me and we both sit on the ground.

"The beach!" she says. "It was all so real. I could feel the sand on my feet. And you…you were so real. I could almost…feel what you were feeling."

"Can I ask you something?"

"Sure."

"What kind of nails would you use to re-roof a house?"

"Galvanized twelve gauge one and three quarter inch roofing nails with a three eighths inch diameter head. Oh my *god*."

We both erupt in laughter, her hand on my knee. I want to kiss her so badly it hurts. Instead, I pull out my gun, remove the magazine, and set it on the ground between us.

"See that rock on the edge? It's your enemy."

Without hesitation she picks up the gun, loads the mag, chambers a round, and blows the rock off the side of the cliff. She hands the gun back to me in slow motion.

Now it's my turn to be speechless.

Finally, she gasps. "Did I…?"

I feel my smile creep back to my face. "Fuck yes you did."

She holds her hands out in front of her, staring at them. "I have never shot a gun in my life."

And I've never had this process go so well for me. She might not even need an adjustment period. "Think you could do it again?"

The furrow in her brow smooths and her eyes narrow, her confusion replaced by competitiveness. She takes the gun from me, aims, and blows another rock off the edge. Triumphant, she lowers the gun casually, like she's done it a million times.

"Do you feel any different?" I'm worried I lied to her when I explained this wouldn't change her as a person. Worried I did just turn her into a killer.

"Not at all. It feels so natural."

She hands the gun back to me. I stick it in the holster and we stand together. I search her face to make sure she's still the same person she was before we came up here. The wind stirs her hair, and she looks up at me curiously.

"You're afraid of me." Her smile fades. I can see this idea bothers her.

"No. I'm afraid *for* you. I didn't expect the change to be so severe."

She looks away, over the bluffs. When she turns back, her face has become playful again. "Didn't I tell you I am your biggest nightmare?"

A vision flashes in my mind of the night she said that to me. Those words are engraved on my core, triggering an explosion of desire in every nerve of my body. My ability to suppress it is missing in action. After all my mental exertion tonight, I have no strength left to fight.

"You shouldn't have said that." It's all I can manage. I close my eyes and reach for her. She's in my arms, drawing me down, her lips against mine. My head swims like I'm about to tumble head first down the side of this mountain. I breathe her in, taste the flavor of her tablet. Of what I've done to her.

She pulls away. I tighten my hold on her, but she places her fingers against my lips.

"We need to go back," she says. "Please. Let's go back."

A slave to her wishes, I pick up my bag, sling it across my shoulder, and take her hand.

CHAPTER 22

LIV

B Y T H E T I M E we get back to the house, I know he's about to collapse. What he did tonight exhausted him, and the long hike back to the house drained whatever he had left. Inside the door, I take his bag, and he falls onto the couch. I pull his arms out of his coat, pull off his boots, his hat, and his jeans. I cover him with the quilt and put a pillow under his head. From his deep and even breathing, I can tell he's already asleep when I turn off the light. I try not to think about what happened because if I do I'll never get to sleep. Despite trying to clear my mind, my body hums with excitement too strong to welcome easy slumber.

In the morning, my palms display proof it wasn't a dream—two round brown stains. As if the new knowledge swarming in my head isn't enough. Today is the day for experimentation, and thinking about what I can do already has me exhilarated. It's like waking up and remembering you have a brand new toy.

I sit on the edge of the couch next to him. "Trey? Can I wake you up?"

He doesn't even stir. I kiss his eyelids, his cheek, his lips. His breathing changes. I kiss his lips again. His hands come alive, searching clumsily, finding my hand, gripping their way up my arm until I am pulled down to him.

"Lay with me."

"Hell no. Get up." I try to wriggle free—a useless effort until he releases my arm. He could snap bones with that grip.

While he showers I pace around the house, tidying up, looking for something to occupy me. I heat up his breakfast, and when he joins me in the kitchen I try to sit still in my chair.

"What are we going to do today?" It's hard not to sound too anxious.

He shrugs. "I'm spent. Won't be very good company to you today."

Disappointment crushes me for about two seconds before my energy ramps back up again. I put on some coffee. He needs to wake up.

"I don't think you should have any more of that." He gives me a sleepy grin.

"I'm not. It's for you."

"If you have something you want to do today, don't let me hold you back."

"It wouldn't be the same without you."

He sighs. It's obvious he doesn't want to disappoint me. He leaves the room and comes back wearing his boots with the laces still untied. With the bucket of potatoes I dug up yesterday, he walks out past the garden. I watch him make a line of the potatoes across the backyard then he comes back inside and retrieves the gun we used last night.

"Practice." His eyes are tired.

"Do you have another nine millimeter?"

He gestures toward the basement stairs. "Help yourself."

I hop down the stairs and come back up with a second loaded nine millimeter and some ear protection. He's already outside on the deck, sipping his coffee. At the railing, I aim both guns and shoot down the line of potatoes two at a time until they are all pulp.

"Did I get them all?" I squint and shield my eyes from the sun. Maybe I missed a few. It's hard to see with the sun in my face.

He explodes in laughter.

I lower the ear protection and hang it around my neck. "What?"

"I've never seen anything like this. This is insane."

He goes inside and returns with an apple. He takes a gun from me, flings the apple into the yard, and shoots it out of the air.

"Okay good," he says. "Just making sure I still had it. You had me worried for a second."

"Worried that I took all your skills?"

"Yeah."

"Why don't you use guns against the people who come for you?"

He drops to his chair and stretches out his legs. "Too easy. There's no challenge. And I need the hand-to-hand combat to keep my skills sharp."

"Will you throw some things for me so I can shoot them like that?"

"We aren't going to have any food left to eat."

I wave a hand across the expanse of his healthy garden like a model on a game show.

"Can I finish my coffee first?"

I go back to the basement to look through his inventory. My hands are itching to try them all, but I settle for a small rifle. I find a compatible magazine and run back up the stairs and outside.

"You're ambidextrous," he says as I rejoin him. His hands are full of apples.

"No, I'm not."

"You shot with your left hand."

I shrug. "So?"

"So if you're not ambidextrous…" He watches me with a look I can't read. "You shouldn't have been able to do that."

Had I known I shouldn't have been able, maybe I wouldn't have tried. But the action felt natural to me. "Are you ambidextrous?"

"I trained myself to be." He continues studying me in that pointed way. "Guess I trained you, too."

He tilts his head toward the rifle. I raise it, aiming toward the yard. He flings an apple, I fire, and it explodes. He flings another, faster this time, and it explodes. He throws two, one right after the other.

"No fair!" I shoot and miss the first, quickly aim and hit the second one. I then go back to the first one and split it just before it hits the ground. "Ha!" I spin to look at him.

He is gaping at me, his mouth open wide.

"Nice try."

"I'm a *fucking* genius."

"You?" I laugh.

"Yes. I'm taking all the credit for this."

Trey says my next training requires new gear, so he drives us to a large sporting goods store near the highway. At the entrance, he pulls the door open for me and I walk directly into Shawn.

"Liv!" Shawn picks me up in his customary giant hug. "I was just thinking about you." He releases me and I take a glance at Trey, who looks like he just tasted something foul.

"Want to do dinner again tonight?" Shawn asks, oblivious of Trey standing behind me.

"Not tonight. Shawn, this is Trey. Trey, Shawn." I step aside, and Trey grabs Shawn's hand, a little more aggressively than necessary.

Shawn turns back to me. "Tomorrow night then. I'll see you after work." He flashes a huge smile to me, nods to Trey, and walks off to his car.

Trey snorts. I can tell he's seething. He's either very bad at hiding it, or he doesn't care that I know he's bothered by Shawn's attention. Maybe a little competition will give him a much needed ego check.

As we move through the store, he continues to fume. I try to make conversation but he's unresponsive and completely irritating. He doesn't own me. If I want to go to dinner with someone, it's none of his business. Maybe I need to make that clear.

"See if these fit you," he grumbles, shoving some boxing gloves toward me.

"You're the one who needs gloves." I try not to make it sound like an accusation.

"I have gloves. But we do need to get some for you."

"Why didn't you wear the gloves?" My voice rises in exasperation. He knows what I'm referring to.

He shrugs. "Didn't think about it."

I look up at him, at his deeply creased brow, his averted eyes. I'm reminded of the scowl that was a permanent fixture on his face when I first met him. The scowl that hasn't appeared in a long time. A reminder is all it takes. I don't want to tell him he doesn't own me. I don't want to tell him I'd go to dinner with another man.

"What's the matter?" I ask instead.

He looks at me but doesn't answer.

I put the gloves on and hold them up. He checks them to make sure they fit before gently taking them off me. I browse around while he looks at heavy bags, and when he's done he finds me.

"What size pants do you wear?"

"It depends. I'd really have to try them on."

He looks at my hand before he takes it in his. I sense an effort to the action, a sweetness to his grasp. I wonder if it's an apology. He leads me over to the military and hunting clothes and points to a display of multi-pocketed cargo pants. "You need a pair of these in black, and a pair in green. Make sure they fit snug. Do you have any close-fitting T-shirts in black or green?"

"Umm…" I try to think. He drops my hand, and I instantly miss the bond.

"Just get some new ones then. On me." There's a dimple in his forehead, a sheepish hang to his head.

I get to work finding my size, and he heads off to another part of the store. In the dressing room is a vent in the wall large enough for a person to climb through. Its metal cover is secured by screws. There would be no quick escape through there. No ambush possible, either. With those two thoughts comes another: Trey Bevan has warped me for sure.

I find him at the gun counter inspecting a Ruger LCP that I know he's buying for me.

"You can't buy me all this."

"Yes, I can." Stacking more stuff on the pile I'm already carrying, he points to some sturdy laced boots. "Grab a pair of those, too."

I shift my pile into his arms, get a pair of boots in my size, and follow him to the checkout, where his boxing bag is waiting for us. We take everything to the truck but he doesn't start the engine.

"He's just a friend, Trey. You don't need to get all bent about it."

He clutches the steering wheel and doesn't answer right away. When he does, it doesn't seem directed at me. "I'm such an ass."

"Let's just forget about it, okay?"

He has more to say, but he doesn't seem to be able to find the words. "I just... I didn't like..."

"Trey, please. Let's drop it."

"Guys like him..."

I put my face in my hands and groan. He seriously can't be this jealous, this possessive. We aren't exactly a couple. Are we?

"You don't even know him." As soon as it's out I wish I hadn't said it. It's only going to egg him on.

He looks at me, still struggling for words. Finally, he lets out an exasperated sigh and turns his whole body to face me. "I want you to be with *me*."

I stare at him, not knowing what to say. He can't just drop something like that on me without warning and expect a rational response.

"It's just, until things are sorted out, it...we...are going to be in limbo."

When I don't answer, he says, "You don't have to say anything. Just tell me you understand what I mean."

"I understand what you mean."

He turns away from me and starts the engine. I wonder if I should say more. Too many seconds pass and I feel like I've lost my chance. We drive home in silence, my brain feverish with unspoken words. It's impossible to express how I feel about him, how badly I want him, while still acknowledging his marriage, his family, and the fact that he may not even be mine to want.

When we pull up to the house, he gets out of the truck but I remain in my seat. He comes around to open my door for me, a question in his eyes.

I slide down from the truck and look up at him. "I understand what you mean, and I agree."

His face relaxes, and I can tell he aches to kiss me like I ache to kiss him. We lock eyes, daring each other to make the first move, until River bursts in between us.

"I'm no good at apologies," he says.

"I don't need one."

CHAPTER 23

TREY

AFTER I HANG the new heavy bag, I pop it a few times to test it out. Too lazy to find the gloves—and too exhausted to face Liv's wrath if I screw up my knuckles again—I go easy. And being honest, I'm more than exhausted. I collect the pieces of the old one and carry it upstairs.

"Another body to dispose of?" she asks when she sees me. "What do you do with them, anyway?"

"Family secret."

"I thought I was in on all the family secrets."

"Not all of them." This reminds me of the last thing I need to tell her. By the end of the day, I *will* tell her. I go through the shopping bags to find the fleece-lined winter gloves I bought her, and her face lights up as I hand them to her. It takes so little to make her happy.

"Why'd you come to the clinic that day after the crash? Why didn't that wound heal?"

I glance at her, surprised by the change of subject.

"I've been meaning to ask you that," she says.

"Just me being careless. Sometimes they don't have a chance to heal. Stitches can help."

"That cut I Steri-stripped at the clinic—you didn't get that when we crashed?"

I try to remember. I should probably keep track of when they come, of how many I kill, but I never thought it was important. "I don't think—"

Wait—that was the guy I was too lazy to meet outside and allowed to come into my house and use one of my own kitchen knives on me. "It was an old cut. It reopened in the crash." Once it finally comes back to me, I'm thankful for the reminder. I'll be dead before I allow myself to become that careless again. Speaking of being dead… "I hope you don't mind if I go to bed early."

She frowns as River stands up on the back door, hackles raised. This does not look good. I step outside with River, pulling the door closed behind me. It's just as I thought. Not good. I go back inside and plod downstairs for a revolver and my rifle with the night vision scope. Liv tenses as she realizes what's about to happen.

"There are three of them out there," I tell her on my way back outside with the rifle, after setting the revolver on the table. I scan the large ponderosa pine that hangs over the house and fire once midway up. Branches break under the weight of the falling body, and a dull thud announces its landing in the yard below.

I go back inside. "That was one of them." I lay the rifle on the table and put my hands on the back of the chair, bowing my head and closing my eyes. "God I'm so damn tired."

"What can I do?"

When I look up, I can't tell if her expression is panicked or excited. Maybe it's a combination. "Just stay inside." I stick the revolver in the back of my pants and go out the front door.

Come on, punks, let's get this over with so I can go to bed. I wait and listen. I move over to the garage for some cover. Motion on the roof of the house sends me sprinting back. He lands next to me and I throw my elbow into his throat. I grab his arm, twisting him to the ground, yanking the knife out of his hand as something hits me in the leg.

Cursing, I fall back and pull the blade out of my thigh. I push away the pain and replace it with rage. I shove myself up and lead them away from the house, away from her. Instantly, they are both on me. I twist, grabbing a throat, and throw him to the ground. The other one catches me in the same thigh with a knife. I hear a growl that must be me. I catch his wrist, break it and take the knife. I remember my gun but can't get to it. In a split second, I'm on my back on the ground. I jab the knife deep into a stomach, and he falls to the side so I flip to my feet. The remaining one kicks my wounded leg, and I fall again. I lunge for his legs, but he moves, and then he's on top of me.

A gunshot sounds from the house, catching him in his shoulder, spinning him, and I see my chance and land my fist in the back of his head. He slumps to the ground, unconscious. I roll away so she can finish him off, but she doesn't shoot. She's on the porch, her gun lowered. I limp back to the house.

"You're hurt."

"It's okay. You saved my ass, do you know that?"

She nods like her thoughts are somewhere else.

"He's not done though. You need to finish him off."

"I know." She hands me the gun. "I can't do it."

I take the gun from her, go out into the yard and put a lethal shot in each of them. She helps me back into the house and sits me down at the kitchen table.

"Really bad night for them to send three." I can barely hold my head up.

"Just give me a few minutes and you can lie down." She's already removed both my shoes and she's pulling off my pants. I put my head down on the table, thankful she's here to do this so I don't have to. I'm vaguely aware of her flushing the wound, and I hear her say, "They got you here twice." Then she makes me move so she can wrap it.

"Give me your hands." She wipes the blood off my hands and dries them. "Now sit up and look at me." I raise my head, and she wipes off my face and neck with a warm wet cloth. The cloth comes back red. I'm not sure if it's my blood or theirs.

"I'm putting you in the bed."

I'm too weak to complain. She leads me to the bedroom, pulls off my shirt, and I fall into bed. The covers stretch over me and the light goes off. She leaves the room and comes back to put a gun on the nightstand.

Sometime later, I awaken to her getting in bed with me. I turn toward her, take her in my arms, and fall into a dead sleep.

In the morning, I wake like I've been in another coma, like I've been washed up on the beach, healed by sun, massaged by waves. It's still early, so I lie in bed and savor the moment. I doze back to sleep and wake up again to her unwrapping my leg.

"How do you feel?" She's wearing one of my T-shirts. Her legs are bare.

"Better rested than I've been in a long time." I drag her into bed with me. Her back is smooth through the shirt. No bra. What's on bottom? I casually skim her hips with both hands. It feels like thin panties.

"You should have the doctor look at your leg. Will you come with me to the clinic?"

"It'll heal today. No worries."

"Please?"

I pull her to me, my lips to her ear. "I owe you big time. If you hadn't been here, I would've fallen asleep on the kitchen floor and bled to death." She smells like citrus. Like something I want to eat, to hold inside me. Although I'd rather be inside her.

"Oh, you wouldn't have bled to death—"

"I would've been dead out there. That makes two times you've saved my ass."

She pushes away. "But it was easy. You don't owe me."

"Yes I do. What do you want? Anything. Except for one thing." Other parts of my body oppose me, and I'm sure she can feel it.

She sighs. "How did I know you were going to say that?"

"Think of something you want. I won't be satisfied unless I can make it up to you."

She presses her lips together. Her eyes move to the side, then back to me. "Take me to dinner. With my gift certificate."

I laugh. "You can have anything, and that's what you want? You're going to have to think of something better."

I suddenly remember what I was supposed to tell her yesterday. Yesterday was my deadline and I missed it. But considering the circumstances, I'll allow myself one more day. I pull her against me and bury my face in her neck, grazing her perfect skin with my lips. Responsibility melts away with all this temptation so close.

She groans. "You are so bad… Oh you are so unfair…"

"Shh." I entertain the thought. Would it be so wrong? I roll, flipping her on top of me. Taking advantage of the new position, my hands slide around the backs of her legs, and I run my fingers along the inside of her thighs as they part on either side of me. She kisses me passionately, and I don't resist. A physical pain similar to drug withdrawal tears through me when she pulls away.

"More?" Her innocent expression is the worst kind of tease.

I pull her toward me and kiss her again. The pressure on my dick is just right. Too right. I grab her ass and press her against me. Two thin pieces of fabric separate us, but they could easily be gone. I feel the layers of my control peeling away, until only a sliver remains.

Yes. It would be wrong.

I lift her off and lay her back on the bed. She reaches for me, and I take her hands and hold them. "This is why I need to sleep on the couch."

She closes her eyes and her chest falls, letting all her breath out. "We need to get up anyway."

We get out of bed, and she flips down the quilt to reveal sheets smeared with blood. She starts stripping the bed. "I'm going to believe this is all your blood, not theirs. It's all over the pillowcases, too."

"It must have been in my hair." I run my hand through my hair to check it. Nothing. At least not anymore.

I take a quick shower, drawing the sound of the water deep into my ears, trying to center myself and regain control. It seems like such a pointless undertaking. As I step out of the tub, my thoughts spring back to her with a vindictive jolt. I towel off and notice my leg bleeding again. I throw on some clothes.

"You're going to have to take those right back off, buddy," she says, noticing my jeans when I join her in the kitchen. "Don't you *ever* shave?"

No time for shaving today. I catch her and kiss her hard. Her lips welcome mine, but when I slide my hands down her back to pick her up, she pushes me away.

After we eat she retrieves the bandages. I drop my pants to the floor, and she wraps my leg. "Does it hurt?"

"Not bad."

"Is that an honest answer or are you being macho?"

"Definitely being macho."

She hands me some ibuprofen and I exaggerate the act of taking them. I'm only taking them for her. Might as well make a show of it.

"Smartass," she says.

Her body beckons me again. Maybe I should just accept my failed willpower. Calming my hunger for her proves to be a wasted effort as soon as she's near me again. I already have a long list of sins, one more isn't going to make a difference, and adultery pales in comparison to the others. I run my finger along her cheekbone, remembering how it felt to be wrapped in her legs, controlled by her whim.

"Stop it. You're the one who keeps saying no." She ducks around me.

She disappears down the hall, and I forcibly block the image of what would happen if I followed her. I go outside and drag the two bodies into the woods so she doesn't have to see them on her way out. The one that fell from the tree is still there so I toss him in the woods too. All three of them left big messes, but there's nothing I can do about that now.

She comes outside dressed for work, and I walk her to her car. I can tell she's trying not to look. I watch her car roll away then clean up the best I can with my less than ideal mobility. I'm going to have to make a short day of it today. As I head to my first job, all I can think of is the heady scent of her neck. It leaves me wondering what I thought about every minute of every day before she came here.

I luck out on my job today—installing some electrical outlets in a new construction. When I finish, I make calls to the next two jobs and find out they aren't even ready for me. I sit in my truck, going through my notebook to find another small job to keep me occupied today. There's nothing. I call Wayne to see if he could use me. He tells me he just hired a new guy but if anything comes up he'll give me a call.

I hit the grocery store for food and first aid supplies. The amount of bandages I'm going through is a clear indication of how much they've boosted their offense. Fuck them.

They're just going to run out of guys faster this way, and I'll get a nice vacation until they stock up again. The cashier looks sideways at me as she rings up six boxes of bandages, and I suddenly feel a smile on my face, which I quickly drop. Maybe I should ask Liv if she can get me a pallet.

When I get home, I unwrap my leg to check the wound. Even I'm surprised how good it looks. I have a few hours to kill and the weather is perfect for a good run, which is probably too strenuous for freshly sealed skin. The guns need cleaning, but it's hard to imagine spending a day like today in the basement.

All of a sudden I think of the Ninja parked in the garage. It's been too long. I grab my riding jacket and go outside. It starts up like a beast, raring to be freed. I happily oblige.

The speed is intoxicating. I push the turns too far, daring myself to go faster. Each dangerous move feeds the next. And out of nowhere, the memory of that guy hugging Liv pops into my mind. I've got to do something about that guy.

CHAPTER 24

LIV

T HERE'S NO WAY I can smuggle anesthetic out, but I take some supplies for the things I can do at home. I know he won't come to the clinic if the wound opens again, so at-home care is what he's going to get. It's one of the many advantages of saving his life. He feels obligated to indulge my wishes. Well, *most* of my wishes. I hurry to get my bag, a physical thrill running through my body at the thought of seeing him soon. As I blast out the door, I hear my name.

Shawn is waiting to walk me to my car. "What's the rush?"

I'm unable to think of an answer that would please him. "You know I'm going to tell you no, right?"

"You don't know what I'm proposing yet."

I laugh. "I think I have an idea."

"It was a tease just seeing you for a minute yesterday. I need at least five. So tell me about your day."

"My day was great, except for the end when I got harassed in the parking lot by this weirdo." I try to remain straight-faced but fail.

"Sounds like you need a bodyguard. At all times. I'm pretty cheap…"

The hot whir of an engine coming closer drowns out our conversation. I see what's making the sound, but it takes a few seconds to hit me. Oh no.

Trey turns off the engine, removes his helmet, swings his leg over the motorcycle. Then he's coming toward us and I've had no time to break away. I look back at Shawn, who doesn't even realize. He brushes my hair out of my eyes, and I'm not fast enough to stop him. Oh *god* no.

"Shawn," Trey says, offering another aggressive handshake.

Shawn meets the handshake and seems to size Trey up for the first time.

"Ready for dinner?" Trey says to me.

"Oh hold on, she hasn't answered me yet," Shawn smiles his friendliest smile and crosses his arms on his chest.

I stare at both of them. Maybe I should just let them brawl it out. That's what it seems like they want. But I really don't want Shawn to get brutally murdered. With the two of them standing side by side, I notice they're both about the same size. Trey only has about an inch on Shawn. Trey has more muscle tone, Shawn carries more mass. They're probably matched in weight. But that's where their similarities end. Trey's dark expression is a harsh contrast to Shawn's light-hearted charm.

And comparing the bodies of fighters to determine the outcome must be another way I've been warped by Trey Bevan.

"How about I get some clubs and you can pretend you're cavemen?"

Neither one of them finds this funny, but I really didn't intend it to be. I glance between the two of them, waiting for someone to make the first mature move.

"I'm sorry. Liv and I already had plans," Trey says, seeming to sense my irritation. His sinister civility, coupled with the predator's stare trained on Shawn, raise a glaring red flag I refuse to acknowledge. This is beyond ridiculous. "I owe her dinner," he adds for my benefit. I'm sure he's hoping I won't blow his story.

Before I can control myself, I say, "We could do it another night."

"I might not be available another night."

Ooh. A threat. He should know better. "That would be a shame."

Shawn chuckles. "You two don't seem to be getting along anyway. Maybe it would be best if you just went on home." He's taken one step and turned in the slightest way, ending up facing Trey and blocking me out of the conversation at the same time.

Sounds around us muffle. Our air has become trapped in an invisible enclosure. Although Trey's made no sign he heard the taunt, I see his muscles become rigid and his eyes fill with violence. His intentions were clear before, but now they have been set in motion. All my hostility toward Trey's behavior is pushed aside by my fear for Shawn.

I step between them, facing Shawn. "I'm afraid I did already promise Trey." I take Shawn's arm and walk him toward his truck. I need to get him away from Trey, and I don't want him to have to stand there, rejected, watching Trey and me leave together.

I realize my mistake when we reach his truck and he gives me a long, drawn out hug. In my ear, he says, "You know you'd have more fun with me than with that guy." He kisses my cheek.

Trey revs his engine across the parking lot.

"Get in." I shove him toward his truck.

I walk back to Trey and get in my car. Since he's already on the motorcycle, I assume I'm following him, so I wait for Shawn to leave then start my car. Trey peels out and I follow him, but it's impossible to keep up. I'm not opposed to going a little over the speed limit, but the speed he's pushing isn't possible on these roads in my car. Every time I lose him, I catch up to him waiting for me on the side of the road. I don't know what he's trying to prove, but this is absurd.

We arrive and park. He comes over to my car with his helmet in his hand, and I glare at him as he opens my car door for me. He throws his helmet into my seat and shuts the door.

"Are you happy?" I hope he hears the sarcasm.

"Yep."

He knows what I mean. He makes no attempt to hide the victory in his eyes.

"So you're okay with being a troglodyte?"

He laughs. "That's a little harsh, don't you think?"

"It's very fitting, actually." My mood is already being altered by the effect we have on one another. My hostility turns to flirtation right before my eyes. It takes my conscious mind a few minutes to catch up and realize I'm not actually mad any more.

He laughs again. "I missed you."

We sit at our table and I look at the menu. He just looks at me. I try to ignore him.

"How's your leg?" I ask him into my menu.

"Fine. Just like I said."

I lower my menu to look at him. "For some reason I don't trust you. You have no sense of self-preservation. What was up with the driving, anyway?"

The server comes with water. Trey orders a scotch.

"So now you don't like my driving?"

"It's not that I don't like your driving. It's just when you're leading another car, you should try to keep it to a speed their vehicle can handle."

"I knew you'd catch up. I can't go slow on that thing."

"You didn't need to go slow. But how about a speed that showed a little responsibility for your health?"

He leans forward. "You know my health is relative."

"That's no excuse."

"Sure it is. I have nothing to lose."

"You have a lot to lose. What if you lost an arm? Would it grow back?"

He ponders that a moment. "I'm not worried. It would never happen anyway, not with my driving ability." He tilts his chin in the air and rubs his knuckles along his lips.

He did look like a professional stunt driver, but I'll never admit that to him, especially not now when he looks so smug. His machismo doesn't need any encouragement. "How did you learn how to drive like that?" I poke an ice cube, trying to make the question appear nonchalant.

His scotch appears in front of him. He takes a long drink. "Easy. When you don't have the fear of death in your mind, you're a lot more willing to try things. Push limits. Do the extreme. And then you get good. Everyone could drive like that, but most people don't ever try."

"Because they're afraid to die."

"Exactly. It's a limitation. On living." His eyes have a glint they've never had before.

For some reason I think he'd be like this, immortality or not. "Were you like this before you knew...?"

"To a degree." He drains the scotch and scans the room for our server.

"If you have another one, I'm going to take advantage of you." I rest my chin on my fist and watch his face, waiting for him to respond.

He meets my eyes with a look that returns full-on seduction so powerful I can practically feel his hands all over my body. If it's just in play, I wouldn't have this body tingle that could bring me to the floor. He has me so charged I'm afraid to touch something metal.

"When can we do the beach again?"

He groans. "I need time to recuperate. It kind of kicks my ass, in case you haven't noticed."

"So we can do it again?"

His eyes focus past me and move around the room as if he's trying to gather his thoughts, but in the end, he says nothing.

"What are you thinking?" He's not getting off that easy.

"Nothing really. I'm just…surprised. By all of this. Who the hell knew. I—" He stares at me intensely for a few moments.

"I, what? You didn't finish. Please finish." I wish our brains could be linked right now.

"I…would've never believed this, if someone had told me it was going to happen. Yet here it is, happening."

I get the impression he's editing himself. Like he's saying what he feels, just not *exactly* what he feels. Either the thoughts are in there and he can't find the words to explain, or he's got them on lockdown. I find myself reaching across the table for him. I want him to trust me. He takes my hand and turns it over to kiss my palm where the mark still dyes my skin. The contact has the strength of an electric jolt—we're the charged particles and his lips are the ground. His grip on my hand tightens as if he's preparing to jerk me across the table into his lap. When he raises his eyes to me I can see the familiar look. He feels it too.

"I'm afraid I have some bad news. I don't have my gift certificate with me."

He holds up his finger, reaches into his back pocket, and drops the gift certificate on the table between us. "Wouldn't be fulfilling your wish without it."

Part of me is sad to see it go. Without it, I won't have an excuse to go out to dinner with him again. "Can we do this again?"

"No. This is it, so you better enjoy it."

"I guess I'll just have to save your life again then."

"I'm counting on it. I plan on driving into a tree on the way home."

"So let's see. You're jealous, reckless, *and* a smartass. Unless I'm forgetting something?" I put my forearms on the table and lean toward him.

He focuses on my mouth, licks the middle of his bottom lip, and looks back up to my eyes. "You forgot vengeful."

"Oh yes, how could I forget vengeful? It's the whole reason for your existence." I laugh and lean back against my seat.

"Should we move on to you? Let's see—"

Our server appears with the bill. Trey hands it straight back with the gift certificate, drops a tip on the table, and stands. "There's a tree out there with my name on it."

Outside, the temperature has dropped several degrees, and the wet mist that developed while we were inside curls my hair. I feel his jacket go around my shoulders and I hold it closed, savoring the smell of him. I unlock my car, and he retrieves his helmet. I pass him his jacket but he puts up his hand to refuse it.

"You're going to freeze in this air. Take it." I push it against his chest and let go. He catches it without effort.

He mounts his bike and blasts ahead of me, the tires slipping on the wet pavement.

"Please be careful," I say to him, although I know he can't hear me. He drives slowly enough for me to keep up until we reach a familiar road, then he shoots away from me, his headlight bobbing under the powerful engine. As he disappears around the corner, his tires slip out from under him but he corrects it and speeds away. I swallow a lump of worry and take my time getting home. I picked the wrong guy to hang out with if I can't handle a little anxiety now and then.

CHAPTER 25

TREY

I GET HOME IN time to get a fire started before she arrives. When she walks into the room, her hair looks different, lush, a little wild. I reach out to take a strand in my fingers.

I'm not going to last. My armor of control is paper thin. We need to go to Virginia and get this over with so I can put Kate behind me. Then there's Aaron—he needs to come live with me, away from them and their lies. He's a young man now and can make the decision for himself. Although he's probably just like them. He's lived his whole life with Kate, if not with them then around them enough to absorb it all.

But so did I.

"How would you feel about living with a teenager?" I ask her before I lose the inspiration. There's no way to know how much of their influence he's had, but I know they've had a tight leash on him. They'd never have allowed my son to grow up free.

"What do you mean?"

"If I can convince my son to come home with us. You okay with that?"

She lays her hand on my arm. "I'd be more than pleased to help you bring your son home."

"Space would be tight. We could build an extension, or finish the basement or something."

She searches my face, and I wonder if she's reconsidering. "There's always my house. I could move back—"

"By yourself? That's not safe. We'll make it work."

"You don't want to see what happens with your wife?"

"Nothing could change my mind. She's out of my life." I squeeze both thumbs in each of my fists. Any harder and I'd break them. It's not hard enough.

She sits on the couch. "I don't think it's fair to you to make any plans until you see her."

"Doesn't matter. I'm ready for all of it to be over. We need to test your sparring." I sit on the couch next to her. Now. I have to do it now. "I need to explain something to you."

She sits up straight, obviously sensing something is up. "Good or bad?"

Now there's a question. With a different answer for each angle you look at it. "That'll be your call." Because there is no answer that simple. "Remember what I told you about my family's prophecy? The one about me?"

She closes her eyes to think for a moment. "Yes. Your heir will destroy them."

"There's more to it than that." I pause to collect the words. "The exact prophecy says, 'The Alignment of the Two will create the Catalyst to our Destruction.'"

"That's in one of your books?"

I pause to remember. Those exact words—have I seen them in writing? "Some of our knowledge is passed verbally."

"And you believe it?" She says this gently, as if treading unknown ground.

There's no way to explain the weight of knowledge shared among my kind. Yes, I believe. It lives in our common blood, our magic, our connection between earth, flesh, and stars. A betrayal of that is unthinkable. "I do. And they believe—they *know*—the Catalyst is my heir."

"How do they prove that?"

"My bloodline. That part is in the books. So let's say we believe their prophecy. Let's say we believe the Catalyst is my heir. That leaves the Alignment." I wonder if there's a gentler way to put it. Decide it doesn't matter. "The Alignment is you and me."

She doesn't speak, and she doesn't look away. She merely watches me, as if I'm still talking.

"I wasn't certain of it until the other night on the bluff."

She makes no sign she understands.

"The beach," I clarify.

"That's...interesting," she says, still watching me.

She wants more of an explanation, but I've got nothing I could put into words. Maybe I should have rehearsed this.

"I just thought you needed to know." I stand, not sure what else to do with myself. I step toward the door, desperate for the cool outside air.

"Wait."

I turn to face her.

"So…" She speaks slowly, thoughtfully. "The heir, the one they're worried about, was never your son at all. That's why he's alive. That's why you're still immortal. They're waiting for a specific heir." She swallows. "An heir coming from you and a different woman."

"Yes." My blood races through my veins as if this moment needs some physical action. Some proof of my words.

"Me."

"Yes," I repeat, crossing the room to put space between us. The two of us—it's a power I cannot fight.

"And it could have already happened," she whispers, almost to herself.

"Yes." My pulse is heavy in my neck.

She goes into the bedroom and shuts the door. I fall into the chair, lean my head back and close my eyes, listening to the rhythm of my breathing, the rhythm of my heart, gradually decreasing both until I feel calm. I stare at the wood in the ceiling and analyze every knot.

Finally, she comes out of the bedroom and stands in front of me. Now that the story is out, our connection, our desire, is an unstoppable force, a tangible object hovering in the room with us. Impatient and undisciplined. Eager to exploit its freedom.

"How do you know it's me?"

It's a struggle to hear her over the static in my mind, the pulsing of my blood, the frenzy of my heart. I stand and walk past her into the kitchen and take a drink of scotch from the bottle. She enters the kitchen on my third belt.

"I looked it up," I say. "The night I fell, certain stars and planets aligned exactly how the prophecy said they would."

"So that's what they mean by Alignment." Her calm can't be shaken. I could tell her the world is ending and she wouldn't even flinch.

"Partially. It also refers to our alignment. It references the text that explains the human magnetism. And when I was in your mind, I just knew." Should I shut up? Should I go on? "This whole time I thought it was me and Kate. But Kate and I...Kate has *nothing* on this."

I take another drink and she steals the bottle from me and sets it on the counter behind her. I already know what she's going to say.

"So it's inevitable?"

"Nothing is inevitable. We just have to control ourselves."

She looks out the window. "What if it already happened?"

"Then we have a war on our hands. They won't give up until they destroy...you think it's bad now?" I laugh bitterly. "They'll send an army. We'll have to leave, and live on the run."

"I could always..." She clears her throat. "We have options. With all this danger—"

"Options?" Then I realize what she means. The threat of my family will not force her decisions. I shouldn't have scared her. I need to think before I open my mouth. "Let them try to get to us. I'll kill every last one."

"But if it did already happen, that means they can kill *you* now."

I'm at a loss. I don't know what to say. "It didn't happen. Everything's fine."

Her eyes lower and settle on my thigh. I can prove it didn't happen. I can show her my healed wound. I unbutton and unzip my jeans and they drop to the floor.

She gasps, and I look down.

Ribbons of flesh lie open and exposed; the entire length of my leg is red and running with blood. I can't believe I didn't notice this. I pick up my pants and sure enough, there's a large stain of blood, but it's not obvious on my dark jeans.

Liv's hands are covering her mouth, and her eyes are full of too many emotions to read.

"It means nothing. I was too careless on the Ninja and reopened the wound." I step toward her and grab her shoulders, leaning down to her level. "This happens all the time. It just needs stitches. I'll sew it up right now and it'll be healed by the morning."

"It's been too long for stitches. I'll pack it and wrap it. It will give me something else to think about."

She leaves to get the bandages and I wet some paper towels and start wiping off the blood. My sock is saturated too. She returns and puts the kettle on the stove. I take the bottle of scotch and sit at the table.

"You're going to kill yourself with that stuff." She shakes her head weakly. Drained. Missing her spark. She cleans the wound and holds a bandage over it, waiting for it to stop bleeding. When she releases the pressure, no blood comes. "There are two cuts here. I'm going to have to do them both."

"Have at it."

She looks at me. "I have no anesthetic."

"Won't be the first time."

She starts ripping a pillowcase into strips. "Don't look at me like that. This is what we use when we have no gauze. You need to buy some gauze." She goes for the kettle. "And a new pillowcase."

I've never had open wounds packed with pieces of pillowcase but when she's finished and wrapping my leg I decide next time I should opt for bleeding to death.

"Not a peep. I'm impressed." She seems happier. Torturing me must improve her mood.

"I have a high tolerance for pain. Goes with the lifestyle."

She sighs. "I'm not going to worry. I'm putting it out of my mind."

"Good." Relief swells inside me.

"But tomorrow morning, we're pulling off that bandage, and it better look pristine."

"It will." I give her my most confident nod.

"I'm holding you to that." She begins to clean up and I get up to help her. "Can you please just sit, tough guy? For the rest of the evening? For me?"

It would be nice to keep myself busy, but it's hard to say no to her. I pick up the newspaper and lie down on the couch, but soon drop it on the floor next to me. I try to plan our strategy but quickly get lost in a maze of my own thoughts. Things have gotten too complicated. An asskicking run would put everything in place right now, but I'm sure she'd kill me.

She lifts my feet and sits underneath them on the end of the couch.

"Can you get some time off work?" I say.

"I'm sure I can."

Without warning, Shawn pops in my head, and I start to think of different ways I could kill him. With my bare hands. A weapon would make it too easy. She'd be mad at me, though, and I don't want that. I wonder if I could get away with it without her knowing, but I don't want to lie to her either. The thought of lying to her makes me feel physically sick.

"What are you thinking about?" Her question interrupts my thoughts like a twenty-man ambush.

"Nothing important."

"You look like you're about to spring off the couch."

I lean back, making an effort to relax. "We'll leave this weekend. Fly to Richmond, pick up a car." This is a perfect excuse to waste some money. "It's a couple hours from there. We can get a room somewhere for the night. The next day, we'll pay our visit."

"I'm not killing anyone," she blurts out. "I just—"

"You won't need to. I'll take the lead, and you'll cover me. You're not opposed to me killing anyone, are you?"

She pulls her knees up, hugging them to her chest. "It's a little late to be asking me that now."

"Our strategy is purely defense. It won't be like the last time I was there. Although that's what they'll expect as soon as they see me."

"What will they expect?"

"Another killing spree. This time I just want some answers. I want to talk to my son. And when I'm finished, we'll leave. No harm done."

"But if Aaron decides to come with you…"

"Then it's hard to know how they'll react. We'll just have to be ready for anything."

CHAPTER 26

LIV

A POWERFUL THOUGHT WAKES me in the middle of the night. Rapid healing and a packed wound probably don't go well together. I need to get that home-made gauze out of his leg now. When I open the bedroom door, I see a light on in the living room.

He's beaten me by about thirty seconds—he's sitting up unwrapping his leg. We must be on the same dream wavelength.

He glances at me. "This is the most uncomfortable shit I've ever—"

"Just let me do it."

He falls back on the couch. He's snoring before I'm finished. What results is a healthy wound and fresh bandage, but we're not in the clear yet.

I wake again but this time it's morning. Too early to get up, but too late for my curiosity. I tiptoe down the hall. I have to see his leg.

How strange I'm using a man's healing wound as my own pregnancy test.

I kneel on the floor next to the couch and gently start working at the corner of the bandage, trying not to tug his skin. He jolts upright, scanning the room fiercely, poised to leap into action.

"Oh—sorry!" I whisper. Regular speaking volume doesn't seem appropriate in the dim light of early morning.

He slams both hands onto his head and leans back. "Shit, Liv. You—"

"I couldn't wait any longer. I have to see. Just go back to sleep."

"Too late. I'm up now."

"No you're not. Close your eyes and stop talking."

I start working at the bandage again. He reaches down and roughly rips it off. I cringe with the sound of dried blood tearing out hair at the root. I squint at the wound. "I have to turn on the light."

"You're really pushing it," he grumbles.

I flip on the light, and he covers his face with his arms. I sit on the edge of the couch.

"It's perfect." The ripped flesh of yesterday has been transformed into a closed, clean pink seal.

"Didn't I tell you it would be?" he says into his arms. "Turn off the light and come back here."

"Why?" I eye him.

"I have to ask you something."

I get up and flip off the light, returning the faint early morning haze to the room. As soon as I'm within reach, he pulls me on top of him and rolls so I'm pinned between him and the back of the couch. His lips touch my ear and brush along my cheek to the corner of my mouth.

"I thought you wanted to ask me something."

"I changed my mind," he says against my cheek, a tease in his voice.

I snuggle into him and sense his restraint. He is working hard to be good. I could make it much more difficult, but I decide not to. This is just too nice.

He slides his hand between my body and the couch, running it down my backbone to the small of my back where it hesitates before planting itself firmly against my skin and pressing me against him. My heart thuds, swollen and hot. He's making it a challenge for me to uphold my decision, but I know if I don't, he will end this now. This intimacy, this pleasure, will end if I make the slightest reaction.

I'm only able to relax when I feel his body surrender to sleep. We doze together until I hear the alarm clock going off in the bedroom.

"I have to get up." The statement is futile. His warm skin has fused to mine. I could die here, completely content.

"I know, I do too. Do you have any idea how bad I want you right now?"

My desire for him surges. "Do you have any idea how bad I want *you* right now?"

"You're not supposed to agree. You're making it worse." He untangles his body from mine.

I struggle to keep my arms from reaching for him, knowing it would cross the border into territory we've just managed to avoid. With no help from him. He must like to push things. But why? To flex his control over his life, or to torture himself?

"You still have to take it easy today, okay?" I say when we meet again in the kitchen.

He leans down to pull on his boots. "Come straight home after work."

"Excuse me?" I laugh. "That's a little controlling, don't you think?"

His head snaps up at me. I wasn't referring to anything specific, but from his expression I can see he thinks I was.

"Oh come on, Trey."

"You're going to get that guy killed."

"Me?"

"Yes." It's so deadpan it can only be serious.

"You have a real problem."

He stands and pulls on his clean shirt. I gather my lunch from the fridge, and when I turn back around, he's still standing in the same spot, his eyes far away, watching something play out in his mind.

"You okay?"

He fills a thermos with coffee and takes his jacket off the back of the chair. Pausing in the doorway, he turns to me and says, "Home after work," and leaves before I can respond.

The day's pace is steady. There's enough to keep me busy, but not enough to keep me from thinking about what Trey's planned for tonight. At the end of my shift, I'm running a little late. I catch a glimpse of Shawn talking to Rachel at the front desk, so I grab my things and slip out the back. It's just…complicated.

My gas tank is low but I can't waste the time. If he's not home when I get there, I'll have to reorganize the whole house just to stay occupied until I can see him.

But it's not his driveway I end up on. It's mine.

The charred corpse of my jeans is a dark blemish on the gravel. I drive toward it. My tires thump hard over something in my path. I can't remember how I got here. I don't recall taking the turn after the bridge, but here I am as if there's something I need. The note is gone, the jeans no longer recognizable. There isn't anything else for me to destroy.

I park and walk behind the car to investigate the bump in the driveway—a line of rocks placed about a foot apart. I follow them into the front yard and down the side of the house where the line continues around the back and up the opposite side. It's a perfectly rounded circle.

Perhaps I shouldn't, but it's too late—I've already picked up the rock near my shoe. I turn it over like I know what I'll see. On one side is an engraved design of a circle with a triangle in the middle, its three sides concave as if being pulled toward the center. The others have the same motif, although slightly irregular. Crudely carved by a human, not a machine.

This must be Trey's doing, and it must have taken days unless he keeps a stock of these in that basement of his. I return the rocks to their positions and when I look up, there's an audience of five coyotes about twenty feet away.

All eyes trained on me, and no River to be our liaison. Time for me to leave. Whatever drew me here will have to wait.

I try to go the speed limit on the way to Trey's house, but my foot keeps pressing the gas harder all on its own. The sight of his truck produces a tug in my belly and a gush in my chest. If I was hooked to a monitor my heart rate would give me away. God, I'm so in love with this guy.

He's out back, taking dried herbs from the eaves.

"Were you at my house?"

He doesn't look at me. "You shouldn't go back there alone."

"Those coyotes—"

"They won't hurt you. Come inside."

In the kitchen, he sets his herbs on the counter and I follow him into the living room, where he dumps a shopping bag out on the couch. "You need to get geared up so you can get used to the feel of it."

I head to the bedroom and put on the clothes we bought together—black cargo pants, black tee, boots. While I'm gathering my hair in a tight ponytail, he joins me to change into his own matching battle uniform. I try not to watch him in the mirror as I pin my bangs to the side.

Back in the living room, we sift through the pile of gear on the couch. I find two sets of drop-leg holsters. How I recognize them in the jumble is a real surprise. Beside me, he holsters two guns like he's gone through the motions a hundred times.

"None of these are loaded. I don't want any more bullets in me. But with this, you'll have to be careful." He lifts my foot onto the couch, slides my pant leg up, and fastens a sheathed knife at my ankle.

Once it's secure, I draw the knife. It's a double-edged dagger with a shiny steel blade and a marble handle.

"This is too beautiful to be a weapon. I hope you didn't buy this just for me." I turn it over in my hand and see the initials L. G. engraved on the blade. My breath turns my chest raw, threatening to breach the cry zone. There are no tears in my eyes when I look at him so I swallow hard, hoping they'll stay back.

"Sorry I didn't know your middle name," he says, dropping his eyes.

Suddenly *I* don't know my middle name.

He takes it out of my hand and sheathes it back on my ankle. "Let's go." He crosses the room, expecting me to follow. "No jackets. It'll be chilly at first but we'll warm up."

Outside, my muscles seize in the cold.

"No rules. Just try to kill me before I kill you." He sprints around the house out of sight.

He can't be serious. I hug myself, trying to conserve the little body heat I have, and begin analyzing ways I could hide. If I could reach the woods without him seeing me, I could use the cover of the trees to get around the house. But he may not be back there anymore.

I sense movement to my right, and I instinctively crouch. Still under the cover of the porch, I know I'm out of his sight. I sneak away from the house. There's a shuffle on the roof. I spin to face it, drawing my Glock as he appears on the roof above me, aiming his gun my chest.

"You're dead." He holsters his gun. "You didn't even leave."

"Nope. Just waiting for you."

He flips off the roof, and I take off for the woods. I hear one hard thud of his boots against earth followed by pounding footsteps, faster than mine. Pushing more power to my legs, I crash through underbrush. Stealth won't help me—I need speed. My good head start is being devoured by his extra-long legs and machine-gun power. I run toward a large fallen tree and as I get near it I leap over, throwing my legs out sideways as my body aligns itself against the side of the tree and the ground. When he comes over the log, I'm aiming right at his head.

"Shit!" He offers his hand. I wait for him to soften his expression before I take it. He pulls me up. I holster my weapon. Our mutual stare becomes a standoff. As soon as he moves, I jump, avoiding his leg as he tries to knock my own legs out from under me.

"Hey!"

"Don't worry, I was going to catch you." He grins. "But I didn't need to."

He moves again, lightning fast, grabbing me and turning me around in one smooth, unstoppable motion. His index finger mimics the slicing of my throat from artery to artery as if it were a knife.

"Sorry," he whispers in my ear. Mocking me only puts him in worse danger.

His clutch eases, and I know he's about to turn me to face him. But as he does, he starts a step sideways which throws off his balance. I take hold of his arm and crouch, pulling downward with all my strength to flip him over my back. I roll aside just before he lands flat on his back, cursing.

"Oh my *god!*" I fall to his side. It worked too well. I don't want to give him head trauma. He's had enough of that lately.

"Perfect. Time for me to up my game." He gently taps my chin with a boxer's right. "It's going to take a lot more than that to hurt me."

Before the words have settled he's up and sprinting toward the house. The man is fast. And that cute little punch? Distraction. It's like all this is programmed into him so well even *he* isn't aware of what he's about to do.

I follow him almost to the edge of the woods, taking my time to keep my footsteps light. When I get to the last row of trees, I don't move until the wind blows, then I take as many steps as I can while the rustling trees mask my tread. Once I'm high enough to have a good view, I survey the yard, taking notice of all the normal shadows and shapes so when something looks out of the ordinary, I will know.

A shadow flashes along the wall of the garage. With no way for me to get to him undetected, I maneuver down the slope the same way as before, only moving when the wind blows. The house is now only a quick sprint away. He has moved to the corner of the garage—running now would put me right in his view. I pick up a branch and throw it as far up the slope as I can. When I hear it hit the ground, I run for the house, along the side and across the back. I peek around the corner. He's sprinting to the front of the house. I sneak around the side toward the front, hesitating at the corner. I've lost my hold on him.

All of a sudden he's behind me. I dodge, and he catches my arm, so I twist my core, breaking his grasp. His body comes down on me. As my back hits the ground his arms come down on either side of me like fence posts, bracing his fall, protecting me from his falling body weight. All motion stops. I stare into his eyes. The rhythm of our rapid breathing is the only sound.

We both look down at the same time to see my dagger drawn and pointed directly at his heart. He looks as surprised as I feel.

It's too much to process right now, beneath the heated power of his body lowering against me, caught in his gaze. All I can do is lay my dagger beside us. Reach up for him with my free hand. He takes my wrist and holds it against the ground. I start to move the other arm but he's predicted it and pins it along with the other, dagger and all.

I open my mouth, astonished to be at his mercy. I withdrew too soon. He doesn't even try to control his winner's grin. I lower my eyes to his lips, daring him to kiss me. At his mercy sounds like a great place to be.

He cannot resist.

A wave of heat runs the length of me as his lips meet mine. I move against the pressure of his body, unable to cling to him with my arms still pinned. He frees my wrists, and I wrap my arms around his neck, pulling myself closer. His lips become more urgent against mine and it's just like that night. We've no option but to do this. It has to be.

One jarring heave breaks my arms from his neck and pulls him away. He rises to his knees, then to the balls of his feet. There's a universe of space between us and it's cold. Unnatural. Wrong. He leans his head back, facing the starry sky, breathing hard. He looks back down at me, intent but pleading, like he wants to be talked out of something. Like he's just made some painful decision he doesn't want to live with.

I'm afraid to move. I know we set rules but I refuse to be the one to shatter this moment.

He picks up the dagger and pulls me up with him to a standing position. He brusquely takes me in the house and closes me in the bedroom by myself. Thirty seconds later he returns to put a gun on the nightstand. "This one's loaded. You can protect yourself. I'm going to run this off. Listen for River."

In the quiet that follows I remember the tip of my dagger so close to his chest. That surprise on his face proves he hadn't predicted my move. His instinct to protect me was the only thing that saved him. He said I wouldn't become a killer? Well, my new reflexes seem to disagree. I trust this man I barely know, but can I still trust myself?

CHAPTER 27

TREY

AFTER A LONG night trying—and failing—to find composure in the woods and a couple restless hours of crappy sleep on the couch, I decide to make better use of my time. There's something in my books downstairs that can ease this torment until I settle things in Virginia, since I can't seem to keep my hands off Liv on my own. It's an easy preparation—even on little to no rest—and I'm back in the kitchen at a normal morning hour like I hadn't been screwing around all night.

Liv joins me just as I'm putting the coffee on, her bangs smashed on one side like she slept hard all night. As she reaches past me for a mug, I see her elbow scraped deep, and the length of her forearm darkly bruised.

She notices me looking. "Yeah, pretty bad, right?"

I know how I could fix this, but it's not an option.

"Do you want to see the one on my leg?" She pulls the robe up her leg.

I turn my back to her. I don't want to see her body wounded, and it's better if I don't see any more of her bare skin. The combination of the two could easily divide and conquer me. They both have a very valid reason for me to take her to bed right now. I won't allow my will to be broken a second time. "No more fooling around. I'm putting an end to it. It's getting out of hand."

"I never mean to do anything. I just have no control over it."

"Me neither. Until now. I made these last night." I pick up the plastic bag of capsules and shake it.

"What is it?" She takes the bag from me for a closer look.

"Liv Gilchrist repellent."

Worry clouds her face. "What do you—it's going to make it like it was before?"

"It's just supposed to suppress desire. Calm lust. I'm taking two a day, a double dose. Just for a while."

"I feel like I should tell you something. It's kind of a weird thing…"

"Weird is relative." I did just craft some weird shit in my basement after all.

"I got pregnant while I was on the pill."

I can't hold back my bitter laughter. "That's great. 'Cause I can get women pregnant with the pill and a rubber."

"What?" She puts a hand to her smashed bangs like I've just broken her brain.

I've been a prisoner to this prophecy my whole life and now she is too. We can't be together yet it drew us to the same damn intersection in the same damn town, like some sadistic dare. They forbid me from fulfilling their prophecy while setting me up so I will. And once I do, they'll end me and tell me it's my fault.

"I know how to keep track of my cycles. I guess you don't have anything you could mix up downstairs?"

"I'd have no idea what I was doing." I wonder if my mother… Maybe she could talk to my mother about that.

"It's just a few days a month you have to abstain. The only problem is it's not one hundred percent safe."

"That's kind of a big problem." It's a deathwish for both of us. I'm quick to blame them, but if they are behind this, they have it backwards. It would be a big disadvantage to them to affect both of us with a problem like this. It could be a coincidence. A fucking unfortunate coincidence. But it fits pretty well into my life.

"What's the matter?"

"Nothing." I get up and take a shower. When I get out, she's pulling on her jacket. Nothing about the action should remind me of what it felt like to be wrapped in her legs, but it does. I wonder how many of those capsules I could take before poisoning myself.

I sit on the couch to put on my boots, and she asks, "Do you want me to examine your leg?"

"I already did."

"How does it look?"

"Fine."

She lingers in the entryway. "You sound angry."

"I'm not." Not any angrier than usual. "Let me walk you out." I feel like I need to say something but I'm not sure what.

I grab my jacket, and we walk outside together into the chilly morning air. A giant flock of rosy-finches is camping out in a nearby aspen, so I click my tongue to move them on their way. They're curious about her. But they make such a mess. The sound of so many flapping wings taking flight is almost deafening. They seem early this year.

"You can talk to birds too?"

"Birds don't talk."

She stops to glance at me before getting in her car. I couldn't guess what she's thinking. In my truck, I follow her up the driveway to the road where we turn in opposite directions.

I check in at Wayne's work site to see how it's going, but he still can't use me so I don't stay long. It looks like I have no work today either. I spend the morning running errands and buying things for our trip.

After lunch, I opt for a haircut. It's long overdue, and I finally have the motivation to drag my ass into town to do it. I take a magazine to the chair so the stylist doesn't think she needs to talk to me. She does anyway. She is relentless. I do my best to ignore her, but by the time I'm paying I feel like I need to punch something. I decide to go straight home before I do.

At home, I mow and clean up the yard and do some work in the garden. As I'm heading into the house to take a shower, my phone buzzes in my pocket. I dig it out, and the display shows an unfamiliar number with a Chicago area code. It has to be her. She never calls me.

"What's wrong?" I answer.

"Trey." Her voice is too calm.

"What!"

"There's an unfamiliar gray car parked near mine. The windows are tinted so I can't see inside. And I think it's idling."

"At the clinic? Stay inside. I'll be right there." I rush into the living room and grab the Glock which I stick in the back of my jeans.

The front wheel of the Ninja lifts off the ground as I blast out of the garage, gravel flying. My pace is crippled by the turns in the road, but as soon as I hit the straight stretch I'm well over one hundred miles per hour. A red light tries to slow me down, so I ride the shoulder past the line of cars. I don't need a big gap in traffic to make it. I'm already far past the intersection when I hear someone honk their horn at me. People are so damn self-righteous.

I turn into the parking lot and see no sign of the car. I circle toward the entrance. Liv comes outside with Shawn behind her.

"Which way?" I ask.

She points. I turn back out on the road and continue in the direction I was going. The engine growls as I rip through the gears to get the bike back up to speed. There are too many intersections, too many turns, too many options. When I remember Shawn standing behind her, I give up and head back.

They're standing by her car when I return, and I can hear her bright laugh all the way across the parking lot. I pull up near them and take off my helmet.

"Looks like your escort is here," Shawn says, leaning down to kiss her cheek.

He just insists on pushing me. I kill the engine and start to dismount. She's already starting her car. I can't let her go home by herself, but I can't leave without dealing with him. He asks for it every time I see him and it's time to shut him down. He watches me, his arms crossed on his chest, and I glance at her car to see it turning onto the road. Screw it. I put on my helmet and peel out. There will be a next time.

I pass a few cars illegally until I'm directly behind her. She seems to be driving slowly on purpose to keep me from going too fast.

"You need to carry a gun," I tell her as soon as she's out of her car at home.

She's taking me in like I've changed more than my hair. I run a hand over my head—yep, I could join the military. "You hear me?"

"Trey, I cannot carry a gun with me to work every day."

"You can conceal it."

She gives me a long look, this time more annoyed than distracted. I take the gun out of my jeans and put it under the seat in her car before following her into the house.

"What did you tell him?" I have several things I'd like to tell him. But I'd feel much better if I broke his nose.

"That I have a crazy ex. It really isn't a lie. What did you want me to tell him? That a family of witches is after me to cut out my uterus?"

I snort. "They wouldn't bother. They'd just execute you." My voice sounds cold, making my words harsher than I intended.

Her smile falls.

With nothing to say, I head into the kitchen. When I turn around, she's taken her usual seat, elbows on the table, chin in her hands. I didn't even hear her enter the room. Either she's getting that good, or I'm really out of it.

"You look handsome," she says softly.

I make a sound at the back of my throat. "Please," I say, disgusted.

"Your hair. It suits you."

If she only knew what I had to endure for a haircut. I need to buy my own electric clipper so next time I can shave my own fucking head. I stare out the window above the sink, unable to remember why I walked in here.

She gets up. Leans her hip against the counter. "What's gotten into you today?"

"What."

"You seem so…down. Not yourself."

Maybe I do feel more irritated than usual. "Guess that car showing up again pissed me off."

"But I noticed it this morning, too."

"Fuck."

"Trey."

She stands on the tips of her toes to be taller. Not satisfied, she hoists herself up to sit on the countertop and checks my pupils before pulling back to look at my face. "Something's wrong."

"You're imagining things." I throw a towel down on the countertop.

She looks at the towel for a drawn out moment before returning to me. "It has to be those capsules you made. How many did you take today?"

"I don't remember."

"Well it's not worth it if they're going to make you more depressed and angry. Please don't take them. I'll take all the responsibility of making us behave."

"Don't make me laugh." Although I don't think I could if I wanted to. She's right—most of what's in the capsules are depressants. And I took a lot more than the recommended dose. I should probably be in a coma.

"Where are they? I'm going to count them."

"You don't need to count them."

"So you're not going to take any more?"

I can't say no to her, so I avoid the question. "I bought some mats for your house. Let's go over there and practice before it gets too late." I pull her off the countertop and set her on her feet. "Go change into some workout clothes."

"I'm not letting this go," she says over her shoulder as she leaves the room.

She comes out wearing the type of clothes dancers practice in and her hair twisted up, pulling on one of my hooded sweatshirts. We take the truck to her house and haul the gym mats to her front door. I suppose I'm being careless not checking the yard and the house first, especially since my circle's been disturbed. I'm not feeling very motivated. It was probably her anyway.

Inside the house, she walks around turning on lights while I roll out the mats. I take off my shoes and start to take off my shirt but decide against it. She comes toward me, pulling the sweatshirt over her head, then stepping out of her shoes.

"So how do you want to die today?" She cracks her knuckles.

"Slowly and painfully," I answer, trying to play back. It comes out sounding as forced as it feels.

"I can arrange that." She steps toward me on the mat.

I decide to take offense and reach for her, but she's too quick. I try again, and she slips away, laughing.

"Do I know Judo?"

"Yes."

"I thought I might."

"You've already used it on me. In the woods, remember? When you flipped me on my back, that was a *Uchi Makikomi*."

Before she has a chance to answer, I strike again. She dodges and goes for my shoulder and I counter with a *Ura Nage* as gently as I can. As she makes contact with the mat, she continues my forceful motion and I end up thrown over her on my back. My technique must be off.

"Now is when I need my dagger." She rolls back to her feet.

I remain on the ground, splayed out.

"Come on, get up!" She puts her fists up, ready to box.

"I think I'm done for the night."

"Oh come on!" She drops her hands and steps just within my reach. I pull her foot out from under her and roll to catch her before she hits the mat.

"You play dirty," she gasps, about to laugh.

"You should know that by now."

She scrapes her fingers against my hair. "I love this, buzzed off. It's so different."

I remove her hands from my head.

"What else besides Judo?"

"Everything." I know it will all become familiar to her once her body carries out the moves. "Even street fighting."

"Which style do you use most often?"

"I'm not disciplined enough to stick with one."

She slips out of my grasp and stands. I get up slowly then throw my arm out, grabbing her throat lightly. An instant later her knee is a millimeter from my groin.

I laugh, and I feel a weight lift off my chest. It feels good to laugh.

She takes advantage of my distraction. Grabbing my shirt at the shoulders, she swings her leg against my ankle and drops her body weight to the floor, taking me with her. She's starting to make me look bad.

"That's it." I stand and pull my shirt off. "You don't need any help from my clothes."

"No fair. I'm taking mine off too."

"Absolutely not." I take her arms and flip her onto the mat, and she manages to bring me down with her. I try to get her in a choke hold, but she's too slippery. I end up on top of her, holding her down with my body weight.

She fakes a cough. "Oh my god, get off, you're killing me." She giggles. It sends a pulse through me.

She slides her knees up, trying to press me off her, and I bear down with more weight.

"Okay okay I give up!" she gasps, out of breath.

I let her up and she clocks me straight in the jaw. Both hands cover her mouth in surprise.

I can't restrain my laughter. "That's going to leave a mark."

"I didn't mean to do that!" She reaches for me and I take her hands and hold them down.

"It's okay, it's a good reflex to have." I can't help but feel a little proud. She is amazing.

"What's your weapon of choice?"

"Bare hands," I answer without thinking.

As I help her stand, she looks up at me. "That stuff must be wearing off. You're coming back."

I drop her hands. "I need water." I head for the kitchen, fill a glass and gulp it down. I fill it again and hand it to her as she enters the room.

"You're holding back on me. You could snap me in half if you wanted to."

I shrug. "Probably. But it wouldn't be easy. You'd probably get away from me before I had the chance."

She takes a long drink and hands the glass back to me.

"What are we going to do?" she asks.

I know exactly what she's referring to, and I have no idea how to answer.

CHAPTER 28

LIV

ONE LOOK AT Trey's face in the morning tells me he's dosed himself again. We'd reached an agreement—or maybe I'd assumed we had. My fault for not being clear. But does he really think this is helpful?

He shakes his head at his breakfast prep like he knows I'm about to complain but he has no time for it. I feel like we've gone back in time, bickering over every little thing.

"Please tell me you didn't take more of those capsules." I'm aware of the anger in my voice but it's too late to control it.

His answering look is all I need to know he did.

"Goddamn it, Trey!" I look around for the bag. He must have it around here somewhere.

"Don't even bother," he mumbles. "I can always make more."

My blood boils. Raw anger has invaded a mind not used to housing it. I walk to the window, struggling to collect my thoughts There is a solution to this. Discussion isn't going to help me here. I need action.

He's seated at the table. I lift his arm from the tabletop, and slide my leg over his lap to straddle him. He freezes. I've caught him by surprise. I wrap my arms around his neck and kiss him like I did that first night. My passion for him swells. Freed.

His reaction is automatic, his defense delayed, so I get a decent kiss before he pushes his chair back from the table, jerking my arms from around his neck and yanking me up to standing. It strains muscles sore from our workout yesterday, but it was worth it.

"What the hell!" The sudden loose rage in his face should scare me, but it doesn't.

"Get used to it. As long as you are taking those, I'm going to be all over you."

"Oh yeah?"

"Yeah."

"Try it." His teeth are half clenched—he can barely get the words out. His features congeal into the likeness of someone unrecognizable to me.

"I just did, and it worked beautifully. And when you least expect it, I'll do it again." My audible calm contradicts the twisting anger inside me. Maybe if I screamed at him he'd understand.

His only response is a look of pure, primal viciousness. He's gone too still, like something's building up. It's obvious he's at a loss for words.

"Oh, and if I can't be physical? I'll talk. Like, remember that night I came home late, and we shared some ice cream, and then—"

"Stop it." His eyes turn wild.

If I didn't have my new skills, I'd probably be afraid of him right now. I'm not just swimming with a great white shark, I'm provoking it. This may be stupid, but I can't stop it.

"And that morning, when we woke up in bed together? Your lips—"

He swings, punching the wall. Drywall crumbles and scatters on the floor.

"Oh, how mature." I cross my arms over my chest. He's acting out because he knows I have him.

He gives me a last feral look and storms out of the room. I hear him yanking on his boots, the laces slapping leather as he ties them, then the front door slams. With the sound comes a bone-chilling shame. That's the most childish thing I've ever done.

So this is how it's going to play out. My acceptance of this new spin on reality that features magic and bloodlines and corpses disappearing in the woods won't be won by some delayed panic I'm forced to confront and deal with rationally. I'm simply going to crack.

I squeeze my eyes shut. When I open them I'm looking straight at his uneaten breakfast. His empty stomach is one of those minor details that has a free pass into the heart, to unleash grief of a disproportionate scale. Like a teddy bear abandoned in triage, or a car accident victim's missing shoes—images sure to haunt me forever when I might not even remember the patients' names. The real source of my distress is our confrontation and I can't help but feel guilty. He's the asshole but I started it. I could have just let it go. But I can't stand by and watch him turn himself into a zombie. And didn't we talk about this yesterday? Did he even listen?

Outside, the driveway's gravel has been scarred with deep tire tracks where his truck peeled out. I give myself a pep talk all the way to work. I can't give in, no matter how much it hurts me to fight with him. He won't listen to me otherwise. He's too strong-willed and he'll continue taking those capsules to dull his brain because he thinks it's what's best for us. He doesn't trust that I can help him, that we have the power to control ourselves. Screw that prophecy. We're in charge here.

The confrontation follows me around all day at work. Every sentence of our exchange repeats over and over in pitiless distraction. That rash, irrational woman was not me, and I hope I never see her again. It's going to be hard to face him. He doesn't know me well enough to understand I'm not that woman. My worry develops into mental and physical drain, and I keep checking the clock to see if it's time to go. But I know when the time comes, it will probably mean another awkward exchange. I'm going to have to practice my best poker face. He's not getting away with any of it, even if I did start it.

I'm reminded of that day he was unconscious, when I was worried about him lying on his living room floor with no one to care for him. And I came home and he was awake, and he came around the house, and he smiled. There is nothing in the world like his smile. Its rarity makes it even more valuable.

I find myself trying to think of things I could do for him that would make him happy, and as soon as I realize my mind has wandered there again I put an end to the thoughts. He deserves nothing from me right now but a middle finger duo. The best thing I can do for him—for us—is stick to my plan. I cannot give in.

A few minutes before my shift ends, I spot Shawn finishing up a delivery. He winks at me from down the hall, and something inside me twists the wrong way. I need to tell Shawn that we can't be anything more than friends. If I don't make it clear, I'm disrespecting Trey. Yeah, we can't be a couple until he sees his wife. Yeah, he's an insufferable wall-punching jerk. Neither of those things seem to matter when you've been set up by the universe.

Shawn isn't going to care about any of that. If he doesn't hear "Trey and I are together," he's going to think he still has a chance. Just like Trey said, we are in limbo.

I'd rather spend the rest of my life in limbo than lose Trey to his wife. I know he already belongs to her, but denial thrives in limbo. Reality is on hold.

Shawn catches up to me while I'm gathering my things to leave. "Do you need an escort to your car tonight, ma'am?"

"Hopefully not." I'm unable to make my voice light.

He squints at me, obviously noticing a change in my regular mood. "Your ex, guess he's a real creep, huh?"

Time to change the subject. "I'm going to be gone all next week."

"Will you at least be in town? Maybe we could meet up."

"No, I won't be in town. Trey's taking me on a trip to meet his family."

He chuckles and looks away. "I see. Well, hopefully they all have winning personalities like him. I'm sure you'll have a great time."

"So, if I don't see you tomorrow, I'll see you when I get back, okay?"

"Looking forward to it. Let me walk you out anyway."

On my drive to Trey's house, my anxiety builds into a tower inside me. I don't know what to say to him. When I pull into the empty driveway, I exhale in bittersweet relief. As much as I was dreading another confrontation, now that he's not here, I long to see him. All day I've fantasized that I'd come home and he'd tell me that I was right, that he won't take any more of that stuff, and that we can be strong enough together to overcome. But in reality I know he's probably staying out late to avoid me.

It's cold inside. Instead of nudging up the thermostat I change into sweatpants, thermal shirt, thick socks, and his sweatshirt jacket. I take two ibuprofen to relieve my aches and pains from yesterday and fuzzy stress headache from today. After wandering through the mocking emptiness of the house, I return to the kitchen and sit at the table.

My thoughts swim through the nastiness of this morning, replaying every word for the hundredth time. As if I need any reminder other than the hollowness of the empty house. I put my head down on my arms on the table and close my eyes. Pleasant thoughts are in me. I just have to find them.

But everything returns to him, and I refuse to be some basket case over a man. I did it too long before I started my life in Black River and I'll do it no more. Staying out late is a weapon he's raised above me and if he thinks I'll expose my heart for goring, he can think again. My heart is officially retracted until his attitude returns to adulthood.

I find myself in the basement, perusing his warehouse of weaponry. Alone in the house, without his presence, my knowledge of every firearm—caliber, capacity, stopping power—settles on me with a humbling finality. As if that's not enough, every one of his knives is a separate and distinct tool, each with a particular use and specialty. A database of information has been dropped into my head. I've gained the ability to defend myself against most attackers, but I've also become something else. To the wrong person, I've become dangerous. If I wanted to, *I* could be the attacker.

The six-inch hunting knife in my hand is a tool I could use efficiently, without thinking. I turn around to face the punching bag that's hanging from the ceiling on the other end of the basement. My aim would be exact. I could throw it to prove it, but I don't want to damage his new bag. As I return the knife to the table, the overhead light glints off the top edge of the blade and there's a blip in my brain. A flash of an image. Blood spilled on snow. A hand in a black fingerless glove gripping that knife, and another hand that feels like mine but I know is not mine taking control, twisting that gloved hand, stealing that knife—

I shove away from the table and cover my face with my hands to stop it from continuing.

Trey's memories must have been tangled in the knowledge he copied to my mind. The violence he's been living with has become my own, not only as an external force ransacking my house and trying to ambush us, but also inside me in graphic memory. I'm sure he didn't intend to include those memories, but I see they'd be impossible to separate out. So much of what we learn comes from experience. If my possession of these memories took some of the burden from him, I'd gladly accept them. But I know it won't.

It leaves me remembering that non-Liv this morning. Rash, unsympathetic, shoot-first-ask-questions-later Liv. It's as if elements of his personality got left behind in my head.

The basement was supposed to be my distraction but here it is reminding me of him. I jerk the light's pull chain and head for the back porch. A chill has settled but I put my hood up and stay outside, watching the night sneak in and take over. None of the vehicles whishing along the road disturb the gravel of the driveway although each one of them has me convinced it's him until it's long passed. When I decide I'd rather not have a warning of his arrival, I go back inside.

Nothing to do in the kitchen. I check the laundry room. Nothing to fold. I look out the front window. No sign of him. I should call him. Something could've happened. They could have overpowered him. If they send enough men he won't be able to fight them off. I return to the kitchen and go back out on the back porch.

"River!" He usually doesn't call for her. I have no idea how he gets her to come. "River!" Maybe it's a bad idea to be calling out in the night when I'm here by myself. They might know he's gone, and now they'll come for me.

I go back inside in search of a pistol. I find a Glock, load it, and carry it to the kitchen with me. River is standing at the back door, so I open it.

"Is everything okay?"

She cocks her head. I have no idea if she understands me. If something was wrong, she wouldn't be this relaxed. I get a piece of cheese out of the refrigerator and suddenly Coyote Dog is behind her. What is it we named him? Tributary. What a horrible name. I hand them each a half of the piece of cheese and close the door.

Where the hell is he?

If he's doing this on purpose to make me worry, he's succeeded. Maybe he hopes that when he finally does come home I'll be so relieved I'll forget all about it. But I really don't think he's capable of being manipulative. He's usually so straightforward. So if he's not staying out late to make me worry, then where is he? He should've been home a long time ago.

I get my phone out of my bag and scroll to his name. My finger hovers over the button. I can't do it. I have to play hard ball.

I bring a gun into the bedroom and lie down on the bed. When I've stared at the ceiling for an hour, I get up. I take the gun to the kitchen. Every sound I make echoes through the house. I wander back into the living room, get my phone out of my bag, and stare at it.

Tires sound on the driveway but something isn't right. I turn off the light and go to the front window. Peeking outside, I see a vehicle but it's a car, not his truck, and it's too dark to make out any other details. I squint, trying to see inside past the glare of the headlights. Two people in the car, maybe more. I sprint to the kitchen so I have a door I can exit if I need to escape. I pick up my gun from the table. Moonlight illuminates the room through the windows, so I stand in the shadow of the refrigerator for cover.

My ears boom, raw to every noise. They got him. And now they're coming for me. They think I'm going to be easy. They are in for a surprise.

The front door opens and slams closed. I'm not at all surprised by their boldness. I aim at the doorway, my finger itching to squeeze the trigger. Not yet. I need a clear shot. I'm only doing this once, and it has to be fatal.

But there were at least two people in the car, and it sounds like only one has entered the front. I turn my body so I have a view of both doorways.

Something moves at the back door. A wagging tail. River! Why is she here? Doesn't she know? The footsteps approach. Something in the back of my mind is arguing with me. I take my finger off the trigger.

The light flips on, blinding me for a split second. He lunges toward me, cursing, pushing the gun up toward the ceiling.

Callous eyes ravage me in search of an explanation.

"I didn't know it was you," I say. "It was a different car."

"Dave drove me home," he snaps. "My truck broke down."

"You could have called." I try to make my voice level. I'm the one who was in the dark, and he's going to be short with me? Maybe I should shoot him.

He snorts and turns away.

And I thought *I* was the one being childish. He must have to win at everything, including this new game we're playing: Who's the Bigger Jackass.

Well, I surrender. I go into the bedroom and sit on the bed in the dark. The noise from him banging around in the kitchen filters down the hallway. I shouldn't have retreated.

Without a good look at him, I have no idea if he's laying off the capsules. He's in such a bad mood it's going to be impossible to tell if it's a hefty dose or his natural temper.

I emerge from the room. My stomach growls on my way to the kitchen. He's at the table, glaring into a plate of leftovers. I stand in front of the sink, facing him. His head swivels slowly toward me, the glare now aimed at its intended target. He's probably wondering about my next move. His temper has turned him animalistic. His face is hard and cold, but the fire is there. He hasn't taken the capsules.

"Thank you," I say softly, watching him, wishing this could be over.

His expression holds and he turns back to his plate.

"Do you mind if I eat with you?" I open the refrigerator.

He makes no response. The whole room seems to cower away from him.

I heat up some food and fill a glass with water. Noticing he has nothing to drink, I fill another glass and set it in front of him. He glowers at it as if it's going to strike. I sit across from him.

"How long are you going to be mad at me?" I ask.

He looks across the table at me. If looks could kill, I would be obliterated. Along with every form of life for miles behind me.

A dull, fuzzy ache throbs through my skull. The shame and guilt return. They've already spoiled the success of my plan. Effective or not, it all feels like a big mistake, a rash move performed by a person I don't know. Has no one ever pushed me like this?

I should've tried to talk to him, holding on to the plan as a backup only if a talk with him didn't work. Who am I kidding? He would've never agreed with me, no matter how rational I was.

He lifts the glass and drinks the entire thing at once. Whether he intends it or not, the action mocks me. I watch his face, hoping to catch something to prove me wrong. All I see is bold thanklessness, as if he's flaunting his avoidance of me and rubbing it in further. As far as he's concerned, that glass of water just materialized in front of him. I'm not here. I'm a ghost, painfully aware of every move he makes yet completely invisible and inconsequential to him. Not even worth the effort of eye contact.

He puts his dishes in the sink and leaves the room. Isolation closes in like it couldn't wait for him to leave. I finish my meal, my head swarming with no relief in sight. I remember what Christian said when he was here.

He has the worst temper.

I see now what an understatement that is. But it seems to only apply to certain situations. People coming to murder him—that, he takes in stride. He has no hard feelings toward them. It's just business. But if someone close to him disagrees with him, he loses it. For a merciless killer, he's quite thin-skinned.

If he was any other man I'd be packing to leave. Maybe I should reconsider my choice to stay with him, but it would be like reconsidering my choice to sleep once I get off a double shift. He's part of my life now. We're bound. He'll have to learn this behavior is wrong.

I take my dishes to the sink and as I turn off the faucet I hear him step into the room. Then he's behind me, against me, running his fingers across the back of my neck to brush my hair to the side. His lips make contact with my skin and he inhales with the slowest, deepest breath. His hands grasp my hips in a gentle snare.

I involuntarily relax into him when an alarm goes off in my mind. He's testing me. He kisses the side of my neck once, twice, and I grip the countertop with both hands to stabilize myself. If I react to him, he's going to win. He's going to say I'm wrong, that my idea will never work, that we cannot be responsible for our self-control.

For a second I want to be wrong. I want to give in and fail his test. Wild heat crawls from the impact of his lips down my chest and back. He pulls me by the hips against his pelvis. He wants me to know he's excited. He'll probably take it all the way just to prove a point. He's fighting dirty, and he thinks I can't say no. Using all my strength, I push against him and twist my hips, slip out, and leave the room.

I close myself in the bathroom and brush my teeth. Once isn't enough to calm me down so I brush them again. When I exit the bathroom, I see him in the living room putting on his running shoes. I hesitate in the shadow, wondering if I should say something to him, if there's anything I could do to remedy this situation tonight. When the front door slams, I know I've lost my chance.

CHAPTER 29

TREY

EVEN AFTER THAT long run last night, I slept like hell. I rise from the couch, rolling my neck and stretching my back. The bag of capsules sticking out of my jeans pocket on the floor catches my eye. I know well enough when I've been defeated, and I'm not afraid to admit it. I grab the bag and take it with me into the kitchen, tossing it onto her spot at the table harder than I mean to.

I make a pot of oatmeal for breakfast and she appears in the kitchen just as I'm sitting down. Our eyes meet, an accident on my part, but I catch her expectant expression. She hopes I'm over it. I look back to my bowl. She joins me at the table, pausing as she sees the bag of capsules. I refuse to look up. She picks it up gently, puts it in the pocket of her scrubs, and takes her seat.

"Can I at least apologize?" she asks.

I ignore her. Anything I say right now will make everything worse.

"I shouldn't have been so rash. I should have talked to you first. And I'm sorry."

I want to forgive her, but I can't manifest a feeling that doesn't live inside me. I make the mistake of looking at her. Her eyes implore mine, and I stare back, my mind an unhelpful blank. I finish my oatmeal and leave the house without a word.

I take the Ninja to the shop to check on my truck. Dave tells me it's just the fuel pump after all and will be done in a few hours, so I ride into town and find an open parking spot at the curb. Something in the window of the facing store catches my eye—a replica of the white shell bracelet I put on Liv's wrist in her mind, and it couldn't be closer to what we both imagined. Maybe I've seen this bracelet here before, and my subconscious mind found the memory and used it. It's hard to believe I'd notice it, much less remember it.

The salesman pokes his head out of the store. "Shopping for a lady friend? That bracelet comes with a necklace and earrings, too."

"How long have you had this bracelet?"

"It's brand new this week, from our newest line. Would you like to see it?"

I follow him into the store. He takes it out of the case and reaches back in for the other pieces.

"Just the bracelet," I say.

"Very well. Is this for a special occasion?"

"Yes."

"For your wife? Girlfriend?"

"Yes."

"I see." He chuckles, placing the bracelet on a velvet cloth on top of a display case.

The damn thing is exact, down to the silver clasp. I nod at him, and he takes it away to wrap. He returns and I pay, sticking the box inside my inner jacket pocket.

Next stop is the liquor store for a bottle of scotch to replace the one I plan to drain tonight. I slip it into my jacket next to Liv's gift and ride out of town, hitting some twisty roads in search of a much needed rush. My truck is ready by the time I make it back to the mechanic. Dave helps me load the Ninja into the bed, and with nothing left I could do, I go home.

Yard work, then to the basement to lift some weights. The workout is exactly the release I need. I'm still at it when I hear her come home. Her presence in the house becomes an immediate distraction, so I add some reps hoping to wear myself out more.

Upstairs, I'm greeted by the smell of Chinese food, my one absolute weakness in life. Besides ice cream. I don't know who she's been talking to. I drink a glass of water while my ears reach for sounds of her. It's curiosity, nothing more, since the house is so quiet. I eye the brown paper bag of food and consider breaking into it before she comes back. But if I do that, she might expect some conditions, like friendly conversation, or my forgiveness, and I'm still in no mood to think about that. Soft footsteps move into the living room so I turn my back to the doorway and refill my glass at the sink.

"Do you like Chinese food?"

It feels like a loaded question, so I don't answer.

"I thought it would be nice if you didn't have to cook for once. You don't have to eat it if you don't like it, I just…" Her voice fades as if she just realized I may not be listening to her.

I catch a glimpse of her face. She is clearly groveling. Regret twists inside me, triggering my endless guilt. No one's safe around me. The ones who don't get murdered have to put up with me. Being murdered is probably the better option. "I'll eat it," I blurt out. It's the first and only thing that comes to my mind.

She's so pleased she can hardly contain herself. She takes the bag to the table and unloads carton after carton of food. I wipe myself down with a towel then grab two plates and a glass of water for her. When I sit across from her, she's waiting with clasped hands and big eyes. Those eyes ready to undo me.

"I didn't know what you liked, so I got a few different—"

"I like it all."

I sense my mood lifting, and my rigid half finally allows it. I don't know what the hell I'm doing. The one person in the world who is wholly on my side, and I'm making her suffer. Yes, there was a breach, but she's admitted it and apologized. And here I am dragging it out. I take a dangerous plunge into her eyes. Her brows lift the slightest, like she's unsure what to expect, but hoping for the best.

We eat in silence, the air between us already changed.

When I finish off the last carton, I lean back in my chair. She throws a fortune cookie, and I catch it, unwrap it, and read the fortune to myself.

"Oh, you have to read it out loud." That playfulness in her voice hangs just below the surface.

"Use patience when change face you head on," I read.

Her laugh is not her usual joyful laugh, but it's an attempt. "They *have* to make the grammar bad. It wouldn't be the same otherwise." She cracks hers open. "An important decision grant you gift to cherish."

I toss the empty cartons and clear the table. The bag I thought was empty contains two untouched cartons.

"Don't do it," she says. "You can't possibly eat any more."

Her words carry the trace of a laugh. I want to smile, but I don't. Yeah, I was considering finishing it off. I can't be that easy to read.

She puts the kettle on the stove and goes for the chamomile tea while I stash the leftovers in the fridge. With her back to me, she stays by the stove, leaning her hip against the counter, waiting for the water to boil. I go into the living room for my jacket, and reach into the inner pocket for the small silver box. I am impulsive by nature. I'm not going to fight it.

She's still in the same position when I return to the kitchen, so I take her hand off the countertop and place the box inside it. She looks up at me then at the box in her palm, her whole arm rigid as if she's holding a bomb.

"What—"

"Open it."

The deep blue velvet case inside gives her pause. For a second I think she's going to hand it back. She lifts it out and peeks inside. Her breath catches, and she backs up a step.

"You've had this—"

"I just found it today."

She removes the bracelet from its case and lays it across her palm. "You didn't know about this when we…"

"I'd never seen it before that night on the bluffs."

She can't seem to look away from me, so I take the bracelet from her and put it on the same wrist she had it on when we were on the beach.

"I love it," she whispers, returning her attention to her wrist. Without warning, she throws her arms around me. "I'm so sorry. I don't know what got into me. That wasn't me."

I close my arms around her, bury my face in her neck and breathe in, feeling myself being lifted, healed, made new again. She's gone quiet and still, so I gently unwrap her arms and hold her in front of me. Her eyes glow electric blue with a line of tears running down each cheek.

"Please forgive me," she whispers.

My body seizes with actual physical pain, and I wipe her tears with my thumb. "Don't—" I can't stand it.

The kettle screams, and I reach blindly behind her to move it and turn off the burner.

"I don't deserve this." She goes for the clasp on the bracelet.

"Don't say that." I remove her hand and enclose it in mine. "It's not your fault I'm such an asshole."

She touches a fingertip to one of the delicate shells. "How can it be the same bracelet?"

I feel a smile creeping up that I don't try to suppress. "Make your tea. I'm going to take a quick shower."

When I get out of the shower I find her in the living room leaning over a book. "Why didn't you teach me some astronomy?" Her focus slips from my face to my chest. I turn around to retrieve a shirt from the bedroom closet.

Her expression is guarded when I return.

"I didn't want to overdo it. But we can do it again."

"When?" Her eyes light up.

"As soon as things calm down." I sit on the couch beside her. How many of them do I need to kill before they'll calm down?

"Trey, I was wondering. When you were in my head, is it possible you unintentionally left some things behind…?"

"Like what?" Shit, I hope not.

"Fragments of memories." The detail comes fast and straight, like it's been rehearsed.

"It's unavoidable. It's like any human interaction. We rub off on one another. I don't think there's a way to withdraw from someone's mind and not leave a trace you were there."

"Not just a trace. It feels more…specific."

I can think of too many specifics I'd rather her not know. "I'll try to be more careful next time."

"So I can blame you for my rash behavior yesterday morning?"

"No, you can't. Because I'm not rash."

"Oh, *right.*" She nods toward the duffle bags I brought upstairs earlier. "What are the bags for?"

"Carrying a shit-ton of firearms onto a plane."

"I hope you're kidding." She gauges my expression and seems to understand that I'm not. "How's that going to work?"

"I have to prepare something in the basement for that. Discretion Effect. It can make people unsee what they see."

"It makes something invisible?"

"In a way. They'll see it, but the impulse will dissipate. Never reach the cognitive part of the brain. I'm sure there's a legal way to get guns onto a plane but this is easier."

"Oh, god. Why am I going along with this?"

"It's a way to be discreet about something you can't hide."

"Should I be nervous?"

"To meet my fucked-up family? No. But it will be entertaining." I pause to think even though nothing's changed. Yes, I'm pushing it. She'll be safer with me. End of story. "We didn't get in as much practice as I wanted, but I don't think you need it."

CHAPTER 30

LIV

THERE'S A COUNTDOWN ticking and once that time ends, Trey could be back with his wife and son. Although I've known it's been a possibility, it hasn't settled on me like it did this morning when I stood in the living room looking at his empty spot on the couch. Of course, back with his family is the natural place for him. It's the place I'd want for him if it didn't feel so wrong.

I hear him in the basement when I go into the kitchen, so I start the coffee and go downstairs. He's hard at work over dozens of books propped open with various objects to hold the pages back. Jars, measuring cups, beakers, a mortar and pestle, a cutting board, knives, and other instruments clutter the table. I stand and watch him for a minute before moving to his side.

When he sees my expression, he says, "It's easier than it looks."

"I'm not going to worry until we walk into the airport carrying bags full of guns."

"I could mix up something for your anxiety."

"No. I want to be myself. Have you had breakfast?"

"Not yet." He rubs his hand against the grain of his shorn hair and turns back to his work.

I hug myself. "Do you want a shirt?"

Negative. I decide not to ask about shoes. Or pants. In his boxers in a chilly basement, he's either immune to the temperature or too engrossed in his task to feel cold concrete under his bare feet. I'm going to miss this. Just the thought of my life without him gives me the sensation of a phantom limb. Only the feeling doesn't involve an appendage—it's right in my chest.

Back in the kitchen, I decide to splurge and make blueberry pancakes. When I have a small stack finished, he appears like a dog following a scent. I bring him coffee and orange juice and join him at the table.

"Only a few more days..." he says under his breath.

I know he thinks everything is going to be settled easily. He seems to have a cut-and-dried view of the world, and I don't think his philosophy is going to apply to what is about to happen. There are so many people involved, along with strong emotion and complicated history. He thinks he has it figured out, but everything is going to change as soon as he sees her.

But I'm no expert either. I can't pretend to make sense of these thoughts that are darting around in my head. So

I decide to keep my mouth shut and enjoy this time with him. It will probably all end as quickly as it began. It's hard to believe we've only known each other for these past few weeks. I feel like I've known him all my life.

I'm going to miss him like I'd miss someone I've known forever.

Pushing his plate away, he shoots me a satiated grin. "You should cook more often."

"But then you'd be used to it, and it wouldn't be special."

"True." He gulps the last of his coffee and starts to gather his dishes.

"Leave it. I'll get it. It looks like you have a lot to do down there."

"You should pack a bag. Very light." He holds my eye like it's some kind of order.

Really? I am the queen of light packing. I moved across the country with only a car full of stuff. I could teach him a thing or two about light packing. Not much later, I dump my packed bag by the front door as he's passing through.

His attention lingers on my initials on the bag. "What *is* your middle name?"

I sigh. "You're not going to like it."

"Why not?"

"It's Catherine."

His face darkens. "With a K or a C?"

"C."

"You're fine then. Kate's is with a K."

A sour feeling erupts within me as he says her name and it feels like jealousy. All I felt for her up until now was compassion, and most of all, I was happy for Trey. After all these years, he could have his family back from the grave—the wildest dream of anyone who's lost a loved one. And

I'm still happy for him. But my sympathy for her is different now, almost nonexistent.

The animosity has put down roots, and whether it happened just now or days ago, it's not going anywhere. Understanding might calm it down. If I was in her shoes, I couldn't have gone so many years without contacting him. I may not have seen Trey's perspective before, but something has moved me from neutral ground to his camp. Had I been her, I wouldn't have let him suffer so long thinking I—or their child—was dead. She allowed their son to grow up never knowing his father, Trey never knowing him. But it's true we don't know the situation, and we can't fairly judge her until we do. I need to remember that.

What caused this change in me? Is it because now I have a valid claim on him? A claim more powerful than hers?

"Liv?"

"What?"

"You were spacing out."

"I guess I have a lot on my mind."

"Don't go freaking out on me now." He runs a finger across my brow, brushing my bangs aside.

Our eyes lock, a standoff of sorts. He's wondering what had me so preoccupied, but it's all too new to explain. I need time with these thoughts before I voice them. Instead of demanding answers, he leans down to kiss me. It's over too fast, and when I rise on my toes for more, he takes my hand and pulls me downstairs.

His workbench is a disaster, but at the end of the table is a pile of individually wrapped packets each tied with string.

"Those are going to get our weapons through security. They go in the duffle bags with the guns. Just gotta warn you—it's been a while since I've done this one."

I lean down to take a deep smell of their earthy, herbal fragrance.

"The spell will attach to their scent. As long as it lasts, so will the spell. I made you immune."

"And what's our story if it doesn't work?"

He shrugs. "I'll just have to wing it."

My experience with him winging it… I doubt that would go over well with airport security.

"Want to bring an M16?" he asks, holding it against his shoulder to aim at the wall.

"Where'd you get an M16?"

"Christian."

"Why'd he give you that?"

"Just Christian being Christian. Punk had the nerve to say I'm lazy enough to use this thing."

I pause to watch him. He could decide to move back to his family in Virginia. Christian would allow him back. They all might want him back. He'd have to accept a truce. I'd have to return here, alone, to my own house. Even the beginning with the nausea, bickering, and captivity seem preferable to life without Trey.

"You're spacing out again," he says, searching my face.

How could I possibly manage living without him?

"What." This time he's not so understanding. His hard tone is like a bad habit—a bully's way to get answers by making demands. He should know better than to try that with me, especially so soon. Some things I just can't humor.

"It's nothing."

"Right." He doesn't buy it. He crosses his arms over his chest. His bad-cop expression holds.

Even if I could find a way to explain all the thoughts in my head, it will change nothing. No decisions can be made until he visits his family. Change the subject. "Why so much firepower?"

"So we're prepared. I might want to approach it differently—"

"Never mind." The less I know the better. I squeeze his forearm and go upstairs. When he comes up he drops a loaded duffle bag onto the floor with a thud, rattling dishes on the counter. There's a finality in the sound and the contrast of silence that follows. It sends a restriction to my esophagus and a weakness to my limbs, like a crippling stage fright. A coordinated effort has been set in motion, and my role is critical. He's counting on me and I can't back out, but too many pieces are out of my control. I'm standing off stage, hearing the sudden hush of the crowd when the curtain rises. I've been cast in *Giselle*. It's perfectly fitting. I have the costume and the title but I've had no time to practice. The music has started, and the show will go on with or without me. My only option is to dance, fully aware that at the end I will die of a broken heart.

After lunch, we head to the sporting goods store. My new gun is ready and waiting at the counter. On our way to the cashier, he asks, "Is there anything else you want?"

"There's nothing else I could possibly want." *At this moment*, I want to add. *Ask me that again in a week, when I could be without you.*

He stops walking and grasps my upper arm to spin me to face him, making me wonder if I spoke it out loud, and I make an instantaneous decision to stop agonizing over something that's out of my control. Nothing is allowed to ruin what could be my last few days with him. I'm not sure what he reads on my face, but whatever it is causes him to run a rough hand against the grain of his hair and lead me straight to the checkout line. His responses to the cashier's pleasantries sound more like grunts than words, and I can tell he's grinding his teeth again.

In the parking lot, I slip my hand into his. "Is this allowed?"

He nods, trying to play it cool, but I notice the slight softening of his eyes, the easier set of his jaw. I could make him smile if I wanted to, but a shield has gone up around that pleasure like it's no longer mine to provoke.

Back at his house, we settle in the living room. He's grown somber, but I figure it's simple apprehension and the best thing is to leave him to his thoughts. All we'd do is talk in circles anyway. Nothing will be solved until he does what he needs to do. I slide my feet into his lap, expecting no response. His warm hands close over them.

Playing with fire, I crawl over to him and rest my head against his chest. When it's obvious I'm not going to seduce him, he stretches out lengthwise on the couch and I match his position, my leg hooked over his. He makes a great body pillow, even when he's in a mood. As I start to drift off to sleep, a shadow lifts away and my world becomes clear. A mixture of comfort and confidence washes through me—a distinct combination I realize has been building up inside me for some time now. Only now, it has matured into a full-blown revelation.

Trey Bevan is mine. And I am going to fight anyone who tries to take him away from me.

CHAPTER 31

TREY

HEAVY MORNING FOG hangs in patches on the road until we hit the highway in the direction of the airport. Liv flips through the channels on the radio, stopping on all the songs I would stop on myself. She keeps sending smiles my way, and I'm not sure what to make of it. If she's happy, the emotion has invaded me as well. I'm thrilled to have her by my side on this day. On every day. Our drive together to pick up her car a few weeks ago happened in another lifetime.

The hours pass quickly, and soon I'm parking the truck in the airport pay lot. I tell Liv to stay in her seat, and I get out and climb into the bed, pulling my page of notes out of my back pocket. It doesn't take long to solidify the effect. The horizon glows in different shades of orange and pink, and by the time we're walking into the airport the sun has just begun to slip out of hiding.

Fluorescent lights buzz inside. I give a nod to the security guard; he nods back. We carry our bags to the ticket counter. While I check our bags, Liv's composure remains as flawless as I expected it to be. She holds my hand on our way to the gate. Several seats near the counter are already occupied—a twenty-something kid with the vacant stare of someone who's been up all night, an older couple reading a magazine together, a woman and a man in suits sitting a seat apart.

"I'm imagining myself in a movie," she says as we take seats facing the windows. "So if anything goes wrong, it's just part of the script, and afterward we can just return to our normal lives."

"In this movie, nothing goes wrong. The good guys win." I long to touch the soft skin on the back of her neck. To inhale against it. To press myself—

"We're the good guys?" She looks up at me.

Fuck them and their rules. They're after me already. I may as well give them a good reason to be.

But maybe not in a busy airport.

"Of course." I rest my arm across the back of her seat. Her eyes move back to the traffic on the runway, and I try to ignore the charged air between us. She unzips her jacket. The pale pink color of her shirt sets off the natural pink of her lips. My earlier lust returns, making it hard not to grab her right now, in front of all these people.

I stand. "Do you want a coffee? A magazine?" A quickie in the handicap stall of the men's room?

"No. Well, maybe some gum." She snags my jeans as I walk away. This simple motion sends a surge right to my crotch. She knows exactly what she's doing to me, and she shows no mercy.

I buy her two flavors of gum and pick out a few magazines. I take a walk, trying to find other options for coffee while calming my hormones. What I'd really like is a drink. When I return, the waiting area has been overtaken by a mob. I take my seat next to her and hand her the gum.

"I got some magazines anyway." I drop them in her lap. All these people are already getting on my nerves. And I don't like them behind me.

"*Guns and Ammo*? Are you trying to give us away?" Her eyes do an exaggerated look around.

"There's a write-up on the Ruger LCP versus the SIG P238."

That has her interest. She flips it open to find the article. I stare out the window and sip my coffee, trying to move my thoughts away from the chaos behind us.

She finishes the article and closes the magazine. "Ruger's better."

"Is that what it says?"

"No, that's what *I* say." She holds my gaze. "Can I kiss you?" she asks innocently.

I stare at her for an eternity because it takes that long to talk myself out of it. "You are definitely pushing it." I break my eyes away from hers and lean forward, resting my arms on my knees.

She pokes me in the ribs. I look up.

"They're loading the luggage on the plane," she whispers.

We watch until our duffle bags ride the conveyor belt to the attendant and get tossed onto the plane.

"Too easy," she says under her breath.

I settle against the seat and a thought nags me. "Is Gilchrist your married name?"

Her fingers playing with her zipper freeze. It takes her a moment to respond. "No. I switched back when I moved to Black River."

"What was your married name?"

She looks at me sideways. "Why?"

"Just curious," I answer, but she's already on to me.

"I don't trust you with that information."

"I could find out very easily." But I'd rather her tell me. I'd never go behind her back.

She sighs. "Aren't there enough people in your life to take out your aggressions on?"

"It's a lot more fun when it's personal."

"How could it be personal? You don't even know him."

"I don't need to know him."

"Please. You don't always have to be so macho." Her voice carries a slight tease. I know she's just trying to soften her seriousness. I've hit a nerve.

"Has nothing to do with being macho. It's about people getting what they deserve."

"It's not even your fight."

"I'm making it my fight."

"Well, don't." She turns away, crossing her arms.

"What about Liv? What's it short for?"

"Nothing. It's just Liv."

Our flight begins boarding. I follow her down the ramp and onto the plane. As I duck through the doorway, I'm reminded how much I hate flying. I feel like a giant in a world designed for elves. Liv takes the middle seat and I take the aisle, and suddenly I realize how difficult this flight is going to be for me.

"Maybe I'll get lucky and this other seat will stay empty," she whispers in my ear as an inferno spreads from my ear to my toes, burning the insulation off a live wire in my groin on its way. An electrical fire in my pants is just what I need to make this plane ride even more hellish.

I say a silent prayer for the seat to stay empty so she can move over there after we take off. A woman with a baby pauses at my shoulder. Prayer is asinine.

I stand, and Liv moves her knees to the side. The woman squeezes in. I'm really paying for my sins now. Not only is the seat taken, but it's taken by two people, one of which will probably scream the entire time. I sit back down and try to catch Liv's eye, but she's busy smiling at the baby. A severe sadness lurks behind her smile, and I feel something tear inside me.

The engines scream. We pick up speed and lift into the air. I glance at her again, but her head remains bowed like she's in a trance. I can no longer empathize with her now that I know Aaron is alive and I'm on my way to see him. But knowing this doesn't dilute the dark creature crawling from its hole and climbing inside me, headed for the vital organs just like old times. I had fifteen years to deal with my loss. Her loss is still a fresh open wound.

I raise the armrest between us and wrap my arm around her, pulling her against me. She lays her head on my chest and I hold her until the beverage cart arrives. When she raises her head, she leaves a wet spot behind on my shirt.

"She was exactly that age," she whispers, her eyelashes wet. She covers her mouth with her hand, staring at the seat in front of her. "She died in my arms. Her cheek went cold against mine." She makes a shaky gasp, as if her mind has taken her back to that exact moment.

Her pain multiplies wildly with the helplessness inside me. If only I could be inside her mind right now, I could take all her pain away, claim it as my own. I find her hand with mine and she clings on. We're trapped on this fucking plane and there's nothing I can do.

Our flight arrives late in Denver. We run through the airport to catch our connection. The last passengers to board, we're somehow lucky to have the row to ourselves this time.

When we're settled and have our breath back, I notice the slump in her shoulders.

"What can I do?" I ask like an idiot. Helpless. I'm no good at this.

She shakes her head. When I turn away, figuring she doesn't want to talk, she says, "It's just hard sometimes. It all comes crashing back."

"It gets easier with time."

"I know."

"What was her name?" I ask and immediately wish I hadn't. I could punch myself.

"Sloane."

I didn't hear that right. I bend to look directly in her face. "What did you say?"

"Sloane. S, L, O—"

"You don't have to spell it." I straighten and look away, shaking my head, exhaling. This is unreal. "That's my mother's name," I say.

"What?"

"That's my mother's name."

"I heard you. It's just…not a common name."

"Yeah I know."

What a sick coincidence. Unless it's not a coincidence. But how could it not be?

"How did you come up with that name?" I ask.

"A dream. When I was pregnant I dreamed her name was Sloane. So I named her Sloane Catherine."

My focus shifts from the top of one head to the top of another. All these people are too damn close to me. I could kill every single person on this plane right now. I knew I hated flying and I signed up anyway.

"What's your father's name?"

My answer is automatic. "Martin. Martin Moore."

She makes the tiniest sound—a short exhale, like the result of a slight jab to the diaphragm. Her grief must be rising again. I can't sit here and let her cry a second time without doing something about it. I should keep her talking. Distract her. "My mother is Sloane Bevan. She didn't change her name. And I think I told you they gave me her name, not my father's."

She stares at me for a long time before she looks away. When she speaks, her words sound guarded. "Yes, I remember. How do you spell Moore?"

I spell it. She focuses on the seat in front of her, raises her thumb to her lips, and bites it.

I try to remember what I said that could've unsettled her, but all I can think about is the seat in front of me that just got six inches closer to my face. The person in that seat. His soft tissue. His breakable bones.

Her hand slides onto my knee. "So there's Sloane Bevan, Martin Moore, what about Christian?"

"He's a Moore. He's my father's brother's son. And Kate is a Bevan. She took my name. Not sure if she still has it though." My words carry a sour tinge, but I don't care.

"Anyone else?" There's still an off tone to her voice. Maybe I'm overwhelming her.

"Aaron of course. And Christian's father, my uncle. My grandmother—my father's mother—she's a Moore. And a million other relatives always visiting. They're scattered around Virginia and the Northeast. All from my father's side."

"What are their names?" She leans toward me. Her eyes look a little wild. Maybe I'm not the only one about to go postal.

"All of them?" I chuckle. She can't possibly be this interested.

She leans back and turns away. A moment later, her hand finds mine, intertwining our fingers.

She changes her question. "Where does Christian live?"

"At the estate with the rest of them." I guess I should have explained this to her.

"Estate?" Her eyes get big.

I exhale. "Yes. We have a family estate. My grandmother, my parents, my uncle, and Christian, they all live there now. And before I left, Kate and I lived there too, along with many more of them..." I can't remember if I told her about that. She looks at me expectantly, so I skip the complicated part. "Each family has a wing of the house, and Christian has one of the stand-alone houses so he can be free to sneak women in and out without the staff knowing."

She coughs. "Staff?"

"Yes. Staff."

"You should have told me you're rich."

"I'm not."

"Your family is."

"Yes. And they don't deserve a penny of it."

She groans. "I'm going to feel so out of place. God, you should have told me." She bows her head, burying her face in her hands.

Sun blasts through the window. We must be turning. The rolling gray storm clouds below us have been replaced by a sea of blue sky. I reach past her and shut the shade. She grabs my arm on its way back to my seat and holds onto it. I concede and let her keep it. She remains thoughtful and quiet for the remainder of the flight. I put all my effort into not strangling the guy in front of me.

When the tires hit the runway, I want to punch through the window and kiss the ground. The people in the rows in front of us take their sweet time getting off. I never knew human beings could move so slowly. It's almost like they're doing it on purpose, just to piss me off. It might be a little conspicuous to snap every one of their necks, but we'd sure get the hell out of here faster.

I stand in the aisle. An overhead bin opens next to my head. Something brushes down my back and I spin to face it. This guy may not know not to touch me, but he's going to pay for it anyway. All I need is his eye contact. Look at me, fucker. You know you want to.

"Sit down," Liv whispers, tugging my arm. For some reason, I allow her to pull me back into my seat.

"Just relax until we can get off. Okay?" She holds my eye, demanding a response.

"Okay." I focus on a piece of lint on the fabric of the seat in front of me. She takes my hand and weaves her fingers between mine, but this time, it's more like a shackle than an embrace.

Once off the plane, we head straight to baggage claim then out the doors to a man holding a sign marked BEVAN. He takes Liv's bag and leads us past the taxis and shuttles to our waiting black Camaro ZL1 with tinted windows just like I requested. We load the bags into the trunk, he hands me the key, and I tip him a fifty. He opens the passenger door for Liv and she gets in.

"I knew I shouldn't have trusted you," she says as I slide into the driver's seat.

"Is that right?" I ask, a little distracted.

"You *are* rich."

"I don't do this often. I just know when it's time to splurge." The engine growls to life, and I press the pedal to hear the throaty exhaust. The odometer has only sixty-three miles on it. It's not even broken in. I glance over at her to see if she's enjoying this as much as I am.

"I take it you like it?"

"Six point two liter V8. What's not to like?" I check my mirror, slip it into gear, and peel away from the curb.

"Did you buy this?" she asks when we're cruising on the highway and I can finally hear her over the engine and my lead foot.

"Nope. Just a loaner. Don't tempt me to buy it."

"You should buy it." She's taunting me. Always taunting me.

We stop for dinner then drive out of the city. By the time we decide to get a motel, I'm about to fall asleep at the wheel. I leave her in the car to get a room with two beds, and when my head hits the pillow I am already asleep.

CHAPTER 32

LIV

HE'S UP BEFORE me. It's strange to see him watching TV. He flips through the channels without pausing like someone who has never seen a TV before and doesn't know you're supposed to find something you like and watch it. I toss the covers down and stretch.

"Gosh, what is up with the channel flipping?"

He continues as if I hadn't mentioned it.

I sit up and pull my pants on. "Why don't you have a TV at home?"

He switches the power off and tosses the remote into the armchair. "I used to have one. Couldn't justify wasting an eternity watching useless TV so I got rid of it."

And he supplies me with an open door for something I've been meaning to talk to him about. I go to the sink to brush my teeth, hoping to make my question more casual. "So, how is your immortality going to fit in to…us? If there is an us after this week. You're this age forever, but I'm not."

"I'm going to talk to them about that." He answers me into the mirror.

"Your family?"

"I'm going to ask them if they'll grant immortality to you, too."

I take the toothbrush out of my mouth and turn to face him. He leans back on the bed on his elbows as if we're talking about the weather. I return to the mirror and finish brushing my teeth. There's no reason for me to get mad. He doesn't understand he needs to consult people about these types of things before moving ahead with them. In the mirror, he's squinting at the powered-off TV like it just insulted his mother. He's oblivious of me, and temporarily safe from the caustic words bubbling up inside me. I don't want to fight with him. I get in the shower before I do.

When I come out dabbing my hair, he's doing push-ups on the floor. I get dressed behind him and blow-dry my hair. The noise covers the silence, allowing me more time to think. By the time I turn off the hair dryer he's lying on his back on the floor.

I stand over him, looking down. "What if I don't want to be immortal?"

He raises up on his elbows. "You don't? Why not?"

"I'm not saying I don't. But shouldn't I have a say?"

"You do have a say."

"Well, what if—"

"I'm asking them anyway. Asking may be the wrong word, but I need to know if it's possible."

His expression has changed in some way that I'm unable to read, so I go back over what I said, wondering if he heard something I didn't intend. I feel I need to clarify. "I just thought I should've been consulted. Before you asked them."

His face seems to lift, and he stands. "You're right. Then I'm asking you now. Would you like to be immortal?"

"It's kind of a big commitment."

"Yeah," he says slowly, sitting on the bed next to me. "That's kind of the point."

My stomach twirls, and I press both palms into the mattress for stability. I see him on the ground in that puddle of blood. His matted hair. His torn shirt. I see him coming around the house that day wearing that first smile. Him joining his palms to mine on that bluff under the night sky.

He speaks again, drawing out each word. "Would you like to be immortal, with me, forever?"

He's stolen my breath. He's muted my common sense. And that evening he kissed me, he revived my heart. It became his.

My answer rises from that place he now owns. "Yes. Forever."

"Don't," he warns, holding my hands down. "I can't say no to you." His restraint, now so close to slipping, has become obvious in his rapid breath, his tense arms, his grip on my hands, which seems more prepared to pull me toward him than keep me away.

I reach within myself to find the control I promised him I had. I pull away and put a few paces between us in the small room.

"You're wearing your bracelet," Trey says.

"Of course."

He smiles at me. It shines in his eyes. I hope with all my heart that today goes well for him, that he gets everything he wants and more.

We gear up. As I'm loading and holstering my guns, I can't imagine having a need to use them today. He is indeed on his best behavior, and with his radiant mood I can only envision him meeting his family joyfully, passing around hugs and high-fives. I put my hair in a tight ponytail, and he hands me my dagger which I fasten to my ankle.

"Let's go, before I take you to bed instead," he says.

I turn and look at him. Shockingly handsome and covered in guns, he is standing in a scene straight out of an action movie. I can only imagine what I look like to him.

"You didn't tell me why we have to wear these clothes."

"In case we need to hide out in the woods for a few days."

I stare at him until he grins. Something tells me he's not kidding. We didn't pack any food so he better not expect me to eat any bugs. He opens the door wide and surveys the parking lot outside.

"Don't worry. Anyone who sees us will just think we're cops." He must see my expression.

"Cops?" I laugh. "Cops are not this heavily armed."

"Okay then, CIA."

"More like the SWAT team."

We walk out into the blinding sunlight together. A dark purple curtain of storm clouds on the horizon makes the brightness more powerful than it should be. We throw all our luggage in the trunk of the car and get inside.

"I guess this is the reason for the dark windows," I say under my breath.

"That, and to keep people from noticing me. I don't want to be spotted before we get there. It's better without them warned."

The Camaro roars its way onto the highway, and I settle into my seat, pulling a magazine out of my bag. A sane person would be a nervous wreck. I'm clothed in weapons, speeding down the highway, about to meet the family of a man I've only known for three weeks and I just agreed to spend eternity with. Oh yeah, and he's a witch. And everyone in his family is too. And he's going to ask them to make me immortal.

Trey's hand slips around my thigh. I glance out the window and can't ignore what I see in the side mirror. Those dark, billowing storm clouds seem to be following us, gaining on us, even though we're doubling the speed limit. I've never had a problem with storms. For some reason, I have a hard time looking away.

"Getting close," he says, slowing down below the speed limit which is now dropping with each quarter mile. Grand homes with wraparound porches stand along the main road. Little shops come next, in the hub of a small town where we're stopped by a red light. Trey watches the light, stolid and uninterested in the scenery. There's a tension in his jaw that wasn't present a moment ago.

He makes a few turns then we're rolling down narrow pavement through thick forest. Now in shadow, we follow the gentle curves in the road until we stop in front of two towering stone pillars supporting a massive wrought iron gate. The black bars continue on either side of the pillars, forming an impenetrable fence at least fifteen feet tall and topped with forbidding spikes. It continues as far as I can see in both directions before disappearing into the forest.

I stare at the polished brass nameplate on the gate. MOORE.

Gunshots shatter the stillness as Trey unloads his P220 into the lock mechanism of the gate. Bracing his feet against the ground, he pushes, and the gate groans under its own weight as it swings open.

"Don't you have a code?" I ask when he slides back behind the wheel. I point to the number pad.

He reloads. "I doubt my code still works. And I'd like to leave an easy way to get out. They won't be able to fix this anytime soon."

We drive through, the road spilling us into sunlight and the lush green grounds of the estate. Perfectly manicured lawns and massive oak trees usher us along the paved driveway. Rounding a bend, the house comes into view and I stifle a gasp. It's a palace. How could he move to rural Montana and give all this up? The Trey next to me now shares no similarities with the Trey I left the motel with this morning. The focused glare and hooded eyes belong to a different person.

A small black cloud passes above, obscuring the brilliance of the sun. It couldn't have been timed more precisely to match Trey's dark mood.

The driveway ends in a circular loop in front of the sprawling white stone mansion anchored by corner turrets gouging the sky. Just as one would expect, a man in a suit comes out to greet us. Trey turns off the engine, takes a long, deep look into my eyes, and nods once. "Ready?"

I nod. He opens his door and I follow.

"Master Trey, welcome home." The man doesn't seem to notice all the weapons we're wearing.

"I'd like to leave the car here."

"Not a problem, sir. Can I help with any luggage?"

"No thank you."

"Shall I make up a room for the lady?"

"We aren't here to stay. Where's my father?"

"In the house, sir. I'll tell him you're here."

"No need. I'll find him."

The man opens the door for us just as the wind picks up, plucking at my back before I make it across the threshold. We step into an entry foyer out of a fairytale, and the door thuds closed behind us. A staircase opening toward us spans most of the width of the vast room. At the top, a landing splits it into two branches, turning toward either side of the second floor. The domed ceiling is ornately painted like that of a Renaissance church.

Trey leads me into a side room—a parlor—where there's simply too much to take in. I know my mind shouldn't be wandering like this. My focus is critical.

We go into the next room—a library—with rows of bookshelves and floor-to-ceiling windows looking over a wide lawn. Two people appear to be practicing archery on the grass.

Trey sucks a breath through his teeth. His body turns rigid.

"Trey." A woman rises from her seat, marking her page and putting down her book. I feel my eyes follow her up to her full height—the female equivalent of Trey's. Straight long dark brown hair, the color and texture of Trey's. She could easily pass for his sister, but he mentioned no siblings. This woman must be his wife.

And she is about eight months pregnant.

"It'd have been better if you had called first," she says in a slow southern drawl.

"The best thing," Trey says, "is if *you* had called. A long time ago. But I see you've been busy."

She gives him a long look. "And what have *you* been up to?" Her eyes slide to me. It's a knowing, patronizing look. She thinks she's in charge here.

My palms tingle with heat, itching for the cool metal of a weapon. I'm surprised it's the dagger I crave. The sound of her voice curling around his name repeats in my mind.

"I'm not the one under interrogation here," Trey snarls. "Where's my son?"

Her eyes move from me to the lawn, giving it away. Trey walks past her to the window, and I remain in position, covering his back and the doorway. I look again at the people on the lawn and recognize Christian, repositioning a young man's arms while he holds the bow and arrow. The young man shoots. He doesn't look like he needs any instruction.

"Please, Trey, he doesn't need to know." Her voice wraps around his name in that disturbing way.

"You didn't tell him?"

"There was nothing to tell."

"There was *nothing to tell*?" His face is grim as he steps in front of her, the top button of his rage coming undone.

A woman enters the room with a pale blue box. Trey and Kate remain locked in a stare so heated either one of them could snap at any second. The woman unloads stacks of cards and envelopes from the box onto the coffee table near

Kate without making eye contact with either one of them, but I can tell by the stiffness of her body that she can't get out of the room fast enough. Her eyes flick to Trey just as she leaves the room. She's afraid of him.

Three men come through the doorway and Trey turns toward them.

"Son, welcome home. We need to relieve you of your weapons."

"My ass." Trey's voice is borderline sadistic, directed at the man who addressed him as his son.

A second man steps forward and laughs at the ceiling before facing Trey. There is no levity in the sound. "*A nia, le do thoil,* let's be peaceful." The bitter edge of the words betrays his deceit.

I don't allow the switch in languages to rattle me. They can't know they're talking over my head. Its mocking tone makes me wonder if he's using the language or the words themselves to unsettle Trey.

"You don't know the meaning of the word," Trey says.

A line of men files through the door behind them, pistols drawn, aimed at us. Trey takes one step, blocking half of me with his shoulder. I use his motion and cover to release the safety on my weapon. Somehow, I know to draw a line down the room in front of us. Everyone to my right is mine.

Trey's father glances behind him at the men and they all lower their guns. He returns his attention to Trey. It's his turn to speak but he's taking his time. If he hadn't addressed his son directly, nothing else about him would reveal his relationship to Trey. They could be strangers. "*A mhic,* you understand our position and we understand yours. But we're open to a conversation. No one has to get hurt."

Trey still studies the other man, the one who laughed. "Some of you need to be hurt. I neglected a few of you last time."

It's his father who answers. "So this is how you want it. Just know—any decision we make will be based on your decision right now."

One of the men in the firing squad behind them raises his weapon. Trey takes no apparent notice. "I'm not responsible for what you do."

"You're responsible for what we must do to stop you."

"No."

"Yes." His father steps toward us and places a hand on the back of an armchair. "*Ní ba chóir dhuit í a thabhairt anseo.*"

"*Má leagann duine ar bith láimh uirthi, maróidh mé sibh uilig,*" Trey says, as naturally as English.

The other man laughs that joyless laugh again. "We miss you, too."

"*Focáil leat.*" Trey spits the words. He turns back to Kate. "I'm not through with you. Try to leave, I'll find you."

He takes my hand and pulls me to the other end of the room, away from the men. My legs struggle to keep up with his pace. We go through a dining room then into a bright kitchen where many people pause in their work to gawk as we stride through. He takes me up a back staircase. At the top of the second flight, we go down a narrow hallway, turn the corner, and the walls open into a much larger hall with high ceilings and grand chandeliers. As he pulls me through a set of open double doors, the maid, folding clothes, looks up. "Trey!"

"Eleanor, is my mother here?"

"Yes, sir. One moment." She drops the shirt she was folding into the basket and looks at Trey like she wants to hug him, like our visit has made her day. Her comfort around him doesn't fit with the behavior of the rest of the people we've encountered so far. She walks to a second open doorway. "Madam? You have some visitors."

Trey's mother comes through the doorway with her arms open wide. "Fearghus, *a chroí!*" She hugs him tightly then pulls back to look at him. "*Amhail is nach ndeachaigh am ar bith isteach.*"

"What did you expect?" He flashes a boyish smile I've never seen before. He steps out of her grasp and turns to me. "*A Mháthair*, this is Liv. Liv, this is my mother."

She takes both my hands in hers and beams at me. We are exactly the same height. Her eyes are the color of Trey's but hold a warmth his do not.

"Hello." I'm taken aback by her grace. I couldn't even begin to guess her age.

"*Bhur fíorghrá?*" she asks Trey while still looking at me.

"She doesn't know the language, *a Mháthair.*" I can tell he feels like they're talking behind my back.

"You didn't teach her? Shame on you." She walks me over to a sitting area near several sets of French doors. She gestures to the couch, and I sit, and she sits next to me. "You make him very happy. This is the happiest I have ever seen him."

I know Trey can hear but he makes no indication. He moves to the window and looks out, his back to us.

"Considering the circumstances," she adds, eyeing him as he watches Christian and Aaron on the lawn.

"Fearghus," she says, and he turns to her. "Sit with us."

He sits across from us, leaning forward with his fore-arms on his knees, intent. "*A Mháthair*, Liv had a daughter who died in infancy. Her name was Sloane."

"I'm so sorry to hear that." Her words are sincere, and she squeezes my hand.

"A coincidence?" Trey asks.

"Yes." She looks away. She is holding something back.

"When did my father lose so much weight?"

She sighs. "You haven't seen him for a very long time. He's been ill."

"With what?"

"You should call him once in a while."

Trey looks at his hands. "He doesn't want to talk to me."

"He would be overjoyed to talk to you."

A woman in a white apron brings a tray with a teapot, three cups, and a bowl of fruit. "Anything else, madam?"

"Could you please tell Martin to have lunch without me? Open up that bottle of wine for him."

"Yes, madam."

I can't imagine Trey growing up here in such a refined environment. I wonder if I'd even recognize the Trey who lived in this house fifteen years ago.

After the woman hurries off, Trey leans back against the couch. "The Alignment."

"Yes." His mother's face lights up.

"I didn't know how to explain it to Liv in English. It was missing something. Can you try to explain it to her?"

"Hmm..." she begins, handing me a cup of tea and taking one for herself. "Alignment. There really is no good English word to explain it all. Liv, are you familiar with the law of conservation in physics?"

I rack my brain. "Energy cannot be created nor destroyed?"

"Yes, that's the one. Energy can only change in form if acted upon by another force. In our universe, we see whole solar systems altered by one meteor strike. You and Fearghus didn't get along well at first, I assume?"

"No. He made me physically sick," I answer honestly.

"Your energy was not aligned. An outside force acted upon you, and your energy was transformed into something new. Much like a meteorite hitting a planet, shifting moons and other planets, creating a whole new solar system."

"When Trey fell off the roof?"

"He fell off a roof? For goodness' sake."

"I was dragged off a roof," Trey clarifies. "By one of their men."

His mother closes her eyes and takes a breath. It's apparent she doesn't like to be reminded of the danger her son lives with every day.

"Why did we have to hate each other?" It can't be as simple as our combined bad luck, or even our individual torment bringing out ill will. Something else must have been at play.

"Fearghus would never have allowed you into his life without a barrier of dislike to keep you at a distance from him."

She's given me a gift with those words. I understand her son more now, and how intricate our fate really is. I'm humbled—and a bit terrified—to be so... chosen.

"Have you met her lover?" Trey asks abruptly, the violence returning to his face.

"Yes." Her calm voice doesn't waver, even though she's watching him like he's a bomb falling through the sky toward us.

"Is he here?"

"Yes."

He stands and paces, finally moving back to the window and staring out at them.

His mother sighs. "Now is a time for patience." She looks pointedly at Trey. "*Is neamhbhuan cogadh na gcarad; má bhíonn sé crua, ní bhíonn sé fada.*"

He spins around. "What is that supposed to mean?"

"Please come and sit. I have some things to tell you, and I need you to promise me that you'll listen to everything I have to say before you leave this room."

"I'll make no promises until I know what's going on." He struggles to control his tone for her sake. I'm impressed. He doesn't sit, but he walks to the couch and places his hands on the back of it as if to appease her.

She sets her cup on the tray and looks up at her son. "Christian is Aaron's father."

I stifle a gasp. I look at Trey's mother, waiting for her to explain. She needs to say something, but she's become still, taking in the room like she's just been deposited here and she's seeing everything around her for the first time. Trey's grip on the couch has become deadly—his fingers are about to pop through the fabric. With every muscle in his body taut, he looks like he's going to pounce.

"Say that again." He can barely form the words.

"Christian is Aaron's father. But you can't blame him. He's not responsible for this."

A table crashes to the floor. The door is ripped open, and he's gone.

"Liv." She takes both of my hands as the words pour out of her. "You have to stop him. He'll go too far, and when he finds out the truth the guilt and regret will kill him. It's not Christian's fault. He's a victim in this even more so than my son. They've been using Christian, manipulating him, and he has no control, no responsibility for what has happened. I'm putting an address in your mind right now. When the time is right, you'll think of it. Take my son there as soon as you can."

Two men burst into the room, and I instinctively crouch, drawing my Glock and aiming for the first one's chest.

"There will be no violence in here." She stands, turning toward the men and staring them down.

Not finding the person they are looking for, they leave through the same door. I begin to follow them but her voice stops me.

"This way." She opens a door leading to a balcony.

I step outside to see Trey already crossing the lawn toward Christian. I sense movement to my left above me and put a bullet in the shoulder of a man with a rifle on a balcony one floor up. He falls back, dropping the rifle.

I climb over the railing and push off with my feet, flipping in the air, landing in a crouch behind a hedge. Thunder rolls in the distance and echoes across the vast side lawn. From here, I can see Kate and Aaron standing on a patio near the house. Now seeing Aaron clearly, I'm surprised I didn't notice the resemblance to Christian earlier, especially when they were side by side. It should've been obvious. The blond hair is exact, and it glows, saturated in the luminescence created by the storm clouds. Aaron studies the balcony I was on, alarmed by the gunshot. Watching him, I get the mental image of a young Robin Hood, standing there with his bow and arrows.

Two men come outside and join Kate and Aaron on the patio. I hear Trey's raised voice across the yard. The men on the patio begin to argue quietly, obviously unsure what to do. The small army we faced upon entering the house is nowhere to be seen.

Christian makes an effort to walk toward the house but Trey catches him, throwing him back to face him. Christian shoves Trey backward. Trey doesn't return the shove, he simply recovers and steps forward, inches from Christian's face. He must be speaking, but this time, his voice is too quiet to hear. Christian raises his hand, and Trey grabs his fingers. Several sharp snaps resound across the yard as four fingers break. Christian cries out, falling to his knees.

Kate and I rush forward simultaneously. I sense her attention shift to me. I should have listened to the haste in Trey's mother's voice. I waited too long. I sprint across the yard, feeling exposed. Trey already has Christian's throat. I'm not going to make it there in time.

"Trey!" I shout. He is incapable of hearing. I stop, aim, and fire.

A sharp heat peels through my back, my chest. My legs give. Lightning flashes in a white hot web across the sky, and I wonder if my aim was accurate as the dark clouds consume me.

CHAPTER 33

TREY

I SEE HER FALL and forget everything. I'm on my knees at her side. I pick her limp body off the ground, out of an already puddling pool of blood. The boy has good aim.

I turn her over to yank the arrow out. Her breath catches then goes faint. Her heartbeat loses momentum. I lay her back down and whip out my guns, unloading them down the side of the house, scattering people and shattering windows. I don't care who gets hit. I hope I hit them all.

I pick her up in my arms running red with her blood. I sprint to the car, vaguely aware of the bullets hitting the ground around my feet. Her body is dead weight as I lay her in the passenger seat. We blast down the driveway and through the open gate. I have to avoid obvious roads. No interstate. No logical path. I take several pointless turns then head north. I'm running out of time. She's fading fast.

I watch the forest blurring beside us, the trees too thick to allow me through but it's becoming sparser by the minute. Then I'm jerking the wheel and we're off the road, thrust into a din of snapping and cracking and rumbling. Underbrush and young trees scrape around and below us until a thick barrier of trees makes it impossible to go farther. Some cover is better than no cover at all.

I pop a new mag in each gun, jam the guns in their holsters and shove out of the car. I fall to my hands and knees. The damp earth gives beneath my palms, and I bow my head, throwing everything I have into it. I never do this. It may not work. Stinging heat fills my head and just when it becomes too much to bear, it's gone. Out of me. I pant, gathering the breath back into my lungs, waiting for my eyes to focus on the blades of green between my fingers.

When I look up, the forest floor is undisturbed, the Camaro's destructive path erased forever. I hate cheating like this, but I have to fight fire with fire. I know it will come back to haunt me. But there's no more time to think.

I carry her as far into the woods as my legs will allow. My skin is sticky with my blood and hers. As I lay her on the ground on a carpet of thick grass, the sky erupts in a violent downpour.

I kneel next to her and brush her hair off her face. Rain pounds my back and puddles against her closed eyelids. The sound swells around us, stealing my vigilance. I rip off our shoes and clothes. It only exposes more blood, when we are already drowning in it. I put my ear by her lips but can't hear her breath through the sound of the hammering rain. I throw my head back and close my eyes, letting the deluge crash against my face.

"Please." It is all I can say.

Her face is in my hands. Large drops run down her temples like tears. All her color has drained, filling the red puddle around us instead of her face. Her lips blend with her skin. She's barely holding on.

"*Tá mo chroí istigh ionat*," I whisper, but I doubt she can hear me.

I cover her body with mine and part her legs with my knee. It has to be done. She'd tell me to if she could speak. So I shut off my mind. Let my body take control.

Afterward, I relax on my back for a while. The rain has turned into a languid drizzle mostly absorbed by the canopy of trees above us. The large drops that fall from the branches calm my skin. Liv feels cold against me. I sit up and pull my arm from under her head. All the blood has washed away except for a small smear on my side where her chest was in contact with me. I watch the rain dilute it, running in reddish streaks down my body and into the grass.

Using my fingers, I dig a bullet out of my arm and toss it to the side. Probably a bad idea because now it's bleeding again. I tug on my wet pants and boots. Inspecting the wound on Liv's back, I wonder if it's just my imagination to see the skin already sealing back up.

After tugging her clothes back on, I study her face, the slight hint of pinkness returning to her skin. The wound on her chest still bleeds. There's nothing to use for pressure. I need to get her indoors and warmed up. I pick up all our gear and carry her back toward the car.

We're lucky for the heavy rain because my careless footprints from our parking spot to our bed of grass have been covered. As I near the Camaro, I draw my gun. The ruts left by the tires have been erased, but anyone could have been tracking me. It's impossible to know what they used, how far they could've gotten.

After laying her in the seat, I circle the car, checking all around. Nothing seems out of place but I'm not about to get sloppy now. I grab a shirt out of my bag from the trunk and yank it on. Hopefully the tires aren't stuck. I ease the gas and we're moving. I back up all the way to the road and head toward Charlottesville. There are too many of them in Richmond.

From Charlottesville, I drive toward the mountains at top speed. Before reaching Waynesboro I turn off the interstate in favor of back roads, passing other cars illegally and pushing the Camaro around the mountain curves on slick pavement. We've gained enough distance that now we need cover, and the deeper we go the better I feel.

I spot a sign for a bed and breakfast and know it's right. The driveway takes us far from the road and around a bend which descends low into a valley. Only one way out, but no one will find us here. Thickly wooded mountains surround us on all sides. I could affect the trees to mask our presence but I doubt it's necessary and there's no time. I park out front, lock Liv inside the car, and go into the office.

The old woman smiles at my appearance when I come in the door. "Did you get stuck in the rain, hon?"

"Had a rough day."

I buy out all three of her guest rooms and take only one key. It doesn't seem to throw her. Privacy must be a common request among her customers. I doubt many of them show up unannounced, soaking wet and bloody and expecting to reserve all three rooms for a romantic getaway. The woman sends her husband to help me with the luggage. I can't find it in me to decline.

"Looks like you wore her out," he says when I lift Liv out of the car. His eyes graze the wound on my arm, but he decides not to say anything.

"She's a deep sleeper." Enough color has returned to her face so I don't look like a liar.

When we get to the room upstairs, I lay Liv on the bed. Our host sets down our luggage and hovers in the doorway. I catch concern flecked with wariness and a long look passes between us. There's no explanation I can give. I'm no good at lying.

He gives me a nod, closing himself out of the room.

I peel off Liv's clothes and dab her body dry with a towel from the bathroom. I pull the covers up to her chin. Test her pulse. Stronger? Maybe—but I squash all enthusiasm. It can get better before it gets worse. After several minutes of picking at the tangled rubber band in her hair, my patience runs out in favor of my knife.

While searching her overnight bag for a dry shirt, I find an entire bag of first aid supplies she fortunately thought to bring. I doubt she thought she'd need them for herself. I apply a bandage to the wound on her back and the one on her chest. The sight of her relieves me even though I know she's unconscious due to traumatic blood loss. Caused by my fucked-up family. By my idea to bring her with me.

I sit in an armchair and wait, enforcing a censor on my thoughts. There's blood under my fingernails—her blood.

I can't reflect on the events of the day until Liv is with me again. Without her balance, I can't trust myself. I will lose control.

Even though it's still daytime, my exhaustion undermines my will, making the bed look too inviting to ignore. I set the deadbolt on the door and climb into bed next to Liv. Her body is warm next to mine and covered in the soothing fragrance of the earth and the rain.

I'm startled awake by Liv sitting up straight in bed. The white bandage on her back glows in the dim light. I sit up next to her and she turns to me. The intensity of my relief cripples me. She's going to be okay.

"3015 Scarlet Lane. Chicago, Illinois."

"What?" I ask.

"3015 Scarlet Lane," she repeats. "I need to write that down."

I get out of bed and write the address on a paper napkin. She slowly scans the room then returns to me. Her hand moves to the bandage on her chest, and she looks down at it.

My clumsy hands tear through our bags to find her a shirt. I find one of mine and pull it over her head. She puts her arms through then reaches to feel the bandage on her back. She squints up at me, not understanding.

"It went through you," I explain.

"Through me? What went through me?"

"An arrow."

"How did…"

"I pulled it out."

She lies back against the pillow and stares up at the ceiling. I remain standing, unsure what to do. I look at the clock. It's 2:24 a.m.

"Please come back," she whispers.

I get back in bed with her, and she rolls over and pulls herself to me, snuggling against my side as I drift back to sleep.

I wake up and feel her against me. I look into her face. Either it's the morning light playing tricks on me, or she looks vibrant as hell. The pink color of her lips has returned in full force, and I can feel the heat of her skin radiating onto mine. As if sensing me awake, she opens her eyes and smiles.

"Hi." I've never been happier in my life.

She slides her arms around my neck and clings to me. "I missed you. It feels like I haven't seen you in forever."

I hold her to me, unwilling to let her go.

She pulls back to look at me.

"How do you feel?" I ask.

"Wonderful. Better than I've felt in a long time." She pauses, trying to guard her smile. "Did you do what I think you did?"

"I had to heal you. It was the only way to save you."

"But what if—"

"It doesn't matter. I had to save you." I don't want to talk about this.

Her lips part as if she wants to say something.

"What?" I ask.

"You almost made it with a dead girl."

"The key word there is 'almost.'"

She gives me a teasing sideways glance. "Isn't there a term for that?"

"Necrophilia."

She laughs. "So I guess you've already thought of that?"

"Yeah, but I've done much worse, so it really doesn't matter," I say, returning a smile. I run my finger along her cheekbone. I don't deserve this.

Her expression turns serious. "What did you say to me, right before…?"

"You couldn't have heard that."

"It was far away, but I heard it."

"I said, '*Tá mo chroí istigh ionat.*'"

"Which means?"

"My heart is within you." I didn't expect to have to translate that.

"Wow. I never would've taken you for a romantic."

"I'm not. I was desperate." But I wouldn't have to be desperate to say it to her again.

She sits up, pulling my arm away from my body to examine it. She must have just remembered.

"I did that." She stares at my wound.

"It was very effective. But not as effective as this." I place my palm on her chest where I know her bandage is. I wonder if her bullet would've been enough to stop me if she hadn't been hurt.

"I can't believe I did that." Her eyes fill with tears. With a sharp intake of breath, her eyes dart back to mine. "I have to tell you something."

I groan. I can't revisit yesterday's bullshit right now.

"You'll want to hear this. It's from your mother." She sits up all the way and crosses her legs underneath her.

I sit up with her.

"After you left the room, she told me that it's not Christian's fault."

"Yeah I heard that part." I can't help my belligerent tone. I knew this was going to happen. Everyone's going to sympathize with that asshole.

"Trey, listen for a second. She said they've been manipulating him, that he has no control over what happened. He's a victim just like you. They've been using him."

"He has no control over who he—" I jam my fists against the mattress. He was fucking her that long ago. Right in front of my face. God I could kill him.

"Think about it. Would Christian do that to you on his own? You yourself said he and your mother are the only ones you can trust."

I look away from her. I don't want to believe this. Because if I do, I'll never be able to take back what I said to him. What I did to him.

Fucker deserved it.

"Your mother wanted me to stop you because she knew what it would do to you once you found out the truth. She knew if you'd hurt him, you'd never be able to live with yourself."

If I hurt him. I did hurt him. She saw it. So did I.

"And I couldn't get to you in time," she continues. "I had to stop you the only way I could. Thank god my aim was good."

"You should've never come out into the open like that. You know better." I try to clear the image of her falling to the ground from my mind. Her lifeless eyes, after I pulled the arrow out. Her blood, all over my hands. "Aaron thought you were aiming at Christian."

"I had no choice."

"You sacrificed yourself. For *me*. Do you know how ridiculous that is? And just to save me from handing out something he deserves. You could be dead!" Her shoulders are in my hands and I'm gripping too hard. I release my hands.

"Not ridiculous at all because here we are. Everything worked out." She smiles.

"That's quite a gamble to have made." Not everything worked out. I need to go back there.

"Oh, and that address. Did you write it down?" She looks around the room, pushing up from her heels to make herself taller on her knees. "Your mother told me I need to take you there."

"She didn't say why?"

"No. Just that I need to take you there." She shrugs.

Something has to be missing. My mother usually isn't so cryptic. "What were her exact words?"

She looks away thoughtfully. "She told me about Christian, and said she was going to put an address in my mind and when the time was right I would think of it. And that I should take you there right away."

"She put it in your mind because she didn't want to write it down. What I wrote last night is useless."

"What do you mean?"

I laugh hard—it shouldn't be so funny. "See that napkin right there on the table? Go look at it."

She hops off the bed and picks up the napkin. "It's blank." She holds it out for me to see.

"Exactly."

"I thought you wrote it down for me!"

"I did. But my mother didn't want a paper trail."

Her hand flies to her mouth. "Please tell me you remember it."

"Umm…" I should draw it out. I love it when she gets worked up like this.

She returns to the bedside and smacks the top of my head. "Trey!"

"You'll think of it again," I say through my laughter, dodging her again. I snatch her and pull her on top of me.

"What if I don't?!" she cries, jabbing me in the ribs.

I roll on top of her, holding her down. "3015 Scarlet Lane," I whisper in her ear.

"You jerk." She squirms under me, giggling.

"Liv." I'm overtaken by something I need to say. "Everything was a lie. They fed me lie upon lie upon lie, and I believed them all."

Her smile fades, and her expression becomes pained. "I know."

"I can't believe my mother and Christian went along with it. I can't believe—"

"They were probably both powerless to say anything." She places her finger over my lips. "You know if they could have, they would've told you the truth."

Deep down I know she's right. I roll off her, onto my back. "Is it wrong to be relieved he's not mine?"

She's as motionless and silent as she was when I first laid her in this bed. I shouldn't expect her to answer a question like that, and just when I think she's not going to, she does. "I don't think so. It's not wrong to be relieved that a boy was not away from his father for fifteen years, that a boy had not been lied to for fifteen years."

Her perspective heals me. I feel some of my guilt lift off and vaporize.

She turns her head. Looks into my eyes. "And all those years you were tormented without him, you can let it go. You are now released from that."

I wrap my arms around her, pull her against me. She nuzzles into my neck, and for a few brief moments I feel cured from the sick poison of guilt mixed with the disappointment of unfulfilled revenge. Like that primal need to watch them all die has been boxed up and tossed off a cliff. Like my past and everything I've done has been erased.

She opens her lips against my neck and whispers, "Fearghus."

I exhale. "Only a matter of time before you brought that up."

"You actually do look like a Fearghus. But how is Trey short for that? Is Fearghus your real name?"

"It's my middle name."

"Trey Fearghus Bevan." She winds her legs around mine and sighs in contentment.

I could stay like this with her forever.

CHAPTER 34

LIV

I CLOSE THE BATHROOM door behind me and rip the bandage off my chest. I have no idea what the wound looked like before, but now it looks like a week-old scar. I strain to rip the one off my back and turn in the mirror to examine what it was hiding. I don't need a close look to see how perfectly the wound has healed. Judging from where the arrow struck, I should have lost enough blood for the wound to have been fatal.

Forget the wound. What did he do to my hair? It's tangled in so many knots I consider cutting it all off. In the shower, I wash my hair twice and load it up with conditioner. When I emerge from the bathroom, he's at the table cleaning and oiling our weapons. I pull my comb out of my bag and join him.

"How is it?" He doesn't look up from his work.

"A mess." I tug the comb through the ends, hoping I don't break too much hair.

He looks up, startled. "Can I see? You have nothing to compare it to."

"Oh, my wound? It's just fine."

"What did you think I meant?"

I hold up a section of my still-knotted hair.

"I had to cut the rubber band out. It was a lost cause." He goes back to his work.

I should have taken my shower before we went to breakfast—our hosts seemed worried about me earlier. I hope my dirty skin and tragic hair didn't give them any reason to be suspicious. No one can blame me for wanting to break a twenty-four hour fast before showering.

"Can I help?" I ask.

"You need to rest. Get back in bed."

"You can't be serious. There's nothing wrong with me."

"Aside from the fact that you almost died a few hours ago?" He pushes away from the table. "I'm going out to clean up the mess in the car. Stay in here, and don't let anyone in. I don't want anyone to see our arsenal."

Alone in the room with nothing to do, I decide to scrub out yesterday's clothes in the bathtub. A river of red-tinged water flows down the drain. This must be why he wanted us dressed in black—it masks the blood. I hang them up in the bathroom to dry. I make the bed, tidy up the room, and repack my bag.

He finally returns to the room. "Looks like we're driving to Chicago. I just bought a car."

"What car?"

"Turns out taking a new car off-roading in the woods is hard on the paint job. So I just decided to buy it." He grins. "Insurance claims are a pain in the ass."

"That's an expensive car…"

"I think I deserve it. I did save someone's life yesterday." He shrugs out of his jacket. "So we'll take a short detour back to Richmond. I need to sign some papers."

My eyes go straight to his gunshot wound. "Why didn't you wrap that? It looks like you opened it back—" I choke on my own voice. I move closer to examine it. He's not healing as fast as he should be.

"It's fine."

"It's not fine."

He grudgingly goes along with my meticulous bandaging of his arm, and then we pack everything up and load the car. I see what he means about the paint job, and I also see he's understating the damage—a broken headlight, dents and tears not only on the front of the car but also the back, scratches along both sides. I go into the office with him to check out so I can thank our hosts properly this time. As we leave, Trey hands the woman a hundred dollar bill. By the time she recovers herself to refuse, we're walking out the door.

Outside, I open my mouth but he speaks first. "Save it." When he sees my fake offense, he adds, "It's hush money. I'm covering your butt."

"How did I ever get stuck with you?"

We get in the car, and he leans over to me. "I ran a red light."

The joy in his eyes shocks my heart.

He pulls onto a narrow road winding through a forest that appears eager to overtake the pavement. We gain elevation as the trees fall away on one side, offering hints of blue sky beyond their tops now almost level with us. Then we round a curve and I see what they've been hiding—hazy mountains in varying shades of blue as far as the eye can see.

As soon as we enter the Richmond city limits, he rolls up both windows and slows down, obviously in an attempt not to draw too much attention. He takes us to a posh car dealership and parks out front among the Jaguars, Porches, and a bright yellow Lamborghini.

Inside, he's recognized immediately and ushered into an office.

"Everything is ready to go, Mr. Bevan. I just need you to sign here, here, and here. And then here, and here." The salesman hands him a pen.

"The funds?" Trey asks.

"Already here," the man answers.

Outside, Trey hands me the key. "Now I own it. So if you wreck it, you owe me a lot of money."

"But what you don't realize is that I don't mind being forever indebted to you."

He takes the passenger seat and slides his seat back as I slide mine forward. I pull the steering wheel closer, adjust the mirrors, and start it up. The car roars awake. "And isn't it already wrecked?"

"Not as well as you'd do it."

I'd try to ignore him if I could, but I'm sure my smile gives me away. I back out of the parking spot and pull onto the road. The power under my foot scares me, but I get used to it after a few minutes and try to drive conservatively while Trey directs me on our route. As soon as we get on the highway, I merge over into the fast lane and mash the pedal to the floor. I can barely hear Trey's laughter over the Camaro's roar. I slow back down and merge to the right.

He overdoes his surprise. "That's it?"

"That's all I need. I'm not an aggressive driver like you. Running lights, wrecking other people's cars…"

He settles back in his seat. "Then I guess you wouldn't mind if I took a nap?"

"Not at all. What's my next turn?"

"81 South to Lexington."

He falls asleep in minutes, and my thoughts wander. It's nice to have some time to myself. My mind replays every minute of yesterday's events, analyzing each detail. The part that keeps resurfacing is that Trey never had the opportunity to finish his conversation with Kate. Which means things still aren't settled between them. Perhaps the news from his mother cancels out his need to settle anything with Kate at all.

What a surprise it was to see how they treated each other when I had myself prepared for some affection between the two of them. But I guess their relationship was over to her fifteen years ago. She just didn't have the decency to release Trey. She held the power over his suffering, and she continued it for so very long. I ease my foot off the pedal when I notice I'm speeding. And suddenly I realize how much I hate her.

And Christian. A sickness twists my stomach when I think of him and how things might have happened differently if I hadn't hesitated. I can only imagine what Trey said to him, as if Trey's violence against him wasn't enough to hurt him. I don't hold Trey responsible for any of it. It was my job to stop him, and I didn't make it in time.

I glance at him sleeping crunched against the window, arms crossed tightly, chin tucked against his chest. I see a fragility. A little boy. When I return my attention to the road, in my head I see a wall of mirrors reflecting a brightly lit room with mats on the floor and a dark-haired little boy facing his reflection, which is somehow my reflection. He turns when two grown men attack then it's flashes of movement—arms, knees, fists—and the peripheral view of the action in the mirrors. Feelings sweep in. A dark desperation, a primal rage. My heart pounds. Whether it's my imagination or one of his stray memories loose in my head, it's a nightmare I don't want to see.

I exit the highway at a rest stop for a bathroom break. Trey doesn't stir, so I leave him there. When I return, he's missing. I take the passenger seat and surf through radio stations. He might have a web of torment in his head, but we're going to make new memories. We'll push all the bad ones out.

The sun is low when he pulls back onto the highway, its angle blinding us.

"I'm not holding back anymore," he says.

It's a matter-of-fact delivery of information that seems out of place. I'm quiet for a moment to digest his meaning.

He could only be talking about backing out of our no sex bargain, our only safe bet against his godlike fertility and his family's army of killers. Which means he's gone crazy.

Probably taking my silence for confusion, he adds, "With you."

"Isn't that dangerous?" I ask an obvious question, for lack of anything better to say.

"I don't care."

"What brought this on?"

"I'm done with them. And all their crap. For all I know, the prophecy is a lie, too."

"So you're just being rebellious?"

"Not at all. I'm doing what I want to do, for once in my life."

I look over at him. His eyes are determined and his jaw is set. He's going to make it impossible for me to keep my promise to him. "I promised you I'd be responsible for us, and I intend—"

"You're officially released from your promise." He smiles mischievously at me and I turn into a puddle of goo—a speechless puddle—which seems convenient because I can tell by his body language that he doesn't expect a response.

When I find my voice, I say, "But you're still married."

"Fuck it," he says dryly. "So are you."

"Maybe we should do something about that." It's only logical. It's what we need to be right now. Not controlled by hormones or lust or spells or bloodlines.

"Too much paperwork."

I can tell he considers the subject dropped, so I do too, knowing we'll have to revisit it later. He's focused on the more important business of finding a restaurant we agree on.

Seated across from him in our booth, I'm so distracted I don't even taste the food, and every look he gives me sends chills to every nerve ending in my body. I wonder if those looks have actual intent, or if it's just my reaction to knowing he has completely given in.

While waiting for our bill, he takes my hand, and kisses the back of it. His lips linger so long it becomes the X-rated version of the back-of-the-hand kiss.

"It's really bad timing." I seem to be out of breath.

The look he gives me tells me he doesn't care. I pull my hand away.

"One week," I say.

He slowly shakes his head, staring at me with an intensity that conveys only one thing.

"This isn't fair."

Our bill arrives and he puts cash on the table and stands, offering his hand. Outside in the chill, he puts his warm arm around me, pulling me against him. When we reach the car he spins me to face him.

"Don't." I brace myself to push him away.

Instead of going for my lips, he goes for my neck, and I allow it knowing it can't possibly lead to anything right here. I inhale deeply, surrendering, taking in the smell of him, drowning in it. When he pulls away, his rough cheek grazes mine, and I remember that feeling on my skin that night he did so much more than kiss me. I break out of his grasp and push around him to the car door.

"Tell me when you get tired, and I'll take over. I can drive us through the night." Avoiding a motel room with him seems like the best game plan.

"Because you know you can't say no to me?"

"Because I don't want to *have* to say no to you," I answer truthfully.

"But you don't have to say no to me."

"But I will, if it comes to that."

He lets me have the last word, but he remains smug. I don't want to have to prove him wrong.

What seems like an instant later I open my eyes to Trey leaning over me taking off my seat belt. I don't even remember falling asleep.

"Don't wake up," he whispers.

"It's okay." I take his hand and get out of the car. "I'm awake now."

We're in the parking lot of a small motel. He carries our bags while I follow him up the stairs to a room on the second level. He leaves me inside to go back for the duffle bags, and in his absence I throw on a tank top and boyshorts while brushing my teeth. By the time he's back, I'm slipping under the covers of one of the two beds next to my bag and discarded clothes which I intentionally left on one side.

"Good night." I turn off the lamp next to my bed.

"Good night."

He stands at the foot of my bed, watching me, and I shut my eyes and try to ignore his heavy gaze that seems to caress my skin through the sheets. I can't fall asleep until I hear his mattress groan under his weight and his lamp click off.

I wake up and fall back asleep over and over in the morning as Trey hits the snooze button at least a dozen times. Having enough, I flip the covers back and swing my legs to the floor. "Maybe we should just get up." I turn off the alarm clock.

He moans into his pillow. It's an unusual picture. I've never seen him sleep in like this, except for one time, but I can't quite remember when it was.

"Do you want to sleep longer?" I hope he doesn't and know if he does, I'll only be tempted to slide into bed with him and soak up the thick morning smell of his skin that will most likely bait me into allowing him to have his way with me.

"We need to get on the road." His voice is an octave deeper. He shoves himself up, stretches his back and rolls his neck. He sits on the edge of his bed across from me. I make the mistake of looking into his eyes too long. My craving for his attention, for a redo of that night, is much easier to hide when he's got a chokehold on his hormones. Now that I know he's game, my only weapon is stubbornness. I said we can control ourselves, and I meant it. His eyes run the length of my body in a dare, and when they return to my face, one corner of his mouth turns up as if predicting my surrender.

I want to give him the finger. The insult might entice him. I shake my head at him instead.

"It's only a matter of time," he says.

"Before what?" I pretend to miss his suggestion.

He places his hand on my knee and runs it up my thigh until his fingers sneak under the edge of my boyshorts. I try not to move, but it's nearly impossible. He's created a flush so powerful I might need a crash cart. Then he's grabbing the backs of my calves with both hands, giving my body a slight jerk in a threat of pulling me off my bed and onto his lap.

I take hold of his wrists. It's a useless defense against him, but it's all I can manage. He could overtake me right now, and I doubt I'd do anything to stop it. "You don't have permission." My voice struggles to remain calm despite the heat rushing from the point of his touch toward every erogenous zone.

"Do I need it?" He doesn't let go.

He's going to win this one. I want him too badly, and he knows it. The air between us builds like the charged heat before a summer storm, and I suddenly remember I need to breathe. I pry his fingers off my legs. He doesn't resist. I give both of his hands back to him and stand. He grabs my hips.

"You're a bad actress."

"And what are you going to do about it?"

"I'm tired of waiting."

I put my hands over his. "You didn't answer my question." I could give in. What's stopping me? My heart pounds, and my better judgment screams in my ears. If it was any other time of the month, we might get away with it. Not now. It's not worth it. I pry his fingers off my hips and slip away to the bathroom without looking back.

We take turns showering, and when I finish mine I find him at the sink shaving his face with my razor. I can't remember the last time I saw him clean-shaven, and I can't decide if he's more handsome since I don't think it's actually possible.

Back on the road, he stops for gas and I pick up some cheesy gossip magazines just to have something to occupy my mind. I read the articles to him in an overdramatized voice and the time passes at an amazing pace.

When I see the Chicago skyline, my throat closes. Tears burn in my eyes. I refuse to let them free.

"Read another one," he says, noticing my silence. He looks over and reaches for my hand.

His touch is an overwhelming jolt of reality, and part of me wants to pull away. My old house might not be empty. He could be there, minutes away. It's unthinkable to mention, to even want to see him, but to be so close and not at least find out—can I live with that?

Anything will be easier to live with than the sick guilt that's just engulfed me from thinking about him, from missing him, while Trey's next to me holding my hand. And there's no way to see him without the two of them meeting. That's an encounter I'd be wise to avoid.

Trey asks, "Is there anywhere you'd like to visit while we're here?"

"No," I answer without thinking. It's easier not to think right now.

3015 Scarlet Lane is a red brick row house in a vibrant middle-class neighborhood. He parallel parks several houses down, and we step out onto the tree-lined street. Each house is similar yet distinct in that turn-of-the-century way. The oaks at the curb were probably planted the same year the houses were built. They loom over us, like this street belongs to them instead of its human inhabitants. Trey slips on his shoulder holster right out in the open. He covers it with a loose gray jacket while I put my holster and jacket on inside the car.

"Do you really think it's going to be dangerous?" I search for the calm in my mind and hold on tight.

He shrugs. "No idea."

He seems more bored than anything, and I wonder if it's a front. We walk to the house and stand on the sidewalk, staring up at its green door.

"Looks harmless enough," he says.

Large pots of overflowing petunias and herbs line the steps. We walk up side by side. At the door, we take a long look at one another, and I ring the bell.

CHAPTER 35

TREY

THE DOOR CREAKS open and I find myself looking into the eyes of the female version of me. And people think *Kate* and I look alike.

"Fearghus?" the woman asks. It is my mother's voice. She steps down off the step toward me, her eyes like slits and her eyebrows pulled together. I stare back at her, and it occurs to me we're making the exact same expression. She turns toward Liv, whose eyes are full of surprise. "Liv?"

"How do you know Liv?" the woman and I say simultaneously, word for word. Her face changes to lightly guarded astonishment, and she whispers, "It *is* you."

I look at Liv. Her gaze jumps back and forth between the woman and me, and I'm caught off guard by a strong embrace. My arms jerk upward into the air and remain there, unsure, until I'm released.

"Well, come inside," the woman says and steps back into the house.

Liv and I exchange a look. I lead the way in.

"Mamó!" the woman calls into the house from the hall.

Grandma. They know my name, and they know the language.

An elderly woman appears at the end of the hall, wiping her hands on her apron. She's thin and hunched at the shoulders. Her hair is tied back by a scarf. The two women share a knowing glance, and Liv and I follow them into a side room where two children are playing on a rug spread with toys.

The elderly woman pats my arm. "Please sit, *a chroí*, so I can have a better look at you."

I obey, understanding my height is a hindrance to her vision of me.

"You are so much like your father in person." Her accent is diluted, but I can still pick it up.

"You know my father?"

She nods to me and turns toward Liv.

The woman who answered the door says, "Mamó, do you remember Liv Gilchrist? She's the client of mine who moved to Montana. Nancy Carter's territory. I had no idea…" She looks at Liv.

"Tara, I'm dying to know how you know Trey." The suspicion and impatience in Liv's voice is a new sound for her.

"I see this is a little more complicated than we thought." The old woman settles down on the couch next to me. "Please sit," she says to Liv.

Liv sits rigidly on the edge of a nearby chair.

"Fearghus." She turns to me. "My daughter sent you here because it is time you know."

"Your daughter?" I try to think of anyone I know who could be her daughter.

"Fearghus," she says again, forcing me to concentrate. "*Is mise do sheanmháthair.*"

Liv's eyes dart to me. She is at a loss. "She's my grandmother," I say to Liv, merely translating the words.

"And Tara here," she continues in English for Liv's sake. "She is your twin sister."

Without a need to translate for Liv, understanding hits me like a punch in the gut. I react to the shock by standing and moving back to the doorway. When I turn back to face them, Liv is aiming an accusatory stare at Tara.

"Liv, I had no idea you were the one. I sent you to Nancy... I sent you to Nancy because I thought you'd be happy there. I had no idea that Fearghus—Trey—was so close. Or that you, and he..." She puts a hand to her mouth. One of the children wanders over to her and she lifts him onto her lap.

The old woman looks across the room at me. "This is a lot to take in at once."

I feel my short breath settling low in my lungs. Trained, preparing for action. No one's a threat here but my control is slipping away. I'm on that plane again, where everyone in my space needs to die. The bulb in the table lamp beside me is a scalding flame. And there's not enough fucking air in this room.

"Please, Fearghus, come back and sit with us."

My life has been an enormous, calculated lie, fed to me by every single person I know, except for one. "Liv," I say. She stands, looking alarmed. I've been deliberately kept in the dark, manipulated, deceived. "Liv," I say again, to no one in particular. To the world. She's the only one I have. And she's here, by my side, and I can trust only her. I feel her fingers slide against my hand.

"It's okay." Her perfect blue eyes comfort mine.

"Let's go." To the car. To drive away from everything.

"It's okay," she says again. Her voice is calm now, when it was so strained before. She drags me back into the room and pushes me down on the couch, then she sits next to me, holding my arm in her lap. I feel my body relax, and she reaches under my jacket and removes my gun. She ejects the mag and checks the chamber before returning it to the holster. She puts the mag in her pocket and pulls my arm back into her lap.

My mind has flatlined. With no outlet for my rage everything simply turns off.

"Did Trey's mother tell you we were coming?" Liv asks.

"No. We had no idea. This is as much a surprise to us as it is to you." Tara looks down at the little boy in her arms who has fallen asleep.

"Not even close," I hear myself say. "At least you knew I existed."

"I waited forty-five years to meet you!" Tara says. "At least you had your ignorance. Your peace."

"Peace is overrated." My voice comes out in a snarl, but I hardly care.

She stands, glaring back at me while carrying the sleeping child to the hall. The stairs creak under her feet. The other child stands, holding a book, gaping at me and Liv.

The old woman pushes herself up. "You two make yourselves at home. I need to check my stew."

Tara returns to scoop up the remaining child and take her upstairs.

Once she's out of earshot, Liv shakes my arm. "Trey, please. If only you knew what it was like to not have any family at all, you'd welcome this. This is a gift. Don't you see that?"

I don't have any words to answer her.

"I don't know what to say. Please, just try. Just for today. Tomorrow, we can go home and you'll never have to think about this ever again. But for now, could you just try? For me?"

I don't meet her eyes. I know what will happen if I do. I will cave.

"For your mother?"

"My mother *lied* to me my *whole life*." A sick feeling strains in my gut. I have never been angry with my mother.

Tara reappears in the doorway. "If you had any idea what our mother has gone through for you—"

"Do you *know* our mother?" The fierceness of my voice outdoes hers without me trying. If she wants to pick a fight, it's on. She didn't appear once in the thirty years I lived in that house yet she's an expert on my mother? I start to stand, but she sits in a chair.

"I'm not going to fight with you." She looks down at her hands.

Liv's fingernails dig into my arm and I realize I'm straining against her. "Please," she whispers.

I don't know whose move it is but I don't care. Tara watches her hands, I watch Tara, Liv watches me. Her last word rings in my head, and enough time passes for me to realize I am incapable of saying no to her. "Are you going to fill me in? Because this is getting really fucking old."

Tara is visibly taken aback. "I really don't know where to start."

"Now." I lean back against the couch.

Tara takes a breath. "This is going to be a lot."

"Spit it out." Try not to sound belligerent.

"You were kidnapped."

I scoff.

"When we were two weeks old."

I shift my weight and look around the room. "Kidnapped by my own mother."

"No, by the Moores. They wanted you. They knew about you. Our mother couldn't allow them to take you alone, so she went with you."

"Why didn't she just tell them no?" I say, intentionally belligerent this time.

Her eyebrows rise. "You're kidding, right?"

Liv chimes in. "He has no idea what he's saying. We've had a very rough couple of days."

"What do you mean they knew about me?" I wonder if she's being vague just to piss me off.

"They knew how important you are to us."

"Meaning?"

"The prophecy. But see, the prophecy you know is the one they taught you. Our version is a little different."

I knew those assholes were lying about the prophecy.

"Our father had already passed away when you and I were born."

"Our father?" Our father is alive and well.

"Martin Moore is not your real father."

I look at Liv. She can't possibly expect me to take any more of this. Every single thing I know is a lie, and the more these people talk the more lies are revealed. Someone's going to pay for this.

Tara continues, "I stayed with Mamó. Máthair went to live with them—enemies of our family—so she could stay with you, to protect you, to raise you as one of us. The Moores thought they had what they wanted. They had you to keep in their control, to train you to be a killer. To fight on their side. They had no idea our mother was working hard to raise you as one of us, so you could ultimately fight against them. Only now, you can fight them at their own game. You know all their secrets."

Something shifts, awakening inside me. Something I knew all along, but it was buried deep. Under layer upon layer of lies.

"Go on," I say as softly as I can manage.

"Their prophecy speaks of your heir as leading them to their end. But in our prophecy, your heir leads us to our beginning. Our rebirth. The Moores have been in power for two hundred years, and our family has suffered at their hands. The whole world is suffering at their hands."

"A little dramatic, don't you think?"

"Fearghus, the things they do…"

I cock my head at her. I lived in that house for thirty years. I'm fully aware of what they do.

She sighs, looking down at her lap. When her eyes meet mine again I can tell she doesn't want to push the subject. "They want to do everything in their power to prevent your heir from being born. And we want to do everything in our power to protect your heir."

"He doesn't exactly exist," I point out.

Tara's eyes move to Liv. "No…" She dwells on the word.

I shrug. "So?"

"I'm sure they told you they applied the effect. Your immortality."

She takes my silence as an affirmative.

"They didn't. The effect came from us. When our family found out the prophecy related to your bloodline, they wanted to do everything they could to protect you, to ensure the Alignment, and to protect your heir in the future. They placed the effect on you, in the womb, to be applied starting in your thirtieth year, knowing that this timing was necessary for the Alignment to take place. What the Moores told you was an attempt to make it look like a gift from them. They were hoping you'd be grateful enough to respect their prophecy. To honor their wishes. To never father a child. They had no idea you'd ever know the truth."

I realize I'm leaning forward, so I relax against the couch.

"But the funny thing is they didn't know I was in there, too. So I got the effect at the same time you did." She smiles.

My twin should be forty-five years old, and she in no way looks like she's forty-five. Just like me, she's been in limbo for fifteen years.

"Although, it will run out for me as soon as it runs out for you. And that's something else—an important part of the effect is how it passes from you to your child. The

Moores were right in telling you as soon as you have a child you will no longer be immortal. It's designed to be passed, so your child has the ultimate protection."

"Never aging?" What is that good for?

"No, it applies to an infant a little differently than it applies to you."

So yet again, here I am, living a life that has already been decided for me. I look at Liv, who's carefully holding her expression neutral. My anger builds. I didn't ask to be in the middle of this and I want the fuck out. Beating the Moores at their own game is tempting, but I don't see how it's possible. And I don't think it's worth all this shit. It would be a hell of a lot easier to just arm myself to the teeth and go in there and blow them all away. That's what I should have done the other day. I don't know how I could have thought being civilized would get me what I wanted.

"Don't you see?" Tara breaks into my thoughts. "You're set up to beat them, the people you've hated all this time."

"How do you know I've hated them." My voice is cold.

"I know," she says gently.

"You can't possibly know." I hear the disgust in my words. I lean my arms on my knees and stare at the floor between my boots.

"Because you are nothing like them."

And I know she's right. I've known this all my life. Now I finally have the reason for it.

"They killed our father." She's unable to control the fury in her voice.

My head snaps up. "Who?"

"Someone you already killed."

"Martin Moore, senior?" It's a guess I somehow know will be right.

"Yes."

The man I thought was my grandfather until today is responsible for killing my real father. Fifteen years ago I thought he was responsible for killing Kate and Aaron. He was the first one I went after that day. Had I known the extent of his responsibility, I'd have enjoyed it so much more. Made it longer. More painful. Drawn more blood, so I could remember every last drop.

"They thought killing our father would break the line," she says.

"But they were too late." Again, Tara and I speak simultaneously.

"Yes," she says. "Our mother was already pregnant with us."

The doorbell rings, and Tara stands. "This is probably Mamó's nurse. I'll be right back."

Liv and I look at each other but don't speak. There are too many things to say. We hear the door creak open then a dull thud. It creaks again, sounding a little strained this time. Liv and I both look toward the hall, then she looks back at me.

"I can't believe you have a twin. This is so surreal."

"Tell me about it."

Voices from the front door rise in volume. There's some sort of confrontation going on. The old woman shuffles into view and moves toward the hallway with a telephone in her hand, watching the doorway like she's waiting for a cue.

I go into the hallway. Some guy appears to be attempting to go up the stairs without Tara's permission.

"They're sleeping." She's forcing her voice low. "Why are you doing this? Don't you know what will happen if I call the police?"

"Don't threaten me." His hand reaches up, grasps her arm, and suddenly his throat is in my hand and I'm in his face, holding his back against the wall.

"Can I help you with something?" I ask him.

"Who the hell are you?"

"Fearghus…" Tara warns, her hand on my arm. "I have a restraining order, all we have to do is call the police."

"The police take way too long," I say, still in his face. I release him, but I don't withdraw.

"So this is your new boyfriend?" The prick sneers at me while speaking to her. It's a perfect way to ask me for a broken jaw.

"Don't be an idiot. He's my brother."

"Don't lie to me. You don't have a brother."

"Yes, she does." I grab him by the shirt and throw him onto the porch. He picks himself up and I stand in the doorway, waiting for him to leave, memorizing his features and the way he moves. I'm sure I'll see him again someday. I hope I do. I watch him drive away in a black Impala before I go back inside.

Tara's right behind me. She's rubbing her arm where the shithead touched her. "Sorry about that."

"Don't be." I feel a little better now. I'd feel a lot better if I could have relocated his nose, but I'm not going to tell her that.

"He's my ex-husband," Tara says as we sit back down in the living room. "He just shows up like that sometimes, convinced he's going to take our kids even though I have full custody. And a restraining order."

"Your children are twins, too?" Liv asks.

"Yes."

"Cooper is your married name?"

"I've thought about changing it back to Bevan, but being in real estate, people just know me as Tara Cooper."

"And you didn't know Trey lives in Black River?"

"No, I didn't. I don't even think our mother knows where he lives. I've just known Nancy forever. She moved to Montana when her husband died. When you came to me wanting a big change for a similar reason, I immediately thought of her."

"It's just really hard to believe," Liv says.

"I know." Tara grins, looking between us like she's about to get up and initiate a group hug.

The old woman returns and sits next to me. "Our lives have been incomplete without you, Fearghus. We've watched you through your mother's eyes, but it was never enough. Tara had a very hard time without you. And your mother, how she suffered without Tara. And how she suffers now, unable to be with her grandchildren. She is a true warrior. That's what her name means."

"Sloane," Liv says.

"Yes. Warrior." The old woman smiles at her. "Your Sloane—" She reaches across me for Liv's hand. "She was born too soon. She was born without Fearghus' blood, without his gift to her, and she was unable to remain in her time."

"What do you mean?" Liv chokes, her eyes instantly moist. I feel her pain like I'm in her head taking command of it. Dragging it to my side of the field. If only I could.

"She had to be taken. The timing was wrong. But be patient, *a chroí*, you'll have her again."

"You can bring her back?" A tear scurries down Liv's cheek.

"No, but you and Fearghus can bring her back. And if my old senses are right, I think you already have."

CHAPTER 36

LIV

I JERK THE DOOR open and hit the air outside. A sob has inflated in my chest and it's too big to get out. I'm stuck between an inhale and an exhale and I don't know which way the air wants to go. I'm trying to make sense of something so impossible, something I want to be true so badly, maybe it will be true if I believe it. Maybe she could have a second chance—she could be back, inside me right now instead of that little coffin buried in a grave. Soon I could see her again, pink and smiling and cooing. My memory of her lifeless limbs could be snuffed from my reality, like waking up and realizing that eternity of crushing darkness was all a bad dream.

Trey follows me outside, and I turn to him, colliding with him, clinging on. The sob breaks and I press my face into his chest. All the things that have changed for him, and I'm the one breaking down.

"I'm so sorry," I choke.

"Why are you sorry?" There's a tinge of a laugh in his voice.

I pull away and look at him. His eyes are glowing, and his face is relaxed. He dabs my cheeks with the sleeve of his jacket.

"All that you've been through, and I'm the one losing it."

"I'll lose it soon. I wanted to let you have a turn first."

He closes the front door and we sit on the porch bench. His brain might be working but my thoughts remain scattered, and I make no attempt to rein them in. It feels as if I'm sitting in the dark in front of a television playing static, and I'm too entranced to switch the channel.

Still staring straight ahead, he says, "I have to say it. Screw everything. I couldn't be happier." He turns to me and smiles broadly. "And I'll be really disappointed if she's wrong."

I wipe my eyes on the arm of his jacket. I need to blow my nose but I don't think it would go over too well. "After everything…?"

"I'm not thinking about anything else right now. Forget all of that. It doesn't matter."

But all of it does matter. It has to matter—all those things we've learned since we stepped off that plane in Richmond. It's an impossible amount of information. One of us should have been taking notes.

"Stop thinking," he says. "Just think about this, right now."

"I can't believe it," I reply in monotone. My mouth is numb.

"Believe it. If she's anything like my mother, she knows these things. Now, how do you feel?"

I feel like it's too good to be true. Instead of just waking from a bad dream, I'm going to wake from this, a good dream, and realize it was all in my mind. My baby is still dead. I look up at him, and his smile transmits across the inches of air separating us. Filling me. I feel myself smiling back. He takes my face in his hands and kisses me, even though I'm salty from crying. It makes me want to cry again.

He pulls away. "We were crazy to fight this."

"We didn't know."

"Everything we knew was wrong." His voice remains light. There is nothing in the world more gratifying than seeing him happy.

"I have a recurring dream about her. Every time, I wake up convinced I'm holding her."

"An omen." He smiles that same broad smile.

I don't know how long we sit there watching the lilac next to the porch wiggle in the breeze, but at some point I find his hand and don't let go.

We linger at the table with Tara that night after dinner, sipping tea—the store-bought kind, a distinction I'd never thought to be so important until now.

"Are you two staying the night?" she asks with a hopeful smile.

"We need to be—" Trey begins.

"Yes," I say. "We'd love to."

Tara's three-year-old twins thunder into the room. The little boy falls down in a fit of laughter, and the little girl stops next to Trey, looking up at him.

"Hi," Trey says.

She makes a face and balances something on his knee.

"Thanks," he says, and she bounds away. He sets the object on the table and rolls it to me. "Smart kid."

It's an exact replica of Trey's new Camaro. I look at Tara for an explanation but then realize she probably didn't see the car we came in.

"She saw that at the grocery store the other day." Tara stands and stacks the dishes. "I try not to spoil them, but she had that I-can't-live-without-this look. She usually doesn't beg me for stuff like that—"

"When?" Trey asks.

"I think it was…" She tilts her head to think. "Sunday?"

"It's the car we came in today. We picked it up on Sunday."

Tara nods like she's already heard this before. "It isn't the first time she's done something like that. What am I supposed to do? Mamó says just to let her be, so that's what I've been doing."

"I wouldn't know either." Trey rests his finger on the roof of the toy car and rolls it slowly back and forth in front of him.

"Okay, so I'm dying to know," Tara says. "How did the two of you meet?"

"I ran a red light," Trey says, deadpan, beating me to the punch.

"He ran a red light *on purpose*," I explain, and as soon as the words are out I know Trey and I are thinking the same thing. We still haven't found out who's been stalking us in that gray car.

"I was chasing a car I've seen around. I saw it the night I came home to find Kate and Aaron gone. And it's been stalking around Black River since I moved there."

"What kind of car?" Tara asks.

"Gray. At least fifteen years old. Tinted windows, spoiler. Some kind of Acura, maybe an Integra or Vigor. Probably modified."

"I can't think of anyone I know with an Acura," Tara says.

"Anyone who works on cars?"

Tara shakes her head and seems to focus on the wall behind us.

"I meant to check the garage when we were at the estate, but I didn't have a chance." Trey pushes away his empty dish.

"You were there?" Tara's eyes focus hard on Trey.

"We didn't stay long."

"Was it like…the last time?"

"It didn't end well." Trey's face hardens.

"How is she?" She must mean their mother.

"She was happy when I left her room. I didn't see her afterward." He looks down for a moment before his head snaps up. "We have to get her out of there."

"I don't know how that's possible."

"I can make it easy. Can Liv stay with you for twenty-four hours?" He pushes his chair away from the table.

"Not with violence, Trey. She wouldn't want that. And she couldn't leave that house and live the life you live. She couldn't protect herself."

"Liv and I can protect her."

Feeling like I need to give them some time to talk, I scoot my chair back. "Where's the bathroom?"

Tara points down the hall.

After I wash my hands and blot away some crystallized tears, I sit down on the toilet lid. Pregnant. Just like that, my baby will be back in my arms, one crippling loss regained. For so long I've dreamed of going back in time, making some change, doing something different to somehow evade her death. I'd never imagined going forward in time would be the key to bringing her back. I know she won't be the same. She can't be—she'll have a different father. That won't stop me from believing it's her. If I believe in magic now, I can believe in reincarnation.

Trey's family has been working so hard to prevent the conception of a baby that now exists because of their very own actions. If they hadn't tried to kill me, Trey wouldn't have needed to heal me and wouldn't have gotten me pregnant in the process. The whole thing is a massive chain reaction, starting with them tricking Trey into thinking Kate and Aaron were dead, and ending with me carrying the child they fear. Fooled and betrayed by their own game.

Instead of returning to the dining room with Trey and Tara, I join the children in the living room. They warm up to me quickly, and before I know it I have a child on either side of me and a stack of books I've read to them. As I'm nearing the end of the final book in the stack, I look down to see two sets of drooping eyelids.

I lean my head back against the couch and relax to the muffled sound of Trey and Tara's conversation from the dining room. For once, I feel no burden. The immeasurable weight of grief has lifted. My soul is at ease.

Mamó joins me, taking the armchair, and picks up her knitting. Time ticks by on an old clock on the mantel, and I feel calm and content, soaking up the peacefulness of the house and my company. How quickly things can change. The world can drop out from under you, and in the blink of an eye, it has returned, and you are in another hemisphere.

Tara sneaks into the room, followed by Trey, and slides her arms under the little girl. Trey takes the little boy and follows Tara up the stairs. When they return, Trey drops to the couch next to me and wraps his arm around me. Tara lights up the gas fireplace and sits on the hearth with an afghan across her lap. The chill in the air was unnoticeable to me snuggled up to two warm sleeping children.

"What time is it?" I ask Trey.

"Almost ten."

"Past my bedtime." Mamó puts down her knitting. "But there's one more thing you must know. Tara, did you tell them about Kate's baby?"

"No, I was leaving that up to you." Tara eyes Trey.

Mamó leans back in her chair to gather a breath. "You already know your unborn child is very special. Am I right?"

"Yes." Trey removes his arm from me and sits up straighter.

"The Moores will have a special child, a leader, born to them soon as well. We know this from your mother, Fearghus. Her inside knowledge is vital to us. She has told us that Kate is carrying this child, and they believe this child is their only hope to protect them if your child is born." She pauses until Trey looks at her. "You'll understand this is their reason for taking Kate away from you; they couldn't have the two of you together, get this child from her and prevent your child from being born at the same time. Their choice of using Christian in this way has tormented your mother. But she is helpless. You must find it in your heart to forgive him."

"I know." Trey looks down at his hands.

Everyone is silent until Trey looks up. "Why was I kept in the dark? My whole life? Was it really necessary?" He can't keep the roughness out of his voice.

"Yes it was necessary," Mamó says. "We had to go on as if your path was not predetermined, because any minor change caused by that knowledge would have altered the path. Simply having the knowledge was enough to do harm. We had to be careful to live as if we had not possessed the knowledge in the first place. This is why your mother had to stay with the Moores. It seemed so wrong, when considering the prophecy. But ignoring the prophecy, it was the only option. And now we see that it was the only way everything could have turned out this way. Had you gone alone, you never would have grown with your mother's influence, never would have had a reason to leave, and never would have met Liv when you met her. And you wouldn't be here right now."

"But that doesn't mean I couldn't have been told. At some point."

"Telling you at any time before now would have altered the course. Think about this. At what point could you have taken this knowledge and stowed it away, refusing to allow it to affect your life at all?"

She has a very good point. Maybe if Trey was patient and thoughtful instead of impulsive, vengeful, and quick-tempered, he could have been told. The Trey I know could never have learned all he's learned today and simply gone on with his life. He'd be on the road back to Richmond to free his mother right now if Tara hadn't talked him out of it.

"You must learn to accept your destiny. Both of you. You must not fight it. You must embrace who you are. Your lives will not be happy until you do." She holds my eye for a moment, and seeming satisfied, she moves on to Trey.

I feel like I already have accepted all of this. But Trey is still in the process of fighting. And I'm not sure how long it will last, or what will determine the end.

Mamó shifts forward in her chair. Tara hops up to help her, and they walk arm in arm up the stairs.

Trey stands and feels for his gun. "I need to take a walk. Clear my head. Magazine?" He extends his open hand.

I twist, exposing my pocket to him. He's cooled off enough to have it back. Those people made him like this. Whether it was their intent or a consequence of growing up in a house of people who hate him, he's developed some kind of blind craze. A mechanical reaction. A defense that shifts to offense, aimed at whomever is unlucky enough to be in his way. It was training. It was abuse. And it's hard for me to blame him. He loses his humanity in that moment because he's conditioned to. They stripped it from him.

He zips up his jacket and walks to the doorway. "Come with me?"

"Sure you don't want to go alone?"

He nods toward the door just as Tara comes back down the stairs. "You're not leaving?"

"Just for a walk."

"Let me get you a key so you can let yourselves back in." She returns with a key and asks if I want to borrow a heavier jacket.

Trey opens the door. "I'll bring in our bags."

Tara walks me to the coat closet and hands me a fleece-lined jacket and a pair of gloves. As I'm putting them on, she says, "Even though we already knew each other, I'm so glad to have met you again, in this new way."

There's a soft sincerity to her voice that touches me deeply. It's almost as if I can feel her decades spent without her brother. And without her mother. I can easily empathize with that. I know it all too well. "I'm glad to have met you again, too."

"Promise me when you leave, you and Trey will keep in touch."

"Absolutely."

"I'll probably be asleep when you get back. Your room is the one at the end of the hall upstairs. I'll leave a night-light on. Help yourself to anything."

"Thanks, Tara. I'll see you in the morning."

Trey comes in lugging our bags and takes them in the living room. He puts a flannel shirt on under his jacket and pulls on a sock hat.

Tara was right to bundle me up. Night brought the cold with it, and I had forgotten about this wind. Memories of my old life in this city flood my mind, and instead of blocking them, I allow them. With the vision of my new path in front of me, leading me toward a new life, the sadness and the torment have been tamed. One part of my past can no longer threaten me. It holds no power over me anymore.

I find Trey's hand, and we walk in the crisp air under the streetlights, each immersed in our own thoughts, yet blissfully united, as one.

CHAPTER 37

TREY

AFTER ABOUT TEN minutes of walking in silence, I feel the urge to speak. "Do you miss it here?"

She looks up at me as if she expected me to say something else. "I feel like I've moved on from this. It almost seems like a different life. Like something foreign."

Two cars blow by, yet it's hardly a distraction due to the rest of the background noise of the city. Activity swarms around us even at this late hour. Main Street in Black River would be a ghost town at this time of night.

"Did you miss Virginia when you first moved away?" she asks.

A plastic bag crinkles above us, trapped in the branch of a honey locust. Two men come out of a house nearby and light cigarettes. The German Shepherd behind the fence between the houses watches us, but has decided not to bark. I tug my sock hat tighter on my head and put my hood up.

"I had a lot on my mind then. I don't remember." I try to take myself back to that time but all I find are bits and pieces of memories, nothing substantial. Christian visited a lot, but so did their men. The visits from their men offered a perfect outlet for the rage that couldn't be dulled by any chemical I consumed. The violence never seemed to quench it either.

Kate's and Aaron's murders were still so new to me. I was out of control. I didn't see it then, but I see it now. If any of their men got through my guard in the slightest way, I'd lose any shred of cool I had. It was Phoenix where one of them broke my arm. Was I drunk? Probably. But hell, I couldn't let it go. It wasn't until I was boarding the plane to return to Virginia for another killing spree that I thought of my mother and reconsidered. I thought she wanted to be one of them. I was afraid that hurting them would hurt her. I thought she chose to be part of their family.

Tara told me that in a way, she does choose to stay with them. That she decided herself to marry Martin Moore because she loved him, and still does. It's beyond my level of understanding how my mother could love one of them now that I know exactly what they are.

And Tara tried to compare it to how I feel about Christian, but it isn't the same at all. Christian was raised by my mother. He may be Moore by blood, but he is Bevan by nature. And for most of his life, the Bevan side of him was dominant. I'm not sure what they've done to him to change him, but my worst fear is it didn't take much.

"Are you cold?" I ask her.

"Not at all. We can keep going if you want."

We stop at a street corner and wait to cross.

"My mother and Tara, they keep in contact with each other through their dreams." I have so much to tell her about my conversation with Tara that this detail is almost insignificant. But it's the first thing that comes out.

"They can do that?"

"Tara told me she reaches out with her mind every night to try to find me. Guess I'm a dud."

"She's found you now. In real life." She smiles, visibly happy for me and Tara. "You are going to stay in touch with her, right?"

"I don't think I have a choice."

"I think you're right. She's so much like you it's scary. When she first opened the door, and the two of you were glaring at each other—"

"She said my mother may not ever want to leave. Can you believe that?" I drop her hand.

"She seemed happy enough." She slides her hand back into mine.

"We should move," I say, aware of myself jumping from subject to subject.

"Move? Why?"

"Maybe we could throw them off long enough for the baby to be born." It comes out in a rush. I use her silence to go over places in my head where we could move. "We could move here."

"No," she blurts, looking away. "I don't want to live here."

"Farther west? Southwest?"

"But I just moved. I don't want to move again." Her voice cracks on the last word, like she can barely get the words out.

"When we did the mind share, and I first came into your mind, what were you thinking about?"

She takes a moment to respond. "What did you see?"

"You were in a small city park. It had to be here."

"Yes," she answers abruptly as if she just remembered. "It was a memory. I used to go to that park with Chase every day after work."

"Chase?" With a name like that he'll be simple to find. I didn't think she'd give it up so easily.

"My dog. That's when I was single. Chase died right after I got married."

"What are you going to tell Shawn?"

She exhales hard. "Your stream of consciousness is unreal. What do you want me to tell him?"

"Tell him to meet me in the parking lot. And I'll tell him."

"Please. You're not impressing me."

"I'm not trying to. I don't need to anymore." I shoot her a playful smile.

"So, should I tell him that we are..." She watches a few cars streak by.

"Together."

"Okay." She nods once.

Police sirens howl in the distance, bringing me back to more serious matters. "Tara's going to talk to our mother tonight, to see how much damage I did on my way out the other day." My words hover in the air. She defuses them with one curative look, and I stop walking and turn her to face me. She needs to understand.

"Things would've been fine if I had just left with you that day. But now I've pissed them off worse. They'll get back at me, with more force this time." Her pull on me takes hold and I forget what I was saying. "I told you, I'm not holding back anymore. So if you keep doing that—"

"Doing what? I'm not doing anything!" She appears to want to say more but two people just rounded the corner and she's waiting for them to pass behind her. Once they're out of earshot, she says, "We really have no reason to hold back anymore. You already ruined it."

I lean toward her lips, trying to remain aware of our public location. If I'm distracted like this we're open to ambush. She tastes impossibly good, and my body aches for more of her on me, against me. She slides her hands underneath my jacket and I grab her elbows, holding her arms.

"Let's go back." I use all my power to pull away.

She leans in for more.

I stand fully so she can't reach. She opens her eyes. "To be continued?"

I am physically unable to answer her. It takes all my effort to turn us around, to walk forward, to ignore the part of my mind planning what I'm going to do to her. She hugs my arm with her other hand, holding on to me while we walk. A gibbous moon has risen, the only visible object in a night sky that's competing with city lights.

"Do you know your way back?" She's noticed me looking at the sky. "You have no stars to help you here. You're on your own."

"I have you. I'm counting on you to get us back."

"I think you've said that before," she says.

She must be remembering the same night I am, the night we took a walk together and I showed her Orion.

"I couldn't stand to be in the same room as you," she says, as if remembering aloud.

"You couldn't?" I fake my surprise.

"You almost…" She extends her arm, as if expecting the bruise inflicted by my hand to still be there. Her words have faded but it doesn't matter. I'll see that bruise forever. "Who knew what one short month could bring," she finishes softly.

"It's been longer than a month."

"No, it hasn't. I moved to Black River on the first. It hasn't even *been* a month."

"Shit. We don't mess around," I say under my breath.

"*You* don't mess around. I wasn't involved."

I laugh. "I'm only going to let you get away with saying that once. Next time…"

"What?" She stops walking, releases my arm, faces me.

I know by the barely covered smile that she's playing along. I turn her forward and pull her with me. "You heard me talking. So you were involved. Involved enough."

She holds my arm as she did before. "What was it you said again?"

"I'm not repeating it. You got it twice. That's it."

"Rip-off. I don't know why I put up with this." She hugs my arm tighter. "Will you tell me what language it is?"

"*Gaeilge.* Irish Gaelic."

We walk together in silence. When we turn onto Scarlet Lane, I feel like we've lost time we made it back so fast. I lead her up the steps and fish out the key. The door opens into a dark and peaceful house. We carry our bags upstairs to the bedroom at the end of the hall, and I secretly thank Tara for putting us as far away from the other bedrooms as possible.

Inside our room, the chilly air seeps through the old windows. We take off our coats, guns, and shoes, and Liv clamps her teeth and rubs her arms in the cold. I pull my shirt off and yank down the covers.

"After you." I hope she's ready for what I'm about to do to her.

My need for her surges with a strength so fierce I can't think straight. I stare at her, those pink lips, the soft skin of her neck, the curves of her body. I feel like I've waited an eternity for this.

She's so beautiful I feel like I've been smacked in the face. I strip down to my boxers and we get under the covers together, colliding in the middle of the bed. I wrap my arms around her to warm her up. She snuggles into me, and my desire unleashes itself, finally freed. I reach over to the nightstand and turn off the light.

"Good night," she says with exaggerated finality. Another tease. She gets off on this.

"Don't think so. I've waited too long…" I close my eyes and kiss along her collarbone, up her neck, to her ear, savoring the feel of her, the scent of her. I sense her body give, and my lips find hers. And just as I promised, I do not hold back.

When I wake up in the morning, she's attached to my back. I turn over and take her against me. She puts her palms against my chest and pushes away to look at my face. Her hair is a wild mess. Her eyes remind me of the endless blue sky at home.

I don't know how I was ever able to stay away from her.

My hands have a mind of their own with their newly found freedom. She runs her fingers against my hair. I have never known such ecstasy.

She wraps her arms around my neck and her legs around my hips. The morning slows our rhythm. I forgot what a different experience this is when I'm still groggy from sleep. I forgot … too much. Now that I've remembered, I'll never be able to forget again. Now that she's mine, I'll never be able to live without her.

"So how does it feel to be thirty and a few days?" Tara asks me later at breakfast.

I shrug. "The same. You?"

"The same. Just don't get any paper cuts. They're going to take forever to heal."

Paper cuts. She must be being sarcastic. I glance at Liv. She's smiling at me but can't cover the worry on her face.

Tara pulls out a chair for Liv. "Please sit. Let's eat before the kids wake up and all hell breaks loose."

I help her serve the food and pour the coffee. When we're both seated, Tara sets a small carved wooden box next to my plate.

"This is yours." She looks at me like I've been handed a microphone.

"I've never seen that." I dig into my food.

"Of course you haven't. But it belongs to you, along with another story."

I stop chewing and look at her. I'm not in the mood for the disclosure of any more lies. After our conversation last night, I thought she'd told me everything. Knowing she kept something from me to reveal on a new day pisses me off.

"Don't look at me like that. This is a good thing."

"I'm getting sick of having things dropped on me." I catch Tara share a glance with Liv just before I stab another egg.

She reaches across the table and grasps my forearm. "Stop being an ass and listen. These have been handed down, father to child, for centuries. Engraved over and over with names of wives and daughters. Our father would've wanted you to have them. It wasn't possible to give them to you until now."

I take the box and open it. Inside, wrapped in a blue velvet cloth, are two silver rings engraved with what appears to be a complex design. Looking closer, I see the design is made up of many names.

"You're named Fearghus after him. Did you know that?"

"No." A memory pops into my thoughts. "I've seen these before."

"There's no way. I've had them the whole time. Look," she says, taking them from me. "There's my name, and there's Máthair's. She had my name added when we were born."

I look and see both names. They appear as part of the design until you focus more closely, then they become letters etched by a tiny tool. "I've seen them before. I saw these when I was in Liv's mind. We did a mind sharing effect, and when I first entered her mind I was wearing them."

"You saw them when you were in *her* mind? Impossible. Maybe if you were in *your* mind. It could be some kind of family consciousness. Were you in control?" She hands the rings back to me.

"Not when I saw them."

We both look at Liv, who shrugs and says, "I have no idea what either of you are talking about."

"Have you seen these before?" I hold them out to her in my palm.

She picks one up to examine it closely. "Beautiful. But no, I've never seen anything like this. Ever." She hands it back.

"Do they fit?" Tara leans forward, like the evidence of them fitting me is something she's waited a lifetime for. In this simple motion I see something new in her I didn't see before—a person who only speaks the truth. Someone I can trust. If I doubted it before, if it seemed like a novelty, it has now become solid: this woman is my sister.

They both only fit on my middle fingers, just like I wore them in Liv's mind. The third finger must relate to the rule of three. My mother taught me the importance of this number like it was some secret code. It can't be too secret, though. The Moores believe in it too. I was raised by two opposing forces and I'll never be able to divide one's teachings from the other.

"Did you tell her what you are?" Tara looks from me to Liv.

I exhale. "Are you always like this?"

Tara directs her question to Liv. "Did he?"

Liv presses her lips together and looks at me. "He told me some things."

"*Máistir na nDúl?*"

Liv hesitantly shakes her head. I go back to eating.

"Master of the Elements?" Tara translates for Liv.

I feel Liv's eyes on me, but she doesn't answer.

"That's what he is. He has a lot of abilities he refuses to use. Don't be freaked out if for some reason he decides to use them."

I'm already glaring at Tara when she looks at me.

"Don't hide things from her. It's not healthy. She needs to know everything."

"Máthair." I say. "Did you contact her?"

"Yes. And you can relax. No fatalities."

"Injuries?"

"A few. Nothing to worry about. But you did manage to graze Kate." She chuckles. "How the hell did you manage that?"

"Don't look at me, I wasn't exactly conscious," Liv says to me.

"I wish I could take the credit for that, but I can't." I didn't even aim. But that's her fate catching up to her. And my subconscious, getting its say in the matter. Although it would have made more of a point to have unloaded into her heart. I'll work on that next time.

"She's *livid*. She thinks it was done on purpose."

"Let her." I did tell her I wasn't through with her. "How's Máthair?"

"She's okay, as usual. She understands. Mostly, she's thrilled to reunite us. She wouldn't stop talking about that. You need to call her more often."

"I'll try." I know I probably won't try hard enough.

"Especially now that they'll probably shoot you on sight if you ever try to go back and visit."

"I can go back anytime I want."

"They can kill you now," she reminds me. "Tell your ego not to forget that. And you're not on your own anymore. You have two other people you have to consider. No, three. Counting me."

"God, will you lay off?"

"Four. I forgot to count Máthair. Oh wait, five. For Christian."

Christian. How could I forget. I search Tara's eyes for any hint of news about him.

"He's missing," she says, with no need for me to ask.

I stare down into my plate.

"He's fine. He'll come back. He probably just needs to shake it off. You know how he is."

And I know she's right. Nothing ever fazes Christian. He always bounces back, unlike me, who can hold a grudge for decades. He should hold a grudge. What I did, what I said, should not be forgiven. I have to make it up to him somehow. Hopefully I'll get an opportunity soon, so I don't have to carry this new weight just when the massive load I have been carrying for fifteen years has finally been lifted.

CHAPTER 38

LIV

"**C**AN'T YOU STAY another night?" Tara asks as we're putting on our jackets in the entryway. She gives me a hug then moves to Trey, who hugs her back tightly.

"*A leanbh na páirte*," Mamó says, coming up behind Tara. She takes Trey's hand. "Be good to your mother. And always remember who you are." She holds his eye for a moment before turning to me and taking my hands. "Liv. I hope you understand what a gift you are to this family. We are forever indebted to you."

"Thank you," I say, humbled, and for the first time I notice how old she really is.

Tara opens the door, and Trey and I walk down the steps. He stops halfway down and turns back.

"I'll call you," he says, simultaneously with Tara.

She laughs as he curses under his breath.

"That could get annoying." He opens the trunk for our bags. He has no idea how lucky he is. To be expelled from the family he's known only to have a new one fall out of the sky in front of him.

"How many hours is it to Black River?" I ask inside the car.

"Too many to think about right now. I'll drive as far as I can then we'll stop and get a room for the night. We'll make good time in this car, but it's going to eat a lot of gas." He revs the engine and pulls away from the curb.

Maybe if he was easier on the pedal it wouldn't eat so much gas. I settle into my seat, flip on the radio, and browse through the stations. "Classical?"

"Fuck no. Get out." He reaches over me, pretending to go for my door handle.

I latch onto his arm, holding it against my chest. He pulls his arm back and smiles broadly at the windshield.

"'80s hair metal?"

"Sounds good to me."

A few hours outside of Chicago we hit a wall of rain. Trey doesn't slow down until I give him an I-don't-want-to-die-young look. We lose our '80s station so I reach for the buttons to find something else. He catches my hand and turns off the radio instead.

"Yesterday," he says, "Tara told me that hundreds of years ago, the Moores massacred our ancestors. Their intent was to wipe the Bevans out, to extinction. Our ancestors' magic was a threat to theirs. The Moores succeeded for the most part, but the remaining Bevans scattered in order to stay alive. They knew that they would be harder to seek out this way, and less of a threat. There is a saying: '*Ni heolas go haontios.*'"

"What does it mean?"

"'There is no knowledge without unity.' What makes our magic work is the wide collection of knowledge, passed down through families. A collective mind. Without that, we have nothing. My books—my family's texts—are sacred and rare. Our early people wrote nothing down. They feared it landing in the wrong hands. There are few copies. Mine are two hundred years old and were guarded by my mother in that house when I was a baby. The Moores never knew they were there."

If those books need protection, under his watch is a perfect place for them. He's quiet for a few minutes, and I watch the windshield wipers move back and forth in their rhythm.

"Tara said they continue to hunt us. Two weeks ago, they found some of our distant relatives, somewhere in the northeast, and executed them."

The engine growls, and the needle on the speedometer starts moving forward.

"Do you want me to drive?" I ask gently.

He eases off the accelerator. "That's why my mother didn't want Tara's address written down. They could come for Tara at any time if they ever find out where she is."

"Oh my god," I whisper. Those men they send after Trey would be coming after her, too. What would they do to women? To children?

"Do you know the danger my mother lived with when I was young? The risk she took, teaching me everything I know? Teaching Christian? Right under their noses." He presses his head against the headrest and exhales, like he's trying to stave off the agitation I already see. "She's lucky my father—my stepfather—loves her. Or she'd have been dead a long time ago. They have to know what she did by now."

"But you've been gone so long. Maybe they think you picked it up yourself."

"It's not really something you can pick up yourself. I'm remembering now, all the times…god, my mother. She was bold."

"Bold about what?"

"She'd do it right out in the open. My father would get so pissed at her for cooking when we had staff to do that. If he'd known what she was really doing… I'd sit on the counter and watch her, and she would cook, but also prepare other things, teaching me right there in front of them. Unless…"

I don't want to be pushy, so I give him a moment. When he speaks again on his own, I'm glad I held my tongue.

"She must have used the Discretion Effect the whole time. I'd always be finding little packs in my pockets. That's—"

He goes quiet and I watch the road, allowing him to have some time to himself. About an hour later, the rain finally eases. He speeds up again, trying to make up for lost time I'm sure.

"So," he says.

I turn to look at him. He is so handsome that my vision demands all of my mind's resources.

"We have a bit of pressure. The remaining Bevans of the world seem to be counting on us to raise the person who will lead them out of hiding. Back to power." He stares through the windshield, talking without looking at me.

"How do they know?"

"They know. They've been waiting a long time."

"Great." I try to downplay it. It's too much to accept right now.

"Tara said we need to prepare her, make her stronger and more skilled than both you and me put together. We have our work cut out for us."

Either it's my imagination, or he's excited about this.

"And how do you feel about this?" I ask nonchalantly.

"Ecstatic." His voice mirrors his words in its intensity.

I don't know what to say. It's a lot to think about, and I've had little time to come to terms with everything else I learned.

"Liv, I've been in limbo for fifteen years. I thought I'd be in limbo for eternity. Living a useless life, forever. I was almost to the point of giving up. And then I met you." He pauses to look at me. "And now this. I now have a reason to exist." He turns back toward the windshield and takes my hand. "You're enough of a reason yourself. But this? Our child? It's an added bonus. I don't deserve it."

"You *do* deserve it." Something clicks, and in a flash he's inside my mind again like some mental relapse. An awareness so strong I can almost taste the tablet on my tongue. His whole life he's been told by the people he thought were his family that he is a threat who must be controlled in order to save them. That he cannot be trusted. And finally he learns this was all a lie to keep him from the calling he's felt all his life.

A harsh edge has settled on his face, lines around his eyes I never noticed before. He doesn't believe he deserves this. Until he's confronted whatever still haunts him, he'll never deem himself worthy. He's been absolved from a broken life, but all he sees is the truth has exposed more lies, more crimes against him, adding another layer to the vengeance he hasn't paid.

Weeks ago I drove this same highway, broken and burdened like he is now. My goal—the only thing I thought could help me—was distraction. It wasn't a cure but it was a coping mechanism, a temporary reprieve until life moved me forward. Time is the cure. If I can keep him distracted, rein him in when his mind clouds with dark thoughts, maybe he can be happy until time can cure him.

I unbuckle and plant a long kiss on his neck. "Ever had sex in a car?" I nuzzle his ear.

"I'm pulling off." He hits the accelerator and passes several cars before an exit sign appears in the distance.

With my offer so easily accepted, now I'm feeling the space between us, the air that's been holding me away from him every day since the coyotes helped me drag him inside. He takes the exit ramp and turns into the closest lot which appears to be an abandoned service station. I lean into him as he pulls the car out of gear and yanks the parking brake. I am spellbound, and I wonder if he actually did put a spell on me. His lips are like a drug, and I am an addict, falling off the wagon. He pushes his seat back all the way and pulls me over the center console. My fingers grope, searching for a path to his skin. His fingers are faster, more successful, and I feel them slide up my back, taking my shirt with them.

His fingers seize up, and he pulls away, staring into my eyes. I start to object.

"Shh." He leans to look in the side mirror. "Oh, *shit.*"

He slides me back into my seat and pulls his seat a notch forward in one fluid motion. A car door slams behind us, and Trey lowers his window and turns off the engine. I study his face now so thoroughly cleared of all expression. A police officer appears at his window.

"Well, I couldn't tell if anyone was in here with that dark window tint. How are we today?"

"Fine," Trey grumbles. He shifts in his seat like this is the most boring thing he's ever had to sit through.

"I need your license and registration."

Trey reaches into the glove box for the papers from the car dealership and slides his license out of his wallet. The officer takes them back to his car.

I feel like a teenager, ashamed for being caught doing something wrong. Trey looks over at me and laughs.

"This is funny?" I ask, shocked by his reaction.

"Yes. Especially since it is *your* fault."

I cross my arms and stare through the windshield. He leans over and kisses my neck while sliding his palm across my belly.

I catch his hand. "I kind of lost the mood."

"It will come back." He holds my gaze.

We wait in silence for a while until footsteps approach.

The officer hands back the license and papers. "You just purchased this vehicle, Mr. Bevan?"

"Yes."

He steps back to take a long look at the car. "With this amount of damage?"

"Exhaust system is trashed too, want to take a look at that?"

"Would you mind telling me why you're parked here?"

"She wanted to screw, so I pulled off the highway." The Trey Bevan direct approach.

The officer chuckles. "Is that right?"

Trey silently holds his position.

The officer leans in to look at me. "Ma'am?"

"Guilty," I mumble, furious Trey didn't even attempt a white lie to save me the embarrassment. I make an effort to lighten the man's mood, and I get this? Next time I'll go for the radio.

"You two are from out east?" he asks, obviously trying to explain our immoral behavior. Because east coast people… like to have sex in cars?

"No. We're heading home to Montana."

"You just came out to pick up the car in Richmond."

"And visit family, yes." Trey's tone falters, and I start to wonder how much longer he can keep his cool. Bringing up Richmond sure didn't help the situation.

"Is there anything in the vehicle I should be aware of?"

Trey's voice rises. "You kidding me?"

"Trey," I warn. The last thing we need to do is piss off a state trooper. We are almost out of this. He needs to stay calm.

And suddenly I remember our arsenal in the trunk.

"I'll take that as a yes?" The officer is visibly pleased he found something on us.

"Take a look yourself," Trey growls, pushes the trunk release and shoves out of the car. The officer is barely out of the way of Trey's door.

He's got to be crazy. I don't want to imagine what he's thinking, what he could do. I twist in my seat, watching them move to the back of the car. Bags shuffle, zippers unzip, and the trunk slams.

"I'll let you get back on your way. Tell the lady to behave herself, and drive safely."

Trey slides back into his seat and slams the door. "Let's get the fuck out of here."

Back on the highway, he notices my silence and glances at me. "What."

"You couldn't have spared me with one little white lie?"

"I'm a bad liar."

"Well then if you can't lie, tell him that *you* wanted to screw. Because you did."

"I guess I could have. But what does it matter?"

"I guess it doesn't," I mumble. It's pointless to be sullen about it. "He didn't see the guns?"

"He saw them. I have a little more faith in the effect now that I know how my mother used it. Should I pull off at the next exit?"

"No. I'm supposed to behave myself. Remember?" I reach for the radio.

"We'll see how long that lasts."

"You are an asshole," I remind him.

"Noted."

We make a stop, and I take over the wheel for a few hours until the sun stares right in our faces on its descent toward the horizon. We stop and eat dinner, and, feeling sleepy, I ask him to drive again.

"Don't fall asleep," he says. "You have to finish what you started earlier."

"Right," I say sarcastically, closing my eyes and snuggling into the seat. "My unconsciousness never stopped you before."

"Okay, you asked for it."

When my eyes open, we're parked under the bright lights of a motel lobby entrance.

"Don't wake up," he says. "I'll be right back."

"I want to come with you." I get out with him and wind my arm around his waist. I wander about the lobby as he registers and pays, then we load our bags into the room.

"I'm awake," I announce after I close the door and set the lock.

"You know that doesn't matter to me," he says, completely serious.

We strip and he follows me to bed, climbing in behind me, his warm body against my back, his lips on the back of my neck. And for the first time, I'm overtaken by something more that lust, something strong and deep and woven through me like it was there all along and I just had to find it. To recognize it. Like Orion in the night sky.

I twist in his arms to face him. "Trey."

He looks into my eyes, captivated, his eyelids lowered, his lips parted, waiting.

"I love you," I say.

"*Tá mo chroí istigh ionat.*" Like he couldn't wait to say it to me again.

When I wake in the morning, he's sitting up, surfing through TV channels with the volume muted. I reach for him and find a discarded newspaper in my path.

"How long have you been up?" I push myself up on my elbows.

"Not long. I get bored fast without you."

"Let's get up. I'm dying to get home to my own bed. Or, your bed." I haven't slept in my own bed in weeks.

We load our stuff into the car and he pulls onto the highway. For some reason, I'm reminded of my solo trip I took down this very same route a few weeks ago. Did I stay at this same motel, take this same entrance ramp? My memories contain a flavor of something that doesn't exist here now.

"We should move into your house," he says. "It's newer. Bigger. Has a better view."

"What about your garden?"

"We'll just have to make trips over there to work on it."

As much as I liked living with him in his house, I'd love to move back to mine. It would almost be like a fresh start for us. We could put all the bad memories behind. "I'd love to move back into my house with you."

"Then it's settled."

"I wasn't here a month before I got pregnant."

He laughs. "You sure it's mine?"

"Not funny."

I look at him, his light-hearted mood, his face free of that scowl he must have worn for fifteen years. And I realize it doesn't matter. What's happened to us has been planned for centuries. The timing was a work of magic. And by consequence, two haunted people have found happiness. "Nancy wanted to get us together. She's gonna tease me to death."

He slaps the steering wheel. "We can make up a story. Something normal. No ancient spells triggered by Pollux and Mars."

"I thought you were a bad liar."

"I am. A story for you to tell. I'm not going to say a damn thing."

"Okay then think of one." I jab him in the arm.

"I am. I'll let you know when I have it."

"Smartass." I laugh. "Was it really Pollux and Mars?"

"And a few others. I'll show you when we get home."

Hours pass with the landscape sliding by. I snuggle under Trey's jacket now acting as a blanket and marvel again at the open space of this land, losing light and contrast with the fading day. After a while I break the silence. "Do you think we'll be home tonight?"

"Yes. We're making good time. There's nothing in our way out here."

The highway stretches out in a featureless straight line in front of us for miles. The needle of the speedometer points to ninety-five. We've been going so fast for so long that I don't even feel the speed anymore.

"I saw you on your motorcycle when I was on my way to Black River."

"When?" He takes his eyes off the road to look at me, more intrigued than I thought he'd be.

"On the day I drove in from Chicago. I stopped for gas in that town—what's it called? We'll be coming up on it soon."

"Casper."

"Yeah, you were there. I almost passed out in the lot. It was the first time I got sick."

"How do you know it was me?"

"Your motorcycle. And the sickness. It had to be you."

"No kidding. I stop there for gas all the time."

"And I was stranded on the side of the road before that. You passed me right before the tow truck showed up." I look out my window.

"That was you?" He doesn't need me to answer. When I look at him, he's shaking his head at the road ahead of us.

I lose myself in the monotony of the drive, and it seems like a miracle when we pass the town marker for Black River. We made it home before sunset. I reach to the floor for my purse, searching blindly for my Chapstick. "I think I left my Chapstick at the last motel."

"Oh, god. Let's turn back."

I check the zipper pocket. My groping fingers close on an unfamiliar object. I pull it out, turning it over in my hand from the smooth side to the textured side which is tarnished and worn with age. In the center is the same motif that's carved on the stones encircling my house. Its simple beauty reminds me of the rings Trey now wears from his father.

"Did you give this to me?"

"A long time ago. It's for protection."

I close my fingers around it, wondering when he would have first wanted to protect me. It warms in my fist.

We turn into his driveway. All I want to do is collapse into bed with him and stay there forever. River dashes out of the woods at us, and he stops the car. "Someone's here."

"No…" I groan, too tired to be worried.

"Something's not right," he says, as if someone being here could ever be right in the first place.

When we reach the house, he lets all his breath out. "That's Christian's car. I probably shouldn't be relieved." Torment has roughened his voice.

"He beat us here?"

He nods slowly like his mind is somewhere else. "We stopped in Chicago."

"Be good." I slide my hand over his. No confrontations tonight. I just want to go to bed.

He stares out the windshield, and I wonder what's going through his head.

"I will," he finally answers with a strange, almost sad tone, a tone I remember hearing coupled with his voice once before. It takes me a moment to recognize it as regret.

He takes another deep sigh and closes his eyes. "Shit," he says more to himself than me.

"He'll understand."

He opens his eyes and looks into mine. "He drove his own car, which means he's going to stay awhile. Let's go in, I'm dead tired."

I'm already pushing open my door.

We head straight into the house, not even bothering to get our bags. The house is dark and quiet. Trey gives me a puzzled look and checks the bedroom while I wait. I'm so tired my feet feel glued to the floor.

"Must be out back," he says on his way back through, and I drag myself behind him to the kitchen and out the back door, closing it behind me.

Christian is standing at the far end of the deck. All four fingers of his left hand are bandaged. Hearing us, he turns around. Bloodshot eyes, rumpled clothes, the shadow of a beard—he's either on something or hasn't slept in days. Or both.

"Trey, god Trey. I can't..." Christian blurts out. He winces as if in pain and presses both of his palms hard against his eyes.

"What?" Trey squints at him.

Christian's hands drop to his sides. His eyes open and cut through me. He pulls a dark object out of the back of his pants, and I find myself looking down the barrel of a gun.

Trey freezes.

"Trey, god, I have these compulsions, and I can't...I'm so sorry."

"Christian. You don't have to do this. Give it to me. I can help you." Trey's voice is controlled, but my ears are tuned to the underlying panic.

"No you can't. Fuck! You can't!" Christian shouts. His eyes don't leave me. His gun doesn't leave me.

I want to run, but there's nowhere to go. I wouldn't get the door open in time. I wouldn't get over the porch railing fast enough. I catch Trey's almost insignificant movements, poising himself to lunge.

"Christian," he says again. Trying to buy some time.

Christian screams words I don't know. I watch his finger pull the trigger once, twice, three times. Time slows. Trey lunges, knocking Christian into the railing. Reflex has thrown my hands out in front of me. The dying sun reflects off an object in my hand, casting an arc of light around my vision, and the only thing I hear is Trey screaming my name.

ACKNOWLEDGMENTS

My thanks go to—

My husband and best friend, who helped me build a life that allows me to write. My happiness, my settled mind, my peace—I owe to you.

My mother, whose enthusiasm keeps me writing, whose desire to share adventure with her children helped build my writer's mind.

Ginny, because the help you offer may be second nature to you, but to me, its value, and the peace of mind it gives, are immeasurable.

My sisters, two non-readers who fought their way through awful early drafts.

My editor Debra Argosy, a language tyrant who's always right. Not just about writing. About everything.

Karen, my lifelong friend, whose praise means so much because I know how discriminating her taste is.

Laura, I will never forget your insight about TB and his garden. Your requests for more to read are the highest compliment because I know how busy your days are.

Kathy, my favorite member of the best book club, who gave an awful early draft of my book as much thoughtful discussion as she'd give to an award-winning bestseller.

Phillip, for telling me my pitch was all wrong in the most straightforward but gentle way.

Rosemary Whittaker, a talented writer whose warmth and encouragement reach across oceans.

Pam Schuster, an expert who injected my book with trustworthiness.

Stephanie and her inspiring website bekindrewrite.com, because sometimes the most rewarding compliments come from strangers.

Ray Rhamey and his website Flogging the Quill, for the best constructive criticism I've ever found on the internet.

The people in the Irish Learner's Forum—your passion for the language is contagious.

the

ALIGNMENT SERIES

The Alignment
The Two
The Oak and the Moon
The Catalyst
The Warrior